International Praise for *Cry Wolf*

"Hans Rosenfeldt…is a grand master of his trade who knows how to skillfully build high tension."

–Kleine Zeitung, Germany

"A suspenseful and well-written crime story."

–Trønder-Avisa, Norway

"Packed with suspense."

–Jyllands-Posten, Denmark

"Dense, spooky and really well written."

–Politiken, Denmark

"Rich in characters, dark events and violence."

–Smålandsposten, Sweden

"Suspenseful—page-turningly suspenseful."

–DAST magazine, Sweden

CRY WOLF

A NOVEL

HANS ROSENFELDT

TRANSLATED BY ELIZABETH CLARK WESSEL

HANOVER
SQUARE
PRESS

**HANOVER
SQUARE
PRESS™**

Recycling programs
for this product may
not exist in your area.

ISBN-13: 978-1-335-42571-3

Cry Wolf

First published in 2020 in Sweden by Norstedts Förlag. This edition published in 2022.

Published by agreement with Salomonsson Agency.

Copyright © 2022 by Hans Rosenfeldt

This edition published by arrangement with Harlequin Books S.A.

Hanover Square Press
22 Adelaide St. West, 41st Floor
Toronto, Ontario M5H 4E3, Canada
HanoverSqPress.com
BookClubbish.com

Printed in U.S.A.

CRY
WOLF

*S*he lay on her side, held by moss and shrubs.

Gnats buzzed around her head, her breathing was labored, and oblivion was only a few breaths away. One eye stared up at the sky, at wisps of clouds with edges glowing pink and orange.

It was the warm time of the year. When the sky never goes dark.

She'd smelled the stench of infection for several days, but that wasn't going to kill her. Nor was it starvation, the hunger. She was full now. For the first time in a very long time.

The wound refused to heal, no matter how much she tried to clean it. The pain and the warmth had spread up her leg. The pack had adapted to her pace. For a while anyway. Three of her young left with the others, but the smallest stayed behind with her. Doomed to destruction.

She couldn't hunt anymore, and he'd never been taught.

The young moose who were easy prey in the light season were unattainable for now. Even the small prey escaped her. Too early for berries, which in an emergency stave off the worst of the hunger. Yesterday they'd found some meat, partially hidden, with an odor that instinctively told her to flee, but it kept them going. Up on the cliffs at the forest edge, they found more. Much more. Huge chunks, more than they could eat.

So she'd lingered on with her youngest until he slowed, whimpering, taking wobbly steps till finally he could no longer stand.

She'd stayed with him until she was sure he was dead, then kept going. Not far. The cramping and trembling made that impossible. She collapsed in the moss, lying on her side.

In the warmth. In the light. In the never-ending light.

Everything had gone according to plan.
First their arrival.

Be the first in place, park the jeep and black Mercedes beside each other on a rutted clearing in the middle of the forest, used by lumber trucks and harvesters for loading and U-turns, then position the coolers to face the narrow forest road they'd just come down. The ruts beneath them, the nocturnal birdsong around them, the only thing besides absolute silence until the sound of engines announced the arrival of the Finns.

A Volvo XC90, also black, drove up. Vadim watched as Artjom and Michail took their weapons and left the Mercedes, while he and Ljuba climbed out of their jeep. He liked Ljuba, thought she liked him, too. They'd gone out for a beer together a few times, and when they asked her who she wanted to drive with, she'd chosen him. For a moment he considered telling her to wait in the car, take cover, say he had a premonition this might go wrong. But if he did that, what would they do afterwards?

Run away together? Live happily ever after?

That would be impossible once she knew what had happened.

She'd never betray Valerij; she didn't like him that much, he was sure of it. So he said nothing.

The Volvo stopped a few meters in front of them, the engine switched off, the doors opened, and four men stepped out. All of them armed. Looked around suspiciously as they fanned out.

Everything was still.

The calm before the storm.

The Finnish leader, a large man with a buzz cut and a tribal tattoo wrapped around one eye, nodded to the smallest of the four Finns, who holstered his gun, walked behind the Volvo, and opened the trunk. Vadim also backed up a few steps to unlock his jeep's trunk.

So far everything was going according to their plan.

Time for his plan.

A bullet from a rifle with a silencer on it entered just beneath the eye of the large Finn closest to the car. The sudden explosion of bone, blood, and brain matter as the projectile made its way through the back of his head made the others react instinctively.

Everyone started shooting at the same time.

Everyone except Vadim, who threw himself behind the shelter of the jeep.

The man with the tattoo on his face roared loudly, hugged his trigger, and immediately took down Michail with four or five shots to the chest. Artyom answered with gunfire. The tattooed man was hit by two bullets, staggered back, but regained his balance and turned his weapon on Artyom, who threw himself behind the cover of the Mercedes, but it was too late. Several bullets hit his legs from the hip down. Shrieking in pain, he landed on dry gravel. The tattooed man continued bleeding, roaring, and shooting as he moved toward the Volvo, determined to make it out of here alive. But a second later he fell to his knees gurgling, let go of his weapon, and pressed his hands to what was left of his neck.

14

Somewhere more shots were fired, more screams could be heard.

Artjom slid up into a sitting position, while trying to stop the blood that gushed from his thigh in the same rhythm as his racing heartbeat. Then another series of shots, and he went still, his gaze turning from desperation to emptiness, his lips forming some soundless word before his head slumped onto his chest.

The third Finn had thrown himself into the cover of a shallow ditch with a good view beneath the parked cars. A round of concentrated fire from his semi-automatic had hit Artjom in the back. Vadim realized that he, too, must be visible and flung himself around the jeep to hide behind one of its large wheels. When he got to the side of the car, he saw the smallest of the four Finns lying dead on the ground.

Ljuba wasn't visible.

Another round of shots sounded from the ditch at the forest edge and bullets hit the metal on the back of the wheel, puncturing the tire. One went through the rubber and hit him in the side, just above his butt. The pain was a white-hot flash through his body. He closed his eyes, swallowed a scream, leaned his forehead against his knees, and made himself as small as he could. As he slowly let the air in his lungs out again, he realized the gunfire had ceased.

It was silent. Completely silent.

No movement, no voices, no roar of pain or betrayal, no birdsong, nothing. As if the very place itself were holding its breath.

He peeked out carefully from behind the jeep.

Still silent. And still.

Slowly, slowly he raised his head for a better view. The sun hung below the trees, but still above the horizon; the scene in front of him was bathed in that particular soft, warm light of the midnight sun.

He rose cautiously to his feet. A bullet was still lodged in his muscle and tissue, but it didn't seem to have damaged any vital organs. He pressed his hand to the wound. Blood, but no more than he could stop with a compress.

"Ljuba?"

Ljuba was leaning against the rear bumper of the Finn's car, breathing shallowly, the front of her gray T-shirt beneath her jacket soaked in blood, the gun still in her right hand. Vadim assessed the damage. The blood was running out at a steady rate, so it hadn't nicked an artery. No air bubbles, so her lungs were probably intact. She might very well survive.

"Who shot us?" she asked, out of breath, grabbing Vadim's jacket with a bloody hand. "Who the fuck started shooting?"

"He's with us."

"What? What do you mean with us? Who is he?"

"Come on."

He gently took the gun away from her, pushed it into his pocket before standing up, leaned forward and helped her to her feet. She grimaced from the pain of exertion but managed to stand. With his arm around her waist and her arm around his shoulders, they walked out into the open area between the cars. When they reached the rise where the tattooed Finn had fallen, Vadim stopped, gently removed Ljuba's arm, released his supportive grip from around her waist, and backed away with two large steps.

"I'm sorry..."

Ljuba's gaze was uncomprehending at first, but she soon realized what was happening, why he'd brought her here. Seconds later a bullet pierced her temple and she was thrown to the ground.

Vadim pressed his hand to the wound on his lower back and stretched, let out a deep sigh.

In the end, everything had gone according to plan.

The city was waking up.

As she always does. Always has.

The Treaty of Fredrikshamn in 1809. One signature and Sweden lost a third of its territory, a quarter of its population. The Czar of Russia took Torneå, the largest trading center in the region, and a new border was drawn down the middle of the river. Suddenly Sweden had no city in the area. You need one, everyone agreed, but where should it be? The proposals were numerous, the discussions long. While they were trying to make up their minds, she waited patiently and grew, from a village with a few farms to a small market town, and finally she received her city charter in 1842. The year she was born.

Haparanda is named after *Haaparanta*, the Finnish word for Aspstrand.

Good years followed, when she grew so fast she creaked. Things always went better for her when they were going badly somewhere else. Being a neutral city near a border during a world war had its advantages. Now and then she was the only gateway open to Russia. The eye of the needle between east and west.

Material, letters, products, people.

Legal, illegal, living, valuable, dangerous.

The world's traffic went through her, no matter what. She prospered. Thrived.

She's a little more tired these days. She's definitely calmer. Slowly she's shrinking. Not in any dramatic way, simply a case of more people dying and leaving her every year than were born or moved in.

She knows her people. Shares their lives, sees and knows. Remembers and waits. She needs them all. She's a city, exists only as long as people choose to live in her. Like a god who disappears the moment no one believes anymore.

So she welcomes the new ones and grieves for those who disappear, while quietly and patiently lying beside the river's eternal flow.

There were plenty of parking spaces to choose from, so Hannah took the one closest to the sporting goods store, climbed out of the car and looked around while tucking her shirt into her uniform. After she left the police station she'd had a hot flash, and even though it only lasted a minute, her face still felt hot and sweat still ran down her back.

The weather wasn't helping.

The thirteenth day of sunshine and temperatures over twenty degrees Celsius, unusually warm for mid-June this far north. Weather like this also meant this shopping center next to the E4 highway—dozens of stores lined up hoping the appeal to nearby Ikea customers—was less busy than usual. Not going too well for them today, Hannah noted, as she made her way to the entrance of the sporting goods shop.

It was cooler inside the store. A few customers were scattered between the round steel racks beneath signs announcing 40–70 percent off the clothes that hung on them. Hannah raised a hand in greeting to the woman behind the cash register. Didn't know her, but knew who she was. Tarja Burell, married to Harald, younger brother of Carin at the reception desk. Her greeting was answered with a nod toward the interior of the store. Hannah saw immediately why she was here.

A young man, she recognized him, too. Jonathan, or Jonte for short, but she couldn't quite recall his last name at the moment, which meant he wasn't one of the most frequent guests in their detention cells. She continued down toward the stacks of shoeboxes, in front of a wall where shoes were displayed according to their sizes. The young man took a few swaying steps toward a couple in their thirties who were doing their best to avoid him without giving him the satisfaction of chasing them away; in other words, they were pretending he wasn't there.

"How about we have a little chat?"

Jonte turned to Hannah. If the waxy face and jerky movements hadn't told her already what she was dealing with—a man suffering from severe withdrawal symptoms—then the enlarged pupils would have left her with little doubt. Heroin, probably. Or Subutex. Supply and therefore abuse had increased significantly in recent years.

"What?" the young man said with an affronted sniff.

"I just want to have a little talk, follow me outside."

"I didn't do anything wrong."

"We'll discuss that. Outside."

She put her hand gently on his shoulder, and he jerked it away so violently that he almost lost his balance and had to take a step back in order not to fall.

"Get your fucking hands off me. I'm only asking for money," the young man said with a dismissive shrug. "Begging. That's not…that's not a crime."

"OK, but when you don't get anything, what do you do then?"

"What do you mean?"

Hannah could see him making an effort to focus his shifting eyes into an indifferent expression.

"You've been threatening to whip them."

"Yes, but… I haven't followed through—"

"No, but you can't go around threatening people, so come with me now."

She again put her hand gently onto his shoulder and the response was the same as last time, a fierce jerk backward that seemed to come as a complete surprise to the rest of his body.

"Take your fat fingers off me."

"OK," Hannah said, releasing his shoulder. "Are you coming then?"

"Yes, but don't touch me."

Hannah took a step aside and gestured with her arm that he should go first. He slowly made his way on unsteady legs toward the exit. As they passed by a bin of store-brand underwear, he reached out and grabbed a few packs, tried to push them inside his thin jacket.

"Seriously?" Hannah asked him tiredly. "You think I left my guide dog outside?"

"What?" Jonte replied, missing her point completely. Hannah sighed, grabbed the underwear and threw it back into the bin. A curt push on his back meant she'd had enough now. The man seemed to understand and headed to the exit without further protest.

When they stepped out into stark sunlight, he paused and raised his hand to shade his sensitive eyes. Hannah gave another little push that steered him in the direction of her parked police car. Halfway there he stopped, put one hand to his stomach and folded slightly forward. Large beads of sweat broke out on his forehead.

"I'm not feeling too good."

"That's because you took a bunch of shit."

Jonte didn't answer, but Hannah saw him give what looked like a nod before continuing.

She got him into the back seat of the car, and soon they were on their way. She glanced down at her hands on the steering wheel as she turned left at the roundabout. Sure, her wedding ring was a little tighter now than it was when she first put it on her ring finger, and there wasn't a chance she'd be able to squeeze into her wedding dress, if for some reason she'd wanted to, but her fingers weren't fat. She wasn't fat. She might have gotten a little rounder in her stomach over the last year, but a few weeks ago she'd put her height and weight into one of those BMI calculators online. It was only 27.

She put her left blinker on at the next roundabout, wondering if she should tell the man in the back seat that her BMI was the same as his IQ. A glance into the rearview mirror indicated that he'd be unlikely to hear her if she did; her passenger's head was slumped against his chest as if he were asleep.

The drive continued in silence. Soon they were on the other side of the E4, heading toward the city center, which was basically deserted. Ikea customers rarely found their way to the old downtown area on the other side of the E4, which in some ways was as much a dividing line as the actual border with Finland a few hundred meters away.

She took a left at a red two-story building, which housed the editorial staff of Haparanda's local newspaper, which delivered only twice a week these days. Then she pulled up to an anonymous-looking brick building, which housed the Swedish Tax Agency and the Swedish Social Insurance Agency and the police station. She parked in one of the two spots in the garage and turned the car off. The garage doors closed behind her as she climbed out. She leaned into the back seat and shook some life into the young man sitting there.

With a bit of effort he was able to climb out of the car, and he started to head for the doors that led to the detention area without needing to be shown the way. Suddenly he stopped, put a hand on the hood of the car, moaning. Hannah walked over to him and saw his blank expression as he turned toward her. Without warning, projectile vomit hit her just below the chin, and she could feel the warmth of it through the fabric of her shirt as it ran down. Its stench struck her immediately.

"Goddamnit!"

She was able to step aside before the next round of vomit landed on the ground next to her, splashing only her shoes and the bottom of her pants.

The young man straightened up, took a deep breath, and smiled with relief. Hannah did her best to breathe through her mouth as she pushed open the door to the booking area, where people were processed before being put into one of the jail cells, all four of which were currently empty. The woman they'd picked up last week for drug possession had been charged and transferred to Luleå, and this weekend they'd had one DUI, issued two fines—one for driving an unregistered vehicle and one for violating trailer regulations—and on Sunday morning they'd assisted the ambulance staff with an inebriated woman who'd broken her wrist, and found a run-over reindeer.

Nothing that would occupy a jail cell.

Morgan Berg was headed down the corridor with a cup of coffee in his hand, but took a step back when he caught sight of what was headed his way.

"Book him," Hannah ordered, pushing Jonte against the wall-mounted bench opposite the small reception desk. Without waiting for either a reply or objection, she turned around, took out her key card, and opened the door behind her. A short corridor, blue plastic cabinets along one wall, a few chairs here and there, another wall-mounted bench. Pipes and cables in the ceiling. It gave the visitor an impression of being in a conduit, but it was the men's dressing room, which one had to inconveniently pass through in order to get to the much smaller women's area. However, since there were only three female employees it wasn't usually a problem.

Hannah went to her locker and started to peel off her clothes. Couldn't tell if it was just the stench or if she'd actually gotten a little vomit in her mouth. She fought off the nausea. She'd always had trouble with it; when the children were little, Thomas always had to deal with it when the kids threw up. She ripped off her shirt, flung it onto the floor in disgust. Bent down and tore off her shoes and socks. Was standing in her bra and uniform pants when her phone rang. She was tempted not to answer, but then saw the screen.

An area code from Uppsala.

Where Gabriel was studying.

Not his number, but it might be a friend, or maybe he lost his phone. Something might have happened. She answered with a curt, "This is Hannah."

"Uh, yeah hey, is this Hannah...Wester?" The voice on the other end of the call was clearly searching to find a last name before saying it.

"Yes, who is this?"

"Sorry, my name is Benny Svensén, and I'm calling from NVI." He paused for a moment as if he were wondering if he should explain what NVI was, but apparently decided to move on. "I'd like to talk to you about the wolves. You're in charge of that, right?"

She supposed she was.

She was the lead investigator on a case involving the illegal hunting of wolves. A German hiker called in Wednesday, upset, and reported in not-so-great English that he'd found a dead wolf. After talking for a while, they managed to pull a location out of him. Once they got there, it turned out there wasn't just *one* dead wolf, but two. A bitch and her pup, barely a kilometer between them. No visible signs of damage, but it seemed unlikely that both would have died of natural causes a few hundred meters apart. Either way, they followed protocol and sent the bodies to the National Veterinary Institute, where apparently Benny Svensén had been assigned the task of reporting their findings to her.

"That's right," Hannah confirmed, resisting the impulse to spit. "If this is about the wolf bitch and her pup we found outside Kattilasaari on Wednesday—"

"Yes, those are the ones; we have no other wolves right now."

"How could I know that?"

"No, of course, but…"

"Forget it, what do you want?" She regretted answering the call, wanted nothing more than to strip off the rest of her clothes and climb into a shower as soon as possible. Also, she knew what he was going to say. The wolves had been poisoned. That would make it a hunting crime, and the case would most likely be closed as soon as her boss presented it to the prosecutor in Luleå. Resource intensive and low priority with a low clearance percentage. Wolves were rarely seen in this area, and there were no preserves that she knew of, but now and then they wandered in from Russia, Finland, or Norway. And if they were discovered, it didn't take long for them to "disappear."

"The cause of death was poisoning," she heard Benny say, and it was as if she could see the autopsy report in front of her.

"Fine, now I know," she said as she unbuttoned her pants and began to step out of them. "I'm a little busy here, so if you could just send me the report, please?" Leaving no room for doubt that she wanted to end the call. Or so she thought. But Benny Svensén seemed oblivious.

"That's one more thing."

"What?" she snapped, unable to hold back her impatience. But when she heard what he had to say, she froze, forgot that she was half naked and covered in vomit. Not sure she'd heard him right.

Couldn't have heard him right.

It ate a human being?" Gordon Backman Niska repeated back to Hannah with his eyes wide. His voice said he didn't want to believe her, but he was also thinking through the consequences if it were true.

"Both of them had, according to NVI." Hannah nodded affirmatively.

Gordon sighed heavily as he stood up smoothly from his ergonomically correct office chair, walked over to the window, and stared out onto Strandvägen and the parking lot on the other side of the street. At thirty-six, he was the youngest police chief they'd ever had in Haparanda, and the slim fit of his light blue shirt said he was probably in the best shape as well. If further proof was required, certificates from three Ironman races and four Swedish Classics hung above the low bookshelf behind his desk. Hannah and Morgan waited in silence while Gordon stuffed a pouch of tobacco under his upper lip.

Sometimes Hannah tasted his tobacco when she had her tongue in his mouth. She didn't like it.

"They've killed and eaten a human being," Gordon continued, his statement one of fatigue as the implications of this started to sink in.

The attention. The headlines.

The issue of predators in general and wolves in particular divided Sweden, and the debate got fiercer with each passing year. Threats, harassment, online screeds from both sides were common. Occasional property damage and violence. No doubt the wolf haters would be in heaven if, rather than talking about a dead hunter or attacks on people in the mountains of Kazakhstan, they could point to a wolf who'd actually killed a human being in Sweden. But the resistance would also intensify, polarize further, spread to things that had nothing to do with hunting. A lot of people hunted in Gordon Backman Niska's precinct.

"They ate someone," Hannah replied. "We don't know if they killed them."

"How else would it have happened?" Gordon countered, and turned to them.

"Someone could have died out there for other reasons," Hannah said, shrugging her shoulders. "A hiker or fisherman had a heart attack, or who knows what."

Possible, of course, but she could hear how hollow it sounded, something Gordon confirmed with his skeptical gaze.

"That doesn't sound very likely, does it?"

"Them killing somebody doesn't sound very likely either," Morgan objected in his deep, calm voice. "Besides the woman who died at Kolmården, a human hasn't been killed by a wolf in Sweden for over two hundred years."

Neither Hannah nor Gordon thought to ask Morgan how he knew that. They were used to the fact that he knew a lot about everything. He'd won 10,000 kronor on *Who Knows the Most* three times. In 2003 he competed in *Who Wants to Be a Millionaire* on TV4 and won the whole thing with two lifelines remaining. Everybody in Haparanda knew, but nobody—least of all Morgan—ever talked about it.

"We're lucky, it was a Swedish wolf with a tracking device on it," Hannah said. Gordon gave her a look that meant she should explain more fully. "The human flesh in their stomachs was there for half a day max, maybe even less, according to SVA. If the county administrative board has tracked them, we might be able to find the rest of the body."

"How far does a wolf go in thirty-six hours?"

"Between twenty and forty-five kilometers a day," Morgan replied.

"The female was injured," Hannah interjected. "She couldn't go that fast."

"An injured female with her young." Morgan nodded. "That changes the situation a bit. In that case she'll go after what she can catch. Slow things…"

"How detailed is the GPS or satellite or whatever it is they're currently using?" Gordon sighed, well aware of what his colleague was implying.

"Don't know," Morgan answered unexpectedly. "I can call and find out."

"Do it. Find whoever's in charge of tracking the wolf in question and try to get as detailed a map as you can."

Morgan tugged on his enormous beard as if he wanted to add something, but then nodded and left the room without another word.

Gordon walked past her and over to the wall where a map of the precinct hung next to a whiteboard, which was currently covered by duty and vacation schedules. Without a doubt, Gordon had the largest office in the building. If Hannah took two steps past her own desk, she'd hit the wall.

"Where did we find the wolves?"

Hannah walked over, quickly located and pointed to a spot about thirty kilometers northwest of Haparanda, a few centimeters outside Kattilasaari. Gordon walked up behind her. Close, so close she could feel the heat of his body.

"Did you get vomited on today?"

Hannah turned to him while sniffing at the collar of her clean shirt. "Do I smell?"

"No, I just heard about it."

"It was Jonte…coming down from something."

"Jonte Lundin."

"That's right. Lundin." She turned her attention to the map again. "We found them here."

"Thirty-six hours, we'll say thirty kilometers per day, that's a forty-five-kilometer radius." Gordon read the scale of the map, took a ruler and a pencil from the desk, measured, drew a circle, and studied his work. "That's a hell of a lot of forest. We're going to need more people."

"Maybe we should wait to see what Morgan finds out first. If those tracking devices aren't accurate enough, we'll never find him."

"Was it a man? Do we know that?"

Hannah thought back to her conversation with Benny Svensén. He'd said "human," but there'd been no mention of gender. "No, sorry, they didn't say."

"Have we had any missing person reports?"

Hannah shook her head. Gordon sighed again and with one last look at the map he went back to his desk and sat down.

"OK, we'll wait on Morgan and then decide what to do."

The meeting was clearly over. Hannah nodded, walked toward the door, but stopped just as she was about to step into the corridor.

"I know you know this, but we should really keep this between the three of us until we're sure what we're dealing with."

Gordon's dark eyes held a seriousness she rarely saw in him. He was usually close to laughter, easygoing, though he took his job seriously enough to maintain his authority. Hannah nodded again, left his office, and walked down the corridor. It occurred to her that this had been a real shitty day so far.

Ten people.

Gordon couldn't remember ever having this many people in the second-floor conference room. They could all fit around the long, blond wood conference table, but Morgan still chose to lean against a wall of floor-to-ceiling bookshelves stuffed with old books whose brown and black leather spines, worn by time and use, made the room feel more like an archive than the modern conference room it actually was. The books dominated the space. The books and an enormous police emblem that hung on the short wall surrounded by rows of yellowing photos of former police chiefs, who everyone had their backs to now, all eyes on Gordon, who was standing in front of a lowered white screen at the room's other end. The projector was buzzing on the ceiling and projecting a map with a thin blue line that zigzagged through northern Sweden until it ceased just outside Haparanda.

"What are we looking at?" asked Roger Hammar, the station's tallest and skinniest employee who despite—or because of—his gangly appearance and deep bass voice was known to everyone as Lurch, a reference lost on anyone under forty. Instead of answering, Gordon turned to one of the four people in the room who was not a police officer and nodded briefly.

Jens, a young, energetic man from the county administrative board in Luleå, who, when Morgan asked him to email them the map, suggested he bring it in person and explain it to them instead.

Morgan clarified calmly that they would probably be able to figure out how the map worked perfectly well on their own, but Jens insisted. Said he was already in the car. Morgan supposed there wasn't usually much excitement at the county administrative board in Luleå.

"You found two dead wolves here last week," Jens said, straightening in his seat while directing a laser pointer at the map. Gordon heard Hannah sigh from her spot by the window beside P-O, who was ten years younger than Hannah, but whose chalky white hair, lean face, and skin that seemed to have loosened a bit made him look ready to retire any day now. Gordon glanced over at Hannah, who was rolling her eyes; they were obviously thinking the same thing as that little red dot appeared next to Kattilasaari. How hard would it have been for Jens to walk over and point to the map? How ridiculous was that laser pointer?

"As you know, one of them had been tagged with a transmitter, so we know the path she took." The red dot started to follow the blue line. "She was part of a larger pack coming up from the south, wandering here, east of Storuman, up between Arvidsjaur and Arjeplog, on toward an area just outside Jokkmokk where she left the pack, headed southeast, probably would have continued into Finland, but she died here." The dot was back at the place outside Kattilasaari again. "She stops moving at 4:33 a.m., and you wanted to know where she was a day and a half before then." He let his little pointer land at a spot to the north of Vitvattnet. "At that time she was here. She walked forty-one kilometers over those last thirty-six hours." Jens turned off the laser pointer and sank back down into the chair, apparently satisfied with his contribution. The room was unexpectedly quiet, until Lurch spoke again.

"OK, but *why* are we looking at this? Why are we tracking a dead wolf?"

A legitimate question, given that Gordon had brought them here without any explanation, convinced that the fewer people who knew, the better.

But the time had come.

Six police officers and four civilians.

He'd called Kalix for reinforcements, but when they couldn't provide any he'd called in Adrian, his brother, who knew how to keep quiet, and Morgan invited his neighbors, a couple in their sixties whom he knew well and could vouch for, to volunteer. And then there was Jens from the county administrative board. When Morgan told him that Jens had insisted on coming here personally, Gordon suspected he must be the type who tried to make himself seem more interesting than he was.

His use of the laser point hadn't done much to change that impression. There was surely a Twitter account somewhere on which this information should not be shared, so Gordon locked eyes with him.

"Until we know exactly what happened, absolutely nothing of what I'm about to say can leave this room," he began, and saw nods in response from around the room; it was hard to mistake the seriousness of his tone. "The wolves we found had consumed parts of a human being."

"Which parts?" Jens asked.

Gordon gave him a look that said, Why the fuck would you say that?

"Does it matter?" he asked rhetorically, and turned back to the others. "We have to find the rest."

Ten minutes had passed since they'd seen another car. Cruise control was set to a steady 80 km/h. The road stretched out straight ahead of them into green. As soon as the snow was gone, spring quickly turned everything a vibrant summer green. Even the ditches were full of flowers in bloom. For Hannah, they were merely anonymous, tiny flashes of color: white, purple, and blue. Thomas would surely know what they were called, maybe Gordon as well. She'd never asked.

Without really seeing, she stared out at the sparse forest outside the car window. The spruces were dark and gloomy and surrounded by the much more numerous newly leafed and ethereally green deciduous trees. Now and then a break in form, a clear-felled area, a rolling field, or a meadow, and she'd catch a glimpse of the mountains on the horizon. Never poking above the treeline, they too rose up green, giving the impression of a wave rolling forward, a soft wave with nothing solid or hard about it.

A swell of forest. Everywhere, only forest.

The view gave her a sense of tranquility and calm. Easy to

imagine distant birdsong mingling with the slight rustle of wind in the trees. Imagine and long for it.

As soon as they left Haparanda, Jens had started talking about his job, how he ended up there, his ideas for changing and improving his department, the reaction he got to them, how it might sound boring, but truly it was very exciting. Not as exciting as this is, of course, but still. If it turned out a wolf really had killed a man, it would inevitably affect the county administrative board's future resolutions on hunting. As for him, he had never seen a corpse, but he supposed most people his age hadn't.

Hannah was fourteen when she saw a dead person for the first time, but she didn't say that.

No one said anything.

The polite follow-up questions and monosyllabic answers from her and Gordon had ceased long ago; the last fifteen minutes were just a monologue from the back seat. Something Jens apparently realized with only a few minutes left to their destination.

"My girlfriend thinks I talk too much," he said, almost apologetically.

"Your girlfriend is right," Hannah stated.

Jens nodded at the not-so-subtle dig and fell silent. Hannah saw Gordon glance at her with an amused smile. It was a bit of an ordeal to have Jens in the car, but he was more useful than they'd expected. He'd downloaded the map to their phones, made sure that they were connected to the same satellites used to track the animals, which would now tell them if they deviated more than a few meters from the path. Neither Hannah nor Gordon really understood how it worked, but the important thing was that it did.

Morgan was taking his neighbors to the site outside Kattilasaari where the wolves were found, and they were going to follow the route to the northwest. Lurch, P-O, and Ludwig from the station had taken Gordon's brother with them to the spot where the animals crossed 398 between Rutajärvi and Lappträsket. They'd split up there. Two would head southeast and hopefully meet Morgan and his neighbors after about ten kilometers. The other two would follow the tracks to the northwest to meet Gordon, Hannah, and Jens at about the same distance. The idea was that the four groups would cover about ten kilometers each, and if everything went according to plan, they should find the body within two or three hours.

They entered Vitvattnet from the south and parked outside the red railway station. Like so many other small towns in Sweden, this village had flourished when the railroad reached it, and like so many others it had depopulated, shrunk, and lost its relevance when the railroad disappeared. Once it also had a post office, a church, cafes, shops, a gas station, and its own school. Today, only a convenience store and two gas pumps remained.

Hannah got out of the car. It wasn't the first time she'd been in Vitvattnet, but like all the other times, she didn't see a single living soul. Work, school, errands, entertainment, everything was done elsewhere. Gordon walked over to her and handed her a bottle of mosquito spray. It was still early in the season and there were no mosquitoes that Hannah could see in this parking lot, but in among the trees, between the shady shrubs, things would be different.

Jens took out his iPad, and they crossed the railway tracks and headed into the woods on the other side.

"Now we're on their route," Jens said, stopping after walking maybe a few hundred meters straight north. A dot on the screen in the middle of the thin blue line. "We'll go there," he continued, pointing into the trees to the southeast.

And they started to hike.

Jens walked with his neck bent, his eyes on the screen. Hannah and Gordon were on either side of him, scanning the ground, over roots and fallen branches, most of it covered with soft green moss, lingonberry and blueberry shrubs. Hannah was thinking about Thomas. Why hadn't she called him when they needed more people? He liked this type of thing: hunting, fishing, being out in nature. Once in a while when the children were smaller, she'd go with him, drumming up a bit of fake enthusiasm. Didn't want her reluctance to be outdoors to infect the kids. She'd pretend to enjoy sitting among the mosquitoes—which always bit her, never Thomas—in a hunting blind somewhere or on some frozen lake, drinking lukewarm coffee out of a plastic mug and eating dry sandwiches.

That was all a long time ago.

They kept walking, eyes to the ground, didn't say much. Now and then Jens adjusted their course. The treetops blocked most of the direct sunlight, but nevertheless it was very warm in the almost windless forest. Hannah unbuttoned the top two buttons of her uniform shirt as her eyes swept back and forth across the speckled green of the forest floor. They crossed the road toward Bodträsk and entered into the trees on the other side. Hannah waved away some monstrous flies buzzing around her, the freshness from her shower at the station long since vanished. Sweaty and breathless, she glanced over at the other two. Jens was focused on his screen. Gordon seemed completely unaffected.

It wasn't quite an hour later—according to Jens, they'd gone about four kilometers—when a few huge black crows flew off as they approached, and Hannah knew immediately they'd found what they were looking for.

"Stay here," she said to Jens as she and Gordon continued forward.

Buried wasn't the right word, the body was only partially hidden under spruce, moss, and twigs. A few smaller stones had been laid on top to keep the arrangement in place. The person was lying on their back with one arm sticking out from beneath the shrub. The hand was missing all its fingers except the thumb, and large pieces of the exposed body had been torn away. At first glance the injuries seemed to have come from the wolves. Further up toward the shoulder and neck and on the side of the body, which wasn't totally covered, there were more minor wounds from the hacking of bird beaks. Thick flies buzzed around the corpse. A sweet, heavy odor filled their nostrils as they got closer. They weren't supposed to touch anything, because there was no doubt that the person they'd found was dead and the technicians would want the site to be as uncontaminated as possible, but Gordon went ahead and carefully removed the shrubs and branches covering the face.

"It's a male," he noted after he'd taken enough away.

"And unless those wolves were very unique indeed, they didn't kill him." Hannah nodded to the makeshift grave. "Looks like we got a murder."

"Yeah, and maybe that's for the best," Gordon said, taking a few steps back. "We have to call it in, get people here. You know exactly where we are, right?" Gordon turned to Jens, who was still standing where they'd told him to. He nodded, pale and quiet. "Give me the coordinates," Gordon said as he took out his phone.

Hannah looked around. They'd crossed a small road a few hundred meters back. It should continue on not too far to her right. She left the site and set off through the forest.

After a minute, she stepped out onto a narrow forest road. Not really much more than two tire tracks rolling forward and a place to pull over onto the shoulder of the ditch for oncoming traffic now and then. Hannah wiped the sweat from her forehead and glanced back at the forest she'd just exited. If the man wasn't murdered where they found him, if the body was brought there to bury it, they would have parked where she was standing, give or take a few meters. Without really knowing what she was looking for, she slowly began to make her way forward.

Traces of blood? Something lost? Tire prints, maybe.

Not much hope of that. The road was dry and hard after weeks of no rain. She continued a few steps along the ditch and stopped abruptly, bent down.

Shards. Different colors.

Transparent white, red, and yellow.

She resisted the impulse to pick them up, but was pretty sure they came from a car. Headlights, brake lights, and blinkers. Which indicated damage to both front and back.

And two cars.

Hannah made her way into the ditch. Her knees protested a little as she squatted by a large rock protruding from the forest side of the ditch. Dark blue along one edge. A scrape of paint. Impossible to say how long it had been there, but its proximity to the shattered glass led her to assume that it was left there at the same time.

She stood up again, looked around as if the empty road could tell her more about what happened here. From inside the forest, the wind brought fragments of Gordon's conversation with Command in Luleå. Sometimes she was too quick to draw conclusions, she was aware of that, but she was pretty sure of one thing.

Nobody came out here to dispose of a body.

Two cars crashed, someone died in the crash and the person in the other car made a hurried decision to dispose of the body. Dragged it into the forest, covered it up to keep it out of sight from the road before moving on.

Hannah stopped. Both vehicles were gone.

So there must have been at least two people in the other car. Or maybe not. A person could drive their own car, then go back and move the victim's. Far-fetched, but not impossible, you could act without being seen and disturbed for hours out here on these lonely roads.

Hannah was forced to admit that the only thing she could be sure of was that a man died, and someone or some people did what they could to make sure no one found the body. And it might have worked too, if two wolves hadn't been poisoned just thirty kilometers from here.

Katja waited.

She was good at waiting.

She'd spent much of her childhood doing just that. It had been impressed upon her that patience was the key to success. When other people wanted time to pass by quickly, she knew they struggled not to think of anything at all. Tried to empty their minds completely, retreating into themselves.

Not her. She got bored too fast for that.

So she wandered around the strange apartment. Two rooms and a kitchen on the seventh floor of eleven on the outskirts of St. Petersburg. She'd already been in the tiny bedroom, sat on the twin bed with its crocheted bedspread and two ornamental pillows, curiously studied the few things in the bedside table, which told her this apartment was the home of a religious woman who needed glasses for reading and had no active sex life.

On the bureau by the window there was a photo of a man she recognized.

Stanislav Kuznetsov.

There were also a few simple make-up items in front of a dressing mirror. Without thinking about it, she moved the items around so that the containers were arranged first by size, then organized by shape (round, square), then the three lipsticks put in order from lightest to darkest, all the time staring out the window toward the other eleven-story buildings that surrounded a courtyard with too few trees and too little green to tempt anyone unless you had small children to take to the soulless and run-down playground.

Underwear, socks, tank tops, handkerchiefs, scarves, and kerchiefs in the two drawers in the bureau. Katja spent a few minutes folding them and putting them in neat piles before opening the wardrobe.

Dresses, blouses, and skirts.

Not much of anything. She quickly rearranged the hangers so that various types of garment hung together, from left to right: blouses, skirts, dresses. With one last look at the insipid art on the dark green walls, she left the bedroom and went into the living room.

A three-seat sofa, definitely from the Nineties, a stained coffee table standing in front of it. Under the table a drab, green shag rug. A sagging armchair. Everything arranged around a TV on the wall, surrounded by a dark bookshelf with about as many photo albums as books, more framed photos of what she took to be family members and relatives.

Katja randomly took down an album and sank into the armchair. The contents were from the late Seventies, she guessed, because the boy, who had to be Stanislav, seemed to be six or seven years old. He and his older sister were in most of the photographs, sometimes with a man Katja assumed was their father, who she knew had died in a car accident eight years ago. In one photo he stood in the doorway of a small cottage somewhere in the countryside squinting under the sun, shading his eyes with his hand and smiling widely.

Without warning, an image of the man she'd called her father for years popped into her head. He too was standing in a doorway, but no smile, and definitely no sun.

Immediately, she pushed away the thought, closed the album, got up, and put it back on the shelf before heading over to the window.

The heavy traffic on Afonskaja ulitsa was a distant roar. Before leaving the living room she put her finger in a flowerpot on the windowsill and found it needed watering, then she went into the bathroom. Gray waterproof wallpaper and a plastic floor in a slightly lighter shade. Six white tiles in a rectangle above the sink. A deep but short iron bathtub with ornate iron claws, and a shower curtain with angels on it.

For a moment she was back in the great hall.

The twelve bathtubs in a row with their four-degree water.

She turned to the bathroom cabinet above the sink. Before opening it, she caught a glimpse of herself in the mirror door. Her black hair in a short bob, the well-defined eyebrows above brown eyes, the high cheekbones, the straight nose, the full lips. No make-up, as always, unless the job demanded it. She knew she was considered beautiful, and it made it easier, simpler to get close. Men in particular were susceptible, but over the years she'd found that everyone, regardless of gender, was more open and welcoming to beautiful people.

The contents of the bathroom cabinet were a mess. She closed the lid on the toilet, started removing them and putting them on there. Bandages, toothpaste, floss, nasal spray, deodorant, skin cream, nail scissors, foot file, hairpins, clip earrings, bath salts, tissues, medicines (some prescription, some not). Still nothing to indicate that the woman whose bathroom cabinets she was emptying had any sex life to speak of. She did, however, have a yeast infection to judge by one of the tubes that now lay on the toilet seat.

When the cupboard was empty, Katja wiped it off with a few wet pieces of toilet paper before replacing everything according to a system where the articles were divided into four main groups: medicines, body care, hair care, other.

Satisfied with how she'd spent the last twenty minutes, she went out into the small kitchen. She could eat something, she realized, and opened the fridge, took out butter, cheese, eggs, and a beer. While the eggs were boiling on the stove, she opened the light green cupboard doors in search of bread, plates, and cutlery. Found what she was looking for and set the little kitchen table by the window. The newspaper that Kuznetsov wrote for was lying in a wicker basket on the floor, and she picked it up and placed it next to the small dish she'd put out for herself. When the eggs were ready, she rinsed them in cold water and put the pan on a hot pad.

Then she sat down to eat, while she read. Realized it would be nice with some music and started to look for a radio or something like it. Couldn't find one, but that was probably just as well. If there was music coming from inside the apartment when they arrived, they might realize something was up. But she didn't think they'd be here for a few hours.

So she waited.

She was good at waiting.

The rest of the afternoon had flown by.

Hannah returned to where they'd found the body just as Gordon was wrapping up his call.

"What did Luleå say?"

"Serious crimes is taking over."

Not exactly unexpected. A buried body was considered murder until proven otherwise, and murders were sent to Luleå.

"Who's there?"

"Erixon."

Erixon with an x and Alexander as a first name, so people called him X. Hannah knew him. Knew and liked him. He'd been the lead investigator on several other matters over the years. Most recently when they fished a body out of the Kukkolaforsen last spring.

She told Gordon what she'd found down by the road, and that she suspected two vehicles were involved, one of which was blue. Gordon listened and nodded before asking her to pick up their car in Vitvattnet.

"Take him with you," he said, nodding to Jens, who was standing idle and superfluous at a nearby uprooted tree.

"Do I have to?"

"Yes."

"Come on." She waved, and they left the same way they'd come, while Gordon started calling the others to tell them to cancel their search and return to town.

Forty-five minutes later, Hannah parked not far away from where they'd found the body. Jens would have to wait in the car while she and Gordon blocked off the road and the area around the grave in the woods. The technicians were still an hour away, probably more—the downside to being in a small town was having most of your resources at least a hundred and fifty kilometers away—so Gordon asked her to drive Jens back and pick up something for them to eat. On her way to the car, she started to feel heat in her face and around her neck, could feel the heat spreading through her body as every pore opened and sweat poured out. Without looking in the mirror, she knew she must be bright red and sweaty as she sat down next to Jens and started the car. She put the AC on full blast, while resisting the impulse to lower the windows.

The second time today.

It was bad enough when she'd been getting these once a week, was this how it was going to be from now on? It felt like doing a workout a couple times a day but with none of the upsides. Just the sweat and beet-red face.

"Can I turn up the temperature?" Jens asked after they'd driven a few kilometers.

"No, you can't."

"It's kinda cold."

"When your body decides to fuck with you on a daily basis, then you can decide the temperature in the car, OK?"

Jens nodded with complete incomprehension, made some attempt to talk to her about the events of the past few hours, but her monosyllabic grunts in response were even less inviting than on the way out, so he remained silent. It wasn't until they turned into the parking lot outside the police station and he stepped out that he opened his mouth again.

"Maybe you can let me know how things go."

"Why?"

"I'm just curious, I feel involved."

"Sure," Hannah lied effortlessly in order to end this conversation more quickly. "Morgan has your contact information, we'll keep you updated. Drive carefully." She waved, pleased to see him off for the last time, and drove down to the Coop grocery store. She actually preferred ICA Maxi, but the Coop was closer. Went to the shelves of ready-made food to choose dinner. Gordon would want something healthy. So, shrimp salad for him. Everything that looked good to her needed reheating, so she settled on a chicken wrap. A small baguette for Gordon, two bottles of Coke and a bag of nacho chips completed her shopping.

Several cars were parked outside the roadblocks when she returned. The technicians were there, Gordon had told them what they knew, the doctor they'd brought with them declared the body dead and now they were all doing their jobs. Now superfluous, Gordon and Hannah sat down on a stone outside the roadblocks to eat, watching as their colleagues worked. They didn't say much. The stillness was bone deep. The sun was still high in the sky, the insects were buzzing in the heat and occasionally fragments of a brief and quiet conversation between the men working inside the barriers floated their way.

When they had finished eating, Hannah offered to go back and get started on the paperwork; surely it was enough if only one of them stayed. Gordon could hitch a ride back with the technicians.

Two and a half hours later he knocked on her doorframe, just as she was closing the document she'd been working on.

"You're still there," he noted, sinking into her visitor's chair.

"About to leave. Did you just get back?"

"Yes, they walked through half the forest."

"Do we know who it is?"

Gordon shook his head and stifled a yawn with his hand.

"No ID, nothing."

"What's our next step? Do we release a picture?"

"We're going to discuss that tomorrow, X and me."

Gordon got to his feet again, as if he'd only realized how tired he was when he sat down. Hannah logged out of her computer, then stood up, and they made their way together down the corridor.

"Preliminary cause of death is a broken neck."

"How long had he been lying there?"

"Difficult to say, apparently. He became wolf food a week ago, so he's been there that long at least."

They were at the end of the hallway. Gordon's office was just before the doors that led to the stairs.

"See you tomorrow," he said, with a nod to his office, indicating he planned to stay a bit longer. To her surprise, Hannah realized that she'd been expecting him to ask her to wait, maybe even offer to keep her company on the way home. Maybe she'd even hoped for it.

Annoying, and unlike her.

"That you will," she said, pushed open the door and disappeared down the stairs.

A minute later, she stepped out of the glassed-in entryway and took a deep breath as the door closed behind her again.

Bright as day, still as night.

A few cars making their way down the E4, but not so many that they drowned out the sound of the river or the birdsong as she made her way home. It struck her that she hadn't talked to Thomas all day, hadn't told him what happened, or why she was so late. But then again, he'd never called her to ask either. Now it was too late. He'd surely gone to bed.

She continued down Strandgatan, turned up Packhusgatan, past the public library. Thomas used to go there all the time when the kids were small; she only went now and then. It had been several years since she'd checked out a book. Or read one, for that matter. She turned left onto Storgatan, not the world's busiest street at any time of the day, but at midnight on a Monday in June, it was completely deserted. She walked past the big yellow wood building that housed Odd Fellow and some other small shops. Realized she was hungry as she walked by a closed cafe. A long time had passed since the chicken wrap and chips. At the next intersection, she paused. Normally she turned right up Köpmansgatan, walked past the square, the City Hotel, the water tower, and on toward home. But something was gnawing at the back of her mind.

A hit-and-run accident. Two cars involved.

Not because she had any high hopes that it would be there, but it couldn't hurt to pass by. Take a look. There were usually quite a few cars parked out front.

So she headed straight instead, past two banks and H. M. Hermansson's trading yard, the large gray-blue wooden building that had stood there since 1832 and which, with its manor house and its twelve other buildings, took up an entire block. The shops then gave way to impersonal three-story brick houses that could have been in any city, though the occasional older wooden house did its best to remind you of Storgatan's glory days. Hannah turned right at Fabriksgatan and looked into the lot behind the first low red house.

The hunch seemed to pay off. The lights were on in the auto shop. She inspected the cars parked outside before opening the small metal door next to the wide dirty garage door, where a sign said they closed at 7 p.m. on weekdays.

The smell of automobiles, oil, and exhaust. The first notes of *Für Elise* rang out, signaling that someone was entering the shop, drowning out the Eighties music playing on the radio for a moment. Four cars stood inside. None of them dark blue.

"What are you doing here?"

UV appeared out of the grease pit, wiped his hands on a rag, but made no effort to approach or take her hand. Not because his hands were dirty. They had met before. Many times. Until a few years ago, there weren't many petty crimes around here that UV wasn't mixed up in somehow.

Theft, burglary, fencing stolen goods, bootlegging...

There was a rumor they called him—or that he had wanted to be called—UV because it was short for Ultra Violent. If so, it was laughably stupid, Hannah thought.

Five years ago he'd gone to prison in connection with an operation they'd done with the Finns. He'd been sentenced to three years for serious drug crimes: 1,500 Subotex pills imported from France.

Back then the market was much larger in Finland, but now that had changed. The customer base had increased in Haparanda, in the whole of Norrbotten. Mostly among young men like the one Hannah had encountered this morning. There were plenty of them, too many, no direction, no plans, no job. Haparanda had the highest unemployment rate in the region. By far. Part of a vicious cycle. The national statistics for ninth graders spoke clearly to this fact. The girls scored much better than the boys, across every subject. The men were far below the national average, lower than the girls. Fell behind. Were left behind when the young women moved away to pursue higher education.

Haparanda wasn't the only small city that was experiencing this trend, but that didn't make the problem any better.

When UV was released from prison after two years he became a father, left the criminal world altogether, took over a car repair shop and here he was, hard at work after midnight.

"You're working late," Hannah noted, taking a few steps into the room. UV leaned against one of the cars, crossed his arms over his chest, and followed her with his eyes.

"What do you want?" he asked tiredly.

"Have you had any crashed cars this past week?" Hannah turned to catch his reaction. Might as well get straight to the point.

"No."

Hannah stopped short. Out of the speakers streamed the first easily recognizable bars of the theme song from *Fame*. The drums and the bubbling synth. She fell silent, took a steadying breath.

"Can you turn off the radio?"

"Why?"

"Can you just turn it off, please."

Her tone didn't invite any objections or further questions. UV shrugged and did as she asked. Hannah closed her eyes briefly, annoyed at not being able to control this, that the walls she'd built could still be torn down so easily. Everything that had to do with her mother and, of course, Elin...

"Happy now?" UV interrupted her thoughts.

"Yes. Thanks."

Now that it was quiet, she collected herself quickly, able to push away unwanted thoughts and return to her case.

"So, no crashed car?"

"Nope."

"A dark blue one."

"No," said UV, emphasizing it by shaking his head. "No dark blue, not any other color either. No collision damage."

"Are you sure?"

"Completely."

She stood there, looking around, calculating whether there was any way to check, and realizing that there was not, not now anyway.

"If anything comes in, you let me know." She walked over to him and held out a business card. He made no effort to take it.

"I know where to reach you."

She held his gaze as she put the card back into her pocket, then she turned and walked toward the door.

"Give my regards to Tompa," she heard as her hand reached the handle. She stopped. Nobody called her husband Tompa. How well did he know UV? Was she supposed to read something into that short goodbye? Other than that he clearly knew who she was, and whom she was married to. She decided to let it go and pushed the door open. *Für Elise* followed her out of the shop again, and she headed home.

UV waited until the door closed and he was sure she wasn't coming back before letting out his irritation and anxiety. They'd left him alone since he got out of prison. He needed everyone to know he'd left that life; he was a decent family man now. He didn't want cops buzzing around. Couldn't have them here.

Would they react to the fact that he was working late?

Start snooping? Start suspecting him again?

He wouldn't be in the shop so late if he didn't have to, if the Social Insurance office hadn't made a "new assessment."

Nothing had changed.

Lovis still couldn't hold her head up, couldn't talk, couldn't laugh, she was basically blind, tube-fed and had epileptic seizures, sometimes several a day. At four years old, in many respects, she was less developed than a newborn, but still they'd decreased the amount of assistance she received. He and Stina had appealed and argued, with the municipality, with everyone, but the decision was final, so they had to try to make it work. Did everything in shifts, one of them always at home with Lovis, at all hours of the day.

It didn't work.

Stina got sick, had to go down to working half-time until she was finally on sick leave completely. He tried to work as much as he could, but they had been brought to their knees, and in order to survive they paid for help when they needed it.

Which was often. It was expensive.

The auto shop was going well, but still they needed more than what you could earn on servicing and tire and oil changes. So when they were at the absolute rock bottom he'd reached out to his old contacts in Finland and started up again.

On a smaller scale. Absolutely no drugs.

Nowadays, most of his extra income came from cars like the Mercedes S-Class. Crashed in the US last winter, repossessed by the insurance company, resold, and shipped to Europe. Everything perfectly legal so far. UV fixed them up, usually with stolen parts, and made sure they ended up in the Swedish or Finnish market. Sold as used with normal wear and tear. No history of a wreck a few months earlier in Florida. There wasn't a lot of money it, but every little bit helped.

And here she comes, the cop. Asking about collision damage.

He decided to give it a day or two, see how things played out. He knew what he knew, but not what he should do with the information just yet. The only thing he knew for sure was that he couldn't go back to prison. Stina and Lovis wouldn't survive without him.

Naked, she climbed out of bed and headed to the bathroom. She knew he was watching her. They'd just had sex. She was good at it, learned how to do it with the same thoroughness as everything else. He'd been better than expected.

Katja had chosen him in a hotel bar. Businessman, foreigner. Probably forty-five, average looking, brown eyes, dark hair neatly trimmed, a few days of beard stubble, and beneath his unusual jacket and light blue shirt, worn open at the neck, he seemed to have taken care of himself well enough. Sitting alone with his computer. Before she made her move, she checked if there was a ring. She didn't care if he was cheating on someone, but it was always easier if they didn't have to make the choice. Worst-case scenario, they get cold feet late in the evening, and she didn't want to waste any time on him if he wasn't going to sleep with her. She went ahead and asked in English if the place opposite him was available, introduced herself as Nadja.

His name was Simon. Simon Nuhr.

From Munich, it turned out.

"I speak a little German," she said with a thick Russian accent. She was able to speak German fluently, without a hint of an accent. German and five other languages, and she could make herself understood in another six or seven more. She was happy to have the opportunity to practice her German, she had told him, making a few easy mistakes, which he laughed at and corrected. She asked if she could buy him a drink, but he wanted to do the buying.

"A glass of white wine then, please."

He ordered a beer. They toasted over his folded laptop. She smiled encouragingly at him and smoothly steered the conversation further. It was clear that he realized she was way out of his league, looks wise, and his joy in her company seemed sincere, his attentions eager, like he couldn't quite believe his luck. Still, or maybe because of that, he'd hesitated when, after a few hours together, she suggested they go somewhere private.

"I'm not a prostitute," she said. He blushed and stammered a protest that he hadn't thought she was. He was lying. When a young, attractive woman introduces herself to a wealthy businessman at a hotel in St. Petersburg, westerners think that means she's a prostitute. Possibly also a blackmailer. Some companies even warned their employees about this, she knew that. So now he hesitated. Cold feet. They'd just met, so saying that she liked him or had any other deeper feelings for him would seem strange and suspicious, but if she was going to get what she wanted she would have to assuage his fears of being drugged, robbed, or worse.

She tried the truth. Or a variant of it.

She leaned forward, lowered her voice, and switched to English.

"I finished a big project today," she said, holding his gaze. "I'm not from here, I'm going home tomorrow, I want to relax tonight, and I like sex." She stared at him with an expression that dared him not to believe in her.

Too much? Too straightforward?

Apparently not. Simon Nuhr nodded, unable to suppress a smile as he told her he had a room on the fourth floor.

Katja came back from the bathroom. Simon was lying in the double bed, looking at her in a way—even if he wasn't aware of it—that showed he still couldn't believe his luck. She let him look.

"Can I turn on the TV?" she asked in her broken German, and took the remote from the small desk.

"Do you want to watch TV now?" he replied, looking at the time.

"Do you want sleep?" she asked, deliberately making a grammatical mistake, with an expression that said she wouldn't disturb him with the TV if he didn't want her to.

"No, no, we can watch TV."

She went back and lay down beside him again. Stuffed a pillow behind her back. The remote in one hand, the other hand resting on his stomach. She could feel his muscles stiffen at her touch. She put one leg over his, the outside of her thigh against his cock, and started to flip through the channels until she found the news.

A major rescue effort was underway at an almost completely destroyed apartment building. One side had collapsed, as if a giant had stamped on it, leveled it to the ground, but the other half of the house's eleven floors remained intact. Search and rescue teams were combing the rubble for survivors. The news anchor and the scrolling text at the bottom of the screen said the same thing. It had now been confirmed that the journalist Stanislav Kuznetsov and his female colleague Galina Sokolova died in the gas explosion that destroyed large portions of a residential building on Afonskaja ulitsa.

Sometimes you had to make it look like an accident. It had been even more important than usual this time. Too many people had too much to lose if the truth came out.

So she buried it.

"What happened?" Simon asked with a nod to the TV where both speech and text were in Russian.

"Gas explosion. A very famous journalist, critical of the Kremlin, and his mistress died while fucking in his mother's apartment."

"They reported that?" Simon asked with surprise in his voice. "That he was unfaithful?"

"No, I just know."

Her phone beeped on the nightstand. She took it, looked at the display. She'd been paid. She allowed herself a pleased smile.

"Good news?"

"Yes."

She put the phone back, picked up the remote, put the TV on silent, and began moving the hand she had on his stomach downwards.

Slowly she's coming to life again.

Haparanda.

As the sun rises for a second week of cloudless skies, she's exposed mercilessly as the aging prima donna she is. She needs a little help, some tenderness, dedication, and nothing as literal as a new coat of paint, some new paneling or tiles to hide her flaws, to cover up that she no longer breathes with the same vitality or optimism she once did.

Does she miss the old days? Of course she does.

There were times when she'd thought she sat at the very center of the world. She had. A real metropolis in the far north. Back when spies, smugglers, revolutionaries, prostitutes, fortune hunters, and artists came from near and far to gather inside her. International politics, business deals, and the fate of humanity were discussed here, agreed upon, arranged in the rooms of her City Hotel.

In April 1917, Lenin stopped here on his way out of exile in Switzerland. Horses with sledges took him across the ice to Tornio and then on to Petrograd, toward October and his role in history. What you think about that depends on who you are;

she assigns no value, merely notes it. There was a time when everyone seemed to know who she was, where she lay, and wanted to go to her.

The sun rises higher, chasing away the shadows, old and new. Warming the ground of the cemetery where Valborg Karlsson is placing new flowers on her husband's grave under the morning light. She misses him. All the time. She wakes up early, especially in the summer, comes here every day. Has been doing so for the past nine years, unaware that a nurse at her husband's retirement home murdered him with an insulin injection.

The little apartment where Jonathan "Jonte" Lundin, sweaty with the hint of a smile on his lips, is sleeping fully clothed on his bed is already warm and stuffy and smells like garbage. It will be a few hours before he wakes up and his relentless pursuit of drugs begins all over again. By then he'll have forgotten he was dreaming, unable to recall the abstract feeling of complete freedom and happiness that he hasn't felt in his waking state for many years.

In the house on Klövervägen, Jennie and Tobias Wallgren are having tender and enthusiastic morning sex. They got married in the Haparanda church only two weeks ago. Tobias made a promise to himself that he would be faithful once they got married, something he'd been unable to accomplish over the four years they've been together, and the two they've been engaged. So far, he's kept his promise. They're making love without protection, and Tobias comes with a long moan into the pillow. One of his sperm will find its way into Jennie's egg, and she'll become pregnant with a child whom everyone will know in twenty-three years, not just in Haparanda, but in all of Sweden.

Stina Laurin is standing at the doorway of her daughter's bedroom. Lovis is sound asleep now, but she had a seizure last night. It was Stina's night, but Dennis woke up and helped her anyway. Even though he worked late. He looked so tired when he headed back to the auto shop this morning, but they need the money more than he needs his sleep. As so often happens lately, she wonders how long they can endure, and when those thoughts arrive, her fear of losing him, she can't hold back the forbidden. That she doesn't love her daughter, that they would be better off without her. And she hates herself for it.

In one of the low, light green townhouses on Kornvägen, Krista Raivio is trying to come up with an explanation for her colleagues to explain her bruises and swollen eye, while she cuts up bread for her son's breakfast. She wonders, as she often does, what it would feel like to plunge this sharp knife into the chest of her violent husband. It will be another three years before she'll find out.

Sandra Fransson leaves her house, Kenneth still asleep upstairs, and heads to work. She's already looking forward to her lunch break, when she'll head to the Rajalla shopping center in Torneå a few hundred meters on the other side of the river, across the border, and buy the vase she wants so much. She has sixty euros folded in the front pocket of her pants. She knows she shouldn't, but she's going to treat herself. She needs to treat herself, she deserves it. Like most other inhabitants of Haparanda she looks up at the clear blue sky and assumes it's going to be another beautiful day.

She doesn't know, no one knows, that the dark clouds are starting to pile up in the east.

Even before turning, Hannah knew the other side of the bed would be empty. That's the way it was these days. Even on weekends. Thomas went to bed early, sometimes as early as nine. Was deep asleep with his back to her when she came to bed hours later. Sometimes she heard his alarm go off at five, but usually not. She wasn't even sure if he set it every morning nowadays. He woke up anyway.

Different circadian rhythms.

He'd always been a morning person, worked out, showered, got the kids ready for school, all before heading off to work. As for her, she treasured those lonely hours when evening turned to night, when the kids were sleeping and the house was quiet. Her time.

But still they used to see each other, talk to each other.

Yesterday they didn't talk once.

Hannah climbed out of bed, pulled on a pair of jeans and a sweater, headed to the kitchen, threw a routine glance at the kitchen table, though she knew there'd be no note, then opened the cupboards, took out the coffee grounds and scooped them into the coffee machine. While she waited for it to brew, she skimmed the first page of the morning newspaper, which Thomas still had delivered to their mailbox. Nothing about the man they found in the forest yesterday. She didn't have to flip through to know that; if it had made the paper it would be front-page news. She picked up the cellphone, dialed a number, and wedged the phone against her shoulder as she opened the fridge. Thomas answered after the second ring.

"Hey, what are you up to?" she greeted him.

"Working—or rather, I'm at work; it's pretty quiet here."

Hannah could picture him, leaning back in his office chair with his feet on the pedestal beneath his tidy desk. His office was in the last building on Stationsgatan overlooking the palatial railway station, built with a great deal of self-confidence and optimism during the First World War. Or the Youth House as it had been called for many years, ever since passenger service was terminated in 1992, and the city stopped using it as a station. There was talk of passenger trains being reinstated, but most said they'd believe it when they see it.

"We found a body yesterday," Hannah said, taking butter, cheese, and juice out of the fridge.

"Did you?"

"Yes, that's why I didn't come home."

"OK."

Not the reaction she expected. She'd expected him to sit up straight in his chair, lean forward, and ask her to tell him more, tell him everything. Not just an "OK."

He had always been genuinely interested. Not only during their years in Stockholm but after they moved back north. Even though she'd never hunted down any cunning serial killers or been part of other exciting cases, he'd always seemed engaged by her work. Much more than she was in his. There wasn't much to talk about when it came to accounting, she felt.

"Might have been a hit-and-run, and the driver hid and buried him in the woods," she continued, despite his lackluster response, while buttering two pieces of crispbread.

"Do you have any suspects?"

"No, we don't even know who he is."

"Who found him?"

"We did. Some wolves had eaten part of him and…it's a long story."

"You'll have to tell me tonight. Will you be home?"

"It depends on what happens, but yes, I think so."

"OK, I'll see you then."

Clearly wrapping this up. He wanted to hang up. Her thoughts from before she got up came back. Not only had they not talked at all yesterday, but when was the last time they did anything together? She couldn't remember. Seen each other, yes, been home at the same time, sure, but actually done something, just the two of them…?

They didn't typically go to many local cultural events, or sports, or entertainment, but now and then Thomas would see something in the paper and suggest they go. Then it struck her that he'd stopped doing that. Since when?

"How do you know UV?" she asked, and started to slice the cheese, unwilling to end the conversation.

"Who?"

"UV. Dennis Niemi."

"The mechanic?"

"Yes."

"He fixes the company cars, and our car and scooter when we need it. Why?"

"Nothing, I talked to him yesterday, and he told me to say hello to you."

Not the whole truth, but simpler this way. Hearing Thomas's name in UV's shop had reminded her of a feeling she'd had for a while: she had no idea what he was up to these days.

What he did with his time, when, or with whom.

Not just a different circadian rhythm. They lived almost separate lives.

He'd been away so much more than usual this past year. Spent more time at work, or hunting, fishing, up in the cabin, more time at his nephew's. Other things held his attention. Maybe someone else, too. She didn't think so, but she couldn't be certain. They definitely had less sex. Hannah had thought it would be the other way around once Alicia, their youngest, moved out last year. Had been looking forward to it. For many years they'd been forced to sneak around, wait for those relatively rare occasions when they were alone in the house so as not to embarrass sensitive teenagers with their parents' sex life. Now it was only the two of them. Full speed ahead, but not that much was happening in the bedroom. Around the beginning of the year she'd decided to keep track on her phone, noting when they had sex by adding a simple "*s*" alongside the date. So far, there were two "*s*"s in the calendar. The latest from April 8. They were now a good ways into June.

"What did you do yesterday?" she asked, and quickly and efficiently pushed away the thought that he might finally have tired of her. Of them as a couple.

"Nothing special."

"You didn't call."

"I assumed you were working, didn't want to disturb you."

She went back to her butter and cheese. Remembered how things used to be. Back when they were newly married and had not long moved to Stockholm. She had no cell phone then, almost no one did. Instead, she had a pager and when it buzzed she'd try to get to a phone as quickly as possible. Thomas was at home with Elin, something might have happened, but no. He just wanted to check in, stay in touch.

Sometimes all he wanted was to hear her voice.

Didn't care that she was working. If he was disturbing her.

"OK," she said briefly.

"Yes."

"But I'll see you tonight."

"Yes, I'll be home at the usual time."

She ended the call, put the phone on the counter, and started eating her breakfast. Flipped through the newspaper. Without much effort at all, this morning's conversation floated away.

Dwelling didn't make anything better.

After a little over twenty minutes of walking, Hannah pushed open the front door, passed by Carin at reception with a hello, pulled out her key card, tapped in the code, and headed inside to change into a uniform.

On her way up to the morning meeting, she heard footsteps behind her on the stairs. Stopped and waited for Gordon, who was coming toward her with a smile on his face and a thin folder in his hand.

"Hey, isn't X with you?" she asked, assuming it was still classified as a murder investigation, even if the crime classification would most likely change to manslaughter, unless the driver was under the influence, then there might be talk of homicide. Assuming they could find him.

"He's waiting until after the medical examiner and technical reports are done before coming up," Gordon replied. "So we're supposed to continue with our work and keep him updated."

"I stopped by UV's yesterday," she said as they headed up toward the kitchenette.

"When?"

"On my way home. Crashed cars, you know, so I thought of him."

"He's retired, isn't he?"

"That's what he says, but he was in his shop after midnight."

"He probably has a lot to do."

"Must be nice to have such a high opinion of humanity."

She smiled at him and pushed open the door to the spacious area outside their meeting room. P-O sat like a sad bulldog in the big blue corner sofa, deeply engrossed in his phone, but he stood up when he saw them. Lurch was standing by the long counter along the wall, waiting for the coffee machine to deliver.

"Hey, guys," Hannah greeted them.

"Hello," Lurch replied as he grabbed his cup.

Gordon headed directly into the meeting room, followed by Lurch and P-O. Hannah pushed the button for a large cup, extra strong, no milk.

In the meeting room, she sat down next to Morgan, who nodded to her. Opposite her sat Lurch, P-O, and Ludwig Simonsson, the newest recruit. Been here for almost a year now. From Småland, educated in Växjö, was a trainee at Kalix, then got together with a Finn living in Haparanda. A single mother. She and her daughter spoke no Swedish, Ludwig no Finnish. But he learned quickly, was understanding more and more. Which was making things easier, and not just on a personal level. One third of Haparandas were born in Finland. Four out of five had Finnish heritage. 'Sweden's most Finnish city,' it was sometimes called, which wasn't entirely uncontroversial among the increasingly small slice of the population that only spoke Swedish. Think what you want about it, the city was now basically bilingual, and it was becoming more and more difficult to get by without Finnish.

"The medical examiner and forensics aren't finished yet," Gordon began, and the low-pitched buzz in the room immediately ceased. "But they've found a lot in a short time. If we start with a forensic autopsy…" He opened the thin folder in his hand and took out one of the documents inside. "As I said, preliminary, but cause of death seems to be a broken neck. Damage to his legs indicates that he was hit by a car."

"So he was outside his car when he was hit," Hannah interjected, more a statement than a question.

"Seems like it. He also had a gunshot wound. Above his right buttocks. The bullet was still there." Gordon flipped through the few printouts in the folder, switched reports. "The technicians say it was 7.62 mm caliber."

"Finnish assault rifles still have that caliber," Morgan informed them.

"No ID, nothing in his pockets except a Russian matchbox, Russian cigarettes, and some of his clothes were purchased in Russia," Gordon continued. "So probably Russian himself, though he's not in our registry," he concluded and closed the folder again.

"What the hell was he doing out there?" P-O asked the room.

"Smuggling something," Lurch suggested, and received a nod from the others.

If there was a border, then there was smuggling.

Haparanda was no exception.

Drugs, of course, but most of the smuggling was the EU's fault; they'd outlawed the tobacco product snus in every member country except Sweden. A product that was forbidden to sell, impossible to buy legally, but which could be found in legitimate abundance only a few hundred meters away. Inevitably it was smuggled. The snus trade attracted not just adventurous young people looking to make a little extra cash driving over the border with a little more snus than was legal. If you moved large enough volumes, big money could be made. So a Russian smuggler on some backroad wasn't at all far-fetched.

"The paint on the stone, do we know if it came from a car?" said Hannah.

"Not yet. Later today probably."

"But surely it must have been somebody local who ran over him?"

"Because?" Ludwig retorted.

"You have to know about that little shitty road, no map or GPS will take you there."

"Good point, so let's concentrate on the Övre area. I'm going to scrounge up some people to start knocking on doors."

Hannah nodded to herself. They had to start somewhere, and this limited the search area even if it still comprised twenty villages with more than 350 inhabitants spread over an area that had a circumference of twenty or thirty kilometers.

"Weren't a couple of Russians involved in that shooting outside Rovaniemi a week or two ago?" said Morgan, his mind apparently still on the Finnish assault rifle and the Russians.

Everyone knew what he was referring to. Some sort of drug deal gone awry. The Finnish police hadn't asked for any assistance, so that was basically all they knew.

"Is there any way they could be connected?" Ludwig asked, as usual with diphthongs and a heavy-r in his broad Småland accent.

"Wouldn't hurt to check."

"I can do that," Hannah offered, and no one objected.

"Rovaniemi, does that mean the Finns will be here, too?"

"We'll have to see," Gordon replied, looking at everyone around the table again. "We found what was left of the meat that poisoned the wolves."

"Did we?" Hannah asked in surprise. "When?"

"My neighbors and I kept searching after you found the body yesterday," Morgan said, putting a whole cracker into his mouth.

"And?"

She waited while Morgan chewed and washed down his cracker with a sip of coffee before answering her with a shrug.

"Nothing special. It was on a cliff. Had managed to kill some birds and a fox, too."

"Do we have any idea who put it there?" P-O asked.

"No, but Hellgren owns the land adjacent."

Everyone except Ludwig nodded almost simultaneously. Morgan didn't need to say more.

Anton Hellgren.

Suspected of serious hunting violations, poaching, animal cruelty.

Accused of illegal hunting of the lynx, king eagle, wolverine, and bear.

Investigated a number of times, but never convicted or even prosecuted.

"What kind of poison was it, do we know?" asked Ludwig. "Can we trace it?"

"SVA said that the wolves died from alpha chloralose poisoning," Hannah replied. "In other words, ordinary rat poison. So no, probably not."

"What should we do?" P-O asked, turning to Gordon again.

"About Hellgren? Nothing—not at the moment anyway," Gordon said, while gathering together the papers in front of him. "Hannah will be in touch with Finland, the rest of us have our jobs. There will be a brief press conference after this meeting, so hopefully we'll get some good tips after that."

"Reckon we'll hit the headlines?" Morgan threw that out with a smile behind his huge beard.

"Preferably not."

"Russian Gangster Eaten by Wolves," Morgan said, underling every word with his hand.

"We're not going to say a word about nationality or wolves, so it won't be that," Gordon said, and stood up with a smile. The meeting was over.

"Too bad, it's the perfect headline. Russians and wolves, guaranteed to scare people more than those 'your headache might be a brain tumor' stories they run every summer."

"Russian gangster eaten by wolves—what's that in Finnish, Ludwig?" asked Lurch. Their colleague pondered for a while, his lips moving silently.

"*Venäläisen gangsterin…syönyt sudet.*"

"So close, any day now you and your girlfriend are going to be able to talk to each other," Morgan said with a smile and put a hand on his colleague's shoulder.

It should be raining, Sami Ritola thought as he leaned back against a birch tree, smoking a cigarette.

It should be a downpour, black umbrellas, surly men in their leather jackets, cops discreetly taking pictures in the background, the widow and her children standing at the open grave. It could have been like a movie. If it had rained.

But it didn't.

The ceremony was over. One by one, rugged men were paying their respects to the widow and her two children, murmuring a few words, nodding, a supportive hand on her shoulder or arm, some gave and received a hug. Sami stubbed out his cigarette, emptied his lungs of smoke, and readied himself. They'd identified six of the seven bodies found in the forest glade outside Rovaniemi. Four of them were members or initiates of MC Sudet, an older motorcycle gang that existed long before the Outlaws and Bandidos, the Shark Riders and Satudarah, or whatever the new gangs were calling themselves these days. In the past ten years, the number of criminal motorcycle gangs had more than doubled in Finland, but MC Sudet was holding its own, had even grown, despite the competition. It was rumored that one reason was their ruthlessness, the other was their Russian connection.

Valerij Zagornij.

Very powerful. Very, very dangerous.

Matti Husu, the gang's red-bearded leader for the past eight years, was walking down the path on his way to the parking lot where motorcycles had been lined up to lean in an impressively symmetric display. The heels of his boots echoed against the asphalt. Sami left his spot beneath the birch and slid quietly by his side as he passed.

Matti gave Sami a look that said exactly what he thought of his presence here without slowing a bit.

"Nice funeral."

No reaction, they kept walking. Sami glanced over his shoulder. The rest of the gang was behind them, all staring disapprovingly at him. Sami nodded to the grave behind them.

"Pentti, what a guy. Loved the tribal tatt around the eye, very cool." He turned back to Matti again. "Did he do that before or after Mike Tyson, do you know?"

"Don't talk about him."

"What should we talk about then?"

"Nothing, we have nothing to talk about."

"Yes, we do, and as I always say: we can do it here or down at the station."

He took a pack of cigarettes from his pocket and held one out to Matti who, after a moment or two of hesitation, took it with a sigh. He stopped, nodded to the others to continue, while Sami fished out a lighter and lit their cigarettes.

"We want the same thing," he said, blowing out the smoke. "Someone shot Pentti's neck off. Can you say that? Shot his neck off... Who the fuck cares, that's what they did anyway. And they killed the others. We want to know who."

Matti didn't say anything, just took a drag on his cigarette and looked over at the rest of the gang waiting by their motorcycles.

"There was a Russian jeep at the scene," Sami continued. "We were able to ID two more. Both Russians. What happened?"

"Don't you know? You seem to know everything."

"Come on, help me out a little here."

"You'll never find him."

"Him. Do you know who did it?"

Matti met his gaze in silence, a look that meant he'd said too much already. Sami shook his head and gave the bearded gang leader a troubled look.

"Matti, here's the deal. The citizens of Uleå have taken over this investigation, and if this stays in the papers, it's going to end up in Helsinki soon. There are political points to be made, you know, getting tough on the gangs, organized crime, blah blah blah. We'll get more men up here, more resources, watch you around the clock. And that will make it harder for you to do business."

He paused, took a drag while holding Matti's gaze, gauging how well his little speech had gone over. At least he seemed to have given Matti something to think about.

"You have a mosquito on your forehead."

"What?"

"A mosquito," Sami repeated, pointing. "On your forehead. I could swat it, but then your guys would shoot me."

Matti ran an irritated hand along his forehead, looking at his fingers and reversing the movement.

"Tell us what you know, we'll take care of him, you can carry on as usual, a win-win."

"Drop it, Sami. He's dead."

Sami met the gang leader's eyes. Could feel his pulse start to quicken.

Was that it? Was he confessing? Could the theory he'd heard and more or less immediately discarded be right? He needed to know more. Like when he died, and more importantly...

"Where is he?... And where is...you know."

"He's dead. He just doesn't know it yet." Matti patted him on the shoulder, threw what was left of his cigarette on the ground and headed off to his motorcycle. The others started their engines when they saw he was on his way, but no one would dare to drive off until Matti started rolling. As they rolled off, the engines shredded the silence of the cemetery.

Sami walked back, watching as the widow and her two small children were cautiously led to a parked car by a couple who were probably her parents. It was a pity, of course, for her, for the kids, but Pentti had spent fourteen of his thirty-eight years incarcerated, had been stabbed twice, shot once, so the fact that he hadn't made it to retirement couldn't have come as a complete shock to her.

The phone buzzed in his pocket, he took it out and looked at the display. Sweden was calling.

"Calling once, calling twice, three times…and sold for sixty-five kronor."

The greasy auctioneer banged his gavel against the piece of wood he had in his hand and wiped his forehead with a handkerchief before announcing the next item for sale. René sat on the far right-hand side, as far away as possible from the windows where the drawn floral curtains struggled vainly to keep out the broiling sun. It was oppressively hot in this room; the huge fan slowly spinning in the ceiling merely redistributed heat rather than cooling. He fanned himself with a folded auction catalog, unwilling to take off his navy blue, double-breasted blazer and sit there in his shirtsleeves only.

He often went to the auctions in Åskogen. He wasn't alone. The yellow assembly room was crowded. Most people were here for the fun of it, something to do, the chance to find a bargain, get something they liked or needed for cheap. The occasional collector came, too. René recognized at least two. Both gentlemen in their fifties whom he'd seen at nearby farm auctions. They tried to hide their knowledge to keep from increasing interest, but René had seen through them a long time ago. They knew exactly what to bid on and for how much.

Just like René, though for completely different reasons.

Today two estates were being auctioned off. Spread all around the room and up on the small stage were items of furniture, china, appliances, lamps, bric-a-brac, art, rugs, tools, mirrors, and the so-called bargain bins, which was what they were auctioning off now. Boxes of various small items thrown together, of too little worth to be sold separately.

"And here we have bargain bin number four," said the sweaty man while his colleague held up the items. "A glass dolphin, three tubs of oil, a snow globe, a pot coaster, and a small garden gnome with a wheelbarrow, among other things. Plenty of nice stuff. Do I hear twenty kronor?"

René waited, looked around; he had an idea who might bid. A woman in the second row raised her hand. One of those on René's list, she'd already bid on a lava lamp, a cross-stitch of the *Mona Lisa*, and one of the previous bargain bins.

"I hear twenty kronor," the auctioneer confirmed.

"Thirty," René said.

The auctioneer called the bid and looked at the woman, who raised by ten.

"Forty kronor," he said, turning back to René, who raised his hand and nodded.

"Fifty."

The woman turned to see who was bidding against her. René let his lips form a smile. The auctioneer repeated René's bid. The woman shook her head.

"Nobody else?... Calling once, calling twice, three times and sold for fifty kronor."

While they moved on to bargain bin number five, René headed to the front and paid. In cash. This was the third lot he'd bid on today; it was enough. With the box under his arm, he left the room, walked past the busy cafe, and out to his five-year-old wine-red Toyota Yaris. He put the box in the trunk alongside the items he'd bought earlier, started the car, and began the drive back to Haparanda.

Once out on the main road, he set his cruise control to 90 km/h and fell into the rhythm of the traffic. An ordinary car among other ordinary cars.

Anonymity. Was there anything better?

He'd been doing business in Haparanda for over two years now. Lived in a one-bedroom apartment downtown. Worked part-time at Max's hamburger restaurant. He told his colleagues he was studying long distance the rest of the time. Archives and Information Science at Mid Sweden University. He'd deliberately selected the course he thought none of them would be interested enough to ask about. He never participated in any activities, never got beers with them, or went to the movies, or to anyone's house. Had no girlfriend or boyfriend. Knew the others at work thought he was a bit of a weirdo with his proper way of dressing and quiet way of speaking, and they'd long since stopped trying to include him in their plans. That suited him perfectly.

Only ten people in Haparanda knew he existed. And of those only four knew what he was really up to.

Others in his position wanted as many people as possible—as long as they were the 'right' people, of course—to know what they were up to. Needed to be feared and admired. As far as René could see, they had no other objective than to get their egos stroked. That sort of confirmation was something he neither needed nor craved.

He knew what he was, and why he was.

Successful because he was ambitious and smart.

When he was fifteen, his parents had him examined. All through his childhood, he'd been different, odd, a lone wolf who didn't make friends. Then after a few incidents at school—which he hated—his parents started to question his capacity for empathy. Predictably, they thought he must be the one who had something wrong with him, not them, the unambitious, low-intelligence, unstimulating, unimaginative people whose home he grew up in.

After a battery of tests, examinations, and expensive psychological visits, they got what they wanted. No, not a grateful son who realized he was wrong, who in future would do whatever he could not to hate every second of their brain-dead middle-class existence. No, they got something better. A diagnosis. A confirmation of what they knew all along.

He was sick.

A high-functioning sociopath. Or psychopath, the difference wasn't exactly clear. However, that was not the most important part of the diagnosis. Not for him. It was his high performance.

Or to put it another way: intelligence.

Later, he took several IQ tests and at best ended up at 139 on the Wechsler Scale. Qualified for membership in Mensa and the like, but he had no interest whatsoever in being in a larger context. Or to expose his superior intelligence in any way.

The car radio was playing Whitney Houston. René turned up the volume. Whitney was pure perfection. She had it all: the voice, the looks, the vulnerability, the strength, the intimacy. A complete artist. He agreed with Patrick Bateman on that, the protagonist of Bret Easton Ellis's novel *American Psycho*. He didn't like the other artists Bateman praised—Genesis, Phil Collins, Huey Lewis and the News—didn't think the book was particularly good either, mostly read it because of the title, hadn't seen the movie.

But Whitney...

He maintained that her first album was the best debut ever, though his personal favorite was *My Love Is Your Love* from 1998.

Her story was perfect too, from its beginning to its tragic end. Childhood singing gospel, supportive but ever more demanding family, abuse, discovery, breakthrough, the absolute pinnacle, the world at her feet, the press, forced to hide her sexuality, family betrayal, the fall, the comeback attempts, the public humiliation, death. A polished Hollywood writer couldn't have created better, and with a moral lesson at the end.

Don't do drugs, kids.

René smiled to himself, turned up the volume further, and continued driving at the speed limit toward Haparanda.

Kenneth was sitting on the stone steps with a beer can in his hand when Thomas turned into the driveway of the big two-story house with asbestos-cement siding and a mansard roof, which along with a handful of other houses comprised the tiny village of Norra Storträsk. Basically low maintenance, the realtor had told them when Kenneth and Sandra had bought it two years ago.

Basically... Some of the asbestos-cement panel tiles had already cracked and needed to be replaced, and the whole house could use a good wash; several of the panels had turned green from what Sandra hoped was algae, but Thomas feared was mold. The white paint had long since flaked off of all the window frames, which had started to rot here and there. The glass in one window was broken, replaced by plywood, and the stairs that Kenneth was now unwillingly getting up from and heading down had started cracking in several places around the rusty iron railing. If you drove by on the road, which not many did, you might mistakenly think the house had been abandoned.

Thomas raised a hand in greeting to Kenneth and climbed out. His sister's son had never exactly radiated health and wholesomeness, but today he seemed even paler and skinnier than usual as he dragged his feet toward the car. Wild shoulder-length hair, dark circles under his eyes, a black T-shirt with a zombie-like creature on it that Thomas knew was called Eddie, dark green shorts that hung wide around his pale, skinny legs, feet shoved into a pair of clogs.

"What are you doing here?" Kenneth asked, giving Thomas a quick hug.

"Slow day at work, so I thought I'd fix your water heater."

"Oh, that's awesome."

"How are you?" Thomas asked over his shoulder as he opened the back of his car, took out his toolbox and some spare parts.

"I'm fine, just fine."

"What are you up to?"

Kenneth shrugged his thin shoulders and raised his hands.

"Nothin' special, just hanging out…"

Kenneth picked a little nervously at his beard, avoiding Thomas's eyes, then turned to walk back toward the house. Thomas surveyed him before falling in behind. Was he imagining it, or did Kenneth seem…nervous? As if he were having to make an effort to appear normal. Thomas found it hard to believe he'd start doing drugs again; Sandra would never allow it, she'd kick him out immediately. Kenneth loved Sandra; he'd never risk what they had together. All the same, something was off.

Thomas had gotten to know his nephew well over the last few years. He'd been the only one in the family who visited him when he was serving his time. After Kenneth got out and decided to stay in Haparanda, Rita asked Thomas to keep an eye on her son, check on him now and then, help him get back on the right track, make sure he was doing OK.

In the beginning, Thomas urged his sister to come visit her son and him and Hannah. But it was never the right time, something always prevented her. She never said it in so many words, but Thomas knew that Stefan wouldn't let her go. His brother-in-law maintained order through discipline, obedience, and control. He didn't have to expressly forbid Rita from visiting, it was enough to let her know how disappointed he would be if she went. So she never came. Almost never called either, and there was no contact on social media. According to Kenneth, she daren't risk it, not with his father combing through her call history every month.

Thomas knew that Stefan had forbidden his son from ever coming home. He could move back to Stockholm, but he was not welcome in their house in the suburbs. Made it clear he had only two children now, not three.

"Is this a bad time?" Thomas asked as they approached the house, giving Kenneth a chance to tell him if something was weighing on him.

"No, it'll be good to get it fixed."

Sandra was showering at work; where Kenneth showered, Thomas didn't know. Maybe he wasn't showering at all. Thomas hoped that wasn't the case, for Sandra's sake if nothing else. The water heater had been broken for over a week.

They entered the small hallway that Thomas had helped them repaper after a leak had caused water damage. He opened the basement door to the left, which was still a bit warped, flicked the black light switch and headed down the stairs. Kenneth followed him down. It was humid and cool, and as usual Thomas thought he could detect a faint whiff of mold down there. He walked over to the old, round water tank. The earth-leakage circuit breaker he'd installed when they moved in had been tripped—probably a coil had cracked somewhere; he'd brought two replacements with him. The boiler was partially built into a shelf system, and Thomas had to clear away plastic tubs of screws and nails, a couple of garden pots, a bag of LECA blocks, a box of rat poison, and some old paint cans to get to it.

"How's work going?" Thomas asked, as he turned off the power to the water heater and started to adjust the knobs in order to drain it.

"Slow."

"Are you looking?"

"Yes, but not right now, haven't for a while."

Thomas put down his wrench, straightened up, and looked at his nephew.

"Is everything OK?"

"Yes, of course."

"You seem a little...off."

Kenneth stood there, arms crossed over his chest, not saying a word. He used to share personal things with Thomas, sometimes in a roundabout way, but he would answer a direct question. Now Thomas was fairly sure his nephew was mulling over a lie.

"No, I'm just a little tired," he finally said with a shrug. "Sleeping badly."

"Why is that?"

"I don't know. The heat maybe."

Kenneth's eyes roved away; he pulled absentmindedly on his beard. Thomas got the same impression as when he first saw his nephew outside. What would you call it? Hunted. Kenneth looked hunted.

"How's Hannah?" Kenneth asked, breaking the silence.

"Fine, working a lot... Can you go empty out the pipes? Use the kitchen faucet."

"Sure."

Kenneth disappeared up the stairs, obviously relieved to be able to leave the basement for a moment. When he came back, Thomas resolved to steer the conversation toward more neutral subjects, away from how Kenneth was doing, away from Hannah. He'd been thinking about her since this morning, since she'd told him about the body in the forest. Could hear that she expected him to show more interest, to engage more with her. Like before.

But he didn't dare. He was afraid to reveal anything.

Something must be weighing on Kenneth, but who was Thomas to go rooting around in things like that? God knew he had his own secrets.

Hannah was sitting at her desk with her third cup of coffee. After the meeting and her conversation with the folks in Finland, she'd skimmed through the reports and reviewed her own notes to see if she could come up with any leads worth pursuing, but there wasn't much to go on. She would have to wait until Sami Ritola sent her his case file, and hopefully an ID for the Russian in the forest. Gordon had submitted an inquiry to Interpol and a DNA test to the Prüm Register; neither had gotten back to them yet. But the dead Finns outside Rovaniemi were in a local motorcyle gang, so if the body was connected to them there was a possibility Ritola could ID him. Hannah had emailed him a picture and crossed her fingers. But still she needed to keep busy with something, so she downed the last dregs of her coffee, and headed down the hall toward Gordon's office.

"I'm going to pay Hellgren a visit," she said, pulling on her uniform jacket.

"Why?"

"Well, we still have to investigate those hunting violations, but honestly, mostly just for the hell of it." Which she was pretty sure was the only thing she'd get out of it. Hellgren had gotten himself out of jams where the evidence was much more damning; what they had to go on now barely qualified as circumstantial.

"Want some company?"

"Sure."

They left the station together. Hannah had expected to see at least a few journalists lingering outside, but no one was there. The press conference, which had been held in Luleå with Gordon on Skype, had been a rather tame affair. They announced that they'd found the victim of a hit-and-run accident, revealed where it happened, and asked the public to call if they'd seen anything suspicious in the area last week, like for example a dark blue car. Nothing about the bullet, the wolves, or any connection to Rovaniemi. But in a town where hitting a moose was front-page news, she thought there'd be at least a little more excitement about the violent death of a human being. Apparently not.

They took Gordon's car, drove up the E4, past Ikea and toward the west. They hadn't been driving for more than a few minutes when Hannah started to feel the now familiar but always unwelcome heat spreading from her chest upwards.

"Goddamn it!" She rolled down the window to let in a cool breeze. Could already feel the sweat running down her neck and in between her breasts.

"What is it?" said Gordon, glancing sideways at her while instinctively slowing.

"You got it so good, you know that?" More anger in her voice than she'd intended, but at least it concealed how close she was to tears. Better angry than sad. "You men, you've got it so damn good."

"OK…"

"I've had my period every damn month for forty years except when I was pregnant, and then I was fat, had to pee constantly, and felt nauseous."

Gordon kept his mouth shut, realized he wasn't expected to say anything.

Hannah swiped the sweat from her face and wiped her hands on her pants in frustration.

"And now it's over, I'm done with that nonsense. But can it just end? No. Now I have to deal with this bullshit instead."

"Do you want me to stop?"

Hannah leaned back against the headrest, closed her eyes and took a few deep breaths. The wind was quite cool, the hot flash was subsiding, and she was starting to regain control.

"No, it's fine... I'm sorry."

"It's OK, mood swings are common when your estrogen balance is disrupted."

She turned her head and looked at him questioningly. Was he making fun of her? He turned his eyes from the road for a moment and met her gaze.

"I read about it."

"You read about menopause?"

"Like I said it, I care about my staff," he declared with a small shrug. Hannah knew he wasn't just paying lip service; no matter what problem his team might face, private or professional, he would have familiarized himself with the subject to see how best the workplace could be of support and help.

He was a good boss, Gordon Backman Niska. A good man.

But she still wanted to believe he was making a little extra effort because it was her. Eyes straight ahead, she put a hand on his thigh. Nothing sexual, just showing her appreciation, communicating a feeling, something she'd always been bad at doing with words. She noticed his glance from the corner of her eye. Then he put his hand on hers and squeezed it lightly.

They drove on in silence, swung off the E4 and continued north. Hannah rolled up the window up again. Ten minutes later they turned off onto a road so small you would have to know it existed to find it. They crept through the forest until it opened into a clearing with five buildings randomly situated on it. The main house was yellow and small. Behind it sat a larger red building with green double doors on its long side. Though it looked like a barn, there were never any animals inside. No living ones anyway. Next to the barn there stood a small woodshed, and next to that was a doghouse where two hunting dogs were announcing the arrival of Hannah and Gordon with nonstop barking. The last building on the plot, a timbered cabin with a mansard roof, looked like something from a camping ground. Hard to say what it was used for, if it had a use.

Gordon parked and they both climbed out. Hannah glanced back at the car as they made their way toward Hellgren, who was standing outside his front door, waiting for them with his arms crossed menacingly over his flannel-clad chest. He looked younger than his sixty years, younger than P-O, Hannah thought, slim and muscular with a face that told of a lot of time spent outside. He had short white stubble and ice-blue eyes, which stared disapprovingly at them from beneath his gas station baseball cap.

"What do you want?" he asked without so much as a hello.

"Do you have any rat poison at home?" Gordon went straight to the point.

"No, I shoot rats if I see them."

He somehow managed to emphasize rats in such a way that Hannah felt like he considered her and Gordon, maybe all police, as pests.

"Mice though? They're harder to hit."

"Traps. I don't keep poison around, I have dogs."

"You're a true animal lover," Hannah interjected. "Do you know why we ask?"

"You've probably found some poisoned animals somewhere," Hellgren said, and somehow managed to look both tired and pissed off at the same time.

"On your land," Hannah said. Not quite true, but there was a small chance that in his anger he might correct her, reveal that he knew the wolves were poisoned just beyond the boundary.

"I have a lot of ground and no fences," Hellgren answered with a shrug.

"Can we look around a bit? Inside the house?"

"No."

Hannah looked at Gordon, who shook his head almost imperceptibly. They could insist on a search of his home right now if the crime was serious enough, and they had reason to believe that there was something inside those buildings crucial to the investigation. The first criterion had been met, but even if they found a whole pallet of rat poison, they would never be able to connect it to the poisoned meat with one hundred percent certainty.

"Was that all?"

Gordon looked around, seemed to be considering something, and then made up his mind.

"Yes, for now, but we may stop by again sometime."

"Why?"

"Why not?"

"Am I suspected of something?"

"No, not right now, but like I said, we'll stop by."

As they headed back to their vehicle, Hannah could feel Hellgren's angry gaze on her back. They had almost reached the car when they heard the sound of an engine; seconds later another car drove into the courtyard and parked. A snappily dressed man in his mid-twenties stepped out and walked with determined steps toward the house in a way that suggested this wasn't his first visit. He gave Hannah and Gordon a disinterested look and a small nod as he passed them.

"Who was that?" Hannah said, turning back to see the young man shake hands with Hellgren, then follow him into his house.

"Don't know, don't recognize him."

Gordon continued on to their car. Hannah hesitated, then took out her cell phone. With a final glance at Hellgren's house, she took a few steps closer to get a clear shot of the license plate on the burgundy Toyota Yarisen that the young man had arrived in.

The little girl on the playground looked about eight.

She was steering a sibling half her age with her hands on his shoulders toward the next game while telling him how much fun this was going to be. Katja watched with an amused smile as the little girl made sure the game was played completely on her terms, and then took another strawberry from the cardboard box beside her on the park bench. Katja loved strawberries. She'd been the same age as that little girl the first time she tried them. She never had any strawberries in the place she thought of as home, no fresh fruit at all that she could remember, except for the little sour apples from the trees growing in the yard.

They came to her at school. The people there thought she lived with her aunt because her mother couldn't take care of her. Katja—or Tatjana as she was called then—didn't know why the lie was important, had asked once but was painfully reminded that she should do exactly as she was told. One morning her teacher had been called out of the classroom; she seemed nervous when she returned a few minutes later and told Tatjana to accompany her into the hall where two men were waiting for her. One approached her with a warm, friendly smile on his lips, squatted down in front of her, and introduced himself as Uncle. The other remained in the background, saying nothing.

Uncle asked if she'd like to go with him to the schoolyard so they could have a little talk. Tatjana had looked at her teacher, who nodded an OK, and so she did.

Outside, they sat on one of the benches behind the gym. The schoolyard was deserted in front of them, everyone was in class. It was autumn with winter in the air, and she shivered inside her thin jacket. Uncle waved to the other man, who came forward and wrapped his big leather jacket around her shoulders.

"Are you still cold?" Uncle had asked with kindness in his voice.

She shook her head, her eyes on the ground. He'd taken out a small case and removed a lozenge, asked if she wanted one, and got another headshake in response. He put the case back in his pocket, stretched a little and blew some warmth into his hands, rubbing them against each other.

"I want you to come with me," he said, straight out into the air. She didn't say anything. "I want to take you away from all this to a new kind of school where you can make new friends."

She had no friends at this school, but she wasn't about to tell him that. She sat with her head lowered, staring at her boots dangling a few inches above the ground.

"What do you say, Tatjana?" he asked as they sat silent for a while. "Do you want to come with me?"

She shook her head again.

"Why not?"

"Mom and Dad," she was able to press out quietly, almost like an exhale.

"They're not your mother and father. They're bad people."

A brief statement that, and as soon as she heard it, she knew implicitly that it was true. She'd had an inexplicable feeling now and then that there had to be someone else, something else. For the first time, she turned her head and looked at him.

"Do you like living with them? Is it a good life?" he asked.

Dad had told her what would happen if she told anybody what it was like at home, if anyone sensed that something wasn't right. She didn't know this man, didn't even know who he was. He seemed kind, but maybe he'd tell Dad what she said. Maybe he was there to test her, see if she was a good girl. So she nodded emphatically.

"I don't believe you," said Uncle, but without any of the anger of Mom and Dad showed when they thought she was lying. "Do you know why I don't believe you?"

She shook her head again, feeling that the less she said the better.

So he started to tell her.

What happened in that house, what they did, what they exposed her to.

He knew everything. All of the details. As if he had been there, lived with them. His voice was emotional and disgusted, as if he had experienced it with her. She cried when he was done, cried until she was shaking, her shoulders drawn up to her ears, hands squeezing her knees so hard her fingers turned red. Felt shame and fear, but also strangely relieved.

"Do you want to go back?" He handed her a handkerchief. She shook her head and wiped away the snot that ran from her nose in two strands. "If you come with me, no one will ever be able to hurt you again."

She looked up at him. Something in his eyes made her believe him.

It turned out to be true.

The little boy received a hard push, fell and started to cry. His big sister helped him up, brushed him off. A man who Katja assumed was their father rushed forward, crouching in front of the boy, turning to big sister. Katja straightened up; corporal punishment wasn't allowed, but that didn't prevent parents from still using it. One of the most important rules was never to use her skills outside of her assignments, but nothing prevented her from mildly reprimanding the man if he chose to physically reprimand the little girl. To her relief, he seemed to reason with the daughter, who clearly knew she'd done wrong, and who ended up giving her little brother an apologetic hug.

Katja's mobile phone beeped. She put one more strawberry in her mouth and picked it up. A message from Uncle.

A new job. In Haparanda.

Everyone at the station had gathered in the conference room. Gordon gave up his spot at the short end of the table, and Alexander "X" Erixon pulled out a chair, rolled up the sleeves of his light blue shirt, and sat down. After talking to Gordon this morning and finding out about the possible link to the murder in Rovaniemi, he had decided to come up and run the investigation from here. A welcome reinforcement. His colleagues liked him, and the feeling was mutual, Gordon thought. Alexander had worked with all of them at one time or another, except Ludwig.

The man in the checkered shirt and leather vest sitting at the far end of the table beneath the police emblem, balancing on the back legs of his chair while chewing on a match, was also new to Alexander, and to Gordon. Sami Ritola, Rovaniemi police. Arrived with the thin dossier that the Finnish police had on their victim in the forest.

Vadim Tarasov, twenty-six years old, born in a small village in Karelia, but a resident of St. Petersburg for many years.

P-O wondered to himself what was wrong with emails and

phone calls these days, because everyone kept insisting on delivering information to them in person.

Then it dawned on them that Ritola was planning on staying to attend the meeting; why else would he spend an hour and a half on the road instead of simply emailing the information they'd asked for.

"I want to see how my investigation is going," Sami replied with the relaxed self-confidence of a Finn. Morgan, sitting next to him, translated simultaneously.

Sami's Swedish was bad, Alexander's Finnish non-existent.

"This is offically our investigation. *My* investigation," Alexander clarified sharply, still sounding like he was doing his best not to sound too pissed. "This concerns the homicide or manslaughter of Tarasov."

"Who was involved in my case before it became yours." Sami nodded.

Gordon couldn't fault Sami's reasoning, considering the connection between the cases, and it never hurt to maintain a good relationship with the Finnish police. It seemed Alexander was thinking along the same lines.

"True, no need to discuss it further," he said with a disarming smile. "The case is ours, but you are more than welcome to attend."

Sami executed a courteous bow in his chair and sarcastically waved his hand in front of his face as if he had received an audience with some eighteenth-century king.

"Thank you most humbly."

Morgan sat in silence, chose not to translate, sure the gist of it had come across anyway.

Alexander turned to the others as he pointed to a picture on the white screen behind his back.

"So, the dead man's name is Vadim Tarasov," he began, then turned to Sami again. "And you think he's connected to the shooting outside Rovaniemi last week."

"A fucking massacre," Sami confirmed. "Seven dead; there was a funeral for one of them this morning."

"Seven dead Finns?" queried Ludwig.

"Four. Three Russians, too."

"Not everyone here is completely up to date with that investigation," Alexander interjected. "Can you briefly summarize what happened in Rovaniemi."

"As I said, three Russians, four Finns. The bodies left behind. The weapons left behind. So we have a pretty good idea what happened."

While Morgan translated, Sami opened the folder in front of him, spread most of the photos it contained on the table in front of them. Bodies. Many bodies.

"We're sure they met to do business. The Russians were sellers, the Finns buyers."

"Drugs?" Lurch asked, though no one really believed it could be anything else.

"Yes."

"Did you know of the Finns before?" asked Gordon, who along with Alexander had stood up to get a better overview of the spread-out material.

"All of them have a connection to Sudet, a motorcycle gang in our area that sells drugs. Among other things."

"What happened?" Alexander prompted.

"They started shooting at each other. This guy—" Sami pointed to one of the pictures, which showed a man of about twenty, lying in front of a black Volvo XC90 "—one of the Finns, never fired his weapon, unlike all the others, so we think he died first."

Sami put his finger on another of the pictures. This man, much older than the previous one, had a large tribal tattoo around one eye. His neck was one huge gaping wound.

"This guy, Pentti, was buried today. He killed this Russian

and injured this one with his automatic rifle before getting his throat shot away."

He pushed over two of the other pictures: two men, barely thirty years old, lying dead on the ground.

"The third Finn had time to take shelter in a ditch. He killed the Russian who was injured by Pentti before he too was shot."

"The girl and that man there then?" Hannah asked, pointing to the two remaining photographs. A thin man who seemed to be the youngest in the gang, and a woman in her midtwenties with a large gaping hole in her temple.

"He's a Finn, she's Russian. They shot each other, but he wasn't the one who killed her. It was the same shooter who stubbed out the other three Finns."

"Didn't you say she was Russian?"

"Yes."

"I don't understand. Was it Vadim who shot her?" Lurch put into words what everyone was thinking.

"In a way." Sami fell silent and looked around the table. "All four had injuries that didn't match any weapon we found at the scene," he went on, then paused, apparently so Morgan would catch up with the translation, but probably just as much for dramatic effect. "From a rifle. A VVS Vintorez."

"A sniper," commented P-O, who was interested in military history and knew most of what there was to know about weapons and war from the age of the great powers onwards.

"Yes, and Vadim did his military service as a sniper, became close friends with this guy."

Took another photo from the folder. Unlike the others, this showed a man who was alive when the picture was taken. He looked to be about the same age as Vadim.

"Jevgenij Antipin. We believe that Vadim told him about the drug deal, and that he was there, hidden in the forest, shooting the Finns and the Russian."

"What was Vadim doing when all this happened?"

"Must have found cover somewhere," Sami said, shrugging. "Didn't go so well, apparently—you say he had a bullet in his ass?"

"Yes."

"So he made sure everyone, both Finns and Russians, was dead, and then he took off with the drugs and the money," Gordon summed up all the information they'd been given.

"That's the theory we're working on, yes."

"So we're missing two?" Alexander picked up the picture of Antipin and studied it closely.

"And how do you know this Antipin was involved?" Hannah cut in before Sami had time to answer.

He smiled at them, as if he expected both questions and was about to unveil a twist.

"We found him with a bullet in his head in a burnt-out Russian-plated Mercedes outside Muurola the day after the massacre. The Vintorezen was in the car."

"And you can tie the Mercedes to the shootings?" asked Gordon.

"Bullets inside it matched the Finns' weapons, so it was definitely there, yes."

"Wait a minute," Hannah said, holding up her hand. "Did I get this right? Tarasov Vadim brings a sniper to a drug deal, makes sure everyone dies, takes the drugs and the money, kills his sniper buddy, drives to Sweden, and gets run over here."

"Seems like it." Sami nodded. "I leaned on the guys in Sudet, tried to find out who we were looking for, but it looks like you've solved it."

Gordon glanced at Alexander, who nodded. Sami was right, the shootings outside Rovaniemi were connected to Vadim Tarasov. There was no one else to hunt or try to prosecute when it came to the massacre in Finland. Everyone involved was dead.

Even if they'd found him useful, the reason for Sami's presence at the meeting was suddenly much less obvious.

"So all you have to do now is find the drugs and the money," Sami said, putting the matchstick into his mouth and leaning back in his chair.

"How much are we talking about?" Ludwig asked, directing a questioning nod at Sami.

"Our source says that the MC Sudet were planning to buy three hundred thousand euros' worth."

Ludwig couldn't hold back a low whistle. They all knew what that meant. Someone was sitting on drugs with a street value of almost thirty million kronor.

"But if we back up a little," Hannah said, turning to Sami again. "Tarasov must have changed vehicles...at the site of the burned Mercedes..."

"Muurola," Sami helped her.

"Muurola, exactly. Do you know what he was driving?"

"We have a list of cars stolen in the immediate area around that time," Sami said, snapping at the folder in front of him on the table and opening it up again.

"Is one of them a Honda? The Luleå technicians say that the paint residue we found at the site is from a Honda."

Sami studied the list in silence.

It was only a page long, Gordon observed, so unless Sami had a hard time reading, the pause was definitely for dramatic effect. He cleared his throat meaningfully.

"A dark blue Honda CR-V registered in 2015 was reported stolen the night before the shootings," came from Ritola at last.

The atmosphere in the room changed; this was a real lead. After this morning's press conference, only a handful of calls had come in, nothing that required follow-up. They'd shared too few details, been too vague. Now they could ask for a specific car, color, and model. It must have headed off somewhere after the accident, and locals tended to keep track of the vehicles that drove through their villages.

"Do we know what kind of drugs we're talking about?" Gordon asked.

"Not exactly. Something synthetic. Amphetamines, most likely."

"Not our biggest problem, but you do see it, of course," Gordon informed them all unnecessarily; Alexander had a good handle on the statistics in most of the local police precincts in the region, Haparanda was no exception. So he was pretty sure he knew the answer to the next question, but asked it anyway.

"If you stumble onto thirty million kronor worth of amphetamines up here," Sami continued, "what do you do? Who do you contact? Where does it end up?"

His questions were met with silence, everyone reluctant to tell him the depressing and somewhat humiliating truth.

"We don't really know," Gordon answered finally. "We don't have a good sense of who or what is controlling the flow these days, unfortunately."

"It won't matter," Hannah interjected, almost as if she wanted to save him. "If some regular panic-stricken Joe Schmo had stumbled onto it, then he'll have no idea what to do with it either."

"He might try to get some money for it," P-O noted briefly.

"How? I'm not sure they'd even realize what it is."

"When you realize what it's worth, you might at least try," P-O insisted.

"I would be satisfied with the money," Hannah stated with a shrug.

"OK, check in with those you know in town who might have some idea, otherwise keep your eyes and ears open," Alexander ended with a glance at his wristwatch. Obviously time to wrap up. "Let's see what tips we get on the Honda; tomorrow we'll start knocking on doors. Begin with Vitvattnet and spread out from there. I'll make sure we get more people here. Thank you for now."

Everyone stood up, but they were stopped by Sami, who leaned over the table.

"Vadim Tarasov worked for Valerij Zagornij in St. Petersburg. Do you know who that is?"

He was met by shaking heads around the table, except for Morgan.

"Oligarch, not one of the very richest, top fifty maybe, rumored to be a mafia boss."

"It's more than a rumor, he's definitely mafia. Very powerful, very, very dangerous."

"And this matters because...?" Gordon asked.

Sami turned to face him and for the first time seemed quite serious.

"Those were his drugs. He'll try to find that Honda."

She was given one of the larger rooms on the top floor of this centrally located and slightly run-down building which looked like a castle. Subdued green-gray walls, a double bed, a desk, two armchairs the same color as the carpet, heavy red-flowered curtains on the three windows that faced the square outside, which didn't really look like a square at all. It was apparently quite unique; its four streets came from each corner of the compass and converged in a roundabout in the middle, while the square itself consisted of four equal-sized areas instead of the more usual unbroken surface with traffic around it.

Katja came out of the bathroom where she'd just unpacked the contents of her bag and placed them in a specific order that made her feel calm. Her clothes were already hanging in the wardrobe or folded in a drawer in the bureau by the full-length mirror inside the door.

The room was rigged. Only the weapons still lay in her suitcase. A Walther Creed with a silencer and laser sight, and a Winchester Bowie knife in its leg holster. She put the gun into the safe and strapped the knife to her calf. She wasn't expecting any problems in the near future, but you never know.

Her name was Louise Andersson, and she was on an eat pray love trip to Norrland. She felt she needed a change of scenery, new impressions, new people, to recharge her batteries. At least that's what she excitedly told the welcoming, talkative woman at the front desk who'd checked her in.

It felt so good to be back in Sweden, to speak and think in Swedish again. So natural. Of all the languages she'd learned, Swedish was the one that came easiest to her. She'd missed using it; she noticed that while lyrically praising the magical light up here and asking the receptionist if there was a yoga studio in town. Now she'd have plenty of opportunities. She was booked for a week to begin with. Should be enough for what she was planning to do.

Katja filled the kettle with water from the bathroom and made herself a cup of instant coffee while spreading the materials she'd brought with her on the desk. Most of what she had on Rovaniemi came from the Finnish police investigation—which had apparently been generously leaked—and clippings from the Swedish and Finnish press.

She read through the documents twice before taking out her laptop, connecting it to her mobile router—avoiding the hotel's unprotected Wi-Fi—and searching to see if anything new had been released. It had, the police were asking for any information on a dark blue Honda CR-V in the area at that time. Good to know, otherwise there wasn't much more about the dead man in the forest.

What little there was though immediately raised one question.

What was Vadim doing out here?

He'd just robbed a very dangerous man who'd do anything to find him. Why not take the major roads, as quickly as possible, try to put as much distance between himself and Zagornij as he could? She was glad he hadn't. After looking at the map, she could see that not just anyone would be driving down that road. Whoever took that route would have needed local knowledge, most likely lived in the area.

Someone just happens to kill him and drags him into the forest.

This person had clearly been in shock, not thinking straight.

According to her meager information, Vadim wasn't even buried, just partially covered. That gave her some hope. She was looking for a local who reacted instinctively.

An amateur when it came to death without consequences.

That meant he'd make more mistakes.

Use the money. Probably sell the drugs. It was time to get to work.

Her assignment from Valerij Zagornij had been clear:

Find the drugs and the money.

Kill the person who took them.

Für Elise played from a hidden speaker as she pushed open the door. Ludwig van Beethoven, probably composed in 1810. One of the countless more or less trivial facts she'd been expected to learn. A muscular man with a clean-shaven skull wearing blue mechanic overalls came out of one of the inner rooms and walked over to her.

"Hello, UV," she greeted him, and offered her hand.

"Hello?"

The hesitation in his voice and eyes gave away how frantically he was searching his memory to figure out if he'd ever seen her before and, if so, where.

"Do you have time to help me for a bit?" Katja asked with a nod to the door and courtyard outside.

"We're closing now," he replied with a glance at the clock.

"It will only take five minutes. Max." A hopeful smile that also signaled a kind of inferiority. A beautiful woman, in need of help, and he was the one who could give it to her. To reinforce how important it was, she placed a hand lightly on his forearm. "Please?"

"Have we met?" he asked, apparently still trying to place her.

"We have some mutual acquaintances."

"OK, sure."

UV followed her out to the courtyard where a dozen cars waiting for pickup or to be repaired were parked tightly side by side. Katja put her sunglasses on again. UV shook a cigarette out of his pack and lit it, then held out the pack to her. She declined.

"What is it?" UV asked.

Katja pointed to the Audi Q5, the one that had been waiting for her when her private plane landed and which was now parked close to the entrance of the auto shop.

"What's wrong with it?"

"Nothing, I think. It's a brand-new rental car."

She continued to the car and leaned against the hood. UV stopped a few steps away, looked at her with a mixture of suspicion and anger.

"What the hell do you want?"

"Вы работали с людьми, которых я знаю," Katja said, so he'd know where she came from. The seriousness of the situation. Perhaps he did get that, but he had no idea what she'd said. "You used to work for some people I know," she translated.

"That doesn't explain what you want," he replied when she translated it into Swedish for him. "I've stopped doing that shit."

UV took a drag on his cigarette, but made no attempt to go back inside. Just stared at her, trying to decide if it was worth staying and listening to the rest. Katja guessed he was hoping she would offer him some kind of business proposal. If she understood correctly, he was constantly in need of money.

"I know that, but sometimes you hear things anyway."

"Why don't you say what you want and then go."

"Has anyone tried to sell you a large batch of amphetamines? Or is there someone new, really new, selling on the street?"

"No idea. I've quit, like I said."

"But you're working on your crashed cars, some stolen goods, protecting criminals…" She left her place by the car, pushed her glasses up onto her forehead and walked over to him. "You still have some idea what's going on."

"Sorry, I can't help you." He stomped out his half-smoked cigarette, and this time he really was about to go back inside again.

"Did you hear about the man they found in the woods?"

Katja could see that he was trying to figure out what that had to do with anything, but he was too smart to ask, knew that he wouldn't get an answer.

"The cops are searching for a dark blue car, that's all I know."

"A Honda."

"Don't know," he said with a shrug. "They were here yesterday, asking if I'd worked on it."

"But you hadn't?"

"Nope."

"Because you would tell me." She managed to make that brief statement sound very much like a threat. "Tell me who brought it in."

"Yes."

She believed him. He wasn't stupid or careless. Even if he didn't know exactly who, he understood she was working for people who would not appreciate finding out later that he could have helped them but chose not to.

"So if they're not selling to you anymore, who do they sell to?"

"Like I said, I don't know."

"Who would know?"

"Maybe our 'mutual friends'?"

"No, apparently not," she said honestly. When she got this assignment, Uncle had tried to find out who in Haparanda could turn Valerij's drugs into money, which would have given her a place to start, but no one seemed to know. The supply was plentiful, which kept prices low, but whoever it was, he used his own channels to bring in product, his own sales network that knew how to keep quiet. So far no one had managed to establish a serious presence.

"I don't know either," UV said.

"You said that, and I believe you, but I was wondering who would know."

He hesitated. Katja was sure she'd get a name. The man in front of her just had to think a little about loyalty, his reputation, maybe his safety. A lot had to be taken into account. She lowered her sunglasses again, turned her face toward the sun, and waited.

"Jonte might know," finally came out reluctantly.

"Jonte who?"

"Jonathan Lundin. He's going at it pretty hard these days."

"Where does he live?"

A heavy sigh, this time one of pure discomfort, he really didn't like this. But she got an address.

She was halfway through her break in the bright modern break room. The snack she'd brought with her was eaten. Sandra rarely left anything on her plate, hardly ever threw away food. It had been fifteen years, and yet she still remembered her mother's words so clearly, a morning cigarette dangling from her mouth while Sandra shoveled down her breakfast. Oatmeal with milk, or more often without.

Make sure you eat a lot at school today, because there won't be any food when you get home.

Now Sandra was full and on her second cup of coffee. So far, this day looked like most. She appreciated that. Routines and regularity were relaxing, made it easier to imagine everything was normal. That she had a job, a boyfriend. That she spent weekends working in her garden, visiting her mother. That she was looking forward to the Felix Sandman concert in Luleå, which she and her friends were going to in early July. That she hadn't helped to bury a strange man just a few kilometers from her home.

As usual, Kenneth had been asleep upstairs when she left for work this morning. She'd climbed in the car standing in the driveway, trying her best not to think about why it wasn't parked in their garage. About an hour later, she'd arrived at the correctional facility. A change of clothes and a cup of coffee, then it was time to let the inmates out of their cells for breakfast, then spend three hours with them in the wood shop, which was one of thirty-nine production units within Sweden. They'd received a large order of pallets and thirteen of the nineteen inmates worked in the workshop five days a week. Then it was time for lunch, which they cooked themselves. Sandra had been there until noon, when she was relieved of duty and went to the staff dining room, hurriedly ate the contents of her lunch box before heading to Torneå to buy the vase she wanted so much. It was in her car now, and she was thinking about the flowers in her garden she'd pick to fill it with as soon as she got home. They didn't have that many beautiful things at home, she and Kenneth.

The afternoon rolled on as usual, and now she was scrolling through Instagram. Friends, acquaintances, people she'd lost touch with, and a few celebrities appeared in her stream. So many smiles, sunglasses, happy children, rosé and cava, a feeling of summer and vacation, all of it perfect. She seldom posted anything. What did she have to show? Barbed wire, fences, and an exercise yard at work, or her dilapidated house in Norra Storträsk. The garden was lovely, of course, nature all around them, the midnight sun—she always got comments, thumbs-up, and hearts for that—but she wasn't comfortable on here, felt hopeless and left out, as if she were still wearing outdated hand-me-downs, never had the right things.

Boring. Poor. Insignificant.

The radio was on in the background, announcing it was time for the local news. The police in Haparanda had found a body in the forest some kilometers north of town. Sandra froze, turned toward the speakers to hear better. Now the authorities were asking for information about a dark blue Honda CR-V seen in the area at that time.

After the subject changed, Sandra rose slowly on unsteady legs. It wasn't even a lie when she said she felt sick and had to go home. Her colleagues understood; she even looked a little pale.

As she turned in to the courtyard, parked and climbed out, Kenneth came out of the house and walked toward her. He looked worried.

"What are you doing home already? Didn't you have a twelve-hour shift?"

Sandra cast a glance at the nearest neighbor's home before taking a few quick steps toward him and lowering her voice.

"They've found him."

"How do you know?"

"They said so on the radio."

They walked back into the house together, went into a kitchen whose worse-for-wear decor matched the house's exterior perfectly. She went to change. Her uniform was replaced by jeans and a T-shirt; she loosened her tight work ponytail and let her hair frame her broad, freckled face. She met her own green eyes in the mirror. Circumstances had changed; she'd gone this far, and now she had to go further. Before leaving the bedroom, she opened the wardrobe and there they lay, thrown in among the shoes, the laundry basket, and Kenneth's comic books.

She still remembered the first time she saw them.

She'd fallen asleep in the car on the way home from the party, which had been fun but it had gotten late. Woke up to the shockingly brutal sound of metal collapsing, glass shattering, and Kenneth swearing.

"Fuck! Fuck! Fuck!"

"What was that?" Despite the sound, her thoughts turned immediately to the most obvious. "Was it a reindeer? Some animal?"

Kenneth sat for a few seconds with his eyes straight ahead,

his breathing heavy, his heart pounding in his chest. Then he turned to her, his voice surprisingly calm.

"No, it wasn't an animal."

They climbed out of the car, saw the man on the ground. She stifled a scream with her hand. Kenneth bent down and put a finger on the man's neck. She searched her pants and jacket pockets. Knew what she had to do. Couldn't find what she was looking for.

"Where's my phone?"

"Why do you need it?" Kenneth asked, getting to his feet.

"We have to call the police."

She went back to the car. Kenneth followed, grabbed her.

"No, wait a minute now, wait just a bit, we have to think. I've been drinking, and my driver's license has been revoked."

Speeding. A moment's stupidity one afternoon last winter. Two hundred kronor if he could get to the liquor store before it closed; 145 kilometers per hour on an 80-road. His license was revoked on the spot. Sheer luck that he didn't end up in prison. Again.

One more bad decision in a long history of them. She had been so angry with him.

"It doesn't matter, we have to call." She was fighting back tears now that the first wave of shock had passed.

"We're going to, we're going to," he said calmly, wiping her tears away with his thumb. "But wait, wait just a little…"

Kenneth took a few steps behind the car, started pacing back and forth, running his hands through his hair. She sank down onto the road, leaned against the fender, arms wrapped around her legs and forehead against her knees. Her thoughts were chaotic, her emotions swirling behind her closed eyelids, but what started to push out everything else was anger. This was so typical of Kenneth. Lands in hot water no matter what. And pulls her down with him this time. She couldn't say how long she'd been sitting there when he finally came back and sat down beside her.

"We should bury him."

Voice steady. Determined. Sandra looked at him with complete incomprehension, as if he'd spoken to her in a foreign language.

"We'll bury him and take the car with us."

"No."

"Nobody knows we were here. No one needs to know what happened."

"No, we have to call the police."

"They'll put me away again. I can't go back. Please…"

She didn't answer, closed her eyes and leaned her head against her knees. Her tears ran down silently. Damn him for putting her into this impossible situation.

"Listen…"

He gently put a hand on hers. She shook free from his touch and punched him hard in the chest. Her red-rimmed eyes gave him an accusatory look.

"How the hell could you run into him?"

"He was standing there, in the middle of the road."

"It's light out, how could you not see him?" She punched him again and he huddled up, looked at her with an expression she knew all too well. The one he wore after he didn't think it through, when it was time to admit he'd done something stupid.

"I… I took your phone, was going to change the music, and then I dropped it."

She didn't need to know more; it didn't matter. She could feel how exhausted she was. Her gaze fell on the Honda behind Kenneth, parked halfway down in the ditch. Suddenly, she was filled with a horrific apprehension, which hit her like a fist in the gut.

What if.

Sandra got to her feet and approached the car slowly, as if sleepwalking. Prayed to a god she didn't believe in that there was nobody else inside. No one else injured or dead. Absolutely, good God, not a child.

She peered through the side window. To her great relief, the car was empty. Of humans. There were three sports bags lying in the back seat. Without really knowing why she opened the back door and leaned inside. Unzipped one of them. Cash. More than she'd ever seen. She opened the next one. More money. Lots of money. Euros. The third bag contained something that had to be drugs. A lot of drugs.

Kenneth came up behind her, peeked inside, and saw what she saw.

"Is that cash?"

She straightened up, nodded, but couldn't take her eyes off the bags. Off the money. A life-changing amount of money.

"What should we do?"

Finally, she turned to face him. He looked so fragile, as if he were already falling apart. So small and afraid of going back to prison again. She was stronger than he was. Both physically and mentally. He leaned on her, needed her, and she loved him. More than anything. She placed a tender palm against his bearded cheek.

It was so easy to convince herself that this was for his sake.

"We'll do what you want, bury him, and take the car with us."

He looked almost as surprised now as he had beside the car, as she laid the bags from the closet on the kitchen table then pulled the curtains in the two kitchen windows closed.

"What are we going to do with those?"

"That's what we have to talk about," she said, sitting down beside him at the table. "What we need to do now."

"Did they say anything about what they thought had happened?" Kenneth asked.

"No, only that they're searching for the Honda."

"Do they have any suspects, any witnesses?"

"Not that they mentioned."

"Damn it, we moved him." Kenneth flew up from the chair,

took a few quick steps, suddenly struck by an insight. "We must have left DNA on him, right? When we moved him."

"I don't know."

"If they find my DNA I'm fucked—they have my DNA in their registry."

"If they find your DNA, they'll come here, and then it's over." Sandra was surprised by how calm she sounded, how calm she felt. Focused. They couldn't make any mistakes now; this was her future. *Their* future, she quickly corrected.

"But if they don't, then we have to have a plan."

Kenneth nodded, but didn't stop pacing around the kitchen.

"Sit down," Sandra commanded, and he obeyed. "We'll start with the cars."

"Ya, I thought about that," he said, almost stumbling over the words, pleased to be able to contribute. Sandra was doubtful they were thinking the same thing, but she nodded for him to continue.

"The Volvo needs a lot of work. UV can fix—"

"We can't get him involved," Sandra interrupted immediately with a resolute headshake.

"But I don't know if I can do it myself, so… I thought it might be good to buy a new one."

"With what?"

His expression was uncomprehending, and he nodded at the bags on the table.

"With that."

Sandra understood, of course. There was money. A lot of money. Why not just buy what they want and need? No one understood that better than her. Her whole childhood had been about longing, wishing for a little of what everyone else seemed to take for granted. But with a low-paid, partially disabled single mother, there was never enough money for anything, except cigarettes and wine, which, strangely, there was always enough money for.

She was so utterly tired of being poor.

She wasn't asking for the Kardashian lifestyle, she was a realist. All she wanted was to treat herself to a little extra now and then without having to give up something else, not always in search of the best deals, finally able to renovate the house.

Nothing luxurious, just what most people wanted.

A good life, some economic security.

So they had to be smart. Fight the impulse to live that good life immediately. Haparanda was a small city. Sure, she had her job at the prison, but her salary was low. Kenneth was unemployed. Spending a lot of money would attract attention. They couldn't risk that.

Especially considering who Kenneth's uncle was married to.

"We'll start by getting rid of the Honda, and we'll hide this lot where no one will ever find it," she assured him, putting her hand onto the three bags on the table, and she could see that Kenneth didn't understand why. "Even if you go to prison, if we both do, this will be waiting for us when we come out."

"Should we hide the drugs, too?"

"What else would we do with them?"

"Sell them."

"No! Absolutely not."

That was even riskier than using the money. She'd been given a chance. No one was going to take it away from her. If she had to live her life knowing she'd been involved in killing and burying a man, at least something good should come from it. She loved Kenneth, but he wasn't going to be the one who changed her life. He wasn't going to take her away from this moldering asbestos-concrete house in Norra Storträsk, give her the opportunities she'd longed for her whole life.

But those bags on the table would.

About 1,580,000 results. It was a joke.

Hannah had written 'herbs' in the search box, trying to remember something about basil, maybe thyme, and suddenly there were 244,000 recipes to read. She skimmed the first two pages, but didn't recognize any of them. Most of it looked good enough, after all this was only a regular weeknight dinner, but she knew what she wanted. It was easy to cook, and Thomas liked it. She swore to herself and closed the search page.

"What are you doing?"

She turned to the door where Gordon stood, apparently ready to leave for the day.

"Looking for a chicken pasta recipe I made a month ago, but I can't find it."

"Come with me instead, and we'll grab a bite."

It sounded tempting, but hopefully the plans she'd made for the evening would also lead to sex.

"I promised Thomas dinner at home, we haven't seen each other in a while."

"Another time," Gordon said with a shrug; if he was disappointed, he hid it well.

"Yes."

Hannah thought he would say goodbye, see you tomorrow and leave, but instead he came in and sat down in his usual spot by the door. Hannah cast an eye at the clock. Change, shop, go home, cook. She could give him five minutes.

"So you think somebody's going to flush thirty million kronor down the toilet."

"I just said ordinary people don't know how to sell drugs."

"You might be right. So what do we do?"

Hannah hesitated, an idea had occurred to her after the meeting; it wasn't developed yet, and she'd been planning to wait to discuss it until tomorrow, but she might as well try it out on Gordon now.

"Maybe it's stupid, but what do you think about announcing that we know what was in the car and offer amnesty for returning it. If you hand it in, then you can stay anonymous."

Gordon thought it over silently for a few seconds. They'd had a weapon amnesty all over the country last year. Three months during which anyone could drop off any weapon, no questions asked, no investigation. Same thing a bit later for explosives. It had been successful, but they'd never done one for drugs. There were no plans in the works for it that Hannah knew of. She was far from sure that the Haparanda police would be allowed to make that kind of exception.

"The problem is they killed the guy when they got it," Gordon said at last.

"We provide amnesty for the drugs only, continue investigating the hit-and-run."

"And we say it's OK to keep the money?"

"I don't know," Hannah sighed and started to regret not waiting until tomorrow, wishing she'd had more time to figure out the proposal's shortcomings for herself. "It wasn't really thought through yet, just an idea I had to get them off the street."

"It's not totally crazy," Gordon admitted.

"Why, thank you very much."

"I'll take it up with X tomorrow, if you want. The higher-ups might let us do some version of it."

Hannah nodded, shut down the computer, and stood up. Gordon stayed where he was, made no effort to move. She guessed that he would follow her down to the changing room. Seemed to be headed home.

"How does it feel to have X here?" she asked as she gathered her things from her desk.

"Good. Why?"

"He came in and took over your investigation."

"He took it over when we found the body."

"But it's another thing to have him here."

This was only the third time since Gordon had become chief that Luleå had taken over an investigation here. Each time it had quickly become clear to everyone that Gordon was no longer in charge, had taken a step down. Hannah didn't really think it was a problem for him that Alexander had arrived, but it didn't hurt to ask, take a little interest in him, too.

"It is what it is." Gordon shrugged. "Not the first time, won't be the last."

Gordon glanced over at the bulletin board on her wall, where the picture of a closely shaven young man with neatly parted hair and a steady gaze stared into the camera. She'd downloaded it from the passport registry; it was one of the better passport photos she'd seen.

"The guy from Hellgrens," he said, taking a few steps closer to the board.

"René Fouquier." Hannah could hear that she pronounced his last name like 'fucker'. "It's French, I don't know how it's pronounced."

"Hopefully not like that, for his sake." Gordon smiled. "What do you know about him?"

"Born in Lyon, family moved to Gothenburg when he was

five. Came here almost three years ago, works half-time at Max and studies long distance. Young guy, twenty-six."

"What's his connection to Hellgren?"

"No idea," Hannah said, taking one last sweeping look at her desk; nothing had been forgotten. "He's not in our database, doesn't even have a parking ticket."

"A model citizen."

"Who hangs out with Anton Hellgren."

"Does he have a hunting license?"

"No, and I couldn't find him on Facebook or anywhere else online, so I don't know what his connection is to hunting and predators."

"Or older men in flannel."

She gave him a questioning look as she turned off the light, and they left her office together. Hadn't even considered that the young man's visit to Hellgren might be sexual or romantic in nature.

"Do you think Hellgren is gay?"

"He's never been married."

"Neither have you."

"But I don't have snappily dressed young men in double-breasted blazers showing up at my house."

"I'm pretty sure that's a stereotype, and not OK to say," Hannah said with a smile.

They walked past Gordon's office, out and down the stairs. Stopped at the door, which led out to reception. She was headed right, past the jail cells, down toward the locker room.

"See you tomorrow," he said with his hand on the door handle.

"What are you going to do tonight?"

"Now that I can't have dinner with you?"

"Yes."

"Nothing. Maybe see if my brother wants to come over and play some FIFA."

It was when he said things like that she really felt her age. Not because she didn't know what he was talking about. She knew exactly what FIFA was, her son had played it with his friends when he was still living at home. Just like Gordon did with his brother. Three years younger. Divorced with two kids every other week. A house in Nikkala. Hannah had met Adrian a few times, had no idea if he knew she was sleeping with his big brother or not. Did siblings tell each other things like that?

She didn't intend to ask, didn't want to know.

"Have fun."

"You, too."

Then he left. Hannah stood there for a second then hurried down the corridor. Her thoughts back on work again. One more thing to catch up on before going home for the evening. It was going to be a late dinner.

Lovis was sleeping. As she usually did at this hour.

A daily rhythm and evening routines were important. Predictability meant security. UV sat on the bed they'd put in her room, listening to a podcast on his phone on low volume. It dinged when he got a Snapchat. From Stina. Half her face and the living room in the house in Kalix in the background. *How's it going?* He pressed the answer arrow, took a picture from above Lovis's bed with the nightlight. *Good. She's sleeping. Everything's fine.* Send.

He could hardly remember the last time he and Stina slept in the same bed. Must have been when they still had assistants here at night. Now one of them always spent the night in Lovis's room, the other usually alone in the double bed, or sometimes, if they really needed to sleep, with a friend, or Stina with her parents, like tonight. That was never an option for him. Her family had never liked him, and when he was sentenced to three years in prison for drug charges, the relationship went from strained to irreparable.

They weren't much help with Lovis either. Didn't know how to behave around her, and since they would never take on the responsibility of being alone with her, they could never relieve them either.

Stina found out she was pregnant while he was in prison. The moment she put the pregnancy test on the table in the visitors' room, he decided to go straight. He just knew. He'd never risk going to prison again.

It was bad enough he wouldn't be there in the beginning, but he planned to be there for the rest, be present, involved, everything he'd wanted from a father when he was growing up.

He wasn't given permission to attend the birth, but the next morning he went to the hospital in Luleå with two guards, was called into a room where a doctor quietly told him about complications, a lack of oxygen during the birth, and multiple indications that there were also chromosome abnormalities. The extent of her disabilities wasn't known at the time, but it was very serious. His daughter was in the neonatal intensive care unit.

He still remembered the sadness that washed over him when he saw Lovis for the first time. He'd been longing for this ever since he saw that blue plus sign in the family room, the moment he and Stina would have a child. Become a family. But instead of being given something, it felt like something was taken away.

He stood beside the incubator, grieving for a living child.

All his plans for the future, all his dreams for this child, who'd already had such an impact on him, already changed him, maybe even saved him, all of that was gone.

Stina was just angry.

At everything. Angry at life, angry that things hadn't turned out like she'd planned.

She hated the other mothers and their healthy children, didn't want to leave her room. After a week she had to go home, without Lovis, and it took another four months for Lovis to join her. By then he'd served two thirds of his sentence and was released conditionally.

Got out and went home to chaos.

Stina's focus was on Lovis around the clock, but she was caught in a cycle of worry and crushed by the feeling that she'd never be enough. Somehow they'd still made it work, through all the hospital visits, checkups, operations, treatments, medicines, all the applications and dealings with the authorities and the municipality. The help from the assistants was invaluable. The same people came day after day and made sure that there was an opportunity for UV and Stina to do what other, ordinary parents did.

Life had rolled on.

Then came the new decision from Social Services about the hours of assistance, and everything collapsed again.

These thoughts were interrupted by the doorbell. A quick glance at the time. Who would be here at this hour? They'd never had much of a social life, and visitors were now few and far between. With a glance at Lovis, he left the room, walked through the apartment, and opened the front door.

The cop, of course. Tompa's wife. Hannah. A little out of breath from the stairs and with an ICA bag in her hand.

"I'm sorry to disturb you this late," she said, sounding like she actually meant it.

"What do you want?"

"I just want to ask a few questions, if that's OK? It won't take long, I promise."

As soon as the woman, who he assumed was Russian or at least connected to them, had showed up talking about amphetamines, UV had known the cop would be back, too. Even though he'd served his time, and, as far as they knew, had been living a law-abiding life for three years now. Really it made him furious, but he knew he had two options.

Run her off and risk having her suspect he was hiding something, start investigating him and his shop more closely, or convince her that he'd done nothing, knew nothing, and get rid of her. Hopefully get some badly needed information out of her in the process. He nodded and stepped aside.

"You can leave your shoes on."

He didn't like leaving Lovis alone for longer than a few minutes, so he walked back through the messy apartment. Housekeeping was a low priority, had been for a while now.

"We can sit in here," he said, showing her into Lovis's room.

Hannah followed him, but stopped a few steps inside the door. The adjustable bed with steel bars on its sides, even though Lovis couldn't move in her sleep, a wheelchair, floor lift, mucus suction, oxygen machine, medicines, creams, belts, harnesses. Not all the hanging mobiles, colorful paintings, or soft toys in the world could change the fact that it looked more like a hospital than a nursery.

"Won't we wake her up?" Hannah almost whispered with a nod to the bed.

"No," UV replied, and went to sit on his bed. "What do you want?"

"The blue car I asked you about..." Hannah began a little hesitantly. Did he just imagine it, or did she look at him differently now? More softly, as if she felt sorry for him? He didn't want her pity. Lovis wasn't the problem.

"Yes?"

"It was a Honda, a 2015 CR-V. I don't know if you heard about that?"

"Still haven't seen it."

"There were drugs in it. Amphetamines."

"OK... Anything else?"

"What do you mean, anything else?"

"In the car?"

She hadn't expected that question; he saw her considering it, hesitating, which told him he was right, though she wasn't going to say it.

"Why?"

"Don't you want me to be on the lookout for it? Talk to people. Isn't that why you're here?"

"Yes," Hannah admitted. "Have you heard anything?"

UV quickly considered whether there was anything more he could get out of this conversation, something that could help him figure out how to move forward, but decided he'd learned as much as he needed to.

"I've quit the business, as I'm sure you know."

"No one will ever find out that you helped us."

He was about to tell her he couldn't help her, but he stopped. The woman with the Audi seemed satisfied to be sent forward. Be given a name. Maybe that was all it would take for the cop to leave him alone.

He pretended to think for a while, even though he'd made up his mind. Looking at Hannah with an expression that he hoped said he was imparting this information very reluctantly, doing her a favor, he said:

"Do you know Jonte Lundin?"

The tiny studio apartment smelled like stale smoke, cigarette butts, dirt, and old wine. The bed stood unmade in one corner, and the sheets were visibly dirty. On the coffee table in front of the stained and sagging sofa was a dead plant turned ashtray, some beer cans, and a plate of what might be dried tomato sauce. Katja tried lifting the plate by grabbing onto the fork stuck to it.

It worked.

The kitchen was in even worse shape. The stove plastered with burnt scraps of food, two pots whose contents had solidified days ago, cans, bottles, fast-food wrappers, empty packages, everything left where it was used or opened.

She didn't like waiting in here.

She started lining up the beer cans along the short side of the coffee table, but realized there were even more in the kitchen, by the bed, and in the bathroom. To organize only a fraction of this chaos would be more irritating to her than leaving it as it was.

So she stood in the middle of the room. Touched nothing. Did nothing. Waited.

The doorbell rang. Katja walked into the tiny hallway and

peered quietly out through the peephole. A woman was standing outside. Around fifty, ordinary body, hairstyle, and clothes. An ICA bag in her hand. Might be Lundin's mother, Katja thought. Here to replenish his pantry and fridge so that her son didn't starve to death. Would she enter with her own key if he didn't open the door? Katja was about to take a step back when she heard voices in the stairwell. She looked out again. A man she recognized as Jonathan Lundin was coming up the stairs, and the woman had gone to meet him. She couldn't hear what they were saying, but Lundin shook his head repeatedly, trying to get past her. The woman held an arm to the wall and stopped him, spoke again, seemed like she was asking him something. Lundin pressed his chin to his chest and continued to shake his head. The woman seemed to realize she wasn't getting anywhere with him and removed her arm. He took a few quick but unsteady steps toward his door. Katja quickly backed up into the room again. Heard the key turning, heard the door open and close, could hear Lundin mumbling to himself as he came into the room and sank down onto the sofa, heavy and loose-limbed. Katja stood still, but was fully visible in the middle of the room. Even so, he didn't seem to notice her. His eyes, body language, and listless movements as he attempted to untie his shoes suggested to Katja that he was a combination of high and drunk.

"Hello, Jonte," she said calmly.

"Hello?" he replied with a smile and friendly tone of voice, as if happy to see her even though he couldn't quite place who she was right now. Slowly, it dawned on him that he'd probably never seen her before. "Wait, are you a cop, too?"

"Who else is a cop?"

"The lady out there."

"I'm not with the police," Katja said. She walked over to him, sat down on the armrest of the sofa. Jonte nodded, seemed content with that, with no interest in knowing why an unknown woman might pop up in his apartment.

"I want to talk to you," Katja continued, trying to catch his unsteady, hazy gaze. "About drugs."

"That's what she wanted, too."

"The cop on the stairs? What did she say? Do you remember?"

"She wanted to know…if anyone was selling. Or who was buying…"

If they were looking for the same person in the same circles then they had identified Vadim, make the connection to Rovaniemi. Good to know.

"And what did you say?" she coaxed.

"Nothing."

"Because you don't know or because you don't want to squeal to a cop?"

"What?"

He looked at her as if that sentence had been at least a few words too long for him to make sense of. Katja studied him where he sat. Who knew what he'd been through or why he chose to dull it all away. If his upbringing had been half as bad as the first eight years of her life, then she understood taking every chance you could get to forget and repress.

It was, of course, possible that he'd had a completely normal, fairly happy childhood, thought drugs were cool and got trapped. Or maybe he'd inherited an addictive personality.

Whatever the reason, he was weak. Weak people could be used.

She took a wad of cash from the front pocket of her jeans and started to flip through it. Jonte's eyes followed her every move like a hungry Labrador. Five 500-kronor bills on the table. As he leaned forward to take them, she put a hand over the cash.

"I need you to answer a few questions first."

Jonte nodded. With some effort he was able to lift his eyes from the money, and she could see him struggling to concentrate.

"Has anyone popped up selling anything? Anyone new? This last week?"

"Not that I know—"

"Have you heard anything about a big batch of amphetamines?"

He shook his head like a two-year-old with a plate of broccoli in front of him.

"Are you sure?" she asked, putting another bill on the table. He took a deep breath, determined to do this.

"No, I haven't heard anything," with uncharacteristic clarity.

"Who might have heard something? Who do you buy from?"

"I don't know."

For the first time, she became impatient, leaned forward and grabbed his cheek hard.

"Yes, you do."

"No, it's true," he said, slurring more than usual as she pressed his lips together into an O. "Used to be UV...but now... I leave the cash, send a text, and they text back...where I can pick it up."

Katja let go, and Lundin leaned back against the sofa, seemingly exhausted by his long exposition. That might explain why nobody around here seemed to know who was behind the business: everything was handled anonymously, with no personal contact.

"Write what you usually write when you contact them, but don't send it."

"What? Why?"

"Take out your phone, write the text you usually do, but don't send it."

Jonte hesitated; somewhere in the fog that was his consciousness he must have realized this was a bad idea, but his eyes were on the cash on the table. Three thousand kronor. With a sigh, he pulled out his phone and, with some effort, put together a short message that he showed Katja.

"Great, where do you put the money?" she asked, taking his phone from him without protest.

"Trashcan at the bus stop. Behind the hotel."

"The City Hotel?"

Jonte nodded and leaned back against the sofa again. A bus stop behind the hotel, she could find it.

"Who told you how to do this?" she asked, straightening herself, preparing to leave.

"Don't remember, long time ago…"

"Too bad," Katja said with a shrug, grabbing the cash off the table.

Lundin stretched out a hand in an exhausted attempt to stop her. "But…but I heard…" it came quietly from the sofa before he trailed off, blinked a few times. Katja leaned over him and gave him two quick slaps.

"Come on."

"Sometimes I hear… I heard…about some Frenchie."

"Frenchie? Like from France?"

"I don't know…a Frenchman."

Definitely something she could work with. How many Frenchmen could there be in Haparanda and its surroundings? Even if it was only an alias, a nickname, it was something to ask about, it gave her a direction. She put two of the five hundred bills back on the table, and Lundin managed to sit up long enough to grab them.

"Don't tell anyone you heard it from me," he said, leaning back again. Katja didn't answer, went to the front door and left him half asleep on the sofa clutching the cash like a security blanket.

She'd put an envelope with 1,500 kronor inside into the green trashcan in the bus shelter, sat down in the car, and sent the text message from Jonte's phone.

Now she waited.

The radio was on at low volume. Some Swedish song about a man who made a point of walking around in a sweater his ex-girlfriend hated. She'd never heard it before, didn't know who was singing it. It was her job to keep up to date, but national pop music was her limit. Still she liked it, drummed two fingers on the steering wheel with her gaze firmly on the mirror.

A young man with dark hair shaved on both sides and hands stuffed in the pockets of an unbuttoned windbreaker came strolling toward the bus stop. He glanced around the empty street and walked to the trashcan. Katja sat up straight in her seat. The man put a hand into the trashcan and took out the envelope, shoved it into the inner pocket of his jacket, and left the same way he'd come.

Katja let him disappear around the corner of a dilapidated yellow building whose storefronts gaped sad and empty, then she left the car and followed him. Past the water tower, which was visible wherever you were in this city, and then down Köpmansgatan. The man turned right into an area that the signs told Katja was Västra Esplanaden. He carried on at a leisurely pace down the right-hand side of the street. Not once had he turned around, obviously wasn't expecting to be followed, but Katja kept her distance, kept on walking until she'd passed the Sports Hall, then watched from across the street as he approached a group of multiple-occupancy houses. He went past the first, but turned off at the second. Katja increased her pace, glancing around before crossing the street, hurrying after the man who was now out of her sight.

She emerged from behind the house in time to see the furthest door of two slowly closing. Not much more she could do at the moment. The nearest house had a lawn in front of it, which gave no options for cover, but a bit further away was a small soccer field with a few trees where she could hide and watch the door without being discovered. The mosquitoes welcomed her the moment she took her place beneath one of the birches. She

ignored them. Mosquito bites didn't bother her, and any movement might draw attention.

She didn't have to wait long.

Minutes later, the young man came out again and headed
back the same way he came. Probably headed out to deliver the
order she'd sent, and where that was going to happen was now of
no interest to her. However, where he picked up his product...

She waited a few extra minutes, just to be absolutely sure he
wouldn't come back, before going over to the door. The glass
pane in the door let in daylight, but she still pressed the orange
glowing light switch on the wall when she entered. The staircase was completely silent. No sound coming from any of the
six apartments. Two on each floor, according to the bulletin
board with a list of tenants on the wall. Katja scrutinized it and
couldn't hold back a pleased smile when she saw who lived on
the second floor.

René Fouquier. It sounded French.

"Sorry about this," Hannah said as she began clearing off the table. "I wanted to outdo myself."

After leaving UV's and then her useless visit to Jonte Lundin, she'd had no desire or time to cook so she'd swung by Leilani and picked up takeout instead. At least they didn't eat directly from the cartons, she thought as she rinsed off the plates and loaded them into the dishwasher. Always something.

"Doesn't matter, it was good," Thomas said, which was hard to believe since most of his pork with broccoli and barbecue sauce was still in its carton.

"Do you want coffee?"

He nodded and she started loading the coffee machine while he cleared the table. Meanwhile she told him about the investigation. About Alexander coming up and the help from Finland, which nobody had asked for. Thomas had listened, nodded, asked a few follow-up questions.

When there wasn't much more to talk about—his job, as always, was quickly covered—they landed, like always, on the subject of the kids.

Gabriel, who moved out three years ago, was studying to

be a speech therapist in Uppsala and had stayed down there to work this summer; maybe he'd come up for a week or two at the end of August. Thomas was saving a vacation week just in case, he said.

Alicia, who'd gone backpacking last September, said she'd be home again for Christmas, but she kept delaying.

At the end of July, she would know if she'd been accepted into any of the programs she applied for, and then would decide if she intended to come home or keep backpacking and apply again next year.

Gabriel and Alicia. Their children.

Never Elin.

Whose birthday was approaching. July 3. She would have turned twenty-eight this year. If it hadn't been for a sudden thunderstorm one afternoon in Stockholm.

If it hadn't been for Hannah.

They never ever talked about her. Not anymore.

Hannah didn't want to, couldn't. Thomas knew that and accepted it.

Thirty-seven years together. She'd just turned seventeen when she talked to him for the first time in the smoking area. Three years after she arrived home from school, started playing the soundtrack to *Fame* in the kitchen, danced over to the door to the living room, and found her mother hanging from a ceiling lamp.

Still so lost.

She had seen Thomas in the hallways, he was hard to miss, so tall, over 1.9 meters and at least twenty kilos overweight at that time. But that wasn't why she noticed him. It was his attitude. He was totally himself. Large and quiet, he walked around and didn't try to fit in, didn't care what people thought of him. He was in the grade ahead of her, but he was two years older. Had started first grade later than everyone else. Not mature enough, they said. Now he was studying economics, had a driver's license and a car, liked a lot of things she didn't like, being outdoors, fishing, and sitting quietly by a fire somewhere, but she liked being with him so she went along.

Hard to say when they became a couple; they just started spending more time with each other and less with other people. But she remembered when she realized it was going to be the two of them.

They were sitting on the bed in his room in the basement of his parents' house in Kalix, *Nebraska* was playing on the stereo, and he asked her for the first time to tell him about her mother. She had immediately gotten defensive.

"Why?"

"Because it must have been the worst thing that ever happened to you, but you never talk about it."

"That's because I don't want to. She fucking ruined my life."

"OK."

"She was crazy, and she hanged herself. What the hell else is there to say?"

He dropped it, suggested they drive down to Luleå and watch *The Return of the Jedi*. Science fiction: one more thing that he liked and she didn't. But she'd gone along. Afterwards he drove her home, parked outside, stopped her before she climbed out.

"It wasn't your fault."

"What?"

"Your mother."

"I never thought it was," she lied.

"Good. Because it wasn't."

They didn't talk about it again. Not until much later. But right there and then, that was it. She hadn't realized how much she needed to hear those words until they were said. Her father had only told her that her mother couldn't take it anymore, but he'd never said why.

After the funeral, they basically stopped talking about her completely. Nothing got better from dwelling on it, as he always used to say. He never tried to understand, never made the connection that her way of acting out, sometimes selfdestructively, might be because she was suffering from a crushing sense of guilt.

Even though the last few years had been full of complaints and outbursts.

I can't cope with you.

Are you trying to kill me?

You'll be the death of me.

How could she not think it was her fault? No one ever told her otherwise. Until Thomas. A brief and straightforward *it wasn't your fault* that not only eased her guilt, it also showed her how well he knew and understood her.

Since then it had been the two of them. The relationship was never particularly passionate, not particularly exciting, more like an extension of their friendship; neither of them was the romantic type. But it was safe. And that suited Hannah; it was what she needed.

Then and later.

Especially after what happened to Elin.

"He's good for you," her dad told her when Thomas walked into the house one day. "Hold onto him."

And she had.

They'd held onto each other, maybe even taken each other for granted, and now that they no longer had any children at home, when they had all their time for themselves, Thomas chose to spend most of his away from her. And she didn't confront him, nothing got better from dwelling. So she'd ended up with Gordon instead.

Now she came up behind Thomas where he was standing by the sink and hugged him.

"Should we go to bed?" she asked, kissing him on the neck while letting her hand run from his chest down to his crotch.

"I promised Kenneth I'd fix their water heater."

Hannah stopped, slowly moving her hands up again, but

maintained the embrace, glad she was behind his back so he couldn't see her face.

"Right now?"

"Might as well get it done, they don't have any hot water."

"Can't it wait until tomorrow instead?"

"I've been promising it for a while, so…"

Hannah still wanted him, but there were limits, she wasn't going to lower herself to nagging for sex, so she let go, went over to grab the coffeepot and poured coffee into the cups he'd place on the table.

Thomas more or less drank his in a gulp in the somewhat strained silence, then stood up, and put his cup in the dishwasher.

"See you later, it might take a few hours."

"Yes, it surely will. Say hello for me."

With a nod he went out into the hall, put on a thin windbreaker and shoes.

"See you soon," he chirped, and left without waiting for an answer.

Alone in the kitchen, Hannah wondered if she should call Gordon, but didn't. Told herself she didn't want to disturb his brotherly game night, but really she couldn't take the chance that he might reject her as well.

No one knew what the little shack was used for originally, but now it was just four ramshackle timber-framed walls with no windows or front door, a crumbling brick wall, and a collapsing roof, which lay a few hundred meters into the woods on Thomas and Hannah's property. Thomas had shown it to him and Sandra one of the first times they'd been out here to visit the cabin. Half-jokingly, Thomas said he was planning to make something of it, maybe a guest house. He was, of course, handy, but the shack was obviously beyond rescue even then. Now it was a ruin on its way back to nature, and Kenneth knew his uncle was planning to let it stand there and decay at its own pace.

Perfect for them.

Especially since in the furthest corner there was a hatch, and beneath it was a space that might once have been a storage room or cellar. Now three sports bags lay inside it, wrapped in black garbage bags. Kenneth was about to close the hatch again, but stopped.

"What if there are rats or something? Do they eat money?"

"Underground?"

"They live in sewers and drains and stuff like that."

He saw her hesitating. Her plan was for the money to stay there for at least three years, assuming they didn't go to prison, in which case it would be there even longer. After three years, they'd gradually start to use it, say they'd been saving, perhaps won some of it, maybe at one of the hundreds of online casinos advertised everywhere.

Hopefully Kenneth would have gotten a job by then as well, making it even more believable that they'd put away a little.

Three years. Sandra was very determined on that point.

Negligence and carelessness were not going to threaten their future. But she too didn't want to come back and discover that their 300,000 euros had become food and nesting material for a bunch of rodents.

"We have rat poison at home, we'll come back here and place some around," she said, nodding to herself. "We can buy some metal or hard plastic boxes as well."

Kenneth closed the hatch. They left the dilapidated cottage and started walking toward Thomas and Hannah's cabin. Though really it was mostly Thomas's, it had belonged to Kenneth's grandmother and grandfather who he'd barely even met because Stefan considered them a bad influence on the children. After they died, Thomas bought out his sister. The cabin was small and very simple. No electricity or hot water, it wasn't really a place to spend weeks at, and Thomas used it mostly for hunting and fishing, things Kenneth knew Hannah had no interest in.

They exited the woods behind the red wooden house, walked around the corner of the house just as Thomas swung up onto the small driveway and parked next to Sandra's car. They exchanged an anxious look, then both waved and headed over to meet him with what they hoped were relaxed smiles. Thomas turned off the engine and stepped out, clearly surprised to see them there.

"Oh, hey, what are you doing here?"

"We…we were…passing by," Kenneth replied, looking unsurely at Sandra. They hadn't expected to have to explain their presence, so they had no credible lie prepared.

"We have a friend who had a baby in Övertorneå, we were there visiting her," Sandra explained, though she knew immediately that Thomas would realize there was no reason for them to 'stop by' the cabin, which was a little over an hour from Haparanda and literally in the middle of nowhere.

"Yes, we swung by on our way back," Kenneth filled in.

"Thought we'd see if either of you were here while we were in the area," Sandra continued. Thomas said nothing, just looked at them with slightly raised eyebrows as they filled in each other's sentences.

"What are you doing out here?" Kenneth asked in an attempt to steer the conversation away.

"I…came to get some stuff. That I forgot," Thomas answered with a nod to the house, and Kenneth got the feeling that he too was lying. But why would he lie? Maybe he and Hannah had had a fight.

"Well, we should head home," Sandra said with a meaningful look at Kenneth. "I've got work early tomorrow so…"

"OK, drive carefully. Nice to see you."

No offer to come in for a while since they were here. Have a cup of coffee. Admittedly, they would have declined, but still. It felt like Thomas wanted to get rid of them.

"Thank you for fixing the water heater, by the way," Sandra said in front of the car.

"It was nothing."

It seemed like he might say more, but he swallowed the rest. Kenneth opened the door to the passenger seat, then turned to Thomas.

"We heard they found a body in the woods. Is Hannah working on that?"

"Yes."

"Do they know who it was?"

"Some Russian, apparently."

"Do they have any suspects?"

"No, they're looking for a car. The Russian's car. A blue Honda."

Kenneth nodded, saw Sandra giving him a look across the roof of the car that said that's enough, but he needed to know more.

"But they don't know anything about the car that hit him?"

"Not that I know."

"Have they found DNA or anything like that?"

"I don't know, why?"

Thomas took a step forward, his eyebrows raised again. Sandra cleared her throat discreetly.

"No, nothing, it happened pretty close to us so, you know, I'm curious, that's all."

"You two can talk more about that some other time. Get in now and we'll be on our way," Sandra interrupted with a slightly too wide smile. "Bye, Thomas, say hello to Hannah for me."

"That I will. Goodbye, you two."

As they exited onto the narrow forest road, Sandra sped up, driving in silence with her eyes pinned straight ahead. There was no need to talk about how annoyed she was or why.

"I asked too much," Kenneth stated.

"Way too much."

"Sorry, I just wanted to know what they knew."

Sandra didn't answer. He thought he had the right to ask; he was the one who woke up with a lump in his stomach every morning which paralyzed him all day, he was the one who would go to prison if they found DNA, he was the one who'd killed a man, but still he didn't like it when they didn't get along.

"I'm sorry," he said again.

They'd already argued once tonight. After they decided what to do with the money, she'd brought in a newly purchased vase from the car.

"Oh, so you can take the money, but not me," he'd said, aware of how childish and peevish he sounded.

"I took sixty euros, you wanted to buy a new car."

"A used one."

"If you can find one that costs sixty euros, then buy it."

"Six hundred, I can't even fix the Volvo for that."

"Then I think we should scrap it."

Kenneth froze. She surely didn't say that, did she? He wasn't allowed to buy a new one or fix the old one. With no car he'd be stuck at the house all day.

"Well then, what am I supposed to drive? How the hell am I supposed to get out of here?"

"It costs money, and we're pretending to save," she said, which didn't answer his question.

"But we have money," he screamed, walked to the kitchen table, opened one of the bags, and grabbed a fistful of cash. "We have shitloads of money!"

"Don't ruin this for me, Kenneth," she said with a dark look in her eyes that he'd never seen before.

"What does it matter if we spend a few thousand?"

"We are not going to touch the money, how hard is that to understand?"

"Unless we need some useless fucking vase!"

He threw the cash down and stormed out, regretting it immediately. So unnecessary. Especially since he knew what it meant to her. To be able to buy something new, something nice. She'd put flowers from the garden in it, photographed it against a bright sky, and put it on Instagram. The first post she'd made in several weeks. He knew she didn't feel like she had anything to show, knew it was partly his fault, because he had no job, didn't bring in any money.

In her darker moments she wondered how long she could go on living like this.

Only an hour left to closing time and just a handful of guests were scattered around the restaurant. Katja walked past the self-service machines up to the checkout, where a young man waited in a white chef's coat with the hamburger chain's yellow-and-orange logo on his chest. Below it was a nametag that confirmed she'd found who she was looking for.

"Hello, René."

"Hello, and welcome, what can I help you with?"

"*Vous préferez parler Français?*"

"No..." he answered in surprise. "Not unless you do."

"I thought you were the *Frenchman*," she continued with a tiny, meaningful smile as she kept her gaze steady to see if he reacted to the label. Nothing. Maybe that was something other people said about him and not to him.

"My father is French," he said, seemingly unclear as to why they were discussing this.

"Do you have time to talk?"

"It depends. I'm working."

"It will probably take a while. Do you have a break soon? Or should I wait until you close?"

René chose not to answer, took a somewhat deeper breath and tried to direct the conversation back to her order with the same professional smile as before.

"Would you like something to eat?"

"Choose, give me your favorite."

"Do you eat meat?"

"Yes."

He turned to the cash register and quickly entered an order on the touch screen; by this time he'd clearly decided she wasn't totally sane.

"Seventy-nine kronor, please."

Katja handed him a couple of bills and waved away his attempt to give her a krona back. He put it in the collection box that stood next to the cash register.

"Do you have a break soon?" she asked again.

"No, why?"

He didn't wait for an answer before going to fetch the bag of French fries standing ready beside the fryers. Clearly he was getting tired of her. When he came back, he froze. A few pieces of a broken garden gnome lay on the tray.

"I thought we could talk about this," Katja said quietly, while gently tapping the shards. René swept them away, and they quickly disappeared beneath his clothes as he looked around vigilantly. None of his colleagues in the kitchen seemed to care what was going on at the checkout counter right now.

"Do you have a break?" Katja asked again, guessing she might get an answer this time.

"Ten minutes, OK?"

"Sure."

She hummed along to the music coming out of unseen speakers while she waited for him to put her food on the tray. Then went and filled a cup with Diet Coke, grabbed some ketchup, salt, pepper and three napkins, then changed her mind about going straight to a table and returned to the cash register instead.

His bosses weren't going to be happy with him, she thought, and there was really no welcome in René's eyes as she walked over to him again.

"One more thing," she said, leaning over the counter. "I'm not a cop, so don't disappear, because I will find you no matter where you go."

With a small nod as if to confirm that they were in agreement, she took her tray and sat down at a table with her back against the wall and an overview of the restaurant. She unwrapped her burger and lifted the meat to peel off the tomato. She could eat it, she could eat anything, but she didn't like tomatoes so she avoided them when she could. She realized how hungry she was as soon as she took a bite of what they advertised as Sweden's best hamburger. She hadn't eaten enough burgers in Sweden to know, but this was good enough for her and filling.

She ate her burger and was sitting there dipping her fries in ketchup one by one when the doors slid open and two men came in. Jeans and big muscles under their tight T-shirts. Katja followed them with her eyes as they ordered coffee and sundaes from the girl who had replaced René at the cash register. They sat down at the table next to Katja and made every effort to pretend they didn't notice her. For a moment, she wondered if she should tell them she knew René had called them and offer to let them sit at her table. But she didn't do anything until René came and sat across from her and caught her eye.

"You've been to my house," he stated calmly.

"Yep, nice apartment. I really appreciate your sense of order."

René inspected her closely, as if trying to judge if she was just crazy or if there was something he needed to know, maybe even worry about before acting. She was convinced he was going to threaten her, possibly sic his gorillas on her, or he might even be toying with the idea of killing her. She didn't know him, didn't know how far he was willing to go or what he was capable of.

"It was stupid of you to come here," he said, confirming her first assumption.

"Is that so?"

"The best thing for you would be to leave here and never come back again."

"Unfortunately, that's not possible," Katja said with exaggerated regret. "I have a job to finish."

"Oh, and what kind of job is that?" René asked with the hint of a smile that said he was playing a game he was sure he could win.

Katja decided to take control of the conversation, leaned forward and lowered her voice even further.

"I don't give a shit about you or your business, I'm not trying to take it over or take it from you." She met his gaze calmly and openly. "I just want information. If I get it, then I'll disappear."

"Information about what?"

"Did someone offer you a large amount of amphetamines this past week, or have you heard anything about a really big consignment?"

"How'd you find me?" The smile was suddenly wiped away, as if the mention of drugs reminded him that, even though he'd managed to stay under the radar so far, there was a weak link in his chain.

"Answer my question first."

"Why do you want to know?"

"Do you want me to leave you alone or not?"

René cocked his head, judging her silently for a few seconds before shrugging his shoulders.

"No, I haven't heard anything about any amphetamines."

"If you do, you get in touch with me," Katja said, took out an orange Post-it with her Swedish phone number on it and pushed it across the table.

"Sure." He picked it up and stuffed it into his pocket without looking at it. "How'd you find me?"

"It wasn't that hard." Katja smiled, took her bag, and made an effort to stand up. René leaned forward quickly and grabbed her wrist. She could free herself in a second, grab the knife at her ankle, and push it into his eye before he realized what was happening, but she stayed still, and met his questioning gaze.

"Tell me. For your own sake."

She looked at his hand around her wrist, then up to René, holding his eyes without blinking.

"Never touch me again unless I give you permission."

They measured each other for a few more seconds before René released her, leaned back in his chair, and opened his arms wide with a disarming smile.

"Please clear my tray." Katja stood up and draped her bag over her shoulder. "Or ask one of your friends to do it," she continued, placing her hand on the shoulder of one of the men at the table next to them. She felt the muscles tighten at her touch. "Keep them busy for a while so they don't get up to any trouble."

Then she walked out into the light and relative warmth. It was only a few minutes' walk back to the hotel, but she was in no rush. With one last look back toward the restaurant, where the three men had their heads close together, she headed down to the river.

66 **I**t's time."

Sandra turned and headed out. Kenneth put down the iPad and got up. He'd stayed half-awake watching Netflix, already tired when they got back from Thomas's cabin, but they were only halfway done. As he walked out into the hallway to grab the keys from the bureau drawer, he thought about how much easier this would be in December when it was dark around the clock. But they had no choice. The police were searching for the Honda, they couldn't discover it here, so it had to disappear. When he got outside, Sandra was waiting by her car, ready to go. Their future economic opportunities seemed to be an inexhaustible source of energy for her.

"Curtains drawn in every bedroom," she said, nodding to their nearest neighbor as Kenneth came downstairs. "Lights off in the whole house. Let's go."

Kenneth opened the garage door and drove out onto the road. Knew he was just imagining it, but it felt like the little car was making way more noise than Sandra's, and he was afraid he'd wake up the whole village. He glanced in the rearview mirror, Sandra wasn't in sight, but that was the plan. Don't follow right behind. If anyone saw the Honda and knew the police were looking for it, they wouldn't be able to make the connection to Sandra's car.

He drove along the lake that gave the village its name, thinking about all the bad decisions he'd made.

So many. For so long.

He blamed his father for being a first-rate asshole. Extremely successful, respected, and admired. But an asshole.

Not a warm man. Never a loving father.

He was a successful entrepreneur who just happened to have a wife and a couple of kids.

His entire identity was his work. Success required total focus, self-control, and no distractions. Order must prevail in their big house in one of the nicer suburbs of Stockholm. The word had shaped Kenneth's upbringing. Order came from discipline, obedience, and control. Mistakes were a sign of weakness, and you were less likely to repeat them if you were punished, if you knew it would hurt.

So much pain over the years. So many bad decisions.

Kenneth's way of rebelling had been to always make the choice he knew his father would hate. Create chaos. He missed, dropped, ignored, questioned, forgot, skipped class, took drugs, robbed…

That's how he'd ended up in Norrland five years ago.

Haparanda prison. Security, second class.

Three years and eight months for robbery. Sandra was working there. Four years older and half a head taller than him. At first she had been friendly, professional. But as the months went by she talked more and more to him, got more personal. Soon they were in love. Relationships between inmates and guards were, of course, forbidden, so they didn't act on it, didn't want to risk transfer or termination. They just longed for each other, got closer to each other every day, but never too close, never too intimate; counting the days. When he got out after two years, he was drug-free and stayed in Haparanda. Had no one and nothing to return to. He moved into her apartment, which they left a year later to buy the house in Norra Storträsk.

Away from the city, away from the temptations that abounded there.

Everything was good. Better than good. Perfect.

But not anymore.

He turned off before Grubbnäsudden and took the back roads down to Bodträsk. There the road got bigger again, but he wouldn't drive far. After a few kilometers he slowed and turned left, swore to himself. Someone was headed his way. He had only a second to decide which would arouse less suspicion: turn left off the road even though there was only one car approaching, or wait to be overtaken.

Wait or turn?

But by the time he made up his mind, being overtaken was his only choice. Kenneth bowed his head and looked the other way as the oncoming car drove past, then quickly and nervously glanced into the rearview mirror. The red taillights disappeared, didn't slow, made no effort to turn. Relieved, he turned onto a small gravel road, continued forward with the forest on one side, a yellowish bog on the other. Turned again when it was just possible to make out the impression of two wheel tracks from some forest machine, even though they were almost completely overgrown. Bushes and undergrowth scraped against the bottom of the car as he approached his destination at a crawl. A few minutes later he arrived, stopped, and climbed out. In front of him was a rocky slope where ferns and blueberry bushes grew sparsely on nutrient-poor soil. The slope ended in a six-meter-high vertical cliff that rose up from the dark lake below.

The plan should work. Nothing in the way, the lake was deep enough.

Kenneth leaned in, put it into neutral, positioned himself at the open door, and started to push. Once about half the car made it onto the slope, it started rolling on its own, and he stepped aside. The Honda disappeared over the edge, and Kenneth thought it sounded like an explosion in the quiet of the summer night as it hit the water's surface a second later. He took a few careful steps down the slope and peered down. The water covered the hood, rushed into the open front door, and filled the passenger compartment as the car sank. Soon, only the damaged back end of the car was visible, and then that too was gone. A few air bubbles rose to the surface, then ceased after a while, and within minutes the lake turned calm and smooth again.

Kenneth made his way back up the slope, started walking toward where they'd decided Sandra would wait with her car and pick him up. For the first time since the accident, he felt a little hopeful. Yes, the man had died, he couldn't do anything about that, but the police hadn't come—apparently he'd been incredibly lucky and didn't leave any DNA on the body—the money was hidden, and the car was gone.

Maybe it would all work out for the best after all.

In the houses and apartments, cups of caffeine are preparing her residents for another day.

One of many. In Haparanda.

They commute, their shifts begin or end, one calls in sick, one takes out a key car, puts on a uniform, one rushes to preschool. Businesses will be opened and managed. Despite everything.

Many work. Many do not.

She remembers how it felt when Ikea opened its doors in her. The northernmost store in the world. Kamprad himself came to inaugurate it. People lined up in the wet snow for hours to get inside. The hotels were fully booked, Swedish and international press came, the cameras were rolling, she was photographed, filmed, seen. Now everything was going to turn. If Ikea comes, so do the other businesses, the customers, the jobs, a growing city, a thriving district. People talking so proudly about growth.

The customers came—to Ikea—but she didn't regain her former glory. Not by a long shot.

Maybe the answer lies in the expression she hears all too often. *Ei se kannatte.*

It's not worth it, in Meänkieli. The smallest of the three languages spoken in her. Even though it's usually said with a smile, more or less as a joke, she still feels how it permeates her. For many, regardless of age, that was their first reaction when they heard about a new venture, whether it was sports, business, tourism, or politics.

She even has the lowest voter turnout in Sweden.

Ei se kannatte.

It was hard to say if it was the chicken or the egg, but so many big ventures proved not to be viable in this city. Self-fulfilling prophecies or an unusually difficult climate for success. A bit of both, she guesses. Either way, there's nothing she can do about it.

The sun is warm as Gordon Backman Niska glances at his wristwatch: 142. Not bad after thirteen kilometers in fifty-four minutes. Six days a week he trains here. Without exception. Usually, these rhythmic steps and even breathing have a meditative effect on him. Now he realizes he's thinking about Hannah. Again. Doesn't want to admit it to himself, but he missed her yesterday, longed for her as he went to bed. Longs for her often. He increases his pace, focuses on his breathing, and forces away those thoughts.

As they cross the border to Finland, Ludwig looks at the quiet seven-year-old in the back seat. His stepdaughter. Summer vacation. He's driving her to her grandmother's house in Kemi, Eveliina will pick her up in the evening. He doesn't look forward to these mornings alone with the girl. The girl doesn't understand his Finnish—or doesn't want to. Ludwig is convinced she invents words when she's talking to him just to make him seem more stupid. He's pretty sure she doesn't like him. He's right, but he'll have bigger problems in a few months when Eveliina joins a cult and takes her daughter with her.

Viggo, his three-year-old Russian blue, moans reproachfully as Morgan Berg arrives home. There's no food, and Viggo wanted to spend this warm summer night outside, not trapped in the apartment. Morgan carelessly pours some dry food and gives the cat fresh water before disappearing into the shower, annoyed. Last night he went over for dinner at the neighbors, and they ended up in bed together as they sometimes do when the mood strikes them. Afterwards they all fell asleep. It annoys him, he likes to wake up at home, he has his routines, and now he barely has time to shower before he heads into the station.

The investigation into her disappearance takes up the entire basement. P-O Korpela has been down there for two hours already this morning. It's become his obsession. She has. Lena Rask. He lost his virginity to her when he was seventeen. Four years later, she and a friend disappeared without a trace. Never to be seen again, never heard from. Their disappearance had been a cold case for many years. P-O doesn't know that he regularly spends time with the man who murdered them both.

It's getting warm, so Lurch opens the window, then looks over at Nora, who's still sleeping in their double bed. He was so happy when they met, is so afraid of losing her now. For a few years she's been talking about them having children. He pretends to share her longing. Last night Nora mentioned IVF for the first time, and now he's standing here gripped by fear that he might be discovered, that an examination would prove the reason they weren't getting pregnant was that he'd gotten sterilized in secret four years ago.

He pulls the curtains closed against the sun and leaves his room and his home. Just like his colleagues, who will all gather at the station in a little over an hour, he thinks this day will be like most of the others.

But it will not.

Hannah didn't hear Thomas arrive home yesterday or get up in the morning. She knew he'd come home because he was lying in their bed when she woke up boiling hot at three a.m. She'd gotten out of bed, pulled the thin summer blanket out of the duvet, and opened the windows wide, then took the opportunity to pee and splash cold water on her face since she was up anyway. She lay down again and listened to Thomas's calm, even breathing. Considered cuddling up to him, falling asleep there, but the heat of his body beneath the covers stopped her.

By the time her alarm clock went off the next morning he was gone.

She stepped out of the shower and opened the bathroom door to let out the heat while drying herself off in front of the mirror. Her waist was no longer the narrowest part of her torso and gravity had taken a firmer grip on her breasts and buttocks, there was no escaping that fact. Her skin was not as elastic as it used to be, especially not around her neck and down into her cleavage. She was fifty-four, and it showed, but she still liked her body. Its appearance, not how it was behaving these days. She only wished Thomas would appreciate it more.

She started applying her make-up while in front of the mirror. A light eye shadow around her warm brown eyes, a little mascara, and some discreet lipstick. Then she pulled a brush through her hair, which she dyed every third month when the gray started to show. Clean panties and a bra, otherwise the same clothes as yesterday, a quick breakfast while looking at the newspaper and so on.

The sun was already hot as she stepped out of their red brick one-story house onto Björnholmsgatan and started to walk toward the city. A few doors down the street she waved to a man leaving his house, but didn't stop to talk. She'd never bothered to make friends with any of her neighbors.

She wanted to keep the fresh feeling of her shower as long as possible, so she slowed down on the hill that led up to the church, turned left on Köpmansgatan toward the downtown area, walked past Tornedals school where both Gabriel and Alicia had studied, though in different programs. Then she was downtown. It took her a little over a quarter of an hour to walk to work, and she did so every day, summer or winter, so accustomed to the path she never registered what she passed by unless a new store opened or if one closed, which unfortunately was more likely.

To her surprise, Gordon and Morgan were waiting for her outside the station when she arrived.

"There you are, I was about to call you," Gordon said when he saw her.

"Anything new on Tarasov?"

"No, but you're late."

"For what?"

"Competence test."

Hannah sighed loudly, hadn't so much forgotten this as repressed it. Every eighteen months, every armed police officer had to take a shooting test in order to carry their weapons. Last winter she'd passed by the smallest possible margin, and she hadn't practiced shooting a single time since then. Never felt any need to. During all her years as a police officer, she'd only drawn her weapon three times, and never fired it.

"Can't it wait?" she tried.

"No, you've already postponed it twice. Do it now, and you'll have a week left to redo it if you fail."

Hannah sighed again, but reluctantly followed them to a low building behind the station, close to the river. Morgan was a few steps ahead of them, staring down at the ground.

"How did it go yesterday?" Gordon asked conversationally.

"How did what go?"

"Dinner, an evening at home."

"It went fine," Hannah said with a shrug that she hoped conveyed that there wasn't much more to say on the subject.

"Did you make chicken pasta?"

"No, we had a takeaway."

She considered telling him why she got home too late to make something, about her visits with UV and Jonte, but decided, since both were dead ends, to let it be.

"How was the game? Did you win?"

"Didn't happen; my brother was busy."

"Too bad," she said, and it flashed through her mind that she could have spent part of the night with him.

They went in through the metal door, Morgan turned on the fluorescent lights, which illuminated a simple, but functional shooting range. Five targets hung along the far wall, silhouettes of the upper half of a human body with a ring on their chests marking the approved area.

Gordon came over with the weapon, magazine, and bullets. Hannah loaded the gun, put on her noise-canceling headphones, picked up the gun, cocked it, and got into position. Precision shooting from twenty meters. Four out of five inside the circle, all of them hitting the paper target in order to be approved. In the berth next to her, Morgan fired shots in quick succession, all hit the middle of the circle. No problem. Hannah took a deep breath, letting out the air as she pressed the trigger. Four inside the circle, though not as centered as Morgan's.

They moved forward thirteen meters for the next two phases: heightened readiness and emergency defense. Morgan landed five out of five on both. Hannah managed the first because Gordon approved two bullets that grazed the circle as hits even though they were mostly outside. She was not able to manage the emergency move—pull out the gun, cock it, and fire the shots within three seconds. One far outside the circle, one outside the target completely.

"We'll do it again next week, it will be fine," Gordon said comfortingly as he took the weapon from her.

"Sure," she said, shrugging, and left the shooting range. She didn't need comforting, was neither disappointed nor worried. What was the worst that could happen? Desk duty until she passed it? Being relieved of her service weapon. It was hardly something she used daily.

After changing into a uniform, she went up to her office and ran into a cleaning lady on her way out. One she couldn't remember seeing before. Both women apologized at the same time, Hannah told her to go ahead.

"No, no, I'm done," said the young blond woman with a clear Eastern European accent. The high turnover of Eastern European cleaning women here probably meant they should look into the terms of employment at the cleaning company they'd subcontracted, Hannah thought, watching as the young woman continued down the corridor to the next room. Hannah went into her office, turned on her computer as the phone rang. Thomas. Was he calling to apologize for yesterday, for leaving when she so clearly wanted him to stay? She hoped so.

"Yes," she replied, sinking into her chair, entering her password.

"It's me," Thomas said.

"I know."

"That Honda you're looking for. I may know where you can find it."

Ten minutes later he pulled up outside the station building.

"Why did this person call you?" Hannah asked as soon as she closed the door behind her.

"He knows we're married," Thomas said, driving toward the E4.

"Why didn't he call us directly?"

"Not everyone wants to talk to the police."

"What kind of clients do you have anyway?"

She got only a slight shrug in response. Hannah understood. Whoever had called wasn't necessarily involved in something criminal or illegal, and it could basically be anyone. People want to take care of themselves first, not get too involved, not get pulled into something. Distrust of authorities was quite widespread in this area, the police were no exception. Distrust and plain antipathy.

"How did it go with the water heater?" Hannah asked, directing the conversation back to yesterday.

"Good, it's fixed."

"That's great."

Nothing else. No excuse. Should she say it? That she missed him. Felt rejected when he left, got sad. That she noticed they'd drifted apart, or rather that he'd drifted away from her. Distanced himself.

Where would that lead?

Would he tell her why, say what it was he'd withdrawn from, that he didn't want to continue, that he thought their time together might be over.

What would she gain from that?

Better not to confront him. As long as nothing was said, anything was possible—you could even imagine things were normal, or that they would be again. So instead she told him that she'd failed her shooting test. He asked her what the consequences would be, and she said nothing. It simply proved what they already knew: that she was a lousy shot. After that, they drove in silence.

"He turned in here," Thomas said after they'd driven for a while, stopping at the side of the road and pointing to a smaller road to the right.

"And he's sure it was the car we're looking for?" Hannah queried, peering into the woods.

"I mean, it was a blue Honda, dented, and had no taillight."

"When was this?"

"At half past two or so."

"What was your friend doing here at that time?"

"First, he's not my friend, and second, that's exactly the kind of question that made him call me instead of you."

With a little smile that warmed her, Thomas started the car again and took the smaller road. They drove on slowly until a few kilometers later the road ended at a makeshift turning area. Hannah sighed in disappointment. Thomas's conversation had given her some hope. Someone or some people had moved the Honda from the crime scene, had hidden it for a while and driven it again yesterday—or early this morning, she corrected herself. That would be difficult to manage without leaving a trace. The car would most likely yield DNA and other technical evidence. But it wasn't here. Maybe the person who'd driven it realized they were lost when they reached this dead end, turned around and drove away again, or perhaps the informant was simply mistaken.

In any case, it wasn't here.

"We'll drive back," Hannah said, leaning back in her seat, disappointed. Thomas reversed and drove forward a few times until the car was turned around, then they started the return journey toward the main road. After only a few minutes, he slowed again.

Hannah straightened up in her seat. "Why are we stopping?"

"Look."

He pointed out her window. She saw it immediately. The undergrowth hadn't yet risen again to hide a pair of tire tracks; easy to make out when you knew what you were looking for. Broken branches that shone white confirmed someone had recently made their way through this patch of sparse forest.

They climbed out of their car and followed the pressed-down vegetation. Just the two of them. Together. Hannah took his hand. For a moment she got the feeling that he wanted to pull it back, but instead he interlaced his fingers with hers, and they continued on hand in hand. Until they came to the sandy slope above the lake. The tracks ended a bit further down the slope; there was no doubt where the car ended up.

"Do you know which lake this is?" she asked, before carefully making her way down the hill toward the edge and peering into the dark water.

"No clue."

It was difficult to estimate how deep the almost black water was, but deep enough to make seeing any car that might be down there impossible.

"Find out. We have to get a diver here," Hannah said straight into the air.

Even though he hadn't slept at all last night, he wasn't tired. An anxious energy drove him on. Questions spun in his head. Many more than there were answers at the moment, and René didn't like it.

Didn't like it at all.

The most important one was probably how the woman who came to his work last night had found him. If she could, then others might as well. Still, that was the least of his worries right now.

She'd been in his home.

Found the broken garden gnome, hadn't touched the drugs from what he could see, but still. Did that mean he'd have to give up his ingenious method of moving product?

The supplier arrived at the auction they'd agreed on when it opened for preview, walked around among the objects and secretly placed a garden gnome, a figurine, a porcelain ornament into one of the small boxes of crap that would be sold in lots, which were ubiquitous at every auction in the area. A text message to René stating which box the goods were located in, and then he went and bid on it.

It worked flawlessly, no one had a clue.

Until now. Until her.

'I Learned from the Best', the fifth single from his favorite album in every category, flowed into the apartment from his expensive and advanced sound system. A modest success by Houston standards, even if some critics compared it to classics like 'Saving All My Love for You', but it only reached twenty-seven on the Billboard charts in the US. Twenty-three in Sweden. Of course, it had deserved better. Even though the Hex Hector and Junior Vasquez remixes topped the dance lists in the US for three weeks, this minor masterpiece still felt sadly forgotten. He'd been playing the record on repeat all morning, but not even Whitney could push away his thoughts, or quiet his questions.

What was she doing in Haparanda?

She'd said was she wasn't interested in challenging him, taking over the business, or replacing him, so what did she want? Searching for a batch of amphetamines. From whom and why? What would she do if she found it? Disappear again? Take a share of the market? So many questions that all led to the same conclusion: he knew too little, she knew far too much, therefore she was a threat.

For the first time, he understood others in his position, realized the advantages of being feared and admired. If he'd made a name for himself, had a reputation for danger, cultivated a myth, this would have worked out different. She would have asked for a meeting, groveled a little to see him at all. Now she could just show up, take him by surprise.

He hated surprises.

Only idiots thought it was fun to relinquish control over future events to someone else, leaving themselves with no means of influencing the outcome. But perhaps he could turn this to his advantage. The best thing about having found him so easily, seeing how he wasn't protected, was that she had probably underestimated him.

What he was capable of. What he was planning.

As soon as she left them last night, he'd sent his four men to search for her. Most visitors stayed at the City Hotel, so they started there. She wasn't there, so they had to ask around. The city wasn't large, and she was rather conspicuous. They'd find her. The next time they met, it would be on his terms. No more surprises. His questions would be answered. Then he'd try to track down those amphetamines and make her disappear.

For good, if necessary.

He had never killed anyone before. Injured quite a few, some at a remarkably young age, but he'd never gone all the way. There were two reasons.

Dead bodies always generated large police operations. Someone who'd taken a beating knew the consquences of failing to keep quiet; they seldom created much of a problem. Once there was a body, everything changed. You could try to make sure it was never found, but sooner or later most popped up anyway, or so it seemed, and disappearances were investigated more carefully as well. Also, they received more media coverage.

The second reason was that he was fairly sure, even worried, that he might develop a taste for it. He loved control, enjoyed power.

Wasn't having the final say over life and death the absolute power? He'd always been completely indifferent to other people's suffering and pain. Didn't enjoy injuring, never got a kick out of it, but also never felt guilt or regret afterwards.

Never felt much at all.

An egg was cracked into a hot frying pan and started to congeal, a key was turned in a car and it started, a fist landed in the face of an eight-year-old, the lip cracked and started to bleed.

Causality. Cause and effect.

An event led to an expected result. No emotions were involved.

Over time, he'd begun to see it as a strength that he didn't care.

About anything, or anyone. Except himself.

The wind section took over after a short acoustic guitar solo, they approached the crescendo at 3:26, drums and then Whitney's goosebump-raising voice conveying the perfect mix of unbridled strength with the right amount of longing and vulnerability as she makes it clear to the man who left her that she won't take him back. She's learned how to break a heart, learned it from the best...

René's phone buzzed in his pocket, and he took it out, let it vibrate in his hand for a moment, waiting to hear Whitney start singing over herself in the chorus before answering.

They had found her.

The day had begun productively. A good morning.

The city didn't seem to be in any hurry. A car now and then, the shops she passed had no customers, only a few people walking around the square. After her threat to his daughter, Stepan Horvat had delivered what she needed; everything had gone according to plan.

Katja had gathered as much information as possible by the time she pushed open the old, beautifully etched glass doors of the hotel and saw the man sitting in a leather armchair by the elevator. He was doing his best not to attract attention, but she recognized him immediately. From last night.

Were they really so amateurish?

What was the idea? That she'd feel threatened? That the young man, who clearly spent several hours a week in the gym, would scare her? It was almost cute. On her way up the wide marble staircase, she wondered if it would be a problem that they'd figured out where she was staying, but waved it away. She'd given René her number, they knew she was in town, where she was staying didn't matter.

On the top floor, she turned right and saw another familiar

face. A second man from yesterday was sitting in one of the two carved rococo chairs that stood near a small table halfway down the corridor. He was flipping through a tourism brochure, but looked up when he heard her coming. Katja slowed down, the man stood up, took a few steps, blocking her way. Big, muscular, like his friend in the entrance, legs wide for optimal balance, but not armed, at least not that Katja could see. She slowed down further, keeping her eyes fixed on him as she heard calm, heavy footsteps approaching from the stairs behind her. The man who'd been in the reception area turned the corner.

"Do you really want to do this?" Katja asked, backing away so that she had her back to the wall and could keep them both in her sights without having to turn her head. Neither answered, neither made a move. Just stood still and stared at her.

She had to finish this fast.

There were plenty of other guests in the hotel, and even though she rarely passed anyone else in the corridor, someone could show up at any moment. Staff if nothing else. Should she call for help? Get rid of them that way? That was what Louise Andersson would have done, but that would draw unnecessary attention. Someone might even insist on calling the police, and she didn't want that. Killing them was out of the question. If she injured them, they'd still need to be able to get out of here on their own. Preferably unseen.

"What's the plan?" she asked, bending down gently, pulling up her pants leg and taking out a knife, letting the wide, arched blade rest against her thigh. Still no answer. "Go back and tell René that, whatever it was, it didn't work."

The men looked at each other, exchanging a short nod before the two began to move forward. Katja chose the one closest to her, shot out of the wall, was in front in a single sweeping motion, quickly changed direction, came in behind, and put her foot against the back of his knee. When he sank to the floor, she locked one of his arms behind him while pressing the Bowie knife to his neck. The other man stopped in his tracks.

"Think again," she said softly. "I'm in a whole other league."

It was the worst possible situation for Louise Andersson to be discovered in, so Katja immediately let go, took two steps back, the knife blade resting against her thigh again. The man in front of her got to his feet, cast a frightened look over his shoulder, and then walked toward his friend. Gave him a push as he walked by to bring him along and both quickly disappeared down the stairs. Katja bent down, fastened the knife in its holster again.

She'd need to have a chat with René Fouquier.

She continued toward her room, turned the corner at the end of the corridor, and had only a moment to register that a third man was waiting, pressed against the wall, before a burning pain shot from her chest and spread to the rest of her body. She began to shake helplessly, struggling with all the willpower she could muster to regain control, stay on her feet, and failed. The patterned carpet came rushing toward her as she fell headlong. On the floor, her well-trained brain still managed to push away the pain, loosen her muscles and she reached for the knife on her ankle. Before she could, she felt a firm grip on her wrist. The two men had returned, joining the third who had shot her with a Taser.

She made one last attempt to free herself but the man she'd released came up next to her. Again he put one leg on the floor, but this time he pulled back his arm, let his fist land in her face with full force, and she lost consciousness.

He felt a little better.

Freshly showered and with a towel wrapped around his hips, Kenneth walked into the kitchen, turned on the coffee maker, opened the refrigerator, and nodded to himself; it wasn't just his imagination.

He felt better.

He was hungry for the first time since it happened, and he'd slept until a quarter past nine. Naturally, as soon as he opened his eyes, his thoughts started racing again, but in a different way. They weren't so preoccupied with the man on the road, or his staring eyes, or the hard vertebrae beneath his skin. His anxiety about killing someone and his fear of going to jail had subsided. It was easier to convince himself that everything was normal. What he'd felt as he watched the Honda sink still lingered in his body, the feeling that they might survive this.

It felt really good.

Now he was thinking more about Sandra. About the two of them. As soon as they got home this morning, she'd gone straight to bed, still angry. She got up at eight o'clock, after only a few hours' sleep. He'd suggested she set her clock as usual, then call in sick and go back to sleep, stay home with him. That made her angry again; everything had to seem normal, didn't he get that?

"But you went home early yesterday because you felt sick," he'd tried. "So it wouldn't seem that weird if you're still sick."

"I'm going to work," she insisted, turning her back on him. End of discussion. He'd considered spooning her, but gave up, lay there staring up at the ceiling instead. Tired, but with adrenaline still coursing through him.

She had saved him.

It sounded dramatic, but it was true. What would he have done after prison if it weren't for her? Where would he have gone? He wasn't welcome at home. Thomas and Hannah were kind but not really an alternative. He would have ended up somewhere alone, unhappy, easily influenced. Making bad decisions. Sandra had been his salvation, his anchor. He wanted to give her everything she wanted because she was an incredible person and deserved it, but he had so little to give.

He thought she wanted to get married. Not just go to the courthouse and go out to eat afterwards, only the two of them, before driving home to Norra Stortäsk and going to bed. She wanted a real party. With lots of people, catering, an open bar, and music. A wedding night at a hotel. A honeymoon. Do it for real, like everyone else. That's why he'd never proposed. Big weddings cost money. Kids, too. She wanted to be a mother someday, he knew that, but they couldn't afford it.

In three years, some of those millions could probably be spent on a wedding and starting a family. Best-case scenario, he might have found a job by then, which she wanted him to do. Then they could live the worry-free life she deserved. He smiled to himself at the thought.

The future looked brighter. That felt good.

The silence in the house was shattered by the doorbell. Kenneth froze, for a moment completely sure it was a cop. He had left some trace after all. They were here to pick him up. He was going back to prison. It was over.

"Who is it?" he asked, and heard a voice that sounded squeaky and not that loud.

"It's me," came from outside. "UV."

Kenneth relaxed and opened the door with a relieved smile.

They'd met in prison; UV was already there when Kenneth arrived. Started talking, got along well and eventually both made the decision to change their lives. They'd kept in touch when they got out, met now and then, but UV had a family that took a lot of his time, and Kenneth moved away, so these days they met less often. The last time had been on that fateful night. They'd been to the same party, UV left at the same time as he and Sandra.

"Are you really going to drive?" he'd asked as Kenneth unlocked his car.

"Sure, why not?"

UV didn't respond, just shrugged in a way that said everything.

"I only drank a few beers."

"OK, see you soon," UV nodded, waved goodbye, and started walking.

"We can give you a ride," Kenneth said to his back, but UV merely raised a hand again in a gesture of no thanks, and continued walking. If he'd agreed to a ride home, none of this would have happened, it occurred to Kenneth now. He and Sandra wouldn't have been on that forest road at the same moment the Russian was stretching his legs. Sandra might have fallen asleep earlier or not at all, he wouldn't have tried to change the playlist at that moment, not dropped his phone, not taken his eyes off the road.

So many meaningless *ifs* and *maybes*.

"Yo," UV said cheerlessly as the door opened. It struck Kenneth how worn out his friend looked. Dark circles under his eyes, the stubble on his chin longer than usual, a nasty cold sore on his lower lip.

"Hey, nice to see you. Come in, come in."

Kenneth realized that he still only had a towel around his waist as he walked past UV, who stopped to pull off his shoes.

"I'm just going to put on some clothes. There's coffee in the kitchen."

"OK."

He hurried up the stairs, pulled on boxers, jeans, and a T-shirt. This morning's relatively good mood became even better with this visitor. He didn't have many friends in Haparanda, hardly any, but he definitely counted UV as one of them. The best one. He found a hairband and pulled his hair back into a loose ponytail before going back to the kitchen again. UV was sitting at the kitchen table, staring out the window, off into the distance. No coffee cup.

"Didn't you want coffee?" Kenneth asked on his way to the kitchen counter.

"No, I'm fine."

"A sandwich?"

"I ate at home."

"How's it going, with work and all that?" Kenneth said over his shoulder as he continued to fix his own breakfast.

"Fine, it's pretty calm."

"Do you get any time off? You look kinda worn out."

UV didn't respond immediately, just sighed. Kenneth watched as he leaned his face into his hands and rubbed his eyes. Something was weighing on him.

"Social Insurance has reduced our assistance. Did I tell you that?"

"No, I don't think so."

"We get forty hours a week. We have to pay for everything else ourselves."

"What did you have before?"

"One hundred and twenty."

"Goddamnit, that's less than half. How do you manage?"

"We don't. Stina is on sick leave again."

"Tell me if there's anything we can do."

He said it more because it was expected than because he actually meant it. He always felt uncomfortable around Lovis, didn't really know how to behave, not just toward her, but toward Stina and UV when she was with them.

"There is one thing…"

Kenneth grabbed his breakfast and sat down across from him. UV glanced down at his clasped hands, then up again. Kenneth had seen that look before. When his mother was being forced to punish him, even though she didn't think he'd done anything wrong. The forgive-me-for-what-I'm-about-to-do look.

"Yeah, what is it?" Kenneth asked with a growing sense that he wasn't going to like the answer. UV hesitated again; whatever it was he was about to ask was taking its toll.

Kenneth was *definitely* not going to like it.

"I came by here a few days ago, thought I'd pick up those socket wrenches you borrowed from me."

"Oh, damn, I completely forgot about those. Sorry," Kenneth said, trying to sound untroubled.

"You weren't home."

"Nope…"

"So I went out to the garage to see if I could just grab them."

Their eyes met across the table. Kenneth sat in silence. What should he say? No excuses in the world could help him now. That knot of anxiety that had dulled this morning came thundering back again like a freight train, almost stealing his breath away. He knew what UV had seen, understood that he'd figured out what they'd done. But it didn't explain his eyes; there was no compassion or understanding there, only sadness, and maybe shame.

What did he really want? Why was he there?

Kenneth tried, but couldn't make sense of it.

"I'm sorry, Kenta, I really am," UV said, puncturing the silence that had arisen. "But you get it. We're falling apart, Stina and me."

That didn't help one bit. What did this have to do with their reduced assistance hours? What did he want him to do?

"No, I don't understand, what…what do you mean?"

"I want seventy-five thousand. Then I'll forget the Volvo and the Civic."

For a moment, Kenneth was sure he was joking, that he'd break into a smile, lean back and laugh, tell Kenneth he should see his face. Priceless. But that didn't happen. So he tried to sort through his emotions, assuming he should feel scared or maybe angry, but to his surprise he felt tears welling up in his eyes.

"Are you kidding me?" He tried to keep his voice steady. "Where the hell am I gonna get seventy-five thousand?"

"Sell some of the drugs. Not to me, but to someone else."

"What drugs?" Kenneth asked reflexively, not even trying to make sense of what was happening anymore. His best friend was sitting in his kitchen threatening him, blackmailing him for money.

"The ones that were in the Honda."

"There was nothing in the Honda."

"Yes, there was."

"How do you know?"

"Someone told me."

"Who?"

UV hesitated again, seemed to have an answer on his tongue, but swallowed it. Kenneth got the feeling that whatever was coming next was not the truth, or at least not the whole truth. Not that it mattered much. The betrayal could hardly be greater.

"The cop," it came at last. "I'm having a hard time convincing them I retired."

"OK…"

There wasn't much more to say.

"We really need the cash," UV said in a tone that Kenneth assumed was not only supposed to explain, but also excuse all of this, so he pushed out his chair and stood up. Kenneth said nothing, didn't even waste a glance on him, but did stop him on his way out to the hall.

"What happens if I don't pay up? You go to the police? You won't get your cash then."

"Isn't it worth quite a bit to you not to end up behind bars again?"

The question was rhetorical. UV knew. They had talked about it. Many times. How Kenneth didn't think he could handle another round. Losing Sandra. Losing everything. Going under.

His confidences and trust were now being used against him. He'd been wrong; the betrayal could feel worse.

"You could have just asked for it." Now the tears came, and he didn't care, let them run down his cheeks. "Without threatening me. I would have helped you. We're friends."

Without a word, UV turned away and left. What was there to say? A few seconds later, Kenneth heard the front door slam, a car drive away. The silence afterwards seemed to suck all the air out of the room. He slid down from his chair, down onto the floor, taking deep breaths, tears flowing.

This morning's lightness, feeling better, was so very, very far away.

S he'd been conscious for almost five minutes.

Hadn't moved, stayed calm, kept her breathing steady, her head hanging heavily against her chest. Her hair hung down over her cheeks, but she didn't dare open her eyes, couldn't move a muscle in her face that might alert them to the fact that she was awake. She tried to survey the situation as best she could. The air she inhaled smelled earthy, like in a root cellar, but there was definitely daylight streaming through her closed eyelids, so she guessed this was a damp building. Four voices, one of which she recognized as René Fouquier's; she assumed the other three belonged to the men from the hotel. Her jaw ached, and she took a few seconds to curse herself.

For letting herself end up in this situation.

Letting herself be captured by a bunch of fucking amateurs.

Yes, he'd been smart, sent the two she recognized, made her feel safe, as if she had an advantage, kept a third waiting for her. But that wasn't why she'd ended up here.

She'd been careless. And she knew why.

Everything had all gone so smoothly since she arrived in Haparanda. UV gave her Jonte who gave her René who looked like accountant, worked in a hamburger joint, and smuggled drugs in garden gnomes. Even the sleepy little town itself had lulled her into a false sense of security, made her lower her guard. She'd simply underestimated him and was paying the price for it now.

Enough self-castigation, time to get out of here.

She was sitting up, always better than lying down. Hands tied behind her back, narrow bands that bit into her wrists. Cable ties or something similar, maybe narrow plastic ties or a cord, definitely not rope. Too bad, rope always gave after a bit. Her legs were tied outside of the pants to the chair legs. The knife, of course, gone. She would have preferred to use her fingers to explore the cable ties around her wrists, but she didn't dare move. None of the voices she'd heard so far had come from behind, but there was always the possibility someone was there anyway, someone who wasn't talking.

"Wake her up," she heard René say suddenly.

"How?"

"Just do it."

Katja slowly moved her head to avoid some amateurish attempt to awaken her. She lifted her head with a small moan that she didn't need to fake. Her neck was sore from sitting in the same position for who knows how long. She made a show of opening her eyes and blinking, making herself seem more groggy than she really was. Every time she blinked, she turned her head to take in as much of the room and her opposition as possible.

Five of them, it turned out.

In something that must once have been a kitchen.

The two from the restaurant stood by a door that was hanging by its lower hinge only; the man with the Taser was leaning against the wall to her right where the wallpaper had come loose or been torn off, René was on his way toward her, and the dark-haired man she'd followed to the apartment was leaning back in a chair drinking a can of beer next to a rusty old stove that lay on its side. No weapons were visible, other than her knife, which lay in its holster on a counter beneath a row of cupboards, all empty, all without doors. The roof had collapsed in one corner, no doubt because of water damage. The paint was flaking everywhere, the two windows in the room lacked glass, and the dented linoleum floor was covered with debris, dragged in by both people and nature.

An abandoned house. Probably secluded. Good choice.

"What's your name?"

Katja looked at René, blinked as if to bring him into focus.

"Huh?" she got out, as if she didn't catch his question or at least didn't understand it.

"What's your name?" he repeated.

"Louise... Louise Andersson."

The slap came without warning. Her head was thrown to the side and her cheek burned. For a second she felt anger bubble up inside, but quickly she forced the slightly dazed look back into her eyes, even let a few tears flow through, never hurts.

"There is a Louise Andersson who has your social security number, but I called her, and she isn't here. She's at home in Linköping."

So he wasn't content to tell her *that* he knew she was lying; he had to explain *how* he knew. Wanted to brag, show how clever he was.

Cleverer than her.

"So who are you?"

Katja chose a strategy. Give them a sense of superiority without playing too weak, too compliant. After her appearance at the hamburger restaurant yesterday, he'd understand that was just a performance.

"My name is Galina Sokolova."

"Russian?"

"What does it sound like? Да русский."

She seemed to detect a certain hesitation. The Russian mafia were portrayed as ruthless villains in so many books, movies, and TV shows, so she guessed he was making the connection, thinking about what he might be getting himself into, whether it was worth continuing.

René nodded at one of the men from the hotel corridor. "Theo said you're pretty good in a fight."

"Yes, I'm good."

"But now you're sitting here."

Implying, *I'm better.* Which suited her perfectly. Play down her own ability, boost his.

"You were smart in the hotel."

"Thank you."

"I underestimated you."

"Yes, you did. Tell me about the amphetamines."

"What do you want to know?"

"Whatever you know."

So she told him about Rovaniemi, the drug deal that had gone south, about Vadim and what probably happened to him out on that forest road, that all parties concerned wanted what they'd lost back. More than she really wanted them to know, but she had no idea what they already knew or had put together themselves. The truth made them relax. They got information, got control over the situation. It didn't matter how much they found out, she didn't intend to let any of them live.

"And they sent you? Only you?"

To her delight, Katja detected a certain mistrust in his voice. As if it were unthinkable that a single woman could manage this. At least this one.

"Yes."

"How did you find me?"

"Sorry, I can't tell you that."

The blow came immediately. Her head was thrown to the side. She took the opportunity to bite hard on the inside of her cheek and made sure the bloody saliva ran out of a corner of her mouth when she straightened up again. It was not enough for them to think they held the upper hand, she wanted them to think they were in control.

"Did that hurt?"

"Yes."

She met his gaze. There was something in the eyes of men who enjoyed hurting others. Something that seemed to move deep inside, like a fog, black and oily. Alive. She'd seen it many times, not least inside the man she'd called her father. Inside René Fouquier she saw nothing at all. No desire, no joy or satisfaction, no drive that could obscure judgment. She got the sense that he didn't feel anything at all. Which made him much more dangerous.

"How did you find me?"

Katja looked at him, then at the others. One was busy with his phone; the man, apparently named Theo, seemed to be having a hard time watching a bound woman get beaten and glanced through the open door rather than at her. The dark-haired man on the chair was drinking his beer. They felt unthreatened. Safe.

It was time to act.

"Do you remember what I said about touching me without my permission?"

Fixed gaze. Open defiance. She'd challenged him. In front of the others. If she read him right, she knew what was coming. She had. The wind-up was longer, the hand fisted, the blow much harder than the previous ones. She followed it with her whole body, shifted her center of gravity, pushed away as best she could, and the chair overturned. As the front chair legs left the floor, she pushed her hips forward, stretched her legs as far and fast as she could, and felt the cable ties slide off the chair legs the second she hit the floor. She was careful to keep her legs pressed in place, hoping no one saw her little maneuver.

René squatted down next to her. "How did you find me?"

"One of your junkies told me how to buy your shit, so I texted you from his phone, said I wanted to buy, and followed him to your home."

A nod to the man in the chair. René gave him a look that said he wouldn't forget it, would take care of it later.

"Which junkie?"

"Jonte something."

"Jonte Lundin," said the man with the beer can, eager to make it someone else's mistake. "He bought yesterday. It must have been him."

René got up again, nodded toward the two men closest to the door. She hoped he wouldn't send any of them away to punish Lundin immediately. She wanted them all gathered in one place.

"Help her up."

They came over to her. One grabbed her upper arms while the other raised the chair. She pressed her calves hard against the chair legs, a critical moment; if they were even a little observant, they'd notice that she was no longer tied. They didn't. She was raised to a seated position, and they returned to their seats. René stepped toward her again.

"Do you have any idea where the amphetamines are?"

"Yes," she said, clearing her throat. Coughed a little, spat some blood. "Can I have some water?"

"We have no water."

"Do you have anything I can drink?" she asked in a weak and raspy voice, looking at the man in the chair. René waved him over; he got up and walked toward her, holding the can to his lips.

She flew up from the chair, kicked it away, jumped as high as she could while pulling her knees up to her chest and bringing her hands under her heels. With her arms in front of her as she landed, she was at the dark-haired man before he had time to react. Wrapped her arms around him, locking herself to his body. He dropped the beer can. It seemed to break the paralysis of the others. René shouted that they should grab her, and two of them started to approach. Hesitant: both had seen what she was capable of in the hotel.

Katja needed a little more time. Holding the man like a shield between herself and the others, she sank her teeth deep into his throat, locked her jaws, and jolted her head back. The man screamed loudly in shock and pain. The blood started to flow in a steady stream down his neck and spread rapidly over the white T-shirt. The sudden attack and the howl of their comrade had the desired effect: the others stopped, looked at each other. What the hell just happened?

Katja spat out the flesh she'd torn from the man's neck and lunged again. This time, she reached what she'd been aiming for all along. Her teeth ripped into the carotid artery, and the blood started to pump out in a thick red jet, out onto the floor. The man screamed even louder if possible while Katja dragged him backward. With his arms still locked to his body, he had no chance to staunch the blood flowing out of his body. Katja spat again and stared at the others, who seemed stunned by the recent turn of events. She flashed her teeth in a bloody grin.

Once she reached the window, she pulled up her arms and let go of the man, who sank to the floor in front of her. Certain he'd bleed out, she threw herself backward, out the window. Landed heavily on her back on the ground below. The fall was just over a meter, and it knocked the air out of her, but she continued as if she'd been programmed. Rolled away, got to her feet and ran as fast as she could away from the place where she landed. Rounded the corner, stopped, forced air into her lungs, rapidly assessed her surroundings and what her options were.

She saw no other buildings. It was a red, two-story house, out in the middle of nowhere. A small yard in front with a car parked there. A green, open meadow along one side, forest everywhere else. Easy to escape, to hide, to plan the next step, but she didn't want the four who remained to have time to split up, perhaps flee from her, on foot or by car. From inside she heard René shouting at his men to go out there, grab her, she couldn't be allowed to escape. From the number of times he had to repeat himself, she concluded they weren't so keen on pursuing her after that exhibition in the kitchen.

She dragged the cable ties against the corner of the house as hard as she could, and after only a few drags they fell off. She was free to return to where she'd come from. René or one of his men would no doubt have seen where she landed and come out to check that she wasn't still there. So that would be the place they least expected her to show up. She leaned against the wall and took a quick glance through the window. The kitchen was empty.

Smooth, quiet and controlled, she slipped inside. Blood everywhere. The man whose neck she'd ripped open was lying dead a few meters into the room, must have crawled there in an unsuccessful attempt to be saved. She stepped over him and went to the bench where her Bowie knife, much to her relief, still remained. She pulled it out of the holster and moved on.

The room outside, which was probably once a dining room, was in as bad shape as the kitchen. Katja continued through as quietly as the leaky, water-damaged wood floors would allow. She stopped, listened. Got the sense that no one was inside the house anymore. She carried on until she came to a small hallway where the wallpaper hung down over the rotting and peeling half panels. The remains of a battered built-in wardrobe, a torn-down hat shelf, and an old dismantled car engine lay scattered across the floor among the pine needles, leaves, and dirt.

She continued toward the doorway, which lacked a door, then peered out carefully. A few steps to the left, the man who'd been waiting down in the foyer earlier this morning had his back to her. They really did not expect her to come from inside the house.

"Can you see her?" he shouted, and Katja saw Theo ten meters away, cautiously making his way to some dense berry bushes, armed with a half-meter-long pipe. Katja turned the knife in her hand, held it at the far end, slid silently forward, and grabbed the young man from behind. Let a surprised little scream escape from him, which made Theo turn around. Katja raised her arm and threw the knife.

Not a perfect hit, but it went into his stomach just below the sternum, probably damaged the liver, punctured the gall bladder. Theo fell backward with a scream, at the same moment Katja swept away the feet of the man she was holding so that he landed heavily on the ground. She put force behind it and stomped hard on his neck, crushing his Adam's apple and trachea, twisted her foot, stood still and heard the man's last futile attempts to draw breath before running to Theo, who was lying on his back in the tall grass, both hands bloody on the handle of the knife. He moaned softly, wordlessly, stared at her pleadingly as she leaned over him and pulled out the knife. She put it back in his chest, straight into the heart.

Three down, two to go.

She straightened up, snuck back toward the house, and disappeared inside. Moved through the building until she came to the windows that faced the other side. The man who was waiting with the Taser in the hotel corridor had just slammed the lid of the car trunk. Had a shotgun in his hands, which he loaded with two cartridges before starting to walk around the house, the weapon in front of him, ready to shoot. Katja snuck out into the hall and up the stairs to the upper floor.

She had a knife. He had a rifle.

She needed to get close. He knew that.

Upstairs there were three small rooms and a toilet where all the porcelain lay smashed on the floor. She orientated herself and headed into what must have been a bedroom once upon a time. Empty except for a stained, moldy bed in one corner. The mattress had been cut and chewed up in several places. She went over to the window, glanced carefully out and down. Sure enough. The man with the rifle was sitting at the corner where the porch jutted out from the rest of the house. It made him difficult to detect, but offered good visibility across a large portion of the yard. Had she tried to reach the car now, she wouldn't have had a chance.

She pulled her head back inside and thought. Second floor. Three and a half, four meters. Maybe a bit more. But with control and something, or someone, to dampen the fall... She made her decision, went over to the window again and carefully put a foot up. Leaned her weight on it, the frame held and made no sound, so she lifted herself up smoothly until she was squatting in the opening. Made sure she'd done it silently, and that nothing had fallen down, but the man below must have sensed something, because he turned and looked up at the moment she let go.

He was fast. Had the fall been any longer, he would have had time to raise his rifle. Now he only managed to get it about halfway with an angry roar before she landed on him and pushed the knife into one of his wide-open eyes with both hands. For a moment, she sat across from him, breathing calmly while mentally scanning her body for injuries. She discovered none and got to her feet. Bent down and picked up the rifle. Backed against the wall while she made a practiced examination of it.

"René! You're the only one left!"

She stood still, listening. Nothing. Only nature, the occasional sound of an engine that the wind carried from cars passing by at high speed somewhere far away. Katja allowed herself to relax a bit. Fairly certain René had no firearm, and that he was too smart to attack her without one. Definitely too smart to think he could negotiate with her, talk himself out of this.

He knew he would die.

His only chance was to escape. Fast and far.

There was a slight possibility he'd already done so. She hadn't seen or heard him since he shouted those orders after she threw herself out the window. After losing control, he'd lost his initiative. He couldn't have gone very far in any case. Must be on his way to Haparanda. She had the car, should be able to get back faster than him. She looked at her watch and up at the sun. Didn't know where she was, but at least had a sense of direction.

Sooner or later she'd find him. It didn't matter if it took a little time.

She was good at waiting.

It had been so long since she was there.

The apartment on Råggatan. She likes it.

A large, spacious two-bedroom. Dark clouds outside. But she can't see them, not from the hall where she's struggling to put Elin into her overalls.

Doesn't know that they're out there.

Springsteen coming from the living room.

She wasn't sure how she'd feel about living in an apartment. In a big city as well. The biggest. But she likes it. The life they have in Stockholm. Elin doesn't want to go without Daddy. Such a daddy's girl. Not so strange, she spends a lot more time with him, always.

Today he's headed to a job interview. Jacket and tie. Stylish. So Elin, who's just turned two, has to go with Hannah. A nice day together, mother and daughter. No matter how much Thomas enjoys being at home, he's started missing that other life, an adult life. Plus a little more money is always welcome.

If she can only get Elin into her coat.

She bribes her. She can take her red patent leather shoes, even though they're not something you wear outside. And she'll get an ice cream while they go shopping, sounds good, right? Finally, arms and legs fall into place. They're going to have fun together. So say goodbye to Daddy. For the last time.

She doesn't know that either.

He's singing in the living room.

Young lives over before they got started. This is a prayer for the souls of the departed.

When she straps Elin into her car seat and walks around toward the driver's seat, she looks up at the sky. Now she sees them. The dark clouds.

Will it start to rain?

Should she run back and grab an umbrella?

She doesn't have the strength to unhook Elin again. Crosses her fingers that it will hold off. Gets in the car and drives away.

"Hey, we're here."

Hannah opened her eyes and blinked, looked around her, a little drowsy. They were parked outside the police station. Engine off.

"You fell asleep," Thomas informed her, completely unnecessarily.

"I slept badly last night," Hannah said, wiping the saliva from her chin while she stretched in her seat.

They'd remained by the lake until Alexander and Gordon got out there and ascertained what Hannah already knew: they needed to get a diver. It would take time for someone to get there, and not everyone needed to stay. Hannah was quick to offer to head back. It didn't happen often, but she always felt a little tense when Thomas and Gordon met. They drove back the same way they'd come, in the same familiar silence as on the way there. After ten minutes Hannah leaned back and apparently fell asleep.

Now she cast an eye at the clock and turned to her husband.

"What do you say to lunch?"

"Sure."

Did he hesitate a bit, or was she imagining it? He started the car again, drove slowly through the sparsely populated city center, up to Leilani, parked outside and they went inside.

Sami Ritola sat at one of the tables at the far end of the room with a man Hannah didn't recognize. He had his back to her, and she made no attempt to go over and say hi. She was a little surprised to see him, thought he'd gone back to Rovaniemi yesterday after the meeting. Alexander had made it clear his services wouldn't be needed, and if they were, he was only a phone call away.

They turned to the left at the counter, walked by the giant burgundy Buddha statue and sat down. After they'd ordered, Hannah took out her phone, pulled up a map, and put her cell phone on the table between them. "To know about that lake, to find the overgrown road that leads to it, to know about the slope...you'd have to be local."

"Maybe so," Thomas replied, pouring himself a glass of water.

"He was hit here, and the lake is here." She pulled with both fingers on the screen so that the map became larger. "So if we focus on this area—Vitvattnet, a bit further away, up toward Norra Storträsk, Grubbnäsudden, Bodträsk—then maybe someone's seen something."

Thomas took a few sips of water with his eyes on the screen. He appeared to be thinking.

"Your not-friend who called, could he make out anything about the driver?" Hannah asked.

"Not from what he said."

"Can you ask him?"

"Sure."

"Thanks."

She put the phone back in her pocket, stretched her hand across the table and laid it on his, running her thumb over his knuckles.

"It was fun being out with you today, doing something together."

"Yes..."

"Even if it was only work."

"Yes."

"I missed you yesterday, when you went up to Kenneth's."

"Did you?"

"Yes, I felt a little…rejected, to be honest."

There. She'd said it. Surprised herself. Hadn't planned to bring it up at all. At least not here and now. Maybe it was because they were on neutral ground. Out for lunch. As a couple. Made it less dramatic. Didn't have to be such a big deal, just something they dealt with while waiting for their food. A topic of conversation, one of several.

Now the ball was in his court.

He didn't answer immediately, looked at her with a seriousness she could only remember seeing in his eyes once before.

Twenty-four years ago. In Stockholm.

When he said they had two choices: go under or move forward.

It scared her. Gave her the feeling that, whatever she'd thought he might say, this was worse. Worse than she could imagine. He took a deep, ominous breath, but seemed to stop, shook his head slightly and let the air out in a long exhalation instead. When he looked at her again, that heavy seriousness was gone.

"I didn't mean to. I didn't know that… I didn't know."

She leaned forward across the table and lowered her voice. If she'd taken it this far, she might as well continue.

"I basically had my hands in your pants, that should have given you some clue as to what I wanted."

"I'm sorry."

"It's been a long time since… As if you are avoiding me."

"Sorry, that wasn't my intention."

He looked so sincerely sad and guilty that she was immediately willing to believe him. He hadn't realized he was hurting her when he, as she thought, so clearly distanced himself. Was it that simple? That they just perceived these situations differently, didn't talk about them, let it be and let it grow, both unaware of how the other was thinking and feeling.

"You can make up for it now," she said with a slight smile.

"Now now?"

"Not here, but both my bosses will be out by the lake for a few hours, so we could go home."

"I have to go to work," he said, pulling his hand ever so slightly away from hers, unwilling to disappoint her again, but enough to mark distance.

"I thought it was quiet at work," Hannah said, making it easy for him by letting go of his hand completely. The lie she had actually been willing to believe no longer held.

"It's pretty quiet, but there's something I have to do. And Perka is going on vacation next week so…"

"Sure. OK."

"But tonight maybe."

"Sure. Maybe then."

The food arrived, and they ate in silence. Both declined to have coffee afterwards; they paid and headed out together. Stopped on the sidewalk outside. Thomas buttoned up his thin jacket and nodded to the car.

"Do you want a ride back?"

"No, I'll walk."

"OK, then I'll see you later."

"Yep, see you then."

She stood and watched him cross the street, hop into his car, and drive away. He waved, and she raised her hand before setting off toward downtown and work. After a few steps, she took out her phone, held it in her hand, hesitated. It wasn't the way it used to be, not the way she wanted it, but what the fuck. She needed it. Wanted it. Dialed a number, waited for an answer, got it.

"How long do you need to be out by the lake?"

"René! You're the only one left!"

Her voice cut through the silence. Reached him where he lay squeezed beneath an uprooted tree a few meters into the forest. He couldn't see her through the brush and branches, nor could he see the car or the house. Didn't dare stick his head up, risk seeing her. With his face pushed down into the roots and the moss, he did his best to keep his breathing as calm as possible. Afraid that a breath might reveal him in the total silence that prevailed after Marcus's roar was interrupted so terrifyingly abruptly not more than half a minute ago. Then her confident:

"René! You're the only one left!"

He didn't doubt for a second that was true. But what did she want? Was it just a way to prove how superior she was, intended to scare him, or was it to call him forward, show that she'd gotten rid of the infantry and now wanted to resume business. Hardly. If he'd known where the amphetamines were, then maybe he'd have something to bargain with, but there was no chance that he'd be able to reach any kind of agreement. He had nothing to gain from making himself known. If she saw him, he was dead.

His only chance was to escape. Fast and far.

When she'd said her name was Galina, he'd hesitated for a moment. He didn't want to get involved in the Russians' business, had turned down offers before. But he hadn't listened to those alarm bells, he had the upper hand, was in control. Because she'd allowed him to believe that. Under other circumstances, he'd be both jealous and impressed. She was so superior. He quite rightly thought highly of himself, knew he was smarter and better than everyone else, but compared to her, he was no more than a trained monkey. When she tore into Norman's throat—which was the craziest, the most insane thing he'd ever seen in his life—and threw herself back out the window, he'd still thought they might win, that they had a chance. Still four against one. Unarmed, but even so. Four against one. Everyone on guard, they wouldn't be surprised like Theo in the hotel corridor or Norman in the kitchen. So he thought. Then he heard the scream, felt the panic, was struck by the expanding silence, and now he was alone.

His only chance was to try to escape. Fast and far away.

So he waited under the uprooted tree. Half an hour turned to forty-five minutes, an hour, one and a half. The cold and damp penetrated his clothes, and he did his best to relax so his teeth wouldn't chatter, but he didn't change position, didn't move a muscle. Mosquitoes and gnats buzzed around his head, and he felt them land on his forehead and neck, but he let them sit there. Not a sound, not a movement would he make. He would survive this. Sure, he would have to move, or rather run away, but that wasn't the end of the world. Apart from his business, there was nothing that kept him in Haparanda. The city was a dump that allowed him to show off and make money. He didn't even have to go by his apartment. There were drugs worth a few thousand there, but the big money he could access from anywhere. He could go far away, abroad, lie low for a while, a few years even. It wasn't for his sake that this killing machine had come to

Haparanda. Her mission was to find the drugs and the money. She wouldn't waste time and resources looking for him, he was sure of it. If he survived this, he could make it.

It was just a matter of being smart, and he was smart.

When he heard nothing but nature's sounds for over two hours, René slowly crawled out of his hiding place, worming his way along the edge of the forest. Hoping that the brush and the tall grass would protect him. Kept going until he could see the house and the yard.

Outside, to the right of where the front door once sat, lay Jari. He couldn't see the others. More importantly, he didn't see her either. He turned his head in both directions, groped beneath the moss, and found a fist-sized rock. Lifted his upper body enough to be able to throw it in a wide, high arc. With a distinct thump, it landed on the tightly packed gravel yard. René made himself as flat as he could and peeked out. No one, nothing. She must have thought he'd left, fled in panic, thought she could take care of him later. She was probably waiting for him inside his apartment right now. To be on the safe side, he threw another stone, waited another ten minutes before rising slowly and stiffly with a deep breath. Stood still and closed his eyes, expecting a knife, or something else, to come flying. Certain she could turn anything into a weapon. But nothing happened.

He took a first careful step out of the woods. Completely unprotected, fully visible. His body was still protesting as he slowly and with all his senses fully alert approached the house. At the house wall he stopped, looked around. Quiet still. Where was she, wouldn't she have acted by now? He continued around the side of the house. The car remained. Looked untouched. He pushed his hand in his pocket to make sure he had the keys—didn't want to climb in and not be able to drive away because he'd lost them. But they were still there. He took a step out of the house wall, felt his breathing get heavier as he started walking toward the car. So close now.

When he felt the metal under his hand, he sobbed with relief. He was going to make it. Get away. Drive out of here and not stop until he was far, far away. He walked over to the driver's side, was about to open the door when he felt something hard pressed against his leg, looked down but couldn't make sense of the rifle barrel against his ankle before a shot went off and more or less tore off his right foot. He stumbled a few involuntary steps backward and fell to the ground screaming in pain. Saw how Louise or Galina or whatever the hell her name was hurtling at him from beneath the car. Like a ghost from a Japanese horror movie he'd seen. The black hair a sticky mess against her cheeks, dirty sweat running down, and blood all over her face and neck, her eyes staring at him. She looked totally insane. René had a moment to realize how scared he was of her, that he didn't want to die, and how much his leg hurt before she was straddling him.

"Please…" was the only thing he managed to get out.

"Please…"

Katja took out the knife and pressed it with both hands into his throat below his Adam's apple. René gurgled helplessly, opened his eyes, tears running down his temples. His hands clawed lamely in the air a couple of times, but soon stopped. After a minute or so, he was dead.

Katja got to her feet, stretched, her body stiff after hours beneath the car. She had had plenty of time to think about what came next. Had to get rid of the bodies. Traces of blood and signs of a disturbance were of no concern. If someone discovered that something violent had taken place out here that was no problem, no one would ever figure out exactly what or find any victims. The easiest way was to get everyone in the car, drive away, get rid of both it and them. Then find a way to get back to the city and work on what she actually came here to do.

A whole day would have to be spent on this.

Without getting one bit closer to either the drugs or the money.

It made her furious even to think about it. But might as well get started.

She was walking back toward the house to gather the other bodies when she stopped. Engine noise. Close and getting closer. Katja slid down against the wall and peeked forward. A black Range Rover drove slowly into the yard. She couldn't see how many people were sitting in it, but at least two. Kill them, too?

More bodies, another car to get rid of.

She was about to step out into the yard and show herself when another car swerved up behind the first one. Too many, too much.

Without knowing what the consequences would be, Katja slowly backed away, turned around, snuck unseen around the house, and disappeared silently into the forest.

They lay in Gordon's huge bed, 180 cm wide even though he lived alone. Too big for his bedroom, which due to its gloomy outdated wallpaper and closet doors of dark wood already felt smaller than it was. Hannah lay on her back, staring up at the ceiling, Gordon was on his side next to her, one arm over her bare stomach, his face burrowed into her neck. His breathing calm and steady, she wasn't sure if he was asleep.

It had been very easy to persuade him to leave Alexander by the lake and come back here to sleep with her. He hadn't asked or seemed to find it strange that she called him in the middle of a workday, merely let her into his apartment where she kissed him as soon as he closed the front door.

Pressed against him, felt him go hard immediately.

He found her attractive, wanted her.

It was too hot in his room, and she kicked off the blanket she'd pulled up to her navel, feeling how the inside of her thighs were sticky with lubricant and Gordon's semen. They didn't use protection, the pregnancy train had left the station and would never roll in again, but lubricant was an absolute necessity nowadays. The mucous membranes were dry, thin and brittle. Hannah laughed when she remembered a stand-up comedian she and Thomas had seen in Luleå a few years ago saying that most forest fires every summer were started by middle-aged women trying to have sex in the woods without lubricant.

Funny cause it's true.

"What is it?" Gordon asked, lifting his head a little.

"I just thought of something."

"What?"

"Nothing, it wouldn't be funny if I told you."

"OK." He rose up on one elbow and pushed a strand of hair from her forehead. "Maybe we should go back to work."

Before she could answer, his phone started ringing. As he reached over to grab it from the bedside table, she heard her phone start to vibrate in her pants pocket on the floor. She managed to see a large "X" on Gordon's display before he cleared his throat and answered.

"Yeah, it's Gordon."

She couldn't hear what the person on the other end was saying, nor did she need to; she could see on Gordon's face that it was serious.

There were already a couple of cars parked on the neglected gravel road. Gordon pulled to the side and parked behind the last one. They got out, Hannah casting a quick glance back at the car as they started walking toward the building the GPS had led them to. A little further on, the road was blocked with blue-and-white police tape, Morgan stood on the other side, lifted it up for them as they approached.

"What happened here?" Gordon asked as he bent down beneath the barrier.

"Who can say."

"Alexander said something about five dead."

"So far, yes."

Gordon straightened up, took a deep breath, and let out a long, loud sigh.

"Damn."

"Yes."

"Is he here?"

Morgan pointed to the other end of the yard. Over at the edge of the forest, Alexander was pacing back and forth with his phone to his ear. Gordon set a course for him. Hannah looked over at the once beautiful red two-story house that now looked like it might collapse at any moment. The roof was gone in places, the chimney collapsed, all the windows knocked out, gutters hanging vertically along the facade, the paint flaking. A family had once made their home here, lived their lives, loved that house, taken care of it, been proud of it. Probably the parents stayed here when the children moved on, and when it was time to inherit, there was no interest in keeping it. Their lives were elsewhere, in a city, somewhere to the south. Impossible to sell or simply not worth it, it was left to decay. Haparanda was by no means unique. As soon as you got outside the larger cities, there were houses like this all over Norrland.

Hannah looked over at the car parked in the yard, a body covered by a blanket lay a few meters away from it.

"What happens now?" she asked Morgan.

"Alexander is calling in technicians, medical examiners, and dogs. Ludwig and Lurch are making a sweep through the forest to make sure there are no more bodies. Some of the people who've been making door-to-door inquiries in Övre Bygden are on their way to help."

"Is it still Alexander's investigation?"

"As far as I know."

Hannah nodded to herself. Not at all certain that this would end up with them.

Five dead. Murdered. A mass murder.

As far as she knew, this had never happened in Haparanda

before, so there was a risk that the higher-ups in Umeå would get involved, or maybe this would end up with NOA down in Stockholm.

"Where are the others?" she asked, nodding at the body under the blanket by the car.

"One inside, the others scattered around the outside of the house."

"All men?"

Morgan nodded in confirmation. "Shot?"

"No, knifed mostly, or so it seems."

"Five people, with a knife?" The skepticism in her voice could not be missed. Morgan shrugged slightly.

"Three at least. The other two are unconfirmed, I haven't looked too closely."

Hannah fell silent, taking in the information she'd received. Five men. Killed with a knife. A close-range weapon. They must have been scattered around, and yet the killer snuck up on them, killing them one by one. Quiet and efficient. Otherwise, wouldn't the others have managed to overpower the perpetrator or escape from here? Hard to say without knowing exactly where the bodies were and in what order they died, but five adult men killed with just a knife sounded unlikely. Unless...

"Several perpetrators?" she asked Morgan, not because she really expected him to answer, more a case of thinking out loud.

As she'd expected, Morgan's reply was, "Who can say."

Hannah realized she was as up to date as she was going to get right now. Had no real desire to look at the victims, there'd be enough photographs and detailed autopsy reports later, so she turned to the black cars that stood in the yard and the four people who sat inside or stood leaning against them, talking to P-O.

"Were they the ones who found them?"

"Yes."

"What were they doing here?"

"That lady there..." Morgan pointed to the only woman in

the group, young, maybe around twenty, who was sitting in the front seat of one of the SUVs with the door open. "...is some kind of influencer. They were going to take pictures here, they said."

"Why?" Hannah asked, mystified.

"It seems the municipality paid her to make ten posts."

"Really?"

"'To put this hole on the map,' as she so diplomatically put it."

Hannah kept her views on influencers to herself. In high school, Alicia had gone through a phase when she was intent on becoming one. For a few months she persevered, but abandoned the project when followers, a breakthrough, and money all failed to arrive. Not that Hannah cared about influencers personally; they were young, smart, and enterprising enough to make the most of this era's fascination with superficial narcissism and the need to fill our screens with strangers telling us what to do, think, like, feel, and above all buy. But the very fact that they existed, that it was considered a profession that you could train for, proved that they lived in the best of worlds in the worst of times.

The sun shone relentlessly onto the open area as Hannah made her way over to the two big black cars, and it occurred to her that she hadn't asked how long the bodies had been here, just assumed that the murders were recent. If they'd been lying in this weather for a few days...well, she was even more relieved she'd opted not to take a look at them. She slipped in beside P-O, who glanced at her before returning to his notebook.

"But you saw no one moving in the area or on the road when you arrived?" he asked.

Glances were exchanged between three well-groomed men in thin, surely expensive, summer clothes and sneakers, then they shook their heads.

"No," replied the woman in the car, whose skin Hannah saw now was completely smooth. Not a pore, not a shadow, slightly glossy, but certainly from sweat. False eyelashes and lips protruded almost as far as the narrow nose. The short black hair that framed her small face, and the thin body reinforced the doll-like impression that she clearly put a considerable amount of time and money into achieving.

"Who are you?" she asked, turning to Hannah.

"Hannah Wester," Hannah replied, resisting an impulse to extend her hand. She sensed that the woman didn't want to risk those inch-long nails on a shake with a local, slightly blotchy, sweaty law enforcement officer. "Who are you?"

"Nancy Q," she said, as if that should mean something to Hannah.

They were interrupted by the sound of a car approaching. Hannah turned around and saw two men jumping out of a dark green Renault and running toward the crime-scene tape, one with a camera held out in front of him, snapping away.

"Hey, hey, hey," they heard Morgan say, holding out his hands as if to stop them from continuing to take pictures.

"Are we done?" Nancy asked, waving toward the newly arrived journalists. "They're here to talk to me."

"Did you call the press?"

Even Nancy must have detected the ice in Hannah's voice, but she met it with a completely uncomprehending look.

"Of course I did."

Hannah looked away from the two men now engaged in a heated argument with Morgan. They weren't from Haparandabladet. So Nancy had called someone, probably from bigger, nationwide media outlet, who in turn picked up some more or less local talent. That would have taken some time.

"You called them before you called us," Hannah stated.

"I didn't call you, Tom did." Nancy nodded at one of the bearded men, it was unclear which, before jumping down from her seat. "Are we done?"

"You can't talk to them about what you've seen here," P-O tried.

"Yes, I can," Nancy replied, making an attempt to walk toward the barricades. Hannah put a hand out and stopped her.

"Did any of you take photos or film before we arrived?"

"Maybe, why?"

"Then I need all your phones."

"No, you have no right to take them."

Nancy challenged her gaze in a way that told Hannah that she wasn't used to being contradicted. Well, this would be a first for her. When she tried to walk by, Hannah grabbed the soft wool of her thin polo shirt, holding onto her.

"If you have pictures and film, that's evidence. If you remove evidence from my crime scene, you will stay here much longer than you want, and no one will be allowed to talk to anyone. Do you understand what I'm saying?"

"Yes."

"So give me your fucking phones, or I'll arrest you here and now."

For the first time, Nancy looked a little unsure, turning to the three others in her group who all had their hands in their pockets, reaching for their cell phones. A dissatisfied grimace let them know she thought they'd all betrayed her. Finally she put her hand in her back pocket and pulled out her own phone with a sigh.

"Can I go now?"

"Yes, please do, then I won't have to look at you."

Hannah saw her take quick steps toward the barrier, crawl under the plastic strap and disappear down the road with the two men. She turned to P-O, who was still standing with his notebook open in his hand.

"Sorry, were you done with her?"

"I think so. No doubt she'll be back."

"Fucking idiot," Hannah muttered to herself, her growing

irritation forcing her to move. She walked out into the yard, put her hands behind her neck, and took a few deep breaths.

"Are you OK?"

She turned. Gordon was making his way to her.

"I'm pissed."

"At?"

"The world in general, Nancy Q in particular."

It was clear that he wasn't really following, that he had more important things on his mind. He stepped closer.

"I took a look at the bodies… The guy by the car is René Fouquier."

For a moment, Hannah thought they were in the wrong place, that this was just a show apartment where no one lived. A single jacket hung neatly on a hanger on the hat shelf in the hall, nothing on the hooks behind it. Two pairs of well-polished shoes on the shoe rack below. The doormat perfectly flush with the threshold of the front door. A Windsor chair against one wall, next to it a small hall table with a lint brush standing in one corner, but nothing else.

While the locksmith was working on getting them in, they'd pulled on simple, white protective suits over their usual clothes, put on shoe covers, gloves, and tucked their hair beneath white shower cap-like hoods that absolutely no one could carry off with any of their dignity intact. They looked like they were on their way to a shift at a Russian nuclear power plant in the Eighties, Hannah thought as they stood inside the door of the one-bedroom apartment on Västra Esplanaden 12 and caught sight of themselves in the wall mirror, which of course had not the slightest smear or fingerprint.

"Neat and tidy," Hannah proclaimed, and took the first step toward the rest of the sterile and so far impersonal home.

"What do you say? I'll take the bedroom, you take the living room, and we'll take the kitchen together?"

"Sure."

Hannah stepped into the small room directly to the right. How was it possible to keep a place this clean, this tidy? Even when it was freshly cleaned and organized, they never achieved anything close to this at home. Not even now, when it was just her and Thomas. It was like walking into the centerfold of an interior design magazine. Or more like a furniture catalog, because the room was completely anonymous and all the furniture seemed chosen for its functionality rather than any particular personal taste. On the coffee table in front of the gray love seat there lay six coasters in a neat row along the left edge, black alternating with red, but that was all. No newspapers or magazines, no candles or knickknacks, nothing that would indicate any hobbies or interests. Perhaps home electronics. A huge flat-screen TV hung on the wall. Beneath it sat a game console with a hand control neatly laid on top. Hannah counted seven speakers in the room so she assumed that meant 7.1 surround sound. There was a stereo next to the sofa that could play vinyl, CDs, and cassettes. The only thing that spoke to anyone actually inhabiting this room, living here, was an LP lying on the black Plexiglas lid of the record player.

Hannah lifted the white record sleeve that was obscuring the cover. Whitney Houston, squatting in a dark blue turtleneck and boots. She put the record sleeve down and started to scan the bookshelf that stood along one wall, opened a few cupboards; not much inside them and what was there were exclusively utilitarian, nothing that could be called decorative or personal, except three large eggs, each one in some kind of holder that kept it upright on a shelf. Hannah got the sense that René Fouquier was a very special kind of person.

"Hannah."

She left the living room and went into the bedroom, also in

exemplary order. The bed stood against the wall, meticulously made, a bedside table to one side with an alarm clock, phone charger, and a bedside lamp. Two anonymous framed posters hung on the walls.

Gordon stood in front of the open closet. Three shelves with neatly folded clothes and beneath them just as many pullout plastic baskets. In the top one there were neat rows of small sealable plastic bags.

Different kinds of pills and tablets in one row, powder in the other. At the far end, closest to the closet door, in slightly larger bags, stood something that could only be cannabis.

"Cocky bastard. He hasn't even tried to hide it."

"Why would he? We had no idea he existed."

"True."

Gordon pulled out the basket beneath it. There was, among other things, a kitchen scale and an old-fashioned ledger with blue binders and a blank label on the front. Hannah picked it up and turned to the first page. Gordon leaned closer to be able to read over her shoulder. She could smell her scent on him. In neat lines there stood information about deliveries. In and out. Who, when, what, and how much. At least three distinct handwriting styles.

"At least we know who's been supplying the city lately," she said, turning the page. Several transactions were noted each day. Page after page. Weeks, months.

"That doesn't explain why he died out there."

"Amphetamines worth thirty million disappeared on the street just over a week ago. Ritola said the Russians would send someone looking for it."

"You think René got a hold of it?"

"It doesn't say here that he sold it," Hannah said with a nod to the ledger. "But we have five people murdered, one of whom was definitely dealing in drugs. Seems pretty likely there's a connection." She turned to the closet and pulled out the last drawer. Empty bags, thin masks, and a large cashbox. Hannah tried to open it. Locked.

"We better call Ritola, find out if he has any idea who they could have sent," Gordon said.

"He's still here, I saw him at lunch. At Leilani."

"Why?" Gordon looked genuinely surprised.

"Don't know, I didn't talk to him."

She continued rooting around in search of a key. Found nothing. Picked up the cashbox and inspected it. On one side was an orange Post-it note with a phone number, which she snatched away.

"What's that?"

"A phone number."

With some effort, Hannah dug out her mobile phone from beneath her protective clothing, typed the number into a search engine.

"Only the provider's details come up, not the subscriber."

"Bring it along, we'll put someone on it."

She pulled out an evidence baggie, put the note inside, and shoved it into her pocket again. Gordon pushed in the drawers and closed the closet door. The rest they left to the technicians.

"René could have gotten a hold of the amphetamines and tried to sell them back to the Russians," Gordon suggested as they left the room and headed for the kitchen.

"Selling them something that was already theirs sounds like a very dumb idea."

"And they died for it."

"He's been operating here for several years and flown completely under our radar. Look at this place. He wasn't careless, nor was he stupid."

"So what the hell happened out there then?"

"I don't know, but we can start by finding out what he was doing at Hellgren's."

He stood in the yard with a box of rat poison in one hand and a car key in the other. Before leaving, he'd thought it through carefully and come to the conclusion that he had no choice, but still he hesitated before opening the garage. It was a big risk, too big. Worst-case scenario, this could ruin everything for them. But what else was he to do? Even if he knew others in the village well enough to ask for a ride, which he didn't, that wasn't an option. Too risky. The people he knew in Haparanda were acquaintances, not friends, and he didn't trust any of them. If he waited until Sandra came home and took her car, she'd ask where he was going and why, and he wasn't sure he could keep from telling her the truth.

He was bad at lying to her.

Lack of practice, probably. He'd never lied to her in the past. But this was something she didn't need to know. So what choice did he have? None. He'd just have to hope for the best.

Kenneth pulled open the garage door. There stood the Volvo. The damage more extensive than he remembered it. For a moment he was back on the forest road.

There and then. Where his life changed.

Even more than when he got caught in a robbery in Stockholm. More than when he ended up in prison, more than when his family cast him off. He pushed all those thoughts away, no room for doubt. Could he somehow hide the worst of the dents and broken headlight? He looked around the garage, but realized that whatever he did would probably only attract more attention, so he threw the small backpack in the car and drove away.

Took the smallest, least used roads that he knew up to Thomas's cottage. Found himself thinking about his family again. He didn't really miss them. Wasn't interested in trying to get them back in his life. But in three years, when he and Sandra officially became millionaires, he wanted them to know.

That he was doing well.

That everything was going fine without them. Better than fine, actually.

They'd gotten married, had an amazing party, didn't invite them, and now Rita and Stefan would never meet their adorable children, nor be a part of their lives. The kids would call Hannah and Thomas Grandma and Grandpa instead.

But first he had to get himself out of the shit he'd landed in. *That UV had put him in*, he corrected himself as he pulled on to the edge of the narrow gravel road and turned off the engine. There was a ways still to go to the cabin, but he didn't dare drive any further. You never knew when Thomas might be there.

He started to hurry forward, swung away with about fifty meters left to the house. The mosquitoes got interested in him as soon as he entered the shadowy, windless woods, and he waved them away as best he could. Stopped when he saw the little house between the trees. No car in the driveway, no one moving on the lot as far as he could see. Half-hidden by the forest, he continued toward the derelict shed, went to the hatch and opened it. Started by spreading the rat poison all around the three bags. If for some reason Sandra discovered he'd been here, he'd say he'd done it to protect their money. Which was true. Not the whole truth, but still true.

Not telling her everything was not the same as lying.

With all the poison from the box scattered, he pulled out one of the bags and opened it. He knew exactly what he was going to see, but still his breath caught.

So much money. Their money.

One euro was about ten kronor, so he needed around 7,500. He took out 10,000. Had a plan for the last 2,500. Hesitated with the bag open, the money in hand. Alone in the house all day, no car, no way to get anywhere. He was starting to get really bored. A PlayStation 4 cost about 4,000 kronor. Nothing compared to all this. He quickly grabbed another 400 euros. With a smart hiding place and a little discipline, Sandra need never know. Not about any of this. She had definitely counted the money when they got back to the house that evening, but did she remember the exact amount? Would she realize that some of it was missing? If she did, he'd have to tell her. By then three years would have gone by, she couldn't still be pissed off then.

Most of it was going toward an emergency anyway, averting a threat: the risk of being exposed.

He put the money into the backpack, closed the bag, and carefully tied the garbage bag again before replacing it and closing the hatch door.

Ten minutes later he was back in the car. Stopped in front of it and examined the damage more closely. Roads out here were one thing, but he couldn't possibly drive into Haparanda. It had to disappear.

Especially since there was a possibility UV intended to keep blackmailing him. He'd already proved that their friendship didn't mean shit to him, so anything was possible.

A scrapyard would be easiest, but what if the police looked into those? Asked them to keep an eye out? Possible, even probable. He thought about burning it. The fire would probably take care of the DNA, but the risk it would be discovered was high. Even if he removed the plates, there were engine numbers and shit like that you could use to identify a car, or was that just a myth? Besides, he might start a forest fire; it'd been weeks since it rained.

Ideally, it would never be found.

The same place where they dumped the Honda?

That had been relatively easy, he knew the way there, but it was stupid to let both cars be discovered together. Though sinking it somewhere did seem like the best option.

Suddenly it came to him.

So obvious that he cursed himself for not having figured it out before. Markku, a guy he knew in prison, locked up for arson, had told him once, or more like given him a tip, when they were sitting in the break room one evening.

"If you're going to get rid of something up here, anything at all...use the Pallakka mine."

Markku had sunk one thing or another there for people who paid him to get rid of things. Wasn't the only one, apparently. Or particularly sought after. About a year ago, Kenneth read a report about someone who sent down an underwater camera to film inside the mine caves. At least eighteen cars, three motorcycles, a boat, and a bunch of mysterious barrels had been found. The municipality had come to the conclusion that the cost of taking everything out would be too high, and the risk that the unknown content of the barrels might start leaking if you moved them was too great. So everything was left as it was.

"If you're going to get rid of something up here, anything at all..."

The mine had first opened in 1672. Zinc and copper ore were transported downriver to the south. It closed at the end of the nineteenth century. Isolated and full of water, it wasn't that far away, not a tourist attraction like the Falu copper mine or a popular bathing spot and destination like some of the other water-filled mines. This was merely a number of holes in the ground. No buildings, no signs, nothing marking it as a cultural monument. Just holes. Eight by ten meters wide, perhaps. Some bigger, some smaller. But all very deep. The deepest a little over 260 meters, if he remembered what Markku said correctly.

Satisfied with his plan, he increased his speed, was there in less than half an hour. The enamel and frame screeched as they scraped their way through the sparse vegetation toward a small body of water. It looked like something from a John Bauer illustration, water dark and still, surrounded by a summer forest.

Kenneth parked as close as he dared, got out and removed whatever he needed from the car. There wasn't much. The most important item was the backpack. Then he sat down in the driver's seat, turned on the ignition, put it into first gear, and released the clutch and handbrake while gently climbing out. The Volvo rolled down toward the small lake, which you could sense was infinitely deep even if you didn't really know it. It continued over the edge, tipped more or less immediately after leaving solid ground, the engine dying as the water flooded inside. The car sank silently from view within a matter of seconds.

Kenneth got to his feet, his body again filled with happiness. Just like when he'd sunk the Honda, like the feeling he'd had in the kitchen this morning, before UV came.

This was going to work out. They were going to make it.

With the Volvo gone, there was no evidence left to connect him and Sandra to what happened. Backpack strapped on, he headed out to the main road. That was as far as his plan went. How was he going to get back to Haparanda? He took his phone from his pocket.

"I have the cash. You have to come pick me up," he said when his former friend answered.

"Can't you just come here?"

"No. If you want it, you have to come and get me."

"Are you at home?"

"No…" Kenneth quickly made some calculations in his head.

Didn't want to mention the mine, didn't want it to be possible for UV to find where the car was. It would take UV over an hour to get here, which would give him time to walk to Koutojärvi.

"How did you end up here?" was the first thing UV said an hour later when he picked Kenneth up at the village's only intersection.

"My buyer dropped me off here."

Kenneth could see that UV didn't believe him, but it didn't matter. If UV thought this was where they were hiding the loot from the Honda, then he could go searching for it if he wanted to. He'd never find it. Not the car either. To his relief, this morning's fears felt far away, replaced by rage and contempt. He unzipped the backpack and flashed the contents.

"Euros?" UV said as soon as he saw the money.

"I sold it to a Finn," Kenneth said in a steady voice. He'd been expecting UV to react to the currency. Invented a lie. Not so far-fetched, UV had all his contacts in the neighboring country back when he was active.

"Who?"

"It doesn't matter."

UV sat quietly for a while, drumming on the steering wheel, seemed hesitant, but then decided.

"Was there money in that car, too?"

"No."

Too fast? Too eager? UV still looked quite doubtful but didn't pursue the subject further, just nodded to himself.

"It's ten thousand," Kenneth said.

"That's too much."

"I want a new car."

"I don't have one to sell right now."

"Fix one."

He sounded hard. Determined. So different from this morning. UV turned toward him for the first time since he'd climbed into the car; clearly he noticed it, too. Found it difficult to meet his eyes.

"I get why you're pissed."

"Good."

"I never would have done this if it weren't—"

"I'm not interested," Kenneth cut him off, managing to keep his voice harsh. "Can you get me a car?"

UV seemed to be thinking it over. Kenneth could see how tired he was, realized how hard this was for him. Saw, understood, and didn't give a shit.

"Yes, I can get a car. For a while," he said eventually.

"Good."

Kenneth tossed the backpack into the rear seat and leaned back, staring out the side window, making it clear he was done talking. They drove back toward Haparanda in silence.

He had waited five minutes. At least. The phone completely silent. Sami glanced at the screen to make sure that the phone was still connected. It was.

They were just making him wait.

He continued walking along the river, unbuttoned his thin jacket. On the other side of the gently flowing water the Alatornio church towers soared majestically above the forest. More beautiful than the black barn they called a church in this town, he thought, and sat down on one of the benches along the promenade. What wasn't better and more beautiful in Finland? Nothing. The world's most stable state, safest country, happiest population, cleanest air, lowest income disparities, highest level of education, the list goes on. Even the Swedish newspapers wrote admiring articles about how their neighboring country had a bit of an edge on most things.

Sami was shaken from his thoughts about his homeland by the ringing of his phone. He stubbed out his cigarette and unconsciously straightened up on the bench.

"What do you want?" asked the deep voice. No greeting, no apologies for making him wait.

This was, after all, Valerij Zagornij.

Sami had been working for him for a couple of years. He'd first been contacted by the Russian organization when they started doing business with MC Sudet. They needed someone who could warn them about upcoming raids, their competitors, and tell them if the police were on their trail. Keep an eye on things basically. And they paid well for it.

After the massacre in Rovaniemi, Matti Husu, the leader of Sudet, and two of his relatives had tracked down Zagornij in St. Petersburg, tried to get their money back. After all, Vadim had worked for Valerij, so it was only right, they thought.

The day after that meeting, Zagornij had contacted Sami. Said that it was the Finns who were behind all this. They had killed their own people *and* his men in the forest in Rovaniemi, made Vadim's body disappear, scapegoating him, while in fact they kept both drugs and money for themselves. Now they were asking to be compensated another 300,000 euros.

There were a lot of holes in Zagornij's theory. First of all, the Finns weren't that ambitious. No one in their organization was enterprising enough to come up with a plan like that. Killing four of their own and risking a war they couldn't possibly win. Things like that required brains, balls, and vision.

The MC Sudet wasn't exactly known for any of those things.

Secondly, they'd never dare. If Zagornij found even the slightest proof, they'd all be dead. Eradicated from the surface of the earth. Along with their families and friends.

Sami didn't raise any of his objections, nor bring up the dead sniper they'd found, which suggested Vadim Tarasov was behind it all.

He promised to investigate. Get close to Sudet. Make inquiries.

When Matti told Sami at the funeral that he "would never find him" and asked him to "let it go" because Vadim was dead, for a moment he thought Zagornij was right, that Matti might just be greedy and stupid enough to try to swindle him. Then the Swedes called: they'd found Tarasov in the forest outside Haparanda.

Zagornij wanted Sami to get involved in the Swedish investigation instead. He'd send someone else too, someone who could concentrate fully on finding the drugs and the money, but it would be good to have a man inside the police if Haparanda surpassed themselves and tracked down what belonged to him.

So Sami crossed the border, gave his Swedish colleagues everything from the Finnish investigation, but also informed them that Zagornij had sent someone. An easy way to redirect attention. Might become important later if he needed to react to information that only the police had, open up the possibility of a leak.

"Did you track down what went missing?" he asked Valerij now, lowering his voice as he looked around, but no one was close by or within earshot.

"No, why?"

"Was thinking the other person you sent might have found it?"

"No."

No more. Just compact, uncomfortable silence that made Sami nervous and unsure he'd done the right thing making contact.

"A local drug dealer has been murdered, so I thought maybe he was the guy, and you got it back," he continued in explanation, even though Valerij did not ask.

"No."

"OK, well...in that case I'll continue."

Silence again, but a different kind than before. Valerij had hung up. Sami put down the phone, took out another cigarette, noticed that his hands shook a little as he lit it. Stayed on the bench in the sunshine. Tried to enjoy the good weather, the water, and the warmth, but couldn't help wondering if Zagornij appreciated the call. He hoped so; if there was one person he really did not want to piss off, it was him.

When the technicians arrived from Luleå, Hannah and Gordon left René Fouquier's apartment and drove out to pick up Anton Hellgren. The radio news led with the story of five bodies found outside Haparanda, but not much more than that was known at present. When they got to the telephone interview with influencer Nancy Q, who just happened to be in town, Hannah turned it off. She absolutely did not want to hear more from that young woman, and couldn't really see the value of those so-called eyewitness accounts. All of them were variations of how "terrible" it was, and "of course I was afraid," and "it's awful when it happens so close to you." What the listener got beyond an unfamiliar voice repeating the obvious was unclear to Hannah.

"This is going to be big," Gordon said as she silenced the radio.

"Yep."

Just like the last time they were there, Hellgren stood outside the door waiting for them as they approached the house. The same or at least similar sweatpants and a flannel shirt. Definitely the same frown beneath his cap.

"What do you want?"

"To talk to you," Gordon replied.

"I'm busy."

"Whatever it is, it'll have to wait, this is more important."

"So you say."

"We're here to talk to you in connection with a murder investigation, so yes, I do say."

"Who got murdered?"

"We'll give you a ride to the station," Gordon said, pointing to the car. Hellgren shrugged, grabbed his jacket from a hook inside the door, and followed them.

As they turned into the police garage about a dozen people with phones and cameras followed them, shouting questions—pointlessly, since they couldn't hear if someone inside the car answered them anyway.

Seemingly unaffected by all the excitement, Hellgren sat down on one side of the table, Hannah and Gordon on the other. Interrogation rooms were tended to be depicted as rather dull. Small and gloomy, often windowless, their murky colors poorly lit. Hannah always took note of that when she saw one in a film or on TV, and then she'd think it was nothing in comparison to this room. It was as if somebody, after all the other rooms were done, had realized they needed an interrogation room as well, cleared out a storage closet on the lower floor, slapped up some sad wallpaper and that was that. Cramped, airless, and with a claustrophobically low ceiling, even without the pipes that crisscrossed it. A simple white kitchen table of laminated particleboard and four plastic chairs on metal stands, all screwed to the floor so they couldn't be used as a weapon. No two-way mirror, no fixed recording equipment, just empty gray walls, two doors, utilitarian furniture lit by cold, hard light from two buzzing fluorescent lamps in the ceiling. Felt like if you left anyone inside long enough, they'd confess if only to get out of there.

Hannah hated it.

Gordon put his phone on the table, started recording, stated who was in the room and what time it was. Hannah took out a notepad and prepared to take notes. When Gordon became chief, he instituted a protocol in which all interrogations would be taped and noted in order to minimize the risk of a defendant challenging interrogation records during a trial.

"Can you tell us about your relationship with René Fouquier?"

Hellgren didn't answer, just calmly returned Gordon's stare with his own ice-blue gaze.

"We know you know each other," Gordon continued. "We saw him with you."

"We know each other."

"How?"

"How? We're acquainted, that's how we know each other."

"How did you meet?"

"Mutual friends."

"Can you give us any of their names?" prompted Hannah.

Hellgren seemed to think about it, but then slowly shook his head. "Sorry, I don't remember."

"What was he doing at your place?"

"Visiting."

"For?"

"A visit."

Hannah could swear she saw a smug smile on Hellgren's face, as if amused by his own non-answers to the questions.

"We have reason to believe that you were engaged in criminal activity together," Gordon continued, not allowing himself to be provoked.

"What kind of activities would those be?"

"Drug offenses, perhaps murder in your case."

"What makes you think that?" Hellgren asked, sounding sincerely curious.

"Do you know if René was planning to meet with anyone today?" Gordon continued, ignoring the question.

"No."

"Did you hear anything about who he might be doing business with?"

"Isn't it easier to ask him all this?" Hellgren said in a weary tone, with a glance at the clock to indicate he was tired of the interrogation.

"René Fouquier is dead," Gordon said dryly and matter-of-factly. "He and four others were killed this morning. That's why we wanted to talk to you."

For a moment, only the buzzing of the fluorescent lights and the hissing of the pipes could be heard as Hellgren processed this new information. He straightened up in the uncomfortable chair.

"I don't know anything about that," he said clearly.

"Not even *why* they were murdered?"

"Why would I know that?"

"Can you tell us about your relationship with René Fouquier?" Gordon repeated. Hellgren didn't answer immediately. Hannah thought she could make out some feverish calculations taking place behind those blue eyes.

"We knew each other," he said with a small shrug. "That's all."

"Did you know what he was involved in?"

"He was flipping burgers at Max and studying, as far as I know."

"So this young man, with whom you had nothing in common, came out to your place every now and then and just…hung out?" It was obvious Gordon didn't believe that for a moment.

Hellgren leaned back, weighing his options. Hannah thought she knew what he would eventually decide—time to tell the truth—but left it to him to get there.

Gordon stood up and began pacing the few steps the room allowed. "Did you hear about the Russian killed in a hit-and-run outside Vitvattnet? The car was carrying thirty million-kronor worth of amphetamines, which now are now missing. We know René Fouquier was selling drugs, but we don't know who hit the Russian or who took the drugs. So we thought, could it have been you, Anton?"

"Was that why René was at your place? To make a purchase?" Hannah filled in.

"Why do you think it was me?" Hellgren asked.

"I don't know. Why not?" Gordon smiled. "But if you tell me why Fouquier was out there, then we can do our best to eliminate you as a suspect."

Hellgren sat quietly with his eyes fixed on the wall in front of him.

Whatever was coming next, Hannah was sure it wouldn't be the truth.

"We did business together," Hellgren said after some reflection. "But not drugs."

"What kind of business then?"

"He bought skins, meat, horns from me, resold it."

"To whom?"

"I don't know, I never asked. Everything I sold to him was perfectly legal."

"Why didn't you tell us that right away?"

Hannah thought she knew the answer. Hellgren was one of the people in this town who considered the police to be the enemy. She saw him hesitate again, and then decide to continue.

"I don't have any receipts or paperwork. Everything was off the books."

"So it wasn't completely legal," Hannah stated.

"What I sold was legal, that's what I meant."

Hannah took notes. Something didn't seem right. During all the years she'd dealt with Anton Hellgren, he'd never admitted a crime. There was only one reason for him to do so now: to cover up an even more serious crime.

There was a knock on one of the two doors and Roger stuck his head in, more Lurch-like than ever because of the low ceiling.

"Gordon..." he said in his deep voice, and nodded toward the corridor.

"We'll take a short break," Gordon said, ending the recording and exiting the room. Hannah put down her pen, leaned back, stared at Hellgren, who sat straight-backed, his forearms on the table and his eyes on the opposite wall. If he was worried about the consequences of his confession, he didn't show it.

"You have no one to blame but yourself for getting mixed up in this," she said when they'd been sitting in silence for a while. Hellgren cast a guarded glance at her. "If you hadn't poisoned those wolves..."

"What wolves?"

"Did you know they were in the area, or did you put the poison out just for the hell of it?"

Before Hellgren could answer, if he intended to do so, Gordon returned with a small stack of papers in his hand. Most were printed-out pictures, Hannah could see when he sat down. Gordon took out the phone again, started recording. Stated that this was the continuation of the interrogation and what the time was before he leaned forward and spread the pictures on the table in front of Hellgren.

"We just started searching your house..."

Hellgren looked at them, let out a deep sigh, and slumped into his chair.

"This is how it's going to be," Alexander began as soon as he stepped through the door after briefing the additional personnel called in from Luleå and Umeå and then sending them home. There was no reason for everyone to know everything about the ongoing investigation, especially now that the media was sniffing around, so only the "regular" Haparanda staff and Sami Ritola were gathered in the meeting room.

"Umeå will send as many personnel as we need, extra technicians to work outside the house and in Fouquier's apartment, medical examiners who will be working around the clock. National is on standby if we need them. I remain in command," he continued, while pulling out a chair and sitting down.

Everyone around the table nodded in confirmation. No one was exactly surprised. The personnel shortage—an ongoing problem all over the country—could, at least in the short term, be overcome for extraordinary events like this one. Alexander glanced down at his notebook and then turned to Gordon.

"This Anton Hellgren, where are we at with him?"

"We have him for several hunting-related offenses," Gordon

said. "We found animal skins, eggs, and some illegal traps, and he's admitted to selling to Fouquier."

"Fouquier had three bird of prey eggs at his home," Hannah interjected. "He's probably sold the rest."

"Good, anything else?"

"No connection to Tarasov and the Honda—none that we could find anyway," Gordon said with a displeased shake of his head. "We brought in a dog from Customs, but there were no signs of any drugs in his home."

Was he mistaken or was that a disappointed sigh coming from Ritola sitting next to Morgan, who was quietly translating everything for him?

"No damage to any of his vehicles, and none of the vehicles registered to him were missing," Hannah concluded.

"Then we'll lower the priority on Hellgren until we come across anything else that might implicate him," Alexander stated. He turned to the others: "The phone number Hannah and Gordon found, where are we with that?"

Ludwig cleared his throat and looked down at the papers in front of him.

"It's connected to a Tele 2 prepaid phone card. I've asked them to find out which store sold that particular number, and if the person who bought it paid by card."

"Which isn't very likely," P-O muttered loudly enough for everyone to hear.

"It's a new number, wasn't connected to any earlier investigations," Ludwig continued without acknowledging the interruption. "It was activated on the same day we identified Tarasov, so that suggests it may be related in some way."

"Next step?" Alexander asked, taking notes.

"Like I said, we'll try to find out which store sold it. We've been pinging it, but it hasn't connected to any tower yet so it's either shut off or destroyed. We'll keep trying."

A small shrug said that was all he had, and P-O took over.

"Ellinor Nordgren, also known as Nancy Q, and her party saw no one at the scene, met no cars, nothing."

"If they did, I'm sure we'll read all about it," Morgan said sourly.

That was most likely true. Nancy had been given maximum exposure. *Aftonbladet* was the first paper she called, but the tabloids weren't the only ones running with the "influencer caught in the middle of murder case" angle on the tragedy. Probably because there wasn't much else to report. The police hadn't released any official statements yet, and Nancy was able to give them the location of the bodies, the nature of the injuries, how they seemed to have died, all in a trembling voice with teary eyes as if she was the one most impacted by these horrors. Not that it seemed to have been too traumatizing. The contents of the confiscated telephones revealed that Nancy and her friends had walked around the crime scene taking pictures and filming for a while before they decided to call the police. Alexander was still wondering if he should pursue that, and if so how.

That question would have to wait.

"I know it's been a long day," he continued, looking at his colleagues, all of whom, with the possible exception of Sami Ritola, seemed to have been affected to a greater or lesser degree by today's events. "But we have five murders, and if we assume that they're linked to Vadim Tarasov and the drugs, considering what René Fouquier was involved in, then... What do you think? There are no wrong answers. Big or small."

No one seemed willing to start until Morgan spoke up and said they'd identified all five victims at the abandoned house, contacted their next of kin, and conducted initial, brief interviews. One of the victims already had a criminal record. Car theft and minor assault. Two didn't have a driver's license, which didn't necessarily mean that they couldn't drive, René and the other two each owned a vehicle, but there was no damage to either of them.

"From what we've found so far and managed to recreate from their cell phones, there is no indication that any of the murdered men was involved in the hit-and-run that killed Tarasov," Morgan concluded his briefing.

"They may have had burners," P-O interjected.

"Sure, but there was quite a bit on those phones related to selling drugs, so it doesn't seem likely."

"Do we think they were out there to sell or buy?" Lurch jumped in.

"Why would he sell to someone?" P-O shook his head. "Better to peddle the stuff to his own customers if he got a hold of it."

"Nothing indicates that," Morgan interjected. "That he got hold of it."

"So, buying, then?" Lurch continued. "From whom?"

"And what are the odds that Tarasov was hit by someone who also knew what René was up to," Hannah mused. "Not even we knew."

"If they were buyers, why were they murdered?"

"Sami, you said that this Zagornij might send someone," Gordon said, turning to his Finnish colleague at the short end of the table. "Could this be their work?"

"Definitely."

"Who could he have sent? Who are we looking for? Do you have any idea?"

"No, I can ask around, but don't get your hopes up."

No risk of that, Alexander thought, looking at his colleague who was once again casually reclining and balancing on his chair with his arms crossed, that annoying matchstick in his mouth, not actually adding much to anything.

"Why are you still here?" popped out, and Alexander realized his irritation had led him to verbalize what should have stayed in his head.

"Not in a rush to get back. Met a girl yesterday…" Sami replied with a shrug, seemingly unaffected by the clear insult in that question.

"So, René and his guys go out there to buy, the Russians show up in the middle of the transaction, kill everyone, and leave," Ludwig tried to pull the conversation back to the matter in hand.

"How would the Russians have known where to find them?" Gordon asked.

"And if they did know, where did the sellers go? Everyone we found out there can be connected to Fouquier," Morgan added.

"Stupid question, but are we sure the stuff is not still in the Honda?" said Lurch.

"We haven't got it up yet, but the divers say it's empty," Gordon replied.

There was a brief silence. Alexander assumed that everyone's thoughts were headed in the same direction. So many variables, so many possibilities, and so much they didn't know. Nothing, if he were being honest.

"If this was my case," Sami said, glancing at Alexander from the other side of the table. "It's not, but if it was... I would continue to work more broadly, assuming that the drugs and money remain in the area."

"Why?"

"Because we don't know what actually happened out there. Not who or what or why, and we can't link the Russians to the place in any tangible way."

The discussion continued for a few more minutes, but when it became ever more circular, Alexander demanded silence and summarized.

"Our first priority remains the five murder victims, but we'll continue searching for both the drugs and money, and assume that they are still in the area." He saw Sami nod contentedly, then ended the meeting, telling everyone to go home and try to get some sleep.

He himself stayed behind; he needed to think through how much of what they'd talked about should be presented in the press conference, and how much should be held back. No one had linked today's events with the body found in the forest or with the seven dead in Rovaniemi. Yet. But that was probably only a matter of time.

Only when she got back to her office did Hannah realize how tired she was. No wonder, a glance at the clock showed she'd been on the go for almost sixteen hours. While stifling a yawn, she took one of the felt-tip pens neatly lined up at the far edge of the desk, went to the bulletin board on the wall where the picture of René Fouquier still hung. She circled the same area on the map that she had during her lunch with Thomas and took a step back.

"What's that?"

Hannah turned around. Gordon was standing in the door-way with his thin summer jacket on, ready to go.

"If we have more help now, and we assume everything has stayed local, I think this is the area we should concentrate on," she replied with a nod to the map.

"Because?"

"The crash, the Honda in the lake, the knowledge of small roads and dumping sites. In any case, we can start there and work our way out."

Gordon nodded approvingly. She grabbed her jacket from the

back of her chair and was about to pull it on and follow him out when heat began to flood through her.

"Damn it!"

A whole day without the slightest hint of a hot flash. She'd felt warm after having sex with Gordon, but that was because of the sex, not menopause. For a moment she'd dared to believe she might have the luxury of a day or two without a hot flash, but of course not. She could feel herself turning bright red, sweat broke out on her back and face, and began flowing down between her breasts. She went to the desk, pulled out the top drawer, and fished out some tissues.

"Hot flash?"

"What does it look like?"

"Like you just ran a half marathon."

Unable to manage a smile, she wiped her face and neck, threw the tissue in the trash, took out a new one.

"Do you have your car?" Gordon asked.

"No, why?"

"There are journalists all over the place—there's a risk they might follow you home if you walk."

Hannah sighed. Looked at the clock. Should she call Thomas and ask him to pick her up? It was late, but she didn't think he was asleep. Hoped he wasn't asleep, she wanted to continue the conversation they'd started at lunch.

"I can drive you if you want."

"Great. Thanks."

She grabbed the top of her blouse and pulled it back and forth to let in some cool air while she turned off the lights and then followed him down the stairs and outside.

As soon as they opened the door, they were surrounded. Gordon politely told them they had no comment and said Alexander Erixon would call a press conference either later tonight or early tomorrow morning. Hannah kept quiet, glaring at anyone who got too close. They made it to the car, climbed in, managed to back out and pull away without running anyone over.

When they emerged onto Köpmansgatan, they saw people gathered on the part of the square that was closest to the City Hotel and the Town Hall. Hannah estimated around fifty people milling about in large and small clumps, several with their arms around each other, some crying. A number of candles had been lit, though they didn't make much of an impact in the still-light night. Flowers lay on the ground, leaning against a low wall, a few stuffed animals were among them, along with handwritten notes and painted cards and plastic-wrapped photos.

"Did we release the names of the victims?" Hannah asked when she saw that the pictures were all of young men.

"X is doing so now, but apparently it's already out on social media."

A few minutes later, Gordon stopped the car outside her house on Björnholmsgatan. Hannah stared past him and up toward her house. Lights off. Only one of their two cars in the driveway. Thomas wasn't home. Which was not something Gordon needed to know.

"Thanks for the ride."

"It was nothing."

She unbuttoned her seatbelt and for a moment felt the urge to give him a quick hug or a kiss on the cheek, but refrained.

"Well, goodbye then. See you tomorrow," she said and slammed the door, saw him drive away before crossing the street, going over to the mailbox. Empty. Either they hadn't received any mail today, or Thomas had been home sometime in the afternoon and taken it in.

She stepped onto their property, noting that the lawn needed to be mowed despite how dry it had been.

She'd started something today. Unlike her, not her usual way. Thomas was the one who took the initiative, talked, not that much but more than she did, when it was needed. But not now, not for a long time, not when it came to this.

What was "this" anyway?

She had to find out, she realized. That look across the table at lunch. The weight of it. The seriousness. It scared her, made things impossible to avoid anymore.

Better to know than to guess, imagine the worst.

She went in to grab her car key. Didn't bother to call his name or check the bedroom to see if he was asleep. She knew he wasn't there. Didn't know where he was, but there were a few places she could look.

A couple of weeks after the day she'd decided was her eighteenth birthday, Uncle had come to her and told her it was time to leave. She was ready. It was time to start taking assignments.

But first he'd had a surprise for her.

They were sitting in the car. Uncle was driving. Far and long. Back to where she'd started. Even though she hadn't wasted a thought in ten years on the place or people there, she recognized it immediately. Noticed her breathing getting heavier. Her pulse increasing. Concentrated on controlling it, pushing it away, focusing. And managed. She looked calmly and deliberately out the side window when Uncle stopped.

"What are we doing here?"

"What do you want to do here?"

She turned to him, uncomprehending. What she wanted, what any of them wanted, was subordinate, unimportant.

"This is your graduation present."

Katja looked out the window again, saw the man on the lawn outside the small white house at the foot of the hill. Ten years older, but still the same. Tatjana might no longer exist, but Katja hadn't forgotten what he'd done to her.

She'd stepped out, and Uncle drove away.

The man on the lawn glanced at the car as it drove by and then at her. No hint of recognition. She stood there, watching herself walk slowly down the hill, into the yard and over to him. She would make sure he knew who she was before slamming his nose into his brain without much effort.

Or she'd cut the femoral artery with a quick incision and watch him helplessly bleed out on the lawn.

Or crush his throat and lean over him as he slowly suffocated. No, she wasn't going to do any of those things.

It was the middle of the day. She knew nothing of her surroundings, the neighbors, who was inside the house. Preparation and patience were the keys to success. Never let your emotions get the better of you.

With a tiny satisfied smile, she walked down the street and disappeared.

Two weeks later, they found him in the river. Under the influence of alcohol, he'd somehow gotten entangled in his anchor chain while on a fishing trip, fallen overboard and drowned.

An accident rarely arrives alone and the next month his wife died when a broken electrical cable turned her stove and sink live. Katja was standing a short distance away with the other curious onlookers as the ambulance came to pick her up. When it drove away without sirens or blue lights, she took out her phone and walked away. A quarter of an hour later, Uncle picked her up.

Now he stood at the window, the man who'd given her revenge, given her a new life. Flanked by flowery red curtains, he was staring down at the small crowd gathered outside while occasionally taking a sip of his hot drink. Katja was sitting in one of the armchairs, watching him, waiting for him to take the lead.

Uncle.

He'd knocked on her door, stepped inside when she opened, asked her politely how she was doing, looked around the room, expressed his appreciation, and wondered if she could make him a cup of tea.

Katja hadn't asked what he was doing here; he'd tell her in good time. Besides, she probably knew his reasons, more or less.

"Well then, five dead was it?" he said in Russian with his gaze focused outside the window.

"Yes."

"And you have what you came here for?"

Katja hesitated for a moment, sure he already knew the answer, but it was hard to say it out loud, to disappoint him.

"No, not yet."

"But you're getting closer."

Again, it took a few seconds for her to answer. A lie would make the rest of the conversation easier, end it faster, but he was the only person she'd never lie to.

"Not really," she admitted.

Uncle took a sip of his Earl Gray and with one last glance at the mourners in the square, he turned to her for the first time since she'd handed him his tea.

"So why did they die?"

"They knew too much."

"About what?"

"About everything. About me. They attacked me."

"They attacked you? At that house? What were you doing there?"

To an outsider, it would have sounded like polite conversational interest, but Katja knew she was being interrogated. Once again the thought of lying flashed through her mind, but she pushed it away. Those who lied to save their own skin or make themselves look better couldn't be trusted, and the organization she worked for was based on trust.

"They managed to capture me," she admitted, forcing herself to meet his eyes, seeing how he raised his eyebrows in surprise, playacting or real, she couldn't decide.

"So they died because you were careless."

"I'm sorry."

Uncle nodded, turned back to the window, to the people in the square.

"Won't it be more difficult now? The police on high alert and the whole town full of journalists. It feels like all eyes are focused here."

Had it been anyone besides Uncle, she would have said the task was difficult enough as it was, on the verge of impossible in fact.

They'd sent her to Sweden to find three bags that anyone could have stolen and hid anywhere. With more than a week's lead, they could be on the other side of the world now.

"I will finish this," she said instead, noticing to her satisfaction that her voice held.

"I assume so. It's Valerij who's a little impatient."

"It's only been a few days."

Uncle didn't answer, just smiled slightly at her. Did it sound too much like an excuse? Excuses were something she'd let go of early on.

"I know, I know."

He put his teacup on her desk, went out into the small hall inside her door, took his thin pork pie hat from the hook he'd hung it on. Katja got up. He was about to leave, his short visit over. She had to know.

"Why did you really come here?"

"I wanted to make sure you were OK. That you had things under control."

Without another word, he left the room. When the door slid closed again, Katja went and locked it before returning to the armchair.

Certainly not the answer she wanted. Until then, the visit had been a low-key but clear display of disappointment. She had hoped that he'd end it by giving her some new information, tell her that was why he was here. Or in the worst case, that one of her colleagues was coming to back her up.

A gentle rebuke. A certain amount of humiliation.

During all the years she'd worked for Uncle, he had never thought it necessary to make sure she had things under control or that she was OK. That wasn't the reason this time either. The short visit was a reminder and a warning. She had a job to do; right now it looked like she was about to fail.

Uncle did not allow failure.

Eventually he'd fallen asleep.

But Sandra still lay there awake, staring as those irreplaceable hours ticked by, her irritation and anger increasing as dawn approached. This wasn't at all what she'd planned; from now on it was supposed to be easy. Relatively easy anyway. They'd killed a man—*Kenneth* had killed a man, she corrected herself—that was impossible to escape. What they'd done afterwards was immoral, unethical, wrong in every way, but it was also surprisingly easy for her to live with. In fact, she barely thought about that night or the man in the woods anymore. The memory of what had happened was being erased day by day, reduced to an unidentifiable discomfort that would eventually go away completely.

Everything would work out. Everything would be so much better.

At lunchtime she'd gone downtown, looked in shops and stores, made a wish list of beautiful things in her head, annoyed that she'd have to wait so long to make it a reality. Three years. But today she'd started playing with the idea that two, maybe two and a half years might be enough. On Storgatan she'd stopped outside one of the nail salons. She'd never had her nails done before. It was the very definition of wasting money you don't have. Bitten, broken, and with ugly cuticles, her nails needed care and love. They'd get it, too. But not now.

As she turned around to move on, she'd more or less run straight into Frida. Frida Aho, she'd been since marrying Harri Aho, the owner of two of the largest snus shops in the city. When the local paper ran periodic headlines about "who earns the most in your municipality," Harri Aho was always on the list. Near the top.

Frida had several hundred more followers on Instagram than Sandra. She posted almost every day.

"Oh hi." Frida smiled and removed her sunglasses while taking the last few steps toward her. Sandra backed up slightly in case Frida might try to give her a hug. "It's been so long since I've seen you."

"Yes."

Sandra flashed a fake smile in her direction, not knowing where to look. Frida seemed so relaxed, so self-assured. Dressed in bright, fashionable clothes. Expensive shoes, a nice haircut, perfect make-up. Sandra on the other hand had no make-up on and was wearing an old windbreaker over her prison officer's uniform. She felt like she always did around Frida.

Poor, ugly, insignificant.

"How's it going?" Frida asked. Did Sandra still work at the prison (*yes*), how was her mother (*good*), and was she still with... Konrad? (*Kenneth, and yes*).

As if they were friends. As if she cared.

Was it really possible that she'd forgotten?

That for years she'd taken every opportunity to be mean and dismissive of Sandra, take cheap shots at her and make jokes at her expense, until Sandra would run home in tears, swearing she'd never go back to school again.

That in the ninth grade she'd given Sandra her little brother's old clothes in front of the whole class, saying that at least they were newer than whatever else Sandra owned and would fit her perfectly because she still had no breasts.

Sandra answered, asked a few questions of her own, got some updates on other mutual acquaintances, then Frida headed into the nail salon. At least she'd had the good sense not to lie straight to Sandra's face by saying something like "hope to see you soon" or "let's try to meet up." The rest of the afternoon Sandra had spent in a bad mood, and it didn't get any better when she pulled into their yard.

"Where did the Mercedes come from?" she'd asked as soon as she stepped into the kitchen where Kenneth was putting the finishing touches to some kind of pasta dinner.

"I borrowed it from UV."

"Where's the Volvo?"

"I got rid of it."

"Where?"

"A mining hole up in Pallakka."

Sounded like a good place. She'd never been there, only heard about it, and the Volvo was the last thing that connected them to the Honda, which connected them to the Russian. One step closer to a better life. So she checked herself. After all, this was Kenneth, she loved him, she really did, but he didn't always think things through. She narrowed her eyes suspiciously.

"How did you get there?"

"I... I drove it."

"Do you want us to go to prison?" she spat out, seeing him collapse a little from the hardness in her voice. "How the hell can you drive around with it in the middle of the day?"

"You know..." he began, and she could see he'd been expecting the question. "It's actually more suspicious to drive around at three in the morning. By day it was only one more crappy Volvo out on the road."

True. She'd thought the same thing when she'd sat in her car waiting for him to come back after ditching the Honda. It's easier to remember which cars you meet if you only meet one or two.

"And it was your idea that we should get rid of it," Kenneth continued defensively. "I was only doing what you wanted."

True again. Like always. So anxious to make her comfortable, to make her happy and satisfied. Like a dog. Whatever happened, she could be sure of one thing: Kenneth would never abandon her, betray her, or turn against her. She should appreciate that more. Harri Aho probably cheated all the time and made Frida sign a prenup.

"You're right," she said softly, and walked over and gave him a kiss on the mouth. "I'm sorry."

She could not hold back a smile when she saw how happy and relieved that made him. If he had a tail, he'd have started wagging it. She gave him another kiss then went and sat down at the kitchen table.

"How did you get back?" she asked, pouring water into their glasses.

"I called UV, he picked me up in Koutojärvi."

"And then he lent you a car."

"Yes."

"What did you say happened to Volvo?"

"Broke down."

Sandra looked at him as he concentrated on draining off the pasta water. There was something else. Something more. In those brief words. Something he wasn't telling her.

"Didn't he want to look at it? That's his job. And how did you get to Koutojärvi without a car?"

His only answer was a deep sigh, and she could see him closing his eyes to keep them from flooding over. He was so bad at lying to her. He knew she knew that, and that was probably why he didn't even try.

★ ★ ★

Now she couldn't sleep, couldn't relax. Goddamn Kenneth. And goddamn UV. Goddamn the whole goddamn thing. Why couldn't things just go the way she wanted? Why was everything so fucking difficult? She had to get ahead of this.

If the worst happened.

If they got caught. For any reason.

If the police came.

Was there any possibility that she could wriggle out of it? Kenneth was the one who drove into the Russian, so what did they really have on her? Protecting a criminal. Theft, probably. Desecration of human remains, perhaps. But if she said Kenneth forced her to help and then made her keep quiet. Threatened her. Hid the loot and never told her where. She'd been too scared to ask, to say anything. Would they believe that? Doubtful. People who knew them knew she was in charge in their relationship.

Thomas knew. Hannah. And Hannah was a cop.

But Kenneth could be persuaded to lie, and say he'd been threatening, violent. For her sake. It didn't matter much if anyone believed it—they had to prove beyond a reasonable doubt that it wasn't true. At best, she could go free, and Kenneth would go back inside.

It sounded wrong.

At best, of course, they would both manage to get away. But if the worst happened, the best they could hope for was that he'd go in for manslaughter, serve a few years, she'd take the bags of money and move somewhere where no one would think it was strange that they had assets. Kenneth would join her when he was released. Not something she wanted. Absolutely not. Several years of not being together. It was plan B if everything went to shit.

She turned, kicked off the blanket; the room was warm, stuffy—she wondered if she'd get any sleep at all tonight. It didn't feel that way. Plan B. She wouldn't have had to come up with a plan B if it weren't for UV.

Ultra Violent.

Maybe he'd started to believe it himself. Kenneth had told her what it really stood for. When Dennis was ten, he'd called in to a quiz show on the radio and they asked him which rays made it possible to photograph bones inside the body, and he'd answered "Ultraviolet." The next day at school, they'd started calling him UV, and it stuck.

That fake little shit.

She'd never been anything but decent to him when he was on the inside. Kenneth looked up to him like a big brother. And in return he'd stabbed them in the back first chance he got. Despite that, Kenneth had still tried to defend him. Told her about Social Insurance's decision, about Lovis, about how bad they had it, not least financially. Sandra didn't give a shit. Who doesn't have it hard? You don't stab your friends in the back because of it. All evening she'd been pissed at Kenneth, but what could he have done differently? He had protected them. As best he could. If UV pointed the police in their direction, they'd bite. Search until they found something. So it was important that he didn't point.

Simple really, once she came up with the solution.

With a glance at her sleeping boyfriend, she left the bed and bedroom, carefully pulling the door shut behind her. Opened the hatch in the ceiling whose ungreased springs whined, lowered the attic steps, climbed up, and turned on the light. The attic was fairly empty, they didn't have that many things to put up there. So her eyes were immediately drawn to a blue box diagonally to the left of the steps.

A PlayStation. Kenneth must have bought it. Using the money they weren't supposed to touch.

Disappointment washed over her, and suddenly she didn't feel as uncomfortable with her plan B. His carelessness jeopardized everything. They'd definitely talk about this, but Kenneth was just a small problem, she could handle him, get him in line again. UV was the one she had to concentrate on. He was the real threat, and if there was one thing she'd learned over the years at her job, it was not to give in to threats. She continued into the attic and finally found what she was looking for. Thomas had paid for a hunting license for Kenneth when he turned twenty-five. He'd given him the license, and something that Sandra didn't want down in the house. Now she lifted it up and examined it.

A used shotgun.

She could tick off yet another place. Thomas was not staying with any of his co-workers. None of them had seen him after he left work at the usual time this afternoon.

Hannah had quickly ruled out the possibility that he'd gone for a beer. There weren't many places to choose from, maybe not a single one at this time of night, when she thought about it. The number of bars and pubs increased slightly during the summer months when tourists made their way to the city, but they still weren't plentiful, and Thomas rarely went out. At least not alone, and since she'd talked to all his colleagues, there was no one left to accompany him. He had some friends. More than she did, but still, not so many.

It occurred to her that he might be with another woman. In which case she'd never find him. But there was nothing to suggest that, except possibly the way he'd distanced himself from her recently. No traces on his clothes or in the car. No scent of anyone else's perfume. No unexplained purchases from their joint account. She didn't know if there were any text messages or emails, hadn't looked at his phone or logged onto their computer, nor would she ever stoop to checking.

She considered calling, but chose not to. He was staying away, wanted to stay away, if she called he wouldn't tell her where he was, just say he'd be home later.

Maybe he'd gone to Kenneth and Sandra's place. He'd gotten really involved with his nephew after his family abandoned him. Hannah had never liked Stefan or understood Rita. It was one thing not to have the best relationship in the world with your children, she could relate to that, but to more or less pretend he never existed was something else. She had no problem understanding how Stefan could do it, but Rita? Not because of gender, but because Stefan was a cold and controlling psychopath, and Rita was not.

Sandra had to go to work early, had an hour commute each day, so she was surely asleep, but Kenneth was unemployed and might be up. Sometimes Hannah wondered what would become of him. He hadn't worked a day since he got out of prison, didn't show any signs of wanting to study or get any kind of education, showed no initiative.

Sandra bore a heavy load. Hannah always got the feeling Sandra could handle most things, but at some point even she would have to reach a limit. How long would she put up with having him totally dependent on her?

Hannah slowed down outside their run-down house in Norra Storträsk. A Mercedes that she didn't recognize was parked outside, so maybe they did have visitors even if the lights were off and nobody seemed to be moving inside. In any case, Thomas's car wasn't there, so she didn't bother getting out and ringing the doorbell. She drove on. There was only one place left she could think of. If he wasn't there, she'd have to give up. Drive home, call him, or accept that he'd met someone else. How would she feel if she found out that was the case? Fight to keep him? Was that even possible? Hadn't he left her because he was tired of her, wanted something better? What were the odds they'd "find their way back" to each other again? Small, she thought. Minimal.

Of course, it depended on what he had with this other woman. If it was just sex, like what she had with Gordon, someone who offered some intimacy and a body, well then maybe. But unlike Thomas, Hannah had offered him that. Many times. Been rejected. If he had someone else, then it was for something more.

To her relief, she was able to push all those thoughts aside. Thomas's car was parked outside the cabin that Hannah had never liked. When Rita showed no interest in it—that is, when Stefan didn't want her to keep it—Hannah had secretly hoped they'd sell the place, but Thomas bought out his sister instead. Hannah never told him how she felt, realizing it was important to him. Let it be his, not theirs.

She parked behind Thomas's car, saw him come out of the tool shed next to the house with something in his hands. He stopped, surprised to see her and not entirely pleased. Hannah stepped out of the car and walked toward him, noticing as she approached that more equipment and tools were scattered outside the shed.

"Hey, what are you doing out here?" he greeted her as she got closer.

"Looking for you. I thought you'd be home."

"No, I drove out here."

"I can see that. What are you up to?" she asked, with a nod to the things on the lawn.

"Cleaning up a bit."

"Why?"

"It was time. I got a bunch of shit that nobody needs." Hannah glanced at the fishing gear, tools, and gardening equipment. It had been a long time since she'd been here, been with him, but she knew he'd bought some of those things fairly recently. She let it go, that wasn't why she'd come.

"You don't seem very happy to see me."

"Sure I am."

"Sure you are?"

Hannah walked over and grabbed one of the lawn chairs he'd leaned against the wall, unfolded it and sat down. Thomas stood where he was, following her with his eyes, still with a net and a hook in his hand. Hannah leaned forward, rested her arms on her knees and looked up at him.

"What's going on? With us."

Thomas didn't answer, just sighed deeply and looked up at the yellow-orange sky. There was complete silence. No cars, no human sounds, even the birds and insects seemed to have left this place in peace. When Thomas looked at her again, the seriousness in his eyes almost gripped her physically, anxiety made her diaphragm contract. When she realized that he wasn't just struggling with the words but also against his tears, it struck her.

Suddenly she knew.

Couldn't explain how. But when the thought came to her, it was so natural, so obvious. He was going to leave her, but not for someone else. She looked at the things scattered about, her brain struggling to catch up, to make sense of this sudden realization.

"These are things the kids and I don't need."

Thomas didn't answer, air left him in a long exhale, and he seemed shrink. Tears began to stream silently down his cheeks, down to his beard.

"You're sick."

Thomas nodded. Sloping shoulders, drooping arms, the fishing gear still in one hand, as if it took all his energy to stay upright.

"I didn't want you to find out."

"How long have you known?"

She probably knew the answer if she thought about it. When had she felt for the first time that something wasn't right at home, when had things stopped being normal between them?

"A year or so."

That made sense, that was when he started to pull away, keep his distance.

"How long do you have left?"

She heard the words come out of her mouth, but had a hard time understanding they were from her. How could she be sitting on a lawn chair by the cabin asking her husband when he was going to die?

"A few months maybe, if I'm lucky."

Hannah found it difficult to breathe. It felt like her heart might explode in her chest. Couldn't think clearly, couldn't handle it. Absolutely did not know what to say, or how to feel either. So many feelings. Several that she wasn't even aware she had.

What should she do?

Scream, get angry, cry, feel deserted, duped, scared?

She heard more than felt how her breathing became heavier, there was a buzzing inside her head, the silence became muffled, subdued, as if her ears had suddenly closed up. A very, very small part of her still seemed to be functioning normally, trying to tell her that she was in shock, but she couldn't do anything with that information. There was absolutely nothing she knew how to react to or deal with.

The solution was to simply get up and go.

"Hannah!" she heard him call out, but didn't even turn around. Just held up a hand to prevent him from following her as she continued walking.

He didn't, she saw when she got in the car. He remained by the shed. Broken, weak, as unable to handle the situation as she was, he could only watch as she started the car, backed out, and drove away.

The wind from the open window almost overpowered the pulse pounding in her temples. But only almost. Her thoughts were racing, elusive, fleeting, impossible to grasp or hold on to. She thought she might be crying, her cheeks were wet, but she didn't feel sadness or grief more than any other emotion.

When she nearly drove off the road at a slight bend, unsure if this was even the way home, she was finally jolted back into something like reality. She pulled over to the side, sat there, hands on the steering wheel, staring blankly ahead of her at the two ruts that cut through the woods like an open wound. The mosquitoes gathered immediately, lured there by a hot engine, and found their way inside. Hannah didn't notice. Even though the windshield was down, she was finding it difficult to breathe, so she unbuckled her belt, amazed that she was strapped in, had no memory of securing the belt, got out of the car, and started walking, straight into the woods.

Panting, on the edge, so close to completely losing it.

Didn't know how long she walked before she sat down on a fallen tree trunk, rubbing her palms against her pants as she rocked back and forth. Forcing herself to slowly regain control, process, and sort.

Confusion was what she finally grasped. Confusion, the feeling of being lost.

Like when she was fourteen. All through middle school. After her mother took her own life. When she lost her footing, when the world became incomprehensible, and she no longer knew her place in it.

Then it was Thomas who'd grabbed hold of her. Got her on her feet again. No big gestures, nothing thought out. He just saw something inside her that he liked. With his calm, his matter-of-factness, and his patience. He'd become the foundation she slowly rebuilt her life on. Made her imagine a future, improve her grades, apply to the police academy, he moved with her to Stockholm, and even managed to give her the strength to move on after what happened to Elin.

Who would give her the strength to do that this time?

The kids. She hadn't even thought of Gabriel and Alicia. They'd lose the parent they cared the most about and, if she were brutally honest, the one who cared the most about them.

No exaggeration. No self-pity.

That's just how it was, how it always had been.

Thomas was closer to the kids than she was. Despite his quiet, slightly withdrawn manner, he'd always been more involved with them than she had been. Was there for them no matter what, whenever they needed him.

Just as he had been for Hannah.

Maybe subconsciously she'd been afraid to connect too deeply, to love unconditionally. She'd done it before. With her mother to some extent, but mostly with Elin, and then Elin disappeared. It almost destroyed her. She remembered thinking about it as soon as she got pregnant with Gabriel. Would she ever be able to love fully again? She couldn't survive that kind of grief a second time. So she'd kept them at a distance.

But hadn't she suffered enough? How much more could be taken from her? Mom, Elin, and now Thomas.

It was too huge. Too much.

She screamed, straight into the silence. Filled her lungs and screamed again. And again. She didn't fall silent until she tasted blood in her throat, noticed she was crying, gave in, and sat sobbing on the tree trunk.

Didn't know how long.

She let it take the time it took, then stood up and went back to the car. Where now? She really didn't want to go home. Couldn't. Thomas might be there, or he might show up. She couldn't bear to meet him yet. She needed more time. Nothing good could come of seeing him now. He probably knew that, too. He hadn't called or texted her since she left him at the cabin.

Forty-five minutes later, she turned into Haparanda on Highway 99 from the north, onto the Västra Esplanaden, drove past René Fouquier's apartment... It felt like an eternity since she and Gordon had been there. The streets were empty, despite the light and warmth. Hannah swung past the square. Individual candles still burned among the flowers and cards, but otherwise the square was deserted. She continued south, past the train station, past the city's other water tower, the ugly one that looked like someone had speared three blue containers on a number of concrete pillars, turned onto Movägen and parked outside one of the identical houses at the end of the street. Was this a good idea? It didn't matter. There weren't many other choices. None, if she were honest.

"Can I stay here tonight?" she asked when a newly awakened Gordon opened the door. He stepped aside and let her in without a word.

Uncle's visit had shaken her.

More than she'd realized and definitely more than she was comfortable with. The essence was clear: a warning, a reminder that failure was not an option. But why now? She'd had much more important jobs that took considerably longer.

And no nocturnal visits.

Collateral damage, innocent people being affected, that was also nothing new. Best to avoid if possible, but it happened. Five people was extreme and unfortunate, but it had happened before.

Without any late-night visits.

So what was different this time? Why was this so important that it warranted Uncle's direct involvement? Was Valerij Zagornij more than just a criminal client with plenty of money? Was there any other reason besides money to make sure he was satisfied? Uncle coming to her room in Haparanda suggested there was. Actually, it was a waste of time to even think along those lines. They were told all they needed to know, seeking out any information on their own about their clients or why those clients chose their victims would, if found out, be severely punished. Still she couldn't let go of it as she drove slowly down the narrow road, the lake shining blue behind the birches despite the late hour. The idyll, the calm, the seemingly randomly placed houses in the murmuring, ethereal greenery stood in stark contrast to the energy and restlessness in her body. Considering everything that had happened, all the mistakes she'd made, it was almost starting to feel like the place itself was against her.

She had never failed. Never in a larger sense.

Haparanda and Vadim Tarasov were not going to be the first time.

She thought this must be the right area. She couldn't be sure, but the information she'd managed to gather, thanks to Stepan Horvat, led her here. North of Vitvattnet, near Storträsk.

Then she saw it. It took a few seconds to make the connection, to stop the car. She backed up a few meters and stared down the driveway of the house she'd driven past. Asbestos-cement siding and a mansard roof. Facade, windows, and paint left exposed to weather and wind. Then what had caught her interest. A Mercedes in the yard. Only a few years old, seemingly in very good condition. In the eighty thousand euro range, like new. Cheaper used, obviously, but it still stood out in front of that run-down house.

She needed to think through the next step, debating if it was even worth it. She noted the address on her phone and returned to the hotel.

Half an hour later she slammed her laptop down and leaned back in her uncomfortable chair. Two people lived there according to the most popular search sites. A youngish couple. He didn't work at all, as far as she could tell. He'd registered a company in his name, but it seemed to be dormant; in any case it hadn't brought in any income in recent years so far as she could discover. The girlfriend had a full-time job in Haparanda. Government employee. Steady, but fairly low salary. The car imported. Temporary registration. Ownership unclear. Recently purchased, no doubt. He didn't seem to be active on social media. Her Instagram was private. On Facebook, she had to approve a friend request. Katja sent a request from one of the fake accounts she had at her disposal, but to no avail during the short time she waited. She was probably asleep, the clock was ticking toward morning.

Katja looked over at the bed she'd made this morning. Early on, she'd mastered the ability to fall asleep anytime, anywhere, even when under pressure, but she didn't need it now. Could manage longer than most with no sleep or only short periods of rest.

So she made up her mind. Drove back.

Slowed down as she passed the house, looked closer. The garden was empty. Nothing except the Mercedes in the driveway that spoke of money. It really wasn't much to go on. There could be any number of reasons why it was there. It might not even be theirs.

But it could also be the tiny change they made after finding 300,000 euros, something they had treated themselves to.

Katja drove a few kilometers away, turned at the first intersection, and parked by the side of the road. She checked that her knife was where it should be, inspected her Walther, screwed on the silencer, pushed it into the pocket of her thin coat, and left the car. Walked quickly back toward the house. Turned off before she got to the driveway, made her way through a denser part of the forest, crossed over the nearest neighbor's property, and entered through the backyard and the overgrown garden. Hid behind some bushes.

It was a real long shot. This search. If Uncle hadn't showed up, if questions and doubts hadn't arisen, would she be acting on so little information as she was now? The question was totally irrelevant.

Uncle *had* come. The questions and doubts were there.

What were the risks? That she was in the wrong place. That

the couple in the house had no connection to Zagornij's drugs or the MC Sudet's money. At worst, she'd leave witnesses or more bodies behind. But what if she did nothing, and they were the ones who drove into Vadim? Sometime soon, one of the journalists reporting from Haparanda was going to link Rovaniemi and Vadim with the five men she'd killed. That would warn them. They'd get away if she took the time to dig deeper.

Uncle demanded results. Quick results.

Might as well get started. At least form an opinion as to whether or not they were worth investigating. Could never hurt.

She left her place behind the bushes and walked toward the darkened house.

Something feels different as she wakes up today.

The river still meanders smoothly, the sun is still shining as it has been for weeks, the traffic crossing the border is getting heavier, people on their way to and from, but there's something muted in the atmosphere. She feels it. Everyone is talking about it, in subdued voices and tiny words. Unlike the headlines and news stories being written about her, their big letters and fraught expressions scream out what happened. Five young men murdered. She's small enough that everyone knows someone who knows someone who at least knew who they were.

Son of a co-worker's sister.

A babysitter's ex-boyfriend.

Someone whose father sold a car to a friend.

Old as she is, she's seen her fair share of lives extinguished. Cholera and typhoid came in waves. More than two hundred prisoners of war waiting to be exchanged during the First World War stayed in her forever. People have drowned in her river, crashed their cars, burned inside her. She's a city. People die here much as they do everywhere. Old age, illness, suicide, overdoses, accidents, the causes are numerous.

But rarely violence. Even more rarely murder.

Chastened, she notices that this is what it takes for someone to pay attention to her nowadays. Tragedies and evil sudden death.

Henrietta Stråhle is up early. Getting ready. Wants to look nice when the mobility service comes to pick her up. They're signing the papers today. After many years, her old, run-down family farm has finally sold. For a hefty sum. She won't miss it. Her childhood was terrible, her parents and grandparents wicked, violent people. Henrietta doesn't know it as she pins the brooch on her chest, but the new owners won't be any better. Quite the contrary. This time the whole of Haparanda will suffer.

Stepan Horvat stares down at his still sleeping three-year-old daughter. He, on the other hand, hardly slept at all last night. Again and again he considers calling the police. But what would they do then? Move? How far is far enough? In his mind's eye, he sees the pictures again. The red dot of a laser designator on her tiny body. He remembers the warning, the command, and just like all the other times, he decides to do nothing.

Lukas hates his studio apartment. Women, chicks, girls. They all use their attractiveness and sexuality as a means of power. Seem interested but then leave you, choose someone better looking or more successful. Denying you the right to get laid. They've gained this power through their fucking feminism, which has become some sort of state religion. He hates them. So utterly. So deep and fundamentally. He's not alone. When he gets on his computer and tells the others about yesterday, how he was rejected and refused, they immediately confirm what he already knows. His hate is justified. He needs to do something about the problem.

Stina is lying in bed in her childhood room. Finally rested after several nights of undisturbed sleep. Thinking about Dennis, who's taken on all the responsibility, who does everything to make this work, whom she always has to defend to her parents, because they see him as no more than a pusher, a fence, a criminal. She misses him. Him, but not Lovis. Not her daughter. Normally it would make her stomach ache to admit that to herself, but yesterday she figured it out. Lovis was the first pancake. The one that didn't turn out right. The failure. The next one will be perfect.

At Kukkolaforsen's campsite, a man named Björn Karhu opens the door of his camper and steps out into the summer air. The two women who are on the trip with him are still asleep. Barefoot and clad only in his underpants, he makes his carefree way down toward the rapids. Swift and wild. Hoping to find a slightly calmer place where he can take his morning dip naked. There's no rush. They don't need to be in Haparanda for at least two hours to meet the front who bought Henrietta Stråhle's parent's farm.

Thomas is sitting in the kitchen, hasn't slept, is waiting, remembers a question he got in school, maybe in the army as well, definitely he's read it somewhere.

What would you do if you knew you were going to die soon?

What would you take care of? The Bucket List. He doesn't have one. He's satisfied. Not with dying, he would have liked to live on for many more years, but with how he's lived. Stands up and grabs another cup of coffee. No Hannah yet. But she'll come. Scared and angry. At being left alone, because he kept it a secret. He has another secret. One she won't know until after he's dead.

The lawn outside is starting to turn yellow from the drought, he sees. The weather forecast still says fine weather is ahead. But that's wrong. The storm is drawing closer.

Thomas's car was in the driveway. For a second Hannah considered driving on, running away from everything, but she swung into the driveway and parked behind him, turned off the car, stared toward the house. Their home. After Alicia left, they'd talked about it being too big for the two of them. What would she do with it when she was left alone? Probably sell it. Settle in some small apartment somewhere. She pushed those thoughts away—they weren't there yet. She didn't really know anything. She supposed it was time to change that, took a deep breath and left the car. She'd had a feeling he'd be sitting there waiting for her. She was right. The second she closed the front door, he called to her from the kitchen. He was sitting at the kitchen table. In the same clothes as yesterday.

Hannah figured he'd been sitting there all night, waiting for her. She stopped in the doorway, unsure of everything, of herself, of how to continue.

"Hello, sit down," he said, nodding toward the kitchen chair opposite.

"I'm so angry at you."

"I know. Sit down anyway."

She couldn't avoid him or the subject forever. The monster was out of the cage, no chance of getting it back inside, might as well grab hold even if the timing couldn't be worse.

All of Haparanda seemed to be in a feverish but lowintensity boil since yesterday. An almost physical change, she'd felt it as she drove home from a sleepless night spent with Gordon. A strangely subdued silence lay over the city. People in small clumps, candles in the square and at the church were multiplying, people seemed to be out about with no real purpose, just looking for other people, exchanging a few words.

All that washed away as she stepped into the kitchen and sat down. She had her own problems in her own world where nothing outside had any major role.

Thomas got up and went to the counter, poured some coffee for her.

"Have you had breakfast?" he asked.

"No, but I'm not hungry."

Thomas nodded, satisfied with that, and to her relief didn't ask where she'd spent the night. He placed the cup on the table in front of her, settled down opposite. Sat in silence, seemed reluctant or unable to begin.

"So you're dying," she said, no idea how else to start, what else did they have to talk about?

"Yes. Cancer."

"What's the prognosis? What does your doctor say?"

"She says it's going to kill me."

"What kind of treatment are you doing? What have you done? Radiation? Chemo? Can they operate?" She knew he'd always been reluctant to seek medical attention, convinced that his body would take care of most things as long as he gave it time and maybe an Advil. Maybe not when it came to cancer, but he could very well have insisted on some milder treatment to begin with, to see how it went. "You haven't lost any of your hair, you haven't been puking your lungs up, not that I've noticed anyway."

"The cytostatics haven't affected the hair follicles, but I feel a bit unwell, although mostly I'm just tired, weaker…"

"Cytostatics, it's chemo then?"

"Yes."

"When is your next appointment? I want to talk to her, your doctor."

"I don't have any more. It didn't help, it's spread."

He reached for her hand across the table. Hannah could see how sad he was, how much he was suffering. Not for his own sake, for hers. Because he couldn't protect her from this. Because he was the one who was causing her pain.

"I didn't want you to worry or feel sorry for me."

"I will never forgive you for not telling me."

"It was my decision. Everyone has their own way—"

"Your way was wrong," she insisted, struggling against her tears. "We do things together."

"Not this."

"Why not this?"

His eyes wandered away, he let out a sigh and squeezed her hand harder.

"I thought it would be a little easier, later, afterwards, if I kept my distance."

"What would be easier?"

"Being without me."

"Are you really that fucking stupid?!" she snapped, letting go his hand, couldn't believe she'd heard him right. "So if you were at home less, and we didn't do much together, and we didn't have sex for a year, I wouldn't miss you as much when you died?! After thirty years? That was your plan?! How the hell did you come up with that?"

"Maybe I was wrong…"

"Yes, you were."

"…but I did it for you."

She stopped, breathing heavily, suppressed her blossoming rage. Understood what he was trying to do. Keep the pain away from her for as long as possible. Withdraw so that her loss might possibly be a tiny, tiny bit easier. He'd been thinking of her. Like always. She didn't deserve him.

"I know," she said at last, taking his hand again.

"So that you can move on. Without me. Because you have to."

"I don't think I can," she said honestly.

"You have Gordon."

"He's nobody," she said reflexively, her conscience chafing her. "He really is nobody," she repeated.

"It's OK," he said calmly, and looked like he meant it. Hannah frowned, the shame of being caught turning to surprise. In this context, it was of course unimportant how he'd found out, how long he'd known, but his reaction made her curious.

"How long have you known?"

"A few months."

"But you didn't say anything?"

"I pushed you away, I had no one to blame but myself, and I thought it might be good for you to have someone. Who can help you. Afterwards."

"You're an idiot."

Not telling her about his illness was one thing, but being OK with her unfaithfulness was too much. Too twisted. There were limits to what he should do to protect her, how good and self-sacrificing he should be. This exceeded them all by a good measure.

"You don't have many people you're close to, and you'll need someone," he continued matter-of-factly. "I know that, and Gordon is a good guy."

"Stop talking about him!"

Hannah almost felt nauseous just thinking about it. Felt the rage wanting to bubble up again, but it was held in check by a reasonable voice in the back of her head. Thomas hadn't forced her, hadn't encouraged her in any way to go to bed with her boss. He simply hadn't openly opposed it when it happened, hadn't confronted her. It had been her choice to end up there, and it hadn't taken much to push her either. Her anger was replaced by a guilty conscience again. She had to change the subject.

"Do the kids know?"

"Of course not."

A little relief there, so she wasn't the only one. The three of them hadn't been keeping a secret from her. Keeping her on the outside.

"When were you planning to tell us?"

"Later. Gabriel needs to concentrate on his studies, and Alicia is doing so well in Australia."

"So one day you'd just be gone, is that what were you thinking?"

"I intended to tell you so that there would be time…to say goodbye." For the first time, his voice broke, and he swallowed and cleared it. Hannah could feel her own eyes immediately fill with tears. "But I didn't want to walk around here dwelling on it for months."

"No good comes from dwelling."

"Exactly."

"I'm going to lose them, too."

She regretted it as soon as she said the words. This wasn't about her. She wasn't the one who deserved pity. Not yet. There would come a day, a time, but it wasn't now.

"Bullshit."

"No, they visit and stay in touch because you're here."

"That's not true."

"Yes, it is. It's my fault, because… I've kept them at a distance."

"You've been a good mother. You know that. You are good."

No matter how hard she tried, she couldn't hold back her

tears. Again: too much, too big. There was so much they needed to talk about, should talk about, but now it felt like even one more thing would make it too heavy to bear. She pushed out her chair.

"I have to go to work."

"You won't stay home today?"

"I can't. I need… I love you, but I can't be here right now."

She felt how true that was when she said it. It should add to her guilty conscience to leave him again, but she needed something else. Surely it wasn't what a psychologist would recommend, but she needed to push her emotions aside for a while. Suppress them. Hang her life on something familiar and ordinary while everything else seemed to be falling apart.

Work. An easy choice. Work was all she had.

The journalists were still outside. They seem to have multiplied since yesterday. Questions, cameras, and phones followed Hannah on her way in. She nodded a hello to Carin at the front desk, who cast a meaningful glance at the clock on the wall. The most important investigation in Haparanda's history, and she'd decided to sleep in. Hannah just pulled out her key card and disappeared down the hall past the cells, toward the women's locker room. Wanted to get into her uniform as soon as possible.

Leave behind civilian Hannah, Thomas's wife.

Become Hannah the police officer.

Clothes changed, she took the stairs and the corridor to her office. The offices she passed on her way were all empty. The morning meeting was probably still going on, but should be over at any moment. No point sneaking in and attracting attention.

The new, young cleaning lady was in her office when she got there, wiping the low bench below the bulletin board with a duster.

"Sorry, done now," she said apologetically when she saw Hannah.

"There's no hurry."

"No, no, done now," she said again, and Hannah could swear she twitched something like a curtsy as she left the room.

Hannah sat down behind the desk, turned on her computer and logged in, sat still, staring at the folders and icons. Where should she begin? What was engaging enough to dispel these thoughts? Change her focus. But she knew the answer. Nothing. She would just have to make an effort to concentrate on work today. At the same time, she needed to succeed. So what to start with? Fortunately, she didn't have to decide. Gordon knocked on her door as he entered her office.

"So you're here now," he proclaimed as he slammed the door shut.

Hannah sighed slightly, knowing exactly why he was closing it. She couldn't just show up in the middle of the night, leave in the morning without a word, and think he wouldn't bring it up as soon as they saw each other.

"How are you doing?" he began quite properly and settled down in his usual place.

"Fine," Hannah said, managing to smile a little. "Better anyway."

"You look tired. Tired and sad."

"I am tired."

"You still don't want to talk about it?"

"No, and I'm sorry I just showed up like that last night."

"It's OK."

"And we can't see each other anymore."

"Not see—"

"Not fuck, we can't have sex anymore. That's over."

Clearly not what he expected. For a moment he seemed shocked. Swallowed a few times while nodding to himself. Did she imagine it or were his eyes a little glossy when he looked at her again.

"Because?"

"We just can't."

"Does it have anything to do with Thomas? Does he know? Is that why?"

There was something imploring in his voice, as if he needed a reason, was trying to understand. She didn't have it in her to give him one.

"I don't want to anymore, it doesn't matter why."

"OK," his voice definitely wobbly, with disappointment he couldn't hide when he stood up and opened the door. "We… we'll deal with it later, maybe. But, well…we have things to do."

Then he left. Hannah watched him go in surprise, but pushed it aside. Whatever that was, she couldn't deal with it now. She was probably reading too much into it. She was off balance. That's why she was here. To achieve balance. Using her job to do it. She was going to work. So she got up, turned left in the hallway, and walked over to Morgan. He was typing at his desk, his computer glasses balanced on the tip of his nose. He took them off and turned to her when she entered and leaned against the doorpost.

"Hey, were you at the meeting?" she asked.

"Yes, where were you?"

"Had some trouble at home."

Safe for her to mention it, Morgan would never wonder what happened or ask if she wanted to talk about it. Neither curious nor particularly interested.

"You didn't miss much," he said with a slight shrug. "They fished out the Honda, sent it to Luleå."

"The phone number we found at Fouquier's?"

"Pinged it this morning. Still off. So far, nothing in the victims' phones or computers explains why they were at the deserted house or why they were killed."

"So none of them drove into Tarasov?"

"Doesn't seem so. Nothing about amphetamines at all that we could find. No one wanting to buy, no one offering to sell."

Hannah thought about what that meant. The telephone number they found, activated in connection with the identification of the body, René Fouquier, who was evidently involved in drug dealing. It must be connected in some way.

"But we still think this has something to do with Tarasov, don't we?" she asked.

"We're working broadly and without bias," Morgan said with a little smile at the tired press conference cliché. "But yes, what else could it be?"

"So what do we do now?"

"Continue the interrogations, knock on doors, wait for technical reports, hope for witnesses."

"Did Ritola say anything about who the Russians might have sent?"

"He wasn't at the meeting."

"Where was he then?"

"Who knows," Morgan replied with a new shrug.

Hannah felt she'd gotten what she came for and walked back toward her own office, glancing down toward Gordon's at the end of the corridor.

The door was closed.

He almost never had the door closed.

She stepped into her office, which, if possible, felt even smaller than usual. Stared at her computer again, not sure what she should do. There was surely some forensic or technical report she should read. Maybe she could spend some time putting together some kind of flow chart. Get an overview. So much had happened, but nothing seemed to hang together. There must be points of contact somewhere. She stood in front of the bulletin board, staring at the map, at the circle. Norra Storträsk lay within it.

Sandra drove quite a bit to and from work.

Kenneth was home all day.

She had to start somewhere, might as well be there, with them.

Might be good for her, too. It wasn't going to be as easy as she'd hoped to have a normal day at work. Yesterday's knowledge and this morning's conversation still hung heavily over her. It occurred to her that it would affect Kenneth as well, Thomas's death. Hit him hard.

Should she tell him? She didn't get any further than that before there was a knock on the door. She was expecting Gordon again, but it was Morgan.

"Am I disturbing you?"

"No, certainly not."

"One of the guys we found, Jari Persson…"

"What about him?"

"He was apparently at the City Hotel yesterday. X released the names, and the receptionist called, wondered if we wanted to know."

"What was he doing there?"

"Unclear. Shall we see if we can find out?"

It wasn't often he felt this way, like it was going to be a good day, so he enjoyed the walk to his shop. Feeling rested. There were assistants in the apartment last night taking care of Lovis, and they'd stayed so he could sleep in a little this morning, eat his breakfast in peace, he even watched an episode of *Rick and Morty* on his phone. Years after everyone else, but he rarely had the time, energy, or interest.

Stina was coming home from her parents this afternoon. Last night they talked. For a long time. To his surprise, she'd told him she wanted to have another child. She needed it, she said. That feeling of unconditional love. Being there when her child sat up, crawled, stretched out her arms for a hug, talked.

Everything she'd longed for, but didn't get.

If she could experience it with another child, she wouldn't miss it so much with Lovis. He understood, but wondered how they'd manage. What would happen if they had another damaged child?

They could barely handle life and their relationship as it was. But Stina had sounded so sure that another child would give her joy and make their lives easier. She'd be stronger, happier, a better mother to Lovis. If so, UV wasn't going to be the one to say no.

He'd told her that he'd been able to get hold of some money, though he didn't say how, and that it would keep them afloat for a while. Of course, she understood that it had to be something illegal, but she was cool with that, as long as she didn't know any details. He still felt the sting of a guilty conscience when he thought about yesterday. He really liked Kenneth, but if he interpreted the information he'd gotten from the Russian and the cop correctly, they wouldn't miss the dough he took, they had more than enough left to live well. And Kenneth got the Mercedes. Worth a lot more than the extra 25,000. Or at least, he could use it for a while. The Pelttari brothers would ask for it eventually, demand delivery, but hopefully by then he'd have found another car Kenneth could use. It was all going to turn out. Kenneth didn't hold grudges, in time UV would be able to repair the relationship.

It would be worse with Sandra. If she ever found out.

But it was Kenneth's car, his friend, his fault that they were blackmailed. One time he'd confided in UV that he was afraid Sandra would get tired of him, his lack of initiative, his general hopelessness, all the bad decisions he made, so Kenneth telling her about this was unlikely.

UV turned into the driveway and noticed that there was a light on in his shop. Good. Raimo was there. Eighteen years old, dropped out of the metalworking program at high school this spring, but a genius when it came to cars. When he showed up. It had been going so-so lately, and UV had been forced to have a talk with him, make him understand he couldn't come and go as he pleased, that UV was counting on him. He pushed open the door and barely stepped inside before Raimo was upon him.

"Did you hear?"

"About what?"

"Theo and the others."

"Yes, I heard."

Hard to avoid. It had been blowing up all over. At first he'd followed the various streams, but soon the theories about what happened and why had turned to fantasy, someone heard something about someone, rumors became truths, those singled out struck back hard with threats and hate and in the end he'd jumped off the carousel of information, misinformation, and speculation that just kept spinning faster and faster.

"I knew Theo. Did you?"

"I knew who he was."

"Apparently he was involved in some white power thing."

"Really?"

"That's what everyone is saying. There was a guy who knew his sister's ex-boyfriend who knew."

UV patted his shoulder and started walking off toward the changing room.

"Let's get to work."

"A customer is waiting for you in the office."

UV stopped, glanced over at the closed office door, as if trying to figure out who was sitting on the other side just by looking at it.

"Who?"

"Kenneth's girlfriend, the prison guard."

So Kenneth had told her after all. Fuck. UV considered leaving. Tell Raimo to wait a few minutes, then go in and tell her he wasn't coming in today. That he was sick. But then she'd go to his home. It didn't matter what he said, where he went, Sandra wouldn't give up. Might as well face the music right away.

He pushed open the door to his office where an awkward filing cabinet and a desk with an old computer and printer on it made the cramped space feel over-furnished. Ad posters, pictures of cars, and a wall calendar from 2012 hung on the dark green walls. Sandra was a straight-backed silhouette on the other side of the desk, lit from behind by the sun that struggled to make its way through a window in great need of cleaning.

"Hello, Sandra."

"Hello, Dennis."

"What can I help you with?" he asked in as relaxed a way as possible and sat down on his old oil-stained office chair.

"What do you think?"

He met her gaze across the table. Hers didn't yield an inch. He remembered that from prison. New arrivals sometimes tried to push her, thinking she'd be easier to scare or gain control over because she was a woman. Something that everyone, without exception, soon realized was a big mistake.

"The money," he said.

"The money," she nodded.

"You can't get it back."

"It's not yours."

"Not yours either."

"More than yours."

UV leaned his elbows onto the desk, his chin in his hands and kept his eyes fixed on her. What did he know? What could he use? He needed to solve this, but how?

"I want it back," she said, interrupting his thoughts. She nodded meaningfully down toward her knees, UV leaned to the side and glanced beneath the desk. He'd always thought she was a bit off, hard to get a handle on, but never realized she was completely fucking nuts. She must be since she had a rifle aimed at him.

"Put that away."

"Do I get my money?"

"Put that away," UV repeated calmly. Sandra shrugged a little, pushed her chair out slightly, and leaned the rifle against the table.

"I'm not planning to shoot you."

"Good to know."

"Not here anyway."

UV searched for any sign she was joking. Didn't see one.

"So if I don't give back the cash…" He nodded to the weapon.

"You will," she replied with certainty.

"But if not, you're gonna shoot me?"

"Or the police will get an anonymous tip that the drugs are here." She spread her arms, looked around the room and then back at him. "Maybe they'll find some."

UV observed her in silence. What did he know? What could he use? How could he solve this? He assumed that the Volvo was gone by now, so he had nothing left to negotiate with. Stupid that he hadn't taken a photograph of it in their garage.

He didn't know her. In prison she'd always kept a certain professional distance, and for the most part she wasn't there when he and Kenneth hung out. The few times they met, she'd always remained withdrawn.

But he was born in Haparanda just like her, knew how she grew up. Heard about how she had it in school, the bullying, her alcoholic mother. Knew from others that she'd always wanted to get further, climb higher. He hoped that was true. Then he'd be able to take care of his problems, at least financially. It was worth a chance.

"The cop said there was drugs in the car. Amphetamines. Asked me to keep an eye out for them," he began, assuming Kenneth had already told her. Sandra sat in silence. "How much?"

She tilted her head a bit and stared at him, probably trying to figure out what he was up to, if he was trying to trick her in some way.

"I don't know," she said at last. "Quite a bit, I think. A bag full."

"What are you going to do with it?"

"Nothing. Too big a risk."

UV took a deep breath, this was the key, the next few seconds would determine the future. Not only for the two of them but for his little family.

"I can sell it for you. Talk to my old contacts."

She probably thought she seemed coldly unaffected, but her body language gave her away, she straightened up a little, leaned forward on her chair slightly, a glimmer of interest in her eyes. She was tempted. He'd been right about her after all.

"Was there money in that car, too?" he continued. She seemed to have grabbed onto the hook, but it wasn't enough, he needed to reel her all the way in.

"Yes."

"How much?"

"Why do you want to know?"

Her suspicions had returned. Tempted, but not convinced. Yet. He explained to her what he knew and thought he knew. That this was about Rovaniemi, a drug deal gone wrong—she must have read about it—how the driver of the car they'd hit fled with both the money and the drugs. The drugs were worth about ten times more on the street than the cash they'd found in the car. So how much?

"Three hundred thousand euros," she said after a long exhale. UV whistled, more than he'd dared to believe.

"About three million kronor more or less."

"Does that mean it's worth thirty million Swedish?"

"On the street. At best, I might be able to sell it for ten."

He wasn't sure she realized it herself, but Sandra smiled, a broad, happy, dreamy smile. So close now, might as well finish it.

"I want twenty percent," he said. "Two, you can keep eight."

"I can count."

UV nodded, let her think. Didn't want to seem too anxious, give her the feeling that he was doing them a favor, offering himself for their sake, not his own. Saw to his delight that she'd made up her mind before she said anything.

"Fifteen. You get fifteen percent."

"Deal."

Time crawled forward.

How should she occupy herself now? The City Hotel hadn't led to anything. The receptionist had indeed seen Jari Persson in the lobby yesterday morning, recognized him, his father was on the same floorball team as her husband. But she'd been back and forth, doing errands around the hotel, working in the office behind the reception, so she didn't notice when he left or if he met anyone. Unfortunately. At some point she came out into the lobby, and he was no longer there, and she couldn't think of anyone at the hotel he might possibly know or be meeting.

Before Hannah and Morgan left, they asked if they could get a list of the guests currently staying at the hotel. They knew what answer they'd get, and sure enough she didn't dare give them that without checking with her boss first.

They received the guest list around lunch. Seventy-eight of the ninety-two rooms were occupied. Hannah spent most of her afternoon poring over the names, but didn't find anything there that stood out to her yet.

Nobody staying at the hotel had been there when Tarasov

was run over and eaten by wolves. A few checked in around the time he was found, but most of those had left again. Of those who remained, none needed further investigation after an initial background check.

It was monotonous and rather boring work, but it fulfilled its purpose, gave her something to do with her day. Kept her thoughts at bay. She couldn't ask for more.

When she finished, she tracked down P-O and offered her services.

Tips had begun to pour in. Extra personnel consisting mostly of senior police officers and the occasional rookie sat in a makeshift call center down by the shooting range taking these calls, then they handed them over to a command group led by P-O, the most analytical—and the most boring—person at the station. His group went through the information, ranked them according to urgency, and sent out people to follow up.

As far as Hannah knew, nothing so far had led to any results; some of the tips they would continue working on tomorrow, but it didn't seem as though the public was going to solve this for them. Not yet anyway.

Now there wasn't much more for her to do, but she didn't want to go home. Not yet. Maybe never. She stretched in her chair, stood up, and looked out the window. Stared up at black clouds for the first time in weeks, gathering on the horizon. She stifled a yawn. Went to grab a cup of coffee. The door to Gordon's office was open. She'd reported to him after the visit to the City Hotel, but he'd referred her to Alexander instead. That was it.

She pushed open the door to the kitchenette. He was sitting on the blue sofa.

"So you're still here," she stated, walking over to the coffee machine. Large cup, extra strong, no milk. Waited for the machine to finish its work, took the cup, and went and sat down on the sofa next to Gordon. Almost expected him to get up and walk away, but he stayed.

"Do you have anything I can do now?" she asked, taking a sip from her cup. He glanced up at the clock hanging on the wall above the door to the meeting room.

"You can go home. Everyone else has."

"I don't want to."

"Is he angry?"

Hannah knew she couldn't avoid this forever. If he wanted to talk she had to give him that. To a point. He deserved it. She put down her cup and turned to face him.

"No, he's not angry."

"But he knows."

"Yes, he knows. He's known for a while, apparently."

Gordon nodded, fell silent, surely thought he'd been told, had it confirmed, that this was why she didn't intend to sleep with him anymore.

Her husband knew. As good a reason as any.

She could have told him the whole truth. He would understand. More than that, he'd help her in every way, ask her how she was feeling, if she needed anything. Care. It was tempting, but she hadn't even figured out how to handle the situation herself yet. Involving someone else seemed like too much. In time he would find out. Be someone she needed. Just like Thomas said. But that was in the future, too close, but still not here. What she couldn't bear was the thought of work turning into a place where she felt uncomfortable, a place she needed to avoid, to escape from. She needed Gordon. As a boss, as a friend. The kitchen door was closed, the building more or less empty, but she still lowered her voice.

"I don't want things to be weird between us."

"I understand that."

"You've been weird today."

"I know. I was surprised, and I didn't take it so well." He

held his arms wide, a hint of a smile that didn't seem completely genuine. "It won't be weird. I promise."

"Good."

"So what happens now? At home?"

"We'll figure it out," she lied easily. "Somehow."

"But you don't want to go home."

"No, not yet. Do you have anything I can do now?"

S he regretted it halfway there. This wasn't what she wanted or needed.

Being alone in a car. Having time to think.

About Thomas, of course, but still she ended up mostly thinking about Gordon. She didn't really understand him. She'd never been very good at reading people, which you might think she would be, given her profession, and she couldn't figure out his reaction today. He wasn't the type to feel rejected. No injured masculinity. But she remembered how he looked when he left her office.

His face had been sad, not angry. His expression, disappointed.

The smile in the kitchenette hadn't really reached his eyes like it usually did.

Hannah knew he enjoyed their meetings at least as much as she did, but had he seen them as more than just sex? Had he been starting to fall in love with her? Idiotic. He was a thirty-six-year-old man in the prime of his career, she was a married mother of two grown children with hot flashes and less than ten years left to retirement.

Why did she think about him more than Thomas?

Why was she thinking at all?

She pushed down on the gas pedal, increasing her speed, wanting to get there as fast as possible. Start working again.

Twenty minutes later, she turned into a driveway where a Hyundai was parked and a man around her age, maybe a few years older, stood waiting. Hannah looked over at the run-down house as she parked.

With its asbestos-cement tiles, its mansard roof, and general air of being a fixer-upper, it reminded her of Kenneth and Sandra's place on the other side of the lake. She climbed out, and the man walked over to meet her quickly, even urgently.

"Hello, I'm Mikael. Mikael Svärd."

"Hello, I'm Hannah Wester."

"I'm so glad you called. The police officer we spoke to this afternoon said that you didn't intend to send anyone."

"But now we did." Hannah pulled out her notebook, flipped to a blank page. "You wanted to report your daughter and her husband missing," she reminded him as she walked toward the run-down house.

"Her boyfriend, they're not married."

"What are their names?"

"Anna. Svärd, and Ari Haapala. This afternoon my wife and I were supposed to return Marielle to them, and they weren't here, we can't get a hold of them."

"And Marielle is their daughter?"

"Yes."

"How old is she?"

"Turned two in May. She's with us sometimes, so Anna and Ari get time to themselves."

Time for themselves. She and Thomas had never had anything like that. Her dad was good with the kids, but only as long as things were fun. No interest in relieving them or taking responsibility. Thomas's father moved to France after the divorce, and by the time Gabriel was born his mother was seventy-five and in the first stages of dementia. Not someone you left a child with. With Elin it was irrelevant, they'd lived in Stockholm.

"Why do you think something happened?" Hannah asked, steering her thoughts away and starting to walk around the house.

"They knew we were coming, they didn't answer their phones, and the car is gone."

"What's the make of the car?"

Hannah stopped and bent down. One of the basement windows was broken. Shards of glass on the ground. Something you would have picked up if you had a two-year-old running around in the yard.

"A Mercedes. They'd just bought it. Scrapped the old one. They won money in a lottery."

"Registration number?"

"I don't know, it was brand new."

Hannah straightened up again and continued walking around the house, all seemed to be in order. Other than the window.

"Do you have a key?" she asked, pointing to the front door. Mikael Svärd nodded and hauled some keys out of his pocket.

"We went in this afternoon, my wife and I, but it was empty," he said as they walked up the stairs together.

"Could they have gone somewhere? Turned off their phones. Maybe taken more time for themselves."

"They knew we were coming with Marielle today. They'd never leave without her."

No, what kind of parent leaves their child, Hannah thought as they stepped through the door into the hall.

Clothes hung along the wall. Shoes in a shoe rack and on the floor. Side by side, neatly arranged in order of size.

"Anna! Ari!" Mikael shouted into the house. Hannah let him go on, had felt his nervous energy as soon as she met him in the garden. Of course, he hoped they'd come back. Popped up. That the hours of worry and anguish would be a quickly forgotten parenthesis. He received no reply. No relief.

Together they continued into the kitchen. It struck Hannah how tidy it was. Admittedly, they only had the one child, a two-year-old, but even when she and Thomas tried to keep up you could always tell there were kids in the house. Here everything was neatly arranged, wiped down, and sorted. Toys along the wall, crumb-free counters, knives on the magnetic strip on the wall, from smallest to largest.

Even photos and notes on the refrigerator were arranged in straight rows with round refrigerator magnets in three different colors. Those that were not in use were lined up neatly along the left edge.

Red, green, blue. Red, green, blue.

"Anna! Ari!" Mikael shouted again and disappeared further into the house. Hannah heard him head upstairs. Shouting their names again. She was about to follow when a sound made her turn around. At first she thought someone had thrown something, but quickly she realized what it was. Rain beating against the windows. First a few heavy drops, but soon the intensity increased, water hammering violently against the glass.

Hannah's gaze fell on a framed photo that stood on the windowsill between two plants. She walked over and picked it up. Marielle. Taken sometime last winter. Laughing with her arms in the air, riding a sled down a hill. Sheepskin fur and a snow hat. Mittens attached to her overalls. Red-cheeked. Like Elin when she came in from the cold. Her sweaty little body, cold cheeks. One of the two winters she experienced. Hannah looked out the window at the wild garden that had lost its contours behind the powerful rivulets running down the window.

It's really pouring down.

The windshield wipers are at maximum speed, but still struggling to keep the water away. People are running for cover from the sudden downpour, their shoulders hunched, holding up whatever they've got above their heads to avoid the worst. The street drains can't handle that much water that quickly. The streets are overflowing, the car wheels splashing torrents onto the sidewalks, soaking the hurrying pedestrians from another direction.

I should have taken that umbrella with me, she thinks as she drives past a row of cars parked next to a small park on Södermalm. Pulls over in front of them, too close to the pedestrian crossing, but pretty sure no meter maid will defy the weather. It'll take five minutes. Max. She turns off the engine. The rain hammers against the metal. Drowning out the radio that's playing 'Cotton Eye Joe' by Rednex. The storm's doing one good thing. The record store is only few meters down the street. Far enough for her to get soaked. Should she wait it out? She glances up at the sky. Completely black. No sign that it's going stop. Or even slow down. She turns toward the back seat. Elin's asleep in her car seat. Her pacifier hangs three-quarters of the way out of her mouth. Hannah pushes it back in place, and Elin takes a few happy sucks, like the king sucking his thumb in Robin Hood. She'll definitely wake up if Hannah takes her out in this weather. Hannah looks over at the record shop that promised to track down a Bruce Springsteen bootleg for her. Not legal, but not illegal enough for her to have a problem with it. Would be perfect to get a hold of it today. Give it to Thomas to celebrate the new job she's sure he got. She makes a decision. Unlocks her seat belt and gets ready.

Opens the door, hunches her shoulders when the water hits her, steels herself, closes the door as quietly as she can before almost doubling over on the street.

Shakes off like a dog when she enters the store. Only one customer ahead of her at the counter. Seems to be there more to chat than to buy something. Stax records are being discussed. She doesn't know if that's a band, a style of music, or a record company. Looks out at the car. Almost difficult to make out in the incipient twilight and through the drapery of rain. Then it's her turn. The man behind the counter remembers her, takes out what she wants, she pays and with the record in a plastic bag she gets ready to face the rain again.

Realizes something is wrong as soon as she steps out, but not really what. Something is sticking out on the other side of the car. Something that shouldn't be there.

An open door.

Elin can't open doors.

Didn't she lock it? She did. She was in a hurry to get out of the rain, but surely she locked it, right? Must have. But the door is open. A cold hand squeezes her heart as she rushes across the street, pure luck that no car is coming, doesn't even think to look for one. Has eyes for only one thing. The open car door toward the park and the trees behind. She arrives, almost falling, drops the bag, regains her balance and goes around the car.

It's empty. The car seat is empty.

She spins around on the sidewalk. Elin has to be there. Anything else is unthinkable. But she's not there. Panic takes hold. She knows what must have happened, but can't, doesn't want to understand.

Screams her name. Screams. Sees people stop in their search for cover. A sound that comes from the depths of pure desperation and terror. A sound you can't just pass by. She sees them approaching, but not one of them has her child. She screams her name again. Then she sees it. On the sidewalk. A little red patent leather shoe. No longer on the leg that carried it. She falls down on her knees. Finding it hard to breathe. Thinks she might have picked up the shoe, but doesn't know. Doesn't remember.

The red shoe turns everything to black.

"They're not here," Mikael Svärd said when he returned to the kitchen. Stopped in confusion when he saw her, and Hannah realized she was crying. Also realized that Mikael Svärd was interpreting her tears as heralding bad news.

"What is it? What did you find?" he asked anxiously.

"Nothing, I'm sorry, your granddaughter reminded me of someone. I'm so sorry."

She wiped her cheeks. Furious with herself. Furious with Thomas. This was his fault. He'd made her weak, vulnerable. She never allowed herself to think about Elin.

"They're not here," Mikael repeated, his eyes wavering a little, uncomfortable with a weeping police officer.

"I heard you say that."

"What are you going to do now?"

She knew what she was going to do, leave here. As quickly as possible. She put the photo back on the windowsill, cleared her throat, collected herself, and became a person of authority again.

"Not much we can do. Most indications point to them staying away voluntarily, so we can't do anything until twenty-four hours have passed."

"Something happened to them. They would never 'stay away.' Something's wrong."

"I'm sorry."

"You can at least look for the car, go out with a search warrant or something?"

"Yes, we can do that," Hannah said, leaving the kitchen, the house, and a seemingly bewildered Mikael Svärd in the driveway as she backed out and turned toward Haparanda.

About halfway back, she felt the need to talk to someone. She'd thought she wanted to be alone with her thoughts, but her memories were so powerful, so vivid that they clung like a thin, slimy membrane to everything else, penetrating and soiling it.

She considered calling Thomas, like always, like things were normal, but she couldn't handle that. Not now. Not yet. Needed to keep her distance. As she always did with every hardship. Every powerful emotion. But she needed to hear a voice other than the one in her own head.

She called Gordon. He answered immediately, asked how it went, and she told him. About Svärd, the house, the broken window, about everything except the rain and her memories.

"I still think we should send a technician out there," she concluded.

"Why?"

She hesitated a moment. Since she'd left the house, a theory had slowly emerged. At first she'd tried to ignore it as wishful thinking, a desire to make this late outing more important, more meaningful than it was, but it stuck, refused to go away. Now she tested out how it sounded.

"We should check if they were the ones who drove into Tarasov."

"Why do you think that?"

"They live in the right area, both are locals, and they recently scrapped their car and bought a new one. I found it in the registry: a Mercedes for almost half a million kronor."

"That's a lot of money."

"The dad said they won a lottery, but maybe that was their way of explaining how they could afford it."

Gordon fell silent. She could see him in front of her, the phone at his ear, trying to get onto the same track as her, ask the right follow-up questions.

"In that case, where are they?"

"I don't know."

"I suppose they wouldn't go away voluntarily without their daughter."

"Maybe they're hiding out, plan to pick her up later, I mean, they know where she is."

"Maybe."

"Or…"

She hesitated to finish the sentence. The rest was more far-fetched than what she'd presented so far, fewer signs pointing to it. Actually none at all.

"Or?" Gordon prompted when she didn't continue.

"*If* it is them, they might have made a mistake."

"Meaning?"

"Meaning that the person or people who took care of Fouquier and his gang got a hold of them, too."

She heard him sigh into the phone, couldn't determine if it was because her theory was so far-fetched, or if it came from contemplating the possibility of more dead bodies.

"Was there anything to indicate that?" he asked with the vague hope in his voice that he might get no as an answer.

"Not really," she admitted. "Everything was in order, but a technician might be able to find traces of blood or something."

"I'll take it up with X, but there's not much to go on."

"I know, but we have resources for once."

"I'll report it right away, but don't hope for too much."

"Is he still there?"

"Talking to the press, giving one last update."

"Anything new?"

"Nothing you don't already know."

"Are you still at the station too?"

"Yes."

"I'll be there in ten minutes, fifteen."

She bit her tongue, immediately regretted it. Why did she say that? Habit, probably. The risk was that he'd interpret it as an invitation, that she wanted him to stay and wait for her. Maybe she did. She didn't know. Not much she could do about it now, done was done, said was said.

"Then we'll probably see each other."

"Yep," she replied shortly, hung up, and continued on through the rain.

"This is for you," the Russian, or whatever she was, said as she got out of the car she'd insisted on driving into his shop. UV didn't understand at all. "You can have it. A present."

"Why?"

"I want you to help me, and I was a little harsh the last time we met." She put a hand on the hood of the silver-gray Mercedes as she walked around it. "It's a peace offering," she said, looking sincere as she offered him her hand. "My name is Louise, by the way."

"Thank you," UV said, shook her hand, his face open and relaxed. "But I can't help you."

It wasn't true. Hadn't been the last time she was here either. He'd known then that the blue Honda was in Kenneth's garage, but had sent her to Jonte instead. Wanted to know more before deciding what to do with the information he was sitting on. Now he knew precisely.

Lying wasn't hard. He was good at it. The more important it was that the truth didn't come out, the better he got. It had never been more important than now. After months of sacrifices, anxiety, tears, and an exhaustion that made his whole body ache, he finally had the chance to solve their problems. The famous light at the end of a tunnel, he never thought would arrive.

So helping her was unthinkable. And he lied freely.

"René is gone," she said in a casual tone, heedlessly leaning against the wet car.

"Who's René?"

"René Fouquier. Don't you pay attention to the news?"

Alarm bells started going off, urging caution, even though she was giving a guarded, almost uninterested impression, it felt very much like she was testing him. He recognized the name, was glad that Raimo had had to leave early.

"I saw the name somewhere, but I don't know who that is."

Which was true, UV had never heard of this René before reading about him today. Now it dawned on him what the woman in front of him was actually saying. She was the reason René was "gone." He and four others. She was dangerous, more dangerous than he'd understood the last time they met, more dangerous than anyone he'd ever met before.

"He was the new you." She turned toward him again. "I thought that if the new you was gone, then maybe people would go back to the old."

UV didn't respond immediately. What did she know? More than she said? If she had any idea about Kenneth and Sandra and the deal he'd made, she wouldn't have come here—she'd have gone straight to them. Got both the drugs and money. Punished him. Not given him a car, asked for his help. These quick conclusions calmed him, but he realized he still needed to proceed with caution. The more distance he could keep from her, the better.

"I don't do that anymore," he said, well aware that it wouldn't be so easy.

"You'll have to start again."

"What do you mean by that?"

"Spread the word that you're back in business."

"I can't do that."

She took a few steps toward him. UV had to fight the impulse to back away. She stopped close, looked him straight in the eye, seemed to hesitate.

"Do you remember I asked about amphetamines last time, Dennis?" she said at last. "A big shipment."

"Yes."

"I need to find it. It's very, very important to me. You're going to help me to track down whoever has it."

Did he hear wrong or was there a hint of desperation in her voice? She looked completely sincere. Or was this a new tactic to get him to help her?

"It's been a while. If René didn't get a hold of it, what makes you think I can?"

"No one knew him. Not even us. You, on the other hand, can spread the word that you're back, and that you want to do business in a big way. Quickly. Get started again…for your daughter's sake."

Even if it wasn't meant as a threat, it sure sounded like one. The easiest way out of this would be to burn Kenneth and Sandra. Give the Russian what she came for, so she could disappear from his life forever.

But she'd take the millions with her.

Their future.

So that wasn't an option. He needed to win this. Get rid of her. Without complicating things. Say he'd help, sell Sandra's drugs to the Finns, let a couple of days go by, get in touch with "Louise" and say that no one bit, no one got a hold of him.

What could she do about that? He was an excellent liar.

Sounded good, if nothing else it would buy him some time, give him the chance to think through all of this.

"What do I gain?" he asked, not wanting to give in too easily and make her suspicious.

"You just got a car."

He met her eyes, looked at Mercedes, seemed to be considering, and then shrugged.

"OK, sure, I'll help…"

Outside, he heard a car park near the entrance. UV glanced out the window, recognized it immediately. Of all the people he didn't want to meet right now…

Seconds later, the first stanza of *Für Elise* played as Sandra stepped inside carrying a large black bag. UV made an effort to relax, but could feel his pulse pounding in his temples as he raised a hand in greeting.

"Hi, go into the office, and I'll be right with you," his voice held, sounded normal. He was going to be fine.

"Sure." Sandra stared for a moment at the woman in front of him, smiled and nodded a greeting. "Louise" smiled back and followed the visitor with interest with her eyes.

"Your lover?" she asked as Sandra disappeared into his office and closed the door.

"What? No, hell no, no," UV laughed involuntarily, maybe a little too eagerly.

"You looked nervous when she came in."

"Well, no, it's not like that anyway."

She didn't say anything, just looked at him encouragingly, apparently wanting to know what was between them if it wasn't 'that.' It would have been better to tell her they were screwing. Too late now. He looked away from the now closed door Sandra had gone through, and when he turned back again, he lowered his voice.

"We're doing a little…insurance thing."

"Good luck with that, but don't forget what we agreed on."

"No, I'll talk to some people right away."

"Thanks."

A smile and then she walked toward the door. Relieved, he exhaled.

"Dennis…"

He turned to where she'd stopped with her hand on the doorknob.

"Get rid of that fast," she said, pointing to the Mercedes.

"Why?"

"Sooner or later, someone is going to come looking for it."

Für Elise accompanied her as she walked out while UV looked at the car. Fuck. She'd given him stolen goods. Or something even worse. It wasn't fully visible; he could decide what to do with it later.

Sandra was waiting in his office.

The candles were still burning in the square as Hannah drove by. More flowers, small stuffed animals and personally written cards and messages now that everyone knew who had died. More people outside than usual, despite the rain, which had let up, but still drifted in a fine mist over the people in the streets. Most of them were on their way to or from the church, which was open all evening. Small groups of people, young and old, were gathering. Few seemed to want to be left alone in this collective grief. They wanted to share it, even if it was with a stranger. Hannah didn't understand what the point was.

The groups thinned out the closer she got to the river and the police station, and there it was basically empty outside. Just one lone journalist sitting on the bench by the entrance. The others had surely given up, gotten as much as they could from the police. Now that it was official who the victims were, they'd be searching for the personal angle, the emotional hook that would make it possible to sympathize with them and their relatives. There were parents, teachers, co-workers, girlfriends to talk to. Ask them if they had any clue why their child, student, colleague, boyfriend might have suffered this fate. Get some quotes about loss, friendship, shattered dreams.

As she drove by on her way toward the employee parking lot, Hannah saw that there were no journalists waiting at all. She stopped.

Thomas. Alone in the drifting rain.

He'd seen her too, but still sat there, a hand raised in greeting. Hannah closed her eyes briefly, collected herself, and got out.

"What are you doing here?" she asked as she approached him on the bench.

"Waiting for you. I didn't know if you were planning to come home."

"I thought I would. Sooner or later. But we have those five murders, you know…"

A partial explanation for her remaining at work. Not the whole, and he knew it. She sat down next to him, could feel moisture seep through the pants of her uniform. Ignored it.

"How long have you been sitting here?"

"A while. Have you eaten?"

"It's been a while." She realized that was true when she said it. He took a flatbread roll with cheese and ham out of the small backpack sitting next to him on the bench. Handed it to her. She peeled back the foil and took a hungry bite.

"I don't deserve you."

He smiled at her and put his arm around her shoulders.

A lump in her throat suddenly made it difficult to swallow. "How are you?"

She almost laughed. So typical of him. Thinking about her, worrying. It hadn't even been a full day since she found out, but still… How was she? She really didn't know.

"I was thinking about Elin today," she said and realized that probably said quite a bit about how she was doing.

"Why?"

"Don't know. I saw a photo and…the rain started and you and just everything. I lowered my guard."

"You should do that more often."

She felt her eyes overflow, her tears mingled with the rain. She leaned her head on his shoulder.

"I love you."

"I know," he replied, and she knew he was smiling. She realized it was a *Star Wars* reference. A reminder of all the things she was going to miss. Could feel it wash over. All those memories, everything they'd done together, gone through together. A whole life. Better every day, thanks to him, and she'd taken it all for granted. Never appreciated it enough.

"I love you, and I'm sorry."

For so many things. For Gordon, obviously, but also and perhaps most of all because she wasn't there for him when, for once, he needed her more than she needed him.

"You don't need to be."

"I want to be there. For you. This…" She nodded toward the police station behind them. "This is…nothing."

"You will be. I know you."

She straightened up, turned to face him. It was important to say it, so that he really understood what she wanted, what she wished she could do.

"I don't know how. I don't how to be with you for months when I know you're going to leave me."

"We'll figure it out. It's a good start for us just to talk."

"We wouldn't have if you weren't sitting here."

"We would have. A little later, but we would have got there."

She put her hands on his wet cheeks, stared deeply into his eyes before leaning forward and pressing her lips against his, hard and long, then she put her arms around him.

"I don't deserve you," she whispered into his ear.

"You said that, but it's not true and you know it. I love every day with you."

She squeezed him harder. Didn't want to let go, but had to if she didn't want to end up totally sopping wet, at one with the rain on the ground. She let go of him, stood up, and wiped her face with the back of her hand.

"I have to go in…to work," she said, nodding at the station again.

"Yeah, I should go home and dry off."

"I'll be home soon. I promise."

"Sounds good."

He took his backpack and started walking home. Hannah took the few steps toward the entrance, turned around, and watched him walk away in the rain until he was completely out of sight.

Carin had gone home, and the reception was empty, the lights were off as she walked by it and pulled out her key card. She stopped at the stairs inside the door. It was the nearest path to her office if that's where she wanted to go. Didn't know. Couldn't really think clearly. Didn't want to go home, but maybe that was where she should go anyway? Follow him. Going up the stairs meant walking by Gordon's office. Didn't want that right now either. She continued straight along the ground floor instead, went to the changing room, got out of her wet uniform and dried herself off. And then?

Where do you go when you don't want to be anywhere.

Finally, she took the back stairs up and landed heavily in her office chair. Didn't even turn on the lights. As if the rest of the world reflected her mood, it was darker outside than it had been for a while. The days of the midnight sun were over for this year. Tonight the sun would eventually set below the horizon. Not that it would make much of a difference, the dark clouds that had rolled in seemed destined to stay.

She closed her eyes, fighting back tears. Couldn't remember the last time she'd cried; now she was trying to prevent it for the third time tonight. For the same reason.

Everything and everyone had been taken from her.

She opened her eyes, her eyes turned blankly toward her bulletin board. The map with the circle, the picture of René Fouquier, the investigation she tried prioritize all day. Everything neatly hung there.

More neatly than she remembered it.

She straightened up in her chair. The order reminded of her something...side by side. Straight lines. The thumbtacks that weren't in use lined up along the left side of the bulletin board.

Red, green, red, green, red, green.

It definitely reminded her of something, something to do with the case... Then it hit her. It took a few seconds for her to truly understand what she'd discovered. Because it was so... unbelievable. Could it really be?

When the realization finally landed, she flew up from her chair so violently that it crashed into the wall behind her and her thighs banged against the desktop. She put her hand over her mouth, held her breath, and knew that she was just standing there staring straight ahead with her eyes wide.

"Oh for fuck's sake," she finally got out before heading into the hallway, with one last glance at the bulletin board, and on toward Gordon's office.

"They were here. It's her," she almost shouted as she came rushing in. He'd heard her running down the hall and was already halfway out of his chair.

"Who was where?" Gordon asked, ready to step in while simultaneously being completely confused.

The words seemed stuck in her throat, all of it wanting to come out at the same time, but then she burst out: "The person or one of the people the Russians sent. The woman who was at Fouquier's place, at Svärd's, and here. She's been here! She cleans here. At the station."

She could see in his face that she wasn't making much sense. Eagerness blended with annoyance. They had to do something.

Immediately. She'd made a breakthrough in the investigation, and he didn't understand.

"She cleans my office. The new cleaning lady. It's her."

"Is she there now?"

"No, goddamnit, of course not," she snapped at him in frustration. "Come. Come with me."

She turned and hurried back with Gordon a few steps behind. As they entered her office, she flicked on the lights and more or less pushed him down in the visitor's chair before going over to the bulletin board.

"Look here, at the thumbtacks: green, red, green, red. Arranged along the edge with alternating colors. At the Svärds' home, they had fridge magnets in *three* different colors, and they also sat along the left edge: red, green, blue, red, green, blue."

She went over to her desk, woke up her computer, and waited impatiently. Gordon was watching her, not fully on board yet.

Then she found what she was looking for. "Here," she said, opening the pictures Technical had sent from René Fouquier's apartment, turning the screen so he could see. "At René's apartment, the coasters on the left side of the coffee table red, black, red, black, red, black."

She turned to Gordon, who seemed to finally understand what she was getting at, the importance of what she was saying.

"I thought it was just his sense of order, but it was her. She put the toys and hung the knives in this kind of order at the Svärd's house as well. And look here…" Hannah pointed to her desk where pencils, Post-it notes, and other office supplies were neatly arranged by color and size. "It's her. She was here."

"How the hell did she get in?" Gordon muttered, but Hannah could see he was already somewhere else in his mind. Where she was.

Closer to a solution.

★ ★ ★

"I knew you'd come," he greeted them softly as he opened his apartment door, then led them into the living room where a woman Hannah recognized sat on the sofa beside an eight- or nine-year-old boy. Sofia had cleaned the station for several years. Ever since Stepan Horvat's company won the contract from the municipality. Hannah nodded to her. Sofia smiled weakly back before looking anxiously at her husband, who sank down next to her on the sofa.

"Who is this?" Alexander asked, going straight to the point.

Stepan glanced fleetingly at the photo that was pushed across the coffee table, as if he already knew what or whom he was going to see.

"I don't know," Stepan said, looking up from the picture.

"This was taken by a surveillance camera outside the police station," Alexander continued, pointing to the photo. "The woman is employed by you. The key card is your wife's."

"But that's not your wife. How do you explain that?" Hannah demanded.

Stepan sighed deeply, glancing at his wife. There was resignation in the looks they exchanged. Sofia stood up and walked over to the bureau that stood against one wall. Gordon took a few steps toward her to see what she was doing. Didn't expect any trouble, but it didn't hurt to be on the safe side. If the woman in the picture was their suspect, then these two were involved in a mass murder.

"She came a few days ago," Stepan said. "Had photos with her."

"Who? The woman in the picture?" Hannah asked. Stepan nodded, while Sofia held a small envelope toward Gordon. He patted his pockets, then turned to face Hannah and Alexander.

"Do you have gloves with you?"

They both patted the outside of their clothes and shook their heads. Gordon carefully took one corner of the envelope between his nails, went forward and laid it on the table, opened it with a pencil and gently shook out the contents. Hannah and Alexander leaned forward.

The pictures were all of a small dark-haired, brown-eyed girl, maybe three years old, taken at various locations: a playground, a preschool, what looked like a garden. What they all had in common was that the red dot of a laser designator was trained on the girl in all of them. On her forehead, on her chest.

"Our daughter," Stepan explained.

"The woman in the car, she gave you these," Hannah asked, looking up from the contents of the envelope. Stepan nodded.

"Why didn't you go to the police?" Gordon asked.

"She told us not to," Sofia said, as if the answer were obvious, and sat down again. The boy huddled against her immediately.

"She wanted to get into the police station. I put her photo on a new ID and gave her Sofia's key card."

Hannah had the feeling they'd received all the answers they were going to get. They knew how and why, but weren't a bit closer to whom. The visit was, on the whole, a disappointment, not at all the breakthrough they'd hoped for.

"Why was it so important for her to get into the station?" Stepan asked with sincere concern in his voice. "Did she do anything? She hasn't hurt anyone, has she?"

"Yes, we believe she has," Alexander replied curtly and stood up.

"I have a better picture of her if you want," Stepan said as he too got up and handed the printout from the surveillance camera back to Alexander.

"Why?"

"She left two photos, for the ID."

He went over to the bureau, came back with a small passport photo taken at a photo booth. The young blond woman smiled casually at them. Hannah took the picture and studied it. There was no doubt that this woman had been in her office.

But there was something else there, too. Something she couldn't quite put her finger on. Something so far back in her mind that it was impossible to grasp, a connection that couldn't be made.

"She had short, black hair when she was here."

"A bob," Sofia cut in and indicated how long it was with her hand. "She had a bob."

"Hannah?"

She looked up, saw the outstretched hand, realized she was staring at the passport photo, and handed it over to Alexander, who put it away. They got ready to go.

"Are you going to arrest her now? Are we safe here?" Stepan asked, gesturing toward his family on the sofa. Alexander looked at his son, who had sat, quiet and serious, next to his mother this whole time, taking in everything that had been said. He smiled calmly at him. The boy's expression didn't change.

"Probably, but if your wife can go away with the kids for a few days, that might be good."

"What about me?" said Stepan, but Hannah got the sense he already knew the answer.

"You'll have to come with us."

She watched Kenneth from across the table. How he gobbled down the last piece of meat, trying to get up as much of the gravy as possible with the help of his potatoes. The fact that she was sitting opposite him was probably all that stopped him from licking his plate like a child eating ice cream at a birthday party. He'd eaten filet mignon. She'd lied and said she'd bought it on sale because it was close to its sell-by date. That wasn't true. She'd paid full price for it.

She'd done a lot of things today.

What she didn't do was tell him she'd decided to sell the drugs. Didn't really know why. It just felt like something he didn't need to know. Maybe because it was her idea from the beginning that they *not* sell them, and she'd forbidden him to even try. She didn't want him pouting for days because it was a bad idea when he came up with it, but good when she said so.

He definitely didn't need to know that she'd made an agreement with UV. She knew how disappointed he was in his ex-friend, and it would hurt him that she'd rewarded that betrayal by giving the man one and a half million.

That hadn't been her intention, she'd gone to his shop determined to get back the money, but UV had made it sound so easy to quadruple their money.

She'd take most of it, and he'd take all the risks.

If he got caught, ratted her out, she'd deny it: he'd just be a former inmate trying to get back at her for some reason. People who knew about their relationship, Kenneth's and UV's friendship, might think it sounded strange, but what evidence would they have? None. Absolutely none.

She'd gotten a taste of what a new life might mean today.

When she went to the shack to pick up the bag of drugs, she'd grabbed some of the money as well. After leaving his shop, she'd crossed the bridge and spent the rest of the afternoon shopping in Tornio. In Haparanda, there was a risk someone might react to her paying with euros. She'd bought new clothes, make-up, shoes, treated herself to expensive underwear, a new watch, some knickknacks for the house, and a LadyShave, which some of the people she followed on Instagram recommended for smooth summer legs and your bikini line. Back in Sweden again, she'd driven downtown, gone to the nail salon, hoping they'd have some drop-in appointments. They did. For over an hour she let someone else pamper her, make her look nice.

Just because she could, because she wanted to, and it made her feel good.

When she stopped to buy food on the way home, she didn't want the day to end with macaroni or fish sticks or whatever they had in the house. So she'd bought filet mignon.

On arriving home, she hadn't taken all the bags inside, worried that Kenneth might start to wonder how she was able to afford everything, but he hadn't noticed. Not the new candlesticks she put in the window, not the new clothes she'd changed into, not her manicure, even though she never did her nails, and now they were glowing a light pink. Only the filet mignon.

In a way, she was disappointed that he didn't pay more attention to her, didn't appreciate how she'd made an effort to look good, to spiff up their home. At the same time, she was happy he didn't wonder how she'd paid for it. If he knew she'd taken money from their stash, it would be harder for her to be furious about his new PlayStation. She hadn't mentioned that she'd found the console in the attic yet, was saving that for when she needed an advantage, wanted to make him feel guilty.

Besides, she had two more pressing problems.

The first was that if Kenneth ever went behind her back again, drove up to the cabin, then he'd notice the bag of drugs was gone, and know she was the one who took them since the other bags would still be there. The second problem was what to do with the money she got from UV.

She thought she'd come up with a solution for both.

After UV gave her her share of the sale, she'd move everything to a new site. Old and new money. Find a place she wouldn't tell Kenneth about. For both of their sakes. He didn't need to know that she'd done business with UV, be disappointed by her, and if the police arrested him, pressured him, he wouldn't have to lie. He would have no idea where the money was.

She'd have to think it through a few more times, figure out if there were any flaws, but not now. This day had been the best one she'd had in a very, very long time. Maybe it would be enough to wait another year before they started using the money. Before she started living her new life.

Before *they* started living their new life, she corrected herself.

Wonder why it was so hard to get that through her head…

He kept his speed steady as he crossed the bridge to the peninsula that was part of Finland. Not too slow, definitely not too fast. Didn't know if Customs had ANPR on the border, but still pulled his cap as low as he could and basically stared down at the floor as he drove across. Sooner or later, someone was going to come looking for it, she'd said. UV was hoping for later.

After Sandra left the shop this afternoon, he'd tried to go back to work as usual, but couldn't concentrate. His thoughts wandered back to the bag in his office, but even more than that they kept going to that fucking car. Eventually he'd just looked at it. The cop hadn't been there since that night, but he didn't dare keep it in his shop. Couldn't go to prison for something so simple. He made a quick decision, made a call, and closed for the day. Now he was driving across the next bridge, which took him to the mainland, and onto the E8 highway, took a left at the first roundabout and a few minutes later he turned into the industrial area near Torpin Rinnakkaiskatu. Mikko was waiting at the door of the garage, and he rolled inside and parked. The door closed behind him as Jyri, twelve minutes older than his brother, came forward and inspected the Mercedes.

"This isn't the car," he stated as soon as UV stepped out.

"I know, it's another one."

"Didn't you say you were coming with the Mercedes?"

"I said I was coming with *a* Mercedes."

"Is it from Florida?" said Mikko, sniffing a pinch of snus while following Jyri around the car. The Pelttari brothers. UV wasn't a small guy, but he looked like he was in junior high next to them.

Both were two meters tall, muscular, buzz-cut blond heads and tattoos. Mikko also had a large red scar over his right eye and down his cheek, which made him look very dangerous.

Which he was. Both of them were.

"It's not done yet," UV lied. Didn't intend to explain how he'd lent it to Kenneth, was sure they wouldn't appreciate that. It was a problem for later.

"Where did you get this from then?"

"A friend stole it."

"So it's hot?"

"Yes, it needs new plates, VIN, repainted, the whole thing," UV said.

"Why haven't you fixed it?" Mikko asked, aiming a kick at one of the rear tires.

"Honestly, I can't have it at my shop. The cops stop by every now and then."

The brothers looked at each other across the roof, and Mikko shrugged a little.

"We'll give you five for it," Jyri said.

Five thousand. Just over 50,000 Swedish kronor. UV didn't really know what he'd expected, but more than that. That was nothing.

"It's worth half a million kronor," he tried.

"If you don't like it, you can drive it back."

UV sighed. Realized he was in the worst negotiating position possible. He absolutely could not take it back to Sweden. Never wanted to see it again.

"Five now and the same amount when I leave the other."

Jyri nodded and the deal was settled. He started to go, UV followed. The office was bigger than his, brighter, cozier, a sofa in one corner and a TV on the wall. Jyri went over to the safe that dominated one wall and opened it, counted out fifty green hundred-euro banknotes then handed them to UV, put the rest back in the cupboard and locked it.

UV stood there staring at the money in his hand. Knew what he had to do, knew why, but it was tough. He was both pissed off and disappointed that the solution to his and Stina's problem was to take several unwilling steps backward. Go back to being a criminal. For real. He thought he'd never touch drugs again. They were shit, he'd seen what they did to people, his friends, people so young that they were almost still children, but mostly it was because he knew he'd go back to prison if he got caught. What would happen to Stina and Lovis then? Society had already let them down, proven that they didn't care. There was no sign that it would step up and take responsibility if he went away. But what choice did he have? None.

"I have something else going on," he said, watching Jyri turn to him with a curious expression. He told them. About the amphetamines. How much it was, what he wanted, started higher than he knew Jyri would go, so they landed at eight.

"We need some time to fix the dough," Jyri said as he reached out to confirm the deal.

"Sure."

"We'll call. Mikko will drive you back."

He left the office and the garage, asked Mikko to be dropped off outside Maxi when they got back to Haparanda. Bought food without even looking at the price. Enjoyed being able to grab what he wanted, what he knew Stina wanted. Pleased despite everything. Despite the circumstances. 5,000 euros in his pocket. Just as much on the way.

That was enough for many hours of assistance and along with

the cash he'd already taken from Kenneth and the fifteen percent he'd soon receive from the amphetamines, everything was looking bright. For a long, long time to come.

Stepan Horvat was in custody; it was up to the prosecutor to decide whether to charge him or not. Personally, Alexander felt sorry for him. The threats against his family were mitigating circumstances, but they couldn't rule out that he'd committed a crime. Worst-case scenario, the blond woman might have obtained information at the police station which led her to Fouquier and the others; if so, it would make him an accomplice to murder.

But all that would have to wait until tomorrow—they had more important things to do.

On his way up the stairs to the meeting room, he'd felt the same nervous anticipation as when Gordon told him about Hannah's breakthrough. The visit to Horvat hadn't yielded as much as he had hoped, but they had a photo. He'd requested material from all the surveillance cameras in the city—there weren't many, but a few—they had facial recognition programs and could run the passport photo against all possible registries. Both Swedish and international. Gordon was still with Horvat, waiting for the technicians they'd sent for. At best, they might get a set of fingerprints or even DNA from the pictures and the envelope.

He pushed open the door to the kitchenette and stopped when he saw a young girl drinking a Coke on the blue sofa, a bag of cinnamon buns and an iPad on the table in front of her.

"Hi..." he said in surprise.

"*Hei*," she replied without taking her eyes off the screen.

"What are you doing here?"

"*Olen täällä idiootin kanssa.*"

Alexander thought he understood the third of those four words, guessed the reason for the girl's presence was in the meeting room, continued inside, and closed the door behind him.

"Whose kid is out there?"

"Mine," said Ludwig. "Or rather, she's my girlfriend's daughter. I couldn't find a babysitter."

Alexander turned around, saw that on the wall behind him a two-part picture filled the canvas. The photo they'd received from Horvat and next to it the one where a black bob had been photoshopped onto blond hair.

"Do we know who she is?"

The silence that met him was an answer in itself.

"Not yet, no," Lurch finally replied when no one else seemed ready to say anything.

"The cameras in town, have they given us anything?"

"Haven't seen her on any of them yet," P-O said. "I started with the ones closest to the station, we don't have many, as you probably know, so there's a risk she made her way here without passing one."

"Or she knows how to avoid them. She seems quite slick," Ludwig added.

Alexander looked at the pictures again, yes, she seemed quite slick.

But Haparanda wasn't big, they had her picture, he had people, resources, technology, and the world's databases at his disposal.

They'd find her. Catch her.

His thoughts were interrupted by the door opening, and Sami Ritola entered with a cup of coffee in one hand and three croissants in the other. Alexander had called him in at the same time as the others, but as usual he'd strolled in late. Sometimes he suspected his Finnish colleague went out of his way to annoy him.

"Nice of you to join us," he said so acidly that his meaning was clear without translation. Morgan said it in Finnish anyway.

"Good people arrive late," Sami replied. He put one of his three croissants into his mouth and continued unhurriedly to his usual spot at the short end of the table. His eyes widened when he saw the pictures on the wall, swallowed, and pointed at them.

"Why is there a picture of Louise up there?"

The whole room stopped, turned to him. Morgan even forgot to translate.

"What did he say?" demanded Alexander. "Is her name Louise?"

"Do you know her?" Hannah asked.

"Not sure you'd say *know*, but I slept with her." He looked at Alexander while Morgan translated. "We're staying in the same hotel."

She was good at waiting.

Didn't mean she always liked it. Right now, for example, when she had nothing to do besides hope that her recent visit to Dennis Niemi would yield results, it made her restless and annoyed. She planned to give it two more days. Let him spread the word that he was dealing drugs again.

It was her best chance. Her only chance.

If it didn't work, she had to rethink completely. Had to realize that the person who ran into and buried Vadim Tarasov didn't intend to sell the drugs. At least not now, and not here. Not in Haparanda.

The money would be impossible to trace. If the person who had it spent it on a house or car, a trip abroad, invested it in shares or in luxury consumption, she'd never know. Access to what amounted to the entire police station hadn't yielded as much as she had hoped. They had, at least as far as she could see, no new theories and hadn't gotten anywhere with their investigation. Her latest track, the circle on the map inside of Hannah Wester's office, had turned out to be a mistake.

Another one. Unusual for her.

But it was an unusual assignment.

The more she thought about it, the more impossible it seemed. Usually she was given the names of one or more people. Sometimes they were protected, had security details around them, alarms, surveillance, and bulletproof glass. Sometimes they were in what they thought were secret locations. Sometimes they were living ordinary lives, no clue that someone had paid big bucks to end that for them. But they were people, with other people around them who could be bribed, threatened, bought, cheated, and deceived. Information about where they were and how to access them was always obtainable, with more or less difficulty.

She had never been sent on a mission to take back something that anyone, anywhere might have in their possession. It had sounded simple enough: go to Sweden, find the bags, kill the person who took them, and come back. Maybe that's why she'd made stupid mistakes. Like a sports team facing opposition that on paper was much worse, then ending up losing. If you realize halfway that it's all going to hell, it's difficult to reboot, come back, and win. Underestimating, that's what it was all about. She'd assumed victory in advance. Then Uncle had showed up and messed with her head.

Last night was due to him.

Frustrating, but she wasn't too worried.

The police wouldn't start looking for the young couple for at least another day. In addition, since there were no signs of violence in the house and everything indicated that they had left voluntarily, it would take even longer before they investigated it seriously.

Before it turned into a police investigation.

Before Uncle found out.

She needed time. Right now it was passing by. In a hotel room in Haparanda. Should she start considering that the money and drugs might have left the city? The police didn't seem to think so, but if Dennis Niemi didn't give her anything, she had to reckon with that possibility. It would raise the odds of getting them back significantly.

The phone she still had on rang on the desk. She got up and went to answer it. Listened for a few seconds and said she'd get back to them.

Finally! Good news. The first in an eternity.

She took her Walther and silencer out of the safe, fastened the knife to her ankle, left her room and the hotel, filled for the first time with hope that she'd soon leave this city and country behind.

With intense concentration, they discussed the next steps, the best way forward. Hannah was sure they all felt the same way, all wanted to rush out of the conference room, over to the hotel, and go in with everything they had. Immediately. But they had to hold themselves back even if it hurt. The expectation of an arrest was so strong that it was like a physical presence in the room.

Electric. Charged.

Alexander interrupted the discussion by first calling the City Hotel, asking if they knew if Louise was in her room or not.

She wasn't.

They had just missed her.

But she hadn't checked out. Alexander instructed the woman at the other end not to leave the reception area and to contact him as soon as Louise Andersson returned. Without her noticing anything, of course. The receptionist didn't even ask why, heard the seriousness of his voice, promised to do as she was told.

They didn't know where she was, but they'd know when she returned, and could plan accordingly. Didn't dare have anyone visibly guarding the hotel. She'd been inside the police station several times, so they figured she recognized them all. If they sent anyone in, it would be Sami. He was staying there, on the same floor even, and she knew he was a police officer—he'd introduced himself as one when he picked her up at the bar.

"Maybe that's why she slept with you," Morgan said thoughtfully. "Trying to get info that way."

"Do you think I'd give her any?" Sami replied, obviously disturbed by the notion that the young woman would have chosen him for anything other than his charm and irresistible good looks.

"You wouldn't be the first," Hannah said dryly.

Sami ended the conversation by turning to Alexander.

"If it's empty now, I think we should put someone in her room."

"Why?"

"Pincer movement. She comes back, you follow her in, she goes up to the room, you're behind her, I'm there waiting."

"You?"

"I volunteer willingly."

Hannah thought it sounded like a good idea. If for some reason they didn't dare approach her among the other guests and she got to her room, a lot could happen. They didn't know what weapons she had, and she was obviously indifferent to human life. It was better not to evacuate the square, would seem suspicious if suddenly the stream of mourners that had been arriving since yesterday ceased. An automatic weapon pointed out the window could soon turn into an unthinkable disaster. Having someone on the inside to prevent that sounded smart, but it was up to Alexander to decide.

Just as it was up to him to call the chairman of the municipal council and make sure someone went and opened the Town Hall. From there, they'd have a clear view of the hotel's main entrance. Morgan was instructed to take up position in one of the offices facing the square.

The entrance at the back, which led out to the hotel parking lot, would be kept under surveillance from a run-down, mostly deserted building on Stationsgatan. The businesses on the ground floor were all empty, brown paper had been taped to the windows for months. If they scratched out a peephole, they'd be able to see out without being detected. There was no time to try to find out who owned it or get in touch. Alexander approved Lurch and P-O breaking in; at worst the police would have to replace a lock or maybe a doorframe.

If Ludwig put on a hoodie and pulled up his hat, he could blend in with the mourners in the square.

Hannah ended up in a car with Gordon, who was supposed to be here any second—Alexander had called him back from the Horvats' place as soon as Ritola dropped his bomb about knowing the suspect. They decided on Packhusgatan, outside the pizzeria. Just enough distance not to attract attention, but close enough to be able to intervene anywhere inside the hotel within a few seconds.

"I'll stay in the office behind the reception desk," Alexander concluded his run-through of orders. "Weapons and vests. All communication, as little as possible, on channel three. And then we strike. I want everyone in place when she returns."

"What about me?" asked Sami.

"You can take her room." Alexander nodded. Sami smiled contentedly when Morgan translated.

Everyone gathered and resolutely got ready to go. A good plan, Hannah thought. They didn't have access to any special training or police equipment. Keeping this among the Haparanda force and not involving any of the reinforcements felt like a real decision.

Newcomers, no matter how good and well-meaning they were, were always cause for concern. Louise was considered armed and extremely dangerous, but they were eight police officers. With an overwhelming advantage. She didn't know they'd discovered her, that they were waiting for her. They should be able to do this.

On the way out the door, Ludwig stopped.

"Damn it, what should I do with Helmi?"

Hannah assumed that was the name of his stepdaughter. She heard an annoyed sigh from Alexander.

"Oh hell, Ludwig. Just take care of it."

"Eveliina won't be home until late tonight."

"Take care of it!"

Hannah didn't stay long enough to hear what solution he found. She hurried down the stairs, armed herself, put her bulletproof vest on under her uniform jacket, grabbed one for Gordon, and went out to wait for him. As she exited the door, he came running toward her.

"We have her?"

"We know where she's going to show up," Hannah said, throwing the vest to him. "You and I will be in a car on Packhusgatan."

"Mine?"

"Why not."

Eight minutes and forty-seven seconds later, all had confirmed via radio that they were in place.

Now all they had to do was wait.

I t smelled different. That was the big difference. Less confined. More open. He hadn't thought about it before, but he noticed now while they sat curled up together on the sofa watching a movie. Stina smelled good, like shampoo, soap, and some lotion she found in the bathroom, but it wasn't just that. The whole apartment felt cleaner, healthier, less like a hospital.

Stina's father had driven her to Haparanda, dropped her off, didn't come in to say hello, to him or to Lovis. She'd barely made it inside the door before he told her he had a surprise. They were going out again. Nothing grand. Ronnie, one of the few childhood friends he still hung out with, was away for a few weeks visiting relatives in the south and going to the Roskilde Festival, so UV was able to borrow his apartment in one of the yellow two-story buildings on Åkergatan. A small one-bedroom, Ronnie and his girlfriend had no children, but he and Stina would get an evening, a night, and a morning together without having to worry in the slightest about any assistants or wake up from the alarm going off in Lovis's room. Twelve, fourteen hours when it was just the two of them.

As soon as they got to the apartment, she hugged him. Didn't let go, kissed him, and started to unbutton his clothes. Did he remember what they talked about last night? He did. Might as well get started, it could take a while for something to happen. She really wanted to be a mother again. Get that second pancake.

They had unprotected sex in Ronnie's bed. Afterwards, Stina lay on her back with the soles of her feet on the mattress and a pillow under her butt. Every now and then she lifted her hips toward the ceiling so that it would "run down," as she put it.

"Listen, about that pancake thing…" UV said after lying quietly for a while, allowing himself to feel totally relaxed next to her. "Yeah."

"You can't talk about that with people."

"Why not?"

"Because bad pancakes get thrown away."

"That's not what I mean," Stina said, and UV could hear that she was hurt he could even think that. "I mean it lovingly…that things just went a little wrong, so you keep going until you get one you're happy with."

UV didn't answer, hoping she would hear herself, that it wasn't getting any better.

"Or, I don't mean it that way either, but you understand, don't you."

He turned toward her. Didn't doubt for a second that she'd lighten up, be happier, and have a lot more strength if they had a healthy child. What he wasn't at all sure about was if she'd become a better mother to Lovis in the process. But what would he gain from bringing that up now? He knew how she struggled. That she wanted so badly to love their daughter unconditionally, worked so hard at it.

"I do," he said, stroking her cheek tenderly. "But you can't talk about Lovis that way."

"OK."

"Good."

She straightened up, tossed the pillow away, and slipped under his blanket and hugged him. They had sex again.

Afterwards, they showered together, changed into sweatpants, pulled out the folding table in the small, brightly decorated Ikea kitchen, and ate what he'd brought. They had wine, Coke—UV didn't drink any, hopefully he'd go out and drive later—chips and nuts into the living room, sat down on the couch and streamed something from his phone on the large flat screen against the wall. Stina chose something on Netflix, and he watched with half an eye and his arm around her, the scent of her freshly washed hair and the apartment in his nose. Relaxed and having a good time. Could barely remember when they'd last sat together like this. When they had so much time for each other, just the two of them. It had been years. But that would change. This would be the new normal.

His phone rang. Jyri. Without pausing the film, he got up from the couch and answered. Took a few steps toward the door, his back to Stina, speaking softly, almost mumbling. Barely thirty seconds later, he hung up and turned back to Stina, didn't go back.

"I have to get out for a bit."

"Now?" Stina asked, straightening up on the sofa.

"Yes, I have to take care of something."

"OK."

She knew, of course, that it wasn't his auto shop that was paying for all those assistance hours or making an evening like this possible. Understood that the occasional scrap car he fixed up for the Finns wouldn't go far enough either, that what he was about to do wasn't legal.

"Are you going to be gone for a long time?"

"An hour, max."

"Be careful."

If she wanted to know more, to know everything, she would have asked. She didn't. So he went to the sofa, bent down, and kissed her.

"You can keeping watching from your phone," he said with a nod to the film, then he left.

The Do Not Disturb sign hung on the handle.

Had hung there since Louise Andersson moved in. No one had been inside to clean since she arrived, said the woman who let him into the room. Still, it was in perfect order, Sami noticed curiously as he made himself at home. The towels were folded over the towel racks in the bathroom, all the porcelain was dry, the small bottles of hotel shampoo, conditioner, and body wash were lined up on one side of the sink, as were the other jars, bottles, and tubes she must have brought with her. Two wig stands with wigs stood next to each other in front of the mirror. The blond one she used at the police station and a shoulder-length, ash blond one with bangs. Inside the room itself, the bed was made, the trashcan was empty, the desk was in impeccable order, her computer placed in the middle. He didn't even try to open it. Surely it was protected. He opened the closet and wasn't surprised to see clothes neatly hung and folded according to what he assumed was a system even if he didn't get it. The safe was open and empty. Nothing here gave any clue to who she was or why she was there. A real pro.

He went to the window, lifted one thick curtain with his

index finger, and peeked out through the gap into the square below. Decided not to wait any longer, time to take the bull by the horns, and he went and sat down in one of the armchairs. Took out his phone and pressed in a number.

"It's Sami. Is he there?" he said when he got an answer. Expecting to wait again, have time to go through everything he wanted to say it again, but heard Zagornij's deep voice in his ear immediately.

"What do you want?"

"They know who she is."

"Who knows who who is?"

"The police know who you sent to get your stuff back," Sami clarified, not allowing the slightest irritation to stain his voice, even though he was pretty sure Valerij understood what he meant the first time. "I'm sitting in her room at the hotel now."

Not a sound from Zagornij. Sami couldn't possibly make out if that long silence was thoughtful or irritated, and it made him uncomfortable.

"How did they find her?" came at last.

Sami thought briefly, there were a number of factors that came into play, the most important being that she'd left tracks or at least behavior that could be mapped. That and that she'd broken into the police station.

"Good police work," he summed up, to make it easy for himself.

"I thought she was better than that."

"Apparently not."

"So how much do they know?"

"What she looks like, but not what her name is. They know that it's her they're looking for and where she's staying."

"How did they find out where she's staying?"

There it came, the reason he was trembling, what he'd rehearsed to himself in order to explain. What he might eventually be blamed for.

"They got a picture of her and... I had to say I knew where she was staying."

"Why?"

It didn't matter how much he'd prepared for this, he knew how it was going to sound, and it wasn't good. But the alternative was to lie, and that was worse. He took a deep breath.

"We met at the hotel, I didn't know you'd sent her, we had sex, and if my colleagues take her and someone here at the hotel remembers seeing us together, how am I supposed to explain that I didn't say anything when I saw a picture of her at the station?"

Long. More a defense speech than an explanation. Silence came from the other end, definitely an annoyed silence this time, or maybe Sami was overthinking it.

"I had to improvise, to save my own skin."

He heard Valerij humming to himself, then he exchanged a few sentences with someone in Russian. Then it was quiet again. For a long time. But he hadn't hung up.

"I thought you needed to know," Sami said in an attempt to smooth over the fact that he was the bearer of bad news. "So you can reach her, warn her, or whatever you want to do."

Not the optimal solution. For him. If she didn't return to the hotel, there was a risk that his colleagues might guess that someone had tipped her off. Would suspicions fall on him? He was the one who came from outside, the one they knew the least about, had the least reason to trust. Alexander Erixon, that stiff shithead, would definitely think it was him. Even wish it were him. Could they prove anything? Doubtful.

"Kill her."

Sami was ripped from his thoughts, surely he must have heard wrong.

"What did you say?"

"Kill her."

If warning her was a bad idea, this would be a hundred times worse. He closed his eyes, felt his breathing get heavier. To refuse was impossible. Valerij Zagornij was not a man you said no to.

Probably not even someone you could influence, but he had to try.

"She's a pro, right? I mean, even if they get a hold of her, she won't say anything," he said and thought that sounded well thought out and rational. "So isn't it better to warn her and make sure that—"

"Aren't you worried about your own skin?" Zagornij interrupted him with ice in his voice.

"I—"

"Then stop talking and make sure she dies."

The rain drifted toward the windshield, but it was enough to turn on the wipers now and then as he drove toward the Western Esplanade. Headed down at the bathhouse, turned left at the large roundabout that would take him past Ikea, then out onto the 99 and further north.

Soon the manicured lawn of the golf course was on his right. Stretched across the river and over the border, it had eleven holes in Sweden, seven in Finland. Every one of them was deserted in this bad weather, but usually the course was popular at this time of year. The midnight sun meant you could play around the clock and, thanks to the time difference between the countries, you could hit the world's longest hole in one if you got lucky. A drive on hole six in Sweden could land one hour and five seconds later in Finland.

UV had never played golf, didn't intend to start.

Jyri wanted them to meet outside Karungi and barely twenty minutes later he was there, turned off the 99 and onto Stationsvägen, which ran along the railway tracks, increased his speed and continued west.

After less than a kilometer, he turned off and pulled up to

their agreed meeting place. A rusty road barrier with a shot up CLOSED TO TRAFFIC sign hanging off it was lowered over a more or less overgrown road. Behind it in a clearing stood a pile of concrete plinths, left over from some building site and dumped here. Maybe by the municipality, maybe by someone else. UV got out of the car, went around the barrier and down toward the clearing. The rain had stopped, but he felt the tall wet grass soak through his sneakers and into his pants. He went down toward the concrete blocks, sat down carefully on the edge of one of them, looked at the time. Seemed to be first on site. Apart from the faint rustle of the wind in the trees, there was no sound. The wet weather had silenced the birds and forced the insects away.

"Didn't you believe me when I said we had mutual acquaintances?" he heard from behind him and quickly got to his feet. Recognized the voice, knew who he'd see even before he turned around. Her, Louise, the Russian or whatever she was. Casually leaning against the concrete foundations with a gun in her hand. She hadn't been there when he arrived, and he hadn't heard her approach. Damn, but she terrified him.

"The Pelttari brothers called me right away," she said, with a look that almost seemed to say she pitied him, though he was quite sure she didn't.

"The shit is in the car," he said, nodding in the direction he parked.

"I know."

"You can take it."

"I plan to."

UV had a distinct feeling that she wasn't going to settle for that, could feel his heart start to pound in his chest. His adrenaline started pumping as he slowly and carefully began to back away. She hadn't moved, there was maybe twenty meters between them. He wasn't fast, not in great shape, but he was scared, terrified, the adrenaline and stress should give him a slight advantage. Mentally, he readied himself to turn and run as he continued to slowly increasing the distance between them.

"Sorry," he said, raising his hands in the air, hoping it would make her relax a bit more. She still hadn't moved. He had one chance, of course he had a chance, please, say he had a chance.

"Who did you get it from?" she asked.

"Sorry," he said again, feeling his tears start to flow. He wasn't even crying, his eyes just seemed to overflow. "Please. I'm sorry." He didn't want to die. He really didn't want to die. He thought of Lovis, of Stina on the sofa at Ronnie's house. He couldn't die.

"Who has the money?"

He shook his head resignedly in response, took a step back, careful where he put his feet, could not allow himself to stumble, looked for something to aim for, seemed to feel a firmer tuft of grass and took a deep breath.

Then he started running.

His legs pumping, his arms swinging violently along his body. He ran. Faster than he had ever run before. Saw his car approaching and pressed on to increase his pace. Didn't know where she was, didn't dare turn his head and look. Just kept running. Up to the barrier now. He could do this. Did he hear some faint puffs or was he imagining it? Was she shooting? With a silencer in that case, or the blood was pulsing so loudly in his head that the shots could barely be heard. She missed anyway. He was unharmed.

When he saw the car sinking down on one side, he realized she hadn't missed at all. She was shooting at the tires, not him. The car leaned forward as the other front wheel was also punctured by a bullet. How fast could he drive without air in the front tires? Fast enough to get away? But to stop at the door, get it open, jump in, start the engine…

He didn't have a chance.

Not if she could hit the tires from God knows how many meters away.

He kept running, chest burning, but he ignored it. Just ran. Across the road, quickly looking around, right, left, praying that someone would come. No one came. Continued down into the ditch on the other side. Thought he tasted something metallic in his mouth, but didn't know, didn't even know if he was breathing any more. Could feel himself losing momentum, pushed on, but his body didn't obey. He forced his way through young birches that whipped at his face and reached the embankment. On the other side was the forest. Real forest. Dense and green. He could hide there. Sneak away, keep his distance. If he could only get across the tracks. He gave everything he had left to those last few steps out of the ditch, came up and was about to disappear down the other side when something slammed into his leg and he fell. Hadn't heard the shot, but understood he was hit when he roared in pain and saw the rocky embankment suddenly coming closer. He rolled headlong down the other side. Felt his face and arms getting scraped up, but nothing could compare to the pain in his leg. But he was out of sight of her for a short while.

He had one chance, of course he had a chance, please, say he had a chance.

He got to his feet and stumbled to the side, among the trees. Didn't get far, couldn't take it anymore, sank down behind a broad spruce and tried to quiet his breathing. His trousers were soaked with blood from the violently pulsating wound in his thigh.

So much blood. Too much blood.

He pressed his hands to the wound, breathing with short, shocked gasps. Heard her making her way down the embankment in a controlled manner. Closed his mouth, breathing shallowly through his nose only. He heard her. Getting closer. Was it the blood? Was it as simple as her following the trail of his blood? He closed his eyes until it became completely silent.

When he opened his eyes again, she was squatting a few meters in front of him. The pistol aimed at the ground.

"Who did you get it from? Who has the money?"

UV just shook his head, weeping. Sweat, tears, and snot ran down his face but he made no attempt to wipe it away. No energy. It was starting to get difficult to focus his eyes, he felt dizzy and nauseous.

"I'll let you sit here if you tell me."

He looked at her blankly, not sure he could answer even if he tried, his breathing was increasingly strained in short bursts. Shock. He was in shock. She leaned forward and grabbed his chin, lifting his head.

"I'll take the stuff from your car and leave and get the money. Stop the bleeding and you will survive."

"If you…stop it… I'll tell."

She looked down at his injured leg and up again. Blurry and less sharp with every passing second.

"Last chance. Who did you get it from? Who has the money?"

No attempt to do anything. To save him. Besides it was too late.

She needed to know what he knew now. He didn't want to die, but he would die. He knew that now.

"Lovis…"

"What did you say?"

"My daughter… She's sick."

In his head it sounded different, more like a declaration of love. How much he loved her even though she could never love him back, how he wanted to give her as good a life as possible, wanted to be there longer for her, needed to be there. For a brief moment, he managed to conjure up an image of her and Stina in front of him, the warmth of seeing them mingled with the worry and sadness of leaving them before he slipped into unconsciousness.

"**F**uck!"

Disappointment flooded her body as she stared at UV, dead, leaning against the tree trunk. A new failure. The drugs were most certainly in his car, but she needed a name in order to find the money. The Finns who tipped her off didn't know who UV got the product from. That was information she needed to get from him.

Surely she could have managed that if she only got the chance, but then he sat down and died. The torn femoral artery in combination with stress and the fact that he was so out of breath from running made him bleed out in no time.

Nothing was going her way, it seemed.

Disappointed, she left UV, crossed the embankment, crossed the road, and approached his car. Locating half of what she was sent to pick up was better than nothing, but not by much. She couldn't go back until she had everything, and right now she had no idea who could give it to her.

So she opened the trunk. Recognized the bag immediately.

The black bag the woman had brought to UV's shop while Katja was delivering the Mercedes. She took a few seconds and tried to remember if she heard UV say a name when he asked her to wait in the office, but came to the conclusion that he hadn't done so. It didn't matter, it wouldn't be hard to find her.

With renewed energy, she started to do what needed to be done.

First, she carried the bag of drugs to her own car, which she'd parked some distance away. Then she went back over the tracks, down into the woods on the other side, fetched UV. She dragged him, with some difficulty, across the tracks, then over the road. Most of her assignments were in urban settings with potential witnesses, cell phones, surveillance cameras all over the place, around the clock. It undoubtedly made things easier to be working in a sparsely populated area in the far north of Sweden. No one had passed by since UV arrived; no one came now while for a few risky minutes she dragged him across the road and lifted him into the now empty trunk. She drove the difficult-to-steer car hundreds of meters before turning into the woods and hiding it tolerably well. The important thing was that it wouldn't be found for the next few hours so that the woman with the bag didn't find out UV was dead, get scared, take the money, and disappear. Half a day, no more, then her mission would be complete.

Tomorrow she'd be back in St. Petersburg.

Progress. Success. Finally.

As she watched Haparanda emerge from the gray weather half an hour later, she could feel how much she truly needed this.

There were only a few people gathered in the square outside the hotel, she noted as she entered Köpmansgatan from the east. The weather and the late hour probably played a role. There were a couple of free spots in the parking lot outside the main entrance. She threw a routine glance up at her window on the top floor before pulling in. Immediately turned off her blinker and continued on at the same speed as before.

A movement. A tiny gap in the drawn curtains, only a few seconds, but definitely there.

Someone was in her room.

She continued forward calmly, forcing herself to think. Most likely it was Uncle. But why another visit, one day after the first?

Nothing had changed. Besides, she wasn't sure he could get in when she wasn't there. Who else could it be? The privacy sign was up, and it was late for any staff. The police? It seemed unlikely that they would have gotten this far so quickly. She could call Uncle, of course.

Hear where he was, if he was waiting for her. A quick call, then she'd know.

It didn't feel good to not be up at the hotel, not good at all, but it couldn't be helped. When he asked Helmi if there was anyone she'd like to visit, anyone he could call, she just shook her head. He suggested classmates or maybe someone from her dance class, but she kept shaking her head and saying that she wanted to go home to her mother. Maybe that was just as well, it was way too late for most seven-year-olds to still be up, and he'd probably seem like the terrible stepdad he was sure Helmi already described him as if he were to call around trying to get rid of her at this time of night.

Out of options, he'd suggested that she follow him to the square, stand there with him. A father and his child participating in the collective grief. It wouldn't endanger her, they still didn't intend to evacuate the square of civilians, and Eveliina could pick her up there when she got back to town.

"And if you have to intervene, what happens then?" Alexander asked.

"She's seven," Ludwig said, glancing at his daughter on the sofa. "She can be alone for a while. Wait for me."

The look Ludwig received in reply told him exactly what Alexander thought of that idea.

Now he sat in front of his computer feeling stupid. It was admittedly much, much later than what could be counted as normal business hours, and they truly had no one who could watch Helmi, but he was the newest one on the team here, didn't want to be seen as not contributing as much as the others.

"How long do we have to be here?" Helmi asked in Finnish, throwing away the pen she'd been drawing with and staring at him angrily.

"Until Mom comes."

She raised her eyebrows in an uncomprehending look, even though he was pretty sure he'd gotten the word order right.

"Not long," he said, pronouncing both words slowly and extremely clearly.

Helmi sighed in a way that made her cheeks puff out like a stuffed hamster and rolled her eyes with boredom.

"You can draw some more," Ludwig suggested, and she held up a handful of drawings with a look that said she hadn't done anything else in the last half hour.

"How about the iPad?"

With another sigh, she left the room in an exaggerated haste, and he soon heard the speeded-up voices from a cartoon. He returned to work, but couldn't concentrate. Might as well pack it up. Just one more thing before he left, mostly to be able to say tomorrow that he'd done it.

To compensate for the fact that he wasn't at the hotel.

He ordered a new ping on the phone number they'd found at René Fouquier's. So far it hadn't given them anything. Tele2 couldn't say which store sold the subscription, and every time they tried to ping it, it had been impossible to locate.

"Helmi, we're going home now," he shouted to the break room, stood up, put on his jacket, and gathered up the pencils and papers she'd spread all over the conference table. "Turn that off and get ready."

He was about to fold his laptop when he froze. Could it be true? Could he really be that lucky? He pulled out his chair and sat down again. Opened the information he'd just received. Felt a knot of excitement in his stomach when he saw the colorful piece of cake on the screen.

"Shall we go then?" Helmi said from the door.

"Soon, just wait a minute," Ludwig replied without looking up from the screen. His daughter turned and stomped back to the sofa. He wavered briefly: radio or phone? Decided on the phone. Called Alexander, who answered on the first ring.

"She's turned on the phone," Ludwig shouted down the line. "I got it."

Katja was standing inside the small white-and-red gazebo in the quadrant of the square furthest from the hotel keeping the building under surveillance.

She planned to give it an hour to start with, wasn't in any hurry.

Every now and then she let her binoculars slide up along the wall, up toward the windows of her room, but she hadn't noticed any more movements. Of course, that didn't mean no one was there, only that they hadn't given themselves away again.

After thinking through the situation and weighing her options, she'd come up with a first step that didn't involve Uncle, and which would hopefully reveal whether or not the police were on her trail. She'd finished her unplanned ride by driving toward the huge station building, turned left toward the water, pondered the huge blue-green railway bridge on its heavy stone foundations that crossed the river, then changed her mind, didn't want to risk any Finnish cell tower picking up the signals too, so she continued back toward the downtown. Stopped at the small playground by the boardwalk and walked down to it. Took out the phone that had been off since she got rid of René and the others out at the abandoned house and turned it on. Opened it with a four-digit code and called 90510 to check the time, had to make sure it would be seen as active. Then she put it into one of the car tire swings and drove back up to the square. Parked the Audi and walked the few meters down to the gazebo with its disproportionately long flagpole on the roof.

Then she waited.

Didn't really know how it worked, but the number she gave to René Fouquier had been on Hannah Wester's bulletin board, so she assumed they'd be trying to track the phone that number belonged to. But she didn't know if they'd put it into a computer program that would automatically react to it turning on again or if they had to manually look it up.

After forty-five minutes, things started to happen.

A car she thought she recognized came from the west and stopped outside the hotel. She raised her binoculars. Sure enough. She'd seen it parked outside the police station. It belonged to Gordon Backman Niska, who was sitting next to Hannah Wester and had someone else in the back she couldn't see. That they'd arrived in the same vehicle and from the opposite direction as the police station didn't necessarily mean they'd been close to the hotel, but she received confirmation a few seconds later when Alexander Erixon exited the main entrance and quickly jumped into the car. They then headed down toward the river.

Katja lowered her binoculars and calmly started to walk back toward the Audi.

What was going on?

A few minutes ago, Alexander had ordered Lurch to leave the property on Stationsgatan, go with Hannah and Gordon, and pick him up outside the hotel.

She'd turned on her phone again. Or at least, he assumed it was her. Her phone.

Messy. Careless.

If this wasn't a distraction, an evasive maneuver.

But in that case, it meant she knew they were on her trail, maybe even that they had the hotel under surveillance. How had she found out? Had Zagornij warned her after all? But then why not just disappear quietly and unobserved?

Sami went over to the window and looked out again. Everything looked normal. Didn't know what he was really looking for. It would have helped if he'd at least known what kind of car she was driving. He released the curtain and checked his gun again to make sure it was ready to fire. He could feel sweat on his hands, wiped them against his pants.

Nervous. More than that, if he were being honest—scared.

Something was going on. She'd turned her phone back on.

He would have preferred to leave the room, the hotel, Haparanda, Sweden. Drive back to his Rovaniemi. But there was no other option. Valerij Zagornij had given him a job. If he stayed here, he at least had a chance at survival. Morgan and P-O were still in place, so they'd tell him over the comms radio when she was approaching the hotel. If they saw her.

He wondered where he should be, where he should wait for her. Sit the armchair in the dark, shoot as soon as she was a silhouette in the doorway? But if he missed, he'd be relatively immobile. Maybe it didn't matter; he got the feeling he'd only have one chance. After all, she'd killed five men armed with only a knife. Should he allow her to get further into the room so as to claim self-defense? Hide in the bathroom, behind the curtains, under the bed?

He took a deep breath, wiped his palms again, and paced as many steps as the room allowed. Stopped.

He hadn't seen that before. Or was he imagining it?

In the hall mirror he caught a faint flashing red light shining on the wall where the bedspread didn't reach all the way to the floor. He closed his eyes briefly, might just be something his tired eyes did after being in the dark for so long. But when he opened them again, it was still there. Was the room being monitored, did it have an alarm, was that why she knew they were there? With a curious frown on his forehead, he walked over to the bed to investigate more closely.

Katja sat in the car, considering what she'd left behind. Nothing that could be traced back to her, and she had very few possessions with any kind of emotional value, never took any of them with her on assignments. There was also nothing in the room that was objectively valuable. The only thing you could never be totally sure of was DNA traces. But there was a protocol to avoid those as much as possible.

She had followed it to the letter.

The room was rigged.

She leaned forward, opened the glove compartment and took out the little black box, opened up the safety guard, put her thumb down, and pressed the detonator. Heard the powerful explosion, saw flames shoot out, throwing glass, wood, and sections of the outer wall out into the parking lot below. The people still milling around the square screamed, followed by the usual moment of shocked silence as they tried to process witnessing the unthinkable.

Katja backed out and drove away without haste. In the rearview mirror she could see the gaping hole beneath the roof of the hotel, the flames and black smoke rising into the cloudy sky.

"Did he have a family, do we know?" Lurch asked, breaking the muffled silence in the meeting room. He didn't have to explain who he meant, everyone understood instantly, it was difficult to think of anything else.

A bomb in the hotel. In the middle of town.

Sami Ritola was dead, two hotel guests slightly injured.

Bombs and explosions had unfortunately started to become commonplace in Sweden, but not in Haparanda.

"Don't know," Morgan replied abruptly, with a shrug.

"He was sleeping with that woman in the hotel, so probably not," came from Ludwig.

The statement was met with silence—no one wanted to discuss whether or not Sami Ritola had been unfaithful. They were tired, needed to rest, but all were reluctant to go home even though they were no longer needed at the hotel. Alexander had called in staff from Boden, Kalix, Luleå and received reinforcements from Finnish colleagues in Tornio. The bomb squad was on its way, NOA—the National Operational Division—and they'd probably get a SWAT team eventually, too.

When reinforcements arrived, Alexander sent them all onwards. They had been close to the explosion, in the case of Morgan and P-O in the building next door, and they'd lost their Finnish colleague. Besides, everyone had worked at least seventeen hours, and tomorrow would be no shorter. The city was already buzzing with rumors and worry.

Tomorrow everyone would know, everyone would wonder. Be scared and feel unsafe.

Demand answers, action, results.

The door to the meeting room opened, and Gordon led in two civilians they'd never seen before. The first was a white-haired man, around fifty, in chinos and a polo shirt that made him look like he'd come straight from a round of golf. The woman was fifteen years younger, dark-haired, brown eyes, wearing a pencil skirt and a white silk blouse unbuttoned at the neck, ankle boots on her feet.

"This is Henric Isacsson and Elena Pardo, they've come from Stockholm," Gordon introduced them and waved them to seats on the short side of the table.

"You were fast," P-O stated skeptically. "Were you already on your way when Alexander called?"

"They're not from NOA," Gordon said.

"Really, what are you then?"

"We work within the international division of the Swedish Security Service," Elena replied as they sat down next to each other. "We were informed that you had searched the database, trying to identify this woman."

She opened her briefcase, pulled something out, and pushed a photo of the woman they still only knew as Louise Andersson across the table. Different hair this time, long, curly, medium blond. The picture was taken from above by a surveillance camera, but there was no doubt this was the same person.

"We can do this tomorrow if you all want to go home," Gordon added. "But it might be good if you're up to date when we start."

The five people around the table exchanged glances and shook their heads; the long day might as well get longer.

"Do you know who that is?" Lurch asked with a nod toward the photograph.

"Yes and no, mostly no," Henric replied cryptically. "We know she's been to Sweden before, that picture is from Ystad a few years ago."

"What was she doing there?"

"We suspect she executed an informant for an ongoing investigation into trafficking. And two security guards."

Hannah picked up the picture from the table, stared at it with the same focused concentration as she had at the passport photo in the Horvat's home earlier.

"We believe that she might be behind the death of a Ukrainian cultural attaché during the Gothenburg Book Fair in 2017 as well," Elena continued. "And a number of other deaths abroad."

"Wasn't that an accident? At the book fair," Morgan asked quietly. "Wind tore down that shop window?"

"We haven't been able to prove that it was *not* an accident," said Henric, staring meaningfully at them.

"What do you know about her?" Hannah asked, putting down the picture, visibly more interested.

"Not much, pieces of information here and there that we're trying to piece together, but she's a trained assassin, and not the only one. There's some kind of organization behind her, but we know almost nothing about them."

"But you know something?"

"We believe they recruit children, very young, and train them to become…like her."

"Where?"

"Russia, as far as we know; they could exist elsewhere as well."

"Why Russia?"

Henric and Elena exchanged a look, and Henric nodded for her to continue.

"Last year, Europol did a comprehensive online search using a new facial recognition program, and we came up with this."

She laid a new picture on the table. An enlargement of a black-and-white photo, an ambulance outside a small house, some curious people gathered outside.

"It's from a local Russian newspaper. Taken in the village of Kurakino ten years ago. The woman on the stretcher was killed by an electrical accident inside her home. She's there."

Elena pointed to a young woman in the back row of the curious onlookers. Everyone in the room leaned forward to get a better look. Ten years younger, different hair, but undoubtedly it was the same woman.

"Why?"

"We think she grew up in that house."

"Is that her mother?"

"According to the Russian police who helped us, neighbors said that the Bogdanov couple had a little girl, Tatjana, living with them once upon a time, but according to Russian records, they never had any children."

"So where did she come from?"

"No one knows. She appeared as a two-year-old and disappeared again when she was eight."

"That was when we think she was recruited," Henric interjected. "If that's the case, she's eighteen in that picture."

Hannah leaned forward and looked again, she was in the background, not in clear focus, but it seemed to be true. A resolute, serious young woman in her late teens. Ten years ago, she'd be twenty-eight today.

"The school she attended says she was the woman's niece," Elena continued. "But that doesn't seem to be true either."

"What happened to the 'father'?" Lurch asked.

"He drowned a few weeks before the 'mother' died."

Everyone let that sink in in silence. Hard to imagine some-one recruiting an eight-year-old, drilling her all through her childhood, and in ten years turning her into a well-trained, pro-fessional killer. As if next year someone were to take Ludwig's stepdaughter and raise her to be a killer. But based on what they knew about the woman in the pictures, of what she was capable of, and what she'd accomplished in this city in recent days, it unfortunately seemed quite likely.

"Neighbors said the girl wasn't treated well, we think she was recruited, trained…"

"…and came back and took her revenge," Hannah finished Henric's sentence, and he nodded in confirmation. "But she came to that family as a two-year-old, you said," Hannah con-tinued.

"She was around two when she showed up in Kurakino, yes."

"When was this?"

"In 1994."

"But you don't know where she came from?"

"No, we only know what the neighbors told us, and now you know as much as we do."

Hannah nodded, leaned forward and took the first photo again, the one from the surveillance camera in Ystad, leaned back and examined it carefully.

"So. Your turn, what can you tell us about her?" Henric asked, picking up a notepad as he glanced around the table.

What could they say?

All their thoughts revolved in one way or another around her, but when they tried to summarize them, they were struck by how little they actually knew. How she looked, that she'd been inside the police station, that she'd killed five people, and blown up a hotel room, that she spoke Swedish.

"She speaks at least four languages fluently, as far as we know," Henric interjected.

"Swedish is an odd one, a small language," Morgan declared.

"She works in Scandinavia. We know she can speak Finnish as well."

He nodded to them to continue, but before anyone could speak, Hannah pushed out her chair and stood up abruptly. With the photo in hand, she left the room and her surprised colleagues without a word.

I t's raining as she slowly wakes to life.

She expects a day of a lot of talking, wondering, and worrying. Despite the rain, many will linger outside the barriers surrounding the wounded hotel and say it feels unsafe here, say they're considering moving.

No one will.

Not for that reason anyway.

She's been through this before. Something happens, a couple of weeks go by, everything goes back to normal. In a year it will be "the anniversary of," and then just one memory among many.

Like the robbery and murder of the mailman in Harrioja in 1906, the cholera outbreak, the explosion in Palovaara during the mine clearance in 1944, the casualties of the Finnish wars, the famine uprising on Seskarö in 1917, the war invalids.

If you ask her residents, they'll answer that she's good, safe, child-friendly, close to nature, a little boring, has some drug problems, unemployment, bad roads, but you still look forward. Believing in a future where she will grow again.

International contacts will put her on the map again. China this time. The new Silk Road. The infrastructure projects have reached Kuovola and could go through her to Narvik. She still has the country's only railway connection to Finland.

She doesn't take anything for granted. Along with most of her inhabitants, over the years she's learned to keep her expectations low. They haven't managed to connect her with Luleå and Boden again, so what about China?

Good things, she hopes.

She misses the spotlight.

Honestly though, she thinks those days are probably gone forever. But that's something only the future can show.

Now the rain saturates the greedily thirsty ground, rinses roofs, cars, and streets clean. Just like the original flood. And the near future is already here.

Not everyone will survive it.

He woke up later than usual, took some painkillers and a sleeping pill last night. Hannah's bed was empty. Didn't look like she'd slept in it at all. She would come home to him eventually. When she was ready. There were a lot of emotions involved, and she'd never been very good at dealing with those. Wasn't encouraged to express them while growing up. A mother who couldn't bear them, a father who never understood the point.

Nothing gets better from dwelling.

Thomas knew how much she'd already lost. Her mother, of course, but mostly Elin. Who they never talked about. Even though she was behind all of that suppressed grief, so much fear, infinite amounts of guilt.

When her mother took her own life, Thomas had helped Hannah move on. She admitted to him, much later, how important it was for her when he told her it wasn't her fault. But with Elin... Nothing he said mattered. He couldn't reach her. If the guilt from her mother's suicide was crushing, it was still nothing in comparison. The grief and the search turned into an obsession that was literally killing her, definitely destroying their relationship.

In the end, he was forced to give her an ultimatum. For the sake of both of them.

Go on or go under.

Leave Stockholm for a start. Begin the healing elsewhere. They moved home. Or close enough. Back to the north. To Haparanda.

Slowly, slowly, Hannah also returned, to the everyday, to life. Three years after Elin disappeared, she got pregnant again. Could have gone either way, but she put herself into it, life with a baby, those hectic toddler years. Slightly more overprotective, slightly less engaged at times, but on the whole a family again. Until now, when she was about to lose him, too.

Thomas got out of bed and left the bedroom. Frowned when he saw that the door to the attic was open.

"Hannah…" he shouted up toward the dark opening. No answer, so he closed the door and went out into the kitchen. She was sitting at the table, a moving box next to her on the floor, one he didn't even know they still had, and definitely hoped he'd never have to see again. Papers, folders, photos spread in front of her on the table. The same clothes she left home in yesterday morning. Slightly red-eyed from lack of sleep, but there was something manic in her gaze when she turned to him.

"It's Elin."

"What?"

"The woman, the woman we're hunting. It's Elin."

Upset, almost breathless, she seemed to be so tightly wound inside that he was surprised she was still sitting down.

"OK, OK, wait a minute…" he said, holding out his hands to her, pulling out a chair and sitting down. He didn't understand, but he could see that no matter what had happened, no matter how she'd arrived at this being related to Elin, that it was all too much for her.

"Calm down, calm down…"

"The young woman we're hunting," she continued without the slightest sign of calming down. "Have I told you about her?" she asked, and he barely had time to shake his head before she began. She didn't remember what she'd told him, so quickly and somewhat incoherently she started with Tarasov, the money, the drugs, how the Russians sent someone, the murders, the disappearances, the bomb in the hotel.

"A bomb was detonated at the hotel?" he managed to interject in surprise.

"Yes, last night. She blew up her room."

Apparently this was barely worthy of a footnote, because she went on, telling him how this woman, who called herself Louise Andersson, had been inside the police station, how they'd met, and then everything that the agents from Säpo told her only a few hours ago.

That the girl just showed up in a village in Russia. As a two-year-old. In 1994.

"It's her. It's Elin," she finished, looking at him, her eyes brimming with tears now, full of anticipation and the hope that he'd share her joy in this discovery.

"No, it's not," he said calmly. Forced to disappoint her.

"Yes, it is. I know it."

"Hannah…it's not Elin."

"As soon as I saw her picture at the Horvats', the people who clean for us," she continued without taking the slightest notice of what he said. "There was something…"

Thomas didn't answer. With sadness in his eyes he watched her search for something among the papers in front of her.

"She looks a bit like Alicia. I didn't think of it when I saw her in my office, with the wig, but look here…" She laid what looked like a surveillance camera photo in front of him. "You see? Surely it's her. Look. There's a better picture of her at the station."

Thomas didn't even look—he pushed the picture to the side, leaned forward and grabbed her hands, kept his serious gaze focused on her.

"Hannah, sweetie, stop this. It's not Elin. Don't do this to yourself."

"It all makes sense…"

"It's not her."

He felt her stiffen before pulling her hands away. She took a deep breath and wiped a single tear away from her bottom lashes. He noticed the change in her whole posture, and then he saw how coldly she was looking at him.

"So I'm just crazy."

"No."

"Like my mother."

"No, you're not crazy," he said as softly and tenderly as he could. Had to choose his words carefully. He was good at that. "You haven't slept, we haven't really talked about, you know, me, the disease, what's going to happen."

He made another attempt to grab her hands, make physical contact with her, reach out, but she shied away.

"You're grasping at straws. I understand that, but you can't start hoping for this. Please. You'll only end up hurt."

"I'm not crazy," she repeated quietly, as if she hadn't heard anything he said.

"But you are sad. You want to take something back, not just have everything taken from you."

"It's her," she asserted firmly, pushing out her chair and rising abruptly, giving him a hurt look, seemed more disappointed that he wasn't sharing this experience with her than angry that he didn't believe her. Then without a word she turned to go.

"It's impossible," he continued to her back. "That girl, everything she went through, the person she became, and then she ends up in Haparanda of all places and is investigated by you."

No answer. He heard her step on the stairs, then the bathroom door slamming shut, the knob turning. He stopped at the table, staring at the pictures, at the investigation from Stockholm, which she'd taken out, the little red patent leather shoe.

He had always known that she wouldn't cope with his death very well, but for the first time he felt worried she might not cope with it at all.

There was something about the rain. When it was angrily hammering against a metal roof, it made her uncomfortable. It had for as long as she could remember. For the most part she didn't mind the rain, or any weather.

But she didn't like sitting in a car when it rained.

Maybe because it so effectively shut out all other sounds, and she wanted all her senses fully functioning. Now she could hear nothing but the persistent splatter against the metal. The downpour also limited visibility. Even though she started the windshield wipers now and then, it was still hard to make out the entrance to the workshop just fifteen meters away.

Her phone buzzed in her pocket. She answered with a short *yes*.

"You closed down the room." Uncle's familiar voice, a statement without even a trace of judgment.

"Yes."

An acknowledgment; not the first time it happened, not a failure, it was what was expected of her in certain situations.

"Why?"

"There were indications that they found it."

"They had found it. A police officer died in the explosion. Zagornij is pissed, it was one of his guys."

"He sent people other than me?" she said, without revealing how much of an unpleasant surprise that was.

"A backup on the inside. If the police found the goods before you."

"Did you know?"

"No."

Nothing else. Zagornij sending others, sending his own people, should be taken by Uncle as a personal declaration of lack of confidence. That he didn't seem to do so made her think again about their relationship and who Valerij Zagornij really was.

"I'm finishing this today. Coming back in," she said to change the subject and avoid the question of how things were going for her, which she was sure would come.

"Are you sure?"

Katja could see someone jogging around the corner of the workshop. Without an umbrella or any other protection from the rain, already soaked. She started the windshield wipers again and saw the young employee, Raimo Haavikko, hurry to the door, pull on it, and then start rummaging for his keys when he realized it was locked.

"Absolutely sure," she said as she saw the young man open the door and disappear inside.

"Good. See you then."

Then silence. She put away her phone, left the car, and ran toward the garage. *Für Elise* met her as she stepped inside, and she wiped the rain from her face. After a few minutes, Raimo came out of one of the inner rooms, about to button his overalls, his short black hair still dripping wet.

"Hi, Raimo," she said, smiling warmly at him. He gave her the same do-I-know-you look that UV gave her the first time they met, took a few steps toward her, and pushed his hand through his wet hair.

"Hi."

"You can help me with something."

Raimo looked around the shop uncertainly, clearly unused or perhaps reluctant to shoulder any responsibility.

"Can you wait until Dennis gets back? He's, you know, in charge around here. He should be in soon."

"No, I can't wait until Dennis comes back." She smiled at him again. "I'm sure you can help me. I'm looking for someone."

"Well, someone here or what?"

"A customer of yours. A woman, fairly tall, maybe 1.75 meters, light brown hair to here." She gestured with her hand to a bit below the shoulder. "Freckles, green eyes."

"Sandra."

Katja had made up a lie in case he asked why she wanted to know, if he felt he couldn't give out their customers' names willy-nilly, but he seemed genuinely happy to be able to help her.

"Sandra?"

"Kenneth's girlfriend. She was here yesterday."

"Kenneth."

"She's a guard. Works up at the prison," he said and gestured in the direction of where the facility was located.

"Does she have a last name? Or even better, an address?"

*S*ave as and then select the USB-stick she inserted. While the computer did its work, she gathered whatever papers from the investigation that she didn't have in digital form, but felt she might need.

She hadn't expected Thomas to believe her unconditionally, but neither did she expect him to dismiss her discovery so easily, so firmly, not even for a second considering the possibility that she'd found their daughter.

But it was what it was. She understood.

Didn't really hold it against him.

He had enough to handle already. Of course, he deserved more involvement from her. She wanted to do it, she would, but first she had to follow this as far as she could. Couldn't be held back by anything.

You want to take something back, not just have everything taken from you. It wasn't about that, there was nothing to get back. Twenty-six years had passed, and the two-year-old Elin no longer existed, she was not who she would have grown up to be.

Dreams, plans, hopes, all of that was gone.

This was about needing certainty. Like how it was important

to find a body even when you knew for sure a missing person was dead. Closure.

She'd made an appointment with Henric and Elena, wanted to know more, to know everything. Said she might be able to help them, but they were the ones who would be helping her. Then she'd drive up to the cabin—didn't want to be at the station, couldn't be at home with Thomas—and sit down in peace and quiet to go through all the material she'd gathered, everything she knew, and decide how best to proceed.

She was interrupted by Gordon appearing in her doorway. He stood there, didn't come inside and sit down. He looked tired, he never usually looked tired.

"How are you?" he asked.

"Good, why?"

"I was thinking after yesterday, I mean with Ritola and everything."

Of course he was. The events of the past week had led to the death of a police officer, naturally Gordon was walking around checking in on everyone.

"I'm fine," said Hannah. "I mean, it is what it is, I guess." She shook her head a little sadly, she couldn't engage much more than that right now. In all honesty, she hadn't given a thought to her dead colleague since the meeting with Henric and Elena.

"What happens now?"

"NOA has come up. X is handing things over right now, I think, so we'll know what they have for us soon."

"I need a few hours off."

"Today?"

She understood his surprise. They had gone from wildlife accidents, some beatings, and drunk drivers to mass murders and bomb explosions. If there was ever a moment she shouldn't ask for time off, it was now, but she couldn't even begin to explain.

"Yes, something has come up."

She could see he wanted to ask if it had something to do with Thomas, and by extension them, but he held back.

"I'm not the one in charge right now, so…"

"Can you just say I'm doing something else today, then I'll figure it out."

"Sure, you go."

"Thanks." She stopped. He looked really tired. "How are you? You look worn out."

"It's fine, we can discuss it another time."

"Are you sure?"

As soon as she said the words, she regretted leaving him an opening. Henric and Elena were waiting, she didn't want to hear what might be weighing on Gordon, she wanted to go down, change into a uniform so that her visit looked more official, and then get out of here as soon as possible. Find out more about Elin.

"Yeah, I'm sure."

So he left; she heard him put his head in Morgan's office further down the corridor and ask how he was doing. Hannah gathered the last of what she needed to take with her.

Impossible, Thomas had said, that the woman they were hunting was their daughter. Impossible. But impossible things happened all the time. Siblings were reunited after thirty years, twins separated at birth found each other in adulthood, dogs came back after being gone for a decade.

Nothing was impossible.

66 |called, but he's not answering."

Sandra could feel the good mood she'd been in all morning start to subside. She'd woken up long before her alarm rang,
with jittery anticipation in her stomach, like the Christmas Eve
she had never experienced as a child. Humming, she'd put on
a bathrobe and made breakfast for herself. Looked at the short
text message she received from UV last night again and couldn't
hold back a smile this time either.

You can pick it up tomorrow / Dennis Niemi, Car Center.

Proper, neutral, as if it referred to a car or a spare part, nothing suspicious if the police were ever able to recreate it for some
reason. Impossible to figure out that he meant eight million
kronor. Which she could pick up. Today. She deleted the message—probably should have done so as soon as she got it, but it
had made her happy just to read it—and got up to get dressed.
Grabbed some of the new clothes she'd bought. New shoes.
Wanted to feel pretty.

She left home at the usual time, arrived at the prison. Changed
into her uniform, answered in the affirmative when one of her

co-workers asked if that was a new sweater. A cup of coffee and then it was time to unlock the cells.

Just like any other day.

But it wasn't. This was a very, very special day. She found herself standing around smiling foolishly several times, thinking about other things. Eight million other things. The plan was to go down to the auto shop on her lunch break, but time crept by, she couldn't wait that long, was going crazy pacing around the woodworking shop.

Apologized and said she wasn't feeling well, apparently something that came and went, changed into her civilian clothes and drove down to the auto shop. Asked for UV when Raimo met her. He wasn't there. Hadn't come in yet. Didn't say anything about being late either.

Raimo didn't know where he was.

"I called, but he's not answering."

Sandra left the workshop, ran through the rain, and got into her car again. Called UV's number as soon as she slammed the door shut. It went straight to voicemail.

Annoyed, she hung up, had to think. The first thing that occurred to her was that he'd swindled her. Taken the money and run. She'd been gullible and naive to trust him, blinded by the possibilities. She felt her breathing getting heavier, her anger expanding like a glowing ball in her diaphragm. Her thoughts turned to the rifle still lying beneath a blanket in the trunk. He was going to regret this. But what about his daughter, Lovis? You couldn't move her that easily. And the girlfriend? Maybe she knew more. Sandra took out her phone and looked up Stina's number.

She couldn't seem to stop crying. For probably the thirtieth time she called and listened.

This is Dennis Niemi at Car Center...

Stina hung up, let her phone sink into her lap again, no idea what she was going to do. Something had gone wrong. Whatever he went out to do, it must have gone wrong. At best, he was lying low somewhere, waiting out whatever happened. In the worst case...

She couldn't even think of the worst case.

She wrapped the blanket closer around herself where she sat in this unfamiliar apartment. Couldn't call the police, couldn't put them on this, but who could she call, what would she do if he didn't call her soon, if something happened to him? The phone vibrated. She threw herself over it. Not him, a number she didn't recognize, but perhaps he'd borrowed someone's phone, got rid of his.

"Yes, hello." So much anticipation and hope in those two short words.

"Hi, it's Sandra. Fransson. Kenneth's girlfriend."

"Yes, hello." Stina cleared her throat, quickly sniffed her nose to cover her crying. Sandra Fransson. The prison guard. What did she want? Was Dennis with Kenneth? Then he surely would have been in touch.

"Is Dennis there?" Sandra asked.

"No, he's not here."

"Do you know where he is?"

"No. Why do you ask?"

"He was supposed to meet me at the shop, we have a...he's helping me with something."

"He's not here. I don't know where he is."

Sandra chewed on her lower lip a little thoughtfully. Stina was trying to hide it, but it was obvious that she was upset, had been crying. Was that something Sandra should just ignore? They didn't know each other. Was she crying because UV dumped her? Took ten million that wasn't his and left them.

"Did something happen?" she asked, trying to sound like she genuinely cared. "It sounds like you're crying."

Stina didn't answer immediately, fought her tears again,

thought about what she could and couldn't say. Sandra was a guard, but she had to talk to someone. She was going crazy from the uncertainty, the worry.

"Stina?" she heard Sandra wondering at the other end, realized she had been sitting quietly for a while.

"He went somewhere last night. Said he had to do something and didn't come back."

"Do what?"

"I don't know, but it was something, you know, not completely legal, you know..."

"I thought he'd stopped all that stuff?" Sandra said, might as well play ignorant so Stina wouldn't realize that she was involved in the not entirely legal thing.

"He did, but they got rid of so many hours and so..."

"Yes, Kenneth told me about that." Sandra poured a little more pity into her voice, didn't actually care, just wanted to know where her money was. In other words, where Dennis was. Pretty sure she wasn't going to find out from Stina.

"We need help," Stina continued croakily. "But it costs so much, so...he was going to go do something."

"And he didn't come back."

"No."

"You have no idea where he is?"

"No."

Sandra believed her. That was all she knew. UV might possibly try to fool her, but he wouldn't leave his family in the lurch. Stina sounded devastated, there was no reason to believe she was pretending to be upset and sad, to think they were planning to disappear together. With her money.

"He'll probably show up soon, you'll see," she said, eager to end the conversation. "And I won't say anything to anyone about what you just told me."

"Thank you."

"Get in touch if you hear anything."

"Yeah, you, too."

Then she hung up. Sandra stared out into the rain. What had happened? Something must have happened. And it seemed likely it had to do with the sale. Who would know anything about it? She opened the door and hurried back in to Raimo again.

"Did you get a hold of him?" he asked as she stepped inside the door.

"No. When he comes in, tell him to call me right away."

"Sure."

"Or even better, *you* call me right away."

She walked toward one of the workbenches while rummaging in her bag for a piece of paper and a pen.

"Did she get hold of you, by the way?" Raimo asked as she fished out a receipt and started scribbling her number on the back.

"Who?"

"There was a girl here earlier asking for you."

Sandra stopped writing, straightened up, and looked at Raimo. "What kind of girl?"

"I don't know. She knew what you looked like, but not what your name was."

"And you told her?"

"Yes…" Raimo said with some hesitation, seeming to realize that might not have been such a great idea now that he thought about it.

"What did she look like?"

Raimo told her, and Sandra knew immediately who it was. The woman with the expensive Mercedes. That UV refused to tell her about after he came into the office. He'd said she was a customer. Now that Sandra thought about it, he did seem unusually nervous. As if the woman with the expensive car had given him more to think about than just a normal customer.

She wrote her phone number clearly on the scrap of paper and gave it to Raimo.

"As soon as he arrives," she said, returning to her car.

A missed call, he saw it as soon as he came out of the shower. Sandra. Kenneth picked up the phone and called her back as he headed into the bedroom to get dressed.

"Hi, you called," he said when she answered on the first ring.

"If UV isn't at work and not at home, do you know where he might be?"

"What? No. Why?"

"He has no, what do you call it, like a hiding place or something?"

"No, why do you ask that?" he said as he pulled on a clean T-shirt.

Could hear her taking a deep breath on the other end before telling him. He only interrupted her when she got to the part about how she'd given UV the drugs so he could sell them. What the hell was she thinking? They weren't supposed to touch them, they'd agreed.

That was something they'd have to talk about later, he was told, now he had to be quiet and listen.

So he was quiet and listened.

A woman had asked for her this morning, the day after UV

disappeared. It was about drugs worth a lot of money. Who belonged to someone else before they ended up with them. What if they'd tracked them down? If UV fucked up in some way? Talked to the wrong people.

"What did she look like?" Kenneth asked as he stood in front of the bedroom window.

Sandra described her in quick, short strokes.

"She's here now," Kenneth interrupted, taking a step back into the room. Could see the Audi parked in the driveway, and a woman around his own age climbing out. Saw her take a gun out and turn the safety off before putting it back in her pocket.

"She's armed," he hissed as he took another step back, fear gripping him.

"Hide."

"What?"

"Don't let her find you. Whatever happens, do you hear me? Hide. Quickly."

Kenneth lowered the phone, looked around the bedroom in panic. Where? Where could he hide? Had rarely played hide and seek as a child, was bad at it the few times he did.

The closet? Under the bed? Behind the curtains?

Those were the first places you'd look. The doorbell rang. Kenneth let out a little whimper, but it released him from his paralysis. He had a whole house to hide in. Sprinted as quietly as he could out of the bedroom. The doorbell rang again. Longer, more aggressively this time. Kenneth went downstairs. Thought about the basement, but the door jammed, and she was standing right outside and would hear it. More ringing from the door. Four, five short rings. Kenneth stood there bewildered. What would she do if no one opened? Give up?

Wait in the car for someone to show up? Then all he'd have to do was stay out of sight, call the police. Why they had an armed woman looking for them, they'd just have to try to explain later, now it was time to get away.

She stopped ringing the doorbell. Kenneth looked around, he was fully visible if she walked into the house. He retreated up the windowless stairs. Could perhaps risk peeking out from upstairs to see if she had returned to the car. She hadn't, he knew when he heard a pane of glass being smashed in the basement. He backed up the stairs, wanting to put as much distance between her and him as possible.

Panic so close. He had to think. Quickly. Not his strongest suit in any case, now it was almost impossible. His mind was completely blank.

Heard the jammed basement door being pushed open. She was inside the house, and he couldn't think of anything. Anywhere was better than where he was, so he snuck carefully into the bedroom again, all the way to the open closet. Their laundry basket. As big as a suitcase in braided wood or birch or cork or something. Thought he could crawl inside it. Close the lid. A really, really bad hiding place, but he couldn't think of anything else.

Managed to push himself down, but he was really squeezed inside, wondered as he closed the lid how long he'd be able to sit like that.

"Kenneth," he heard from below, and held his breath reflexively. "Sandra? Is anybody home?"

Heard her moving down there, going through the rooms, coming up the stairs. Closed his eyes. Nothing, except possibly the Mercedes outside, said he was home. He could be out and about. In the rain. Got picked up by someone. She couldn't be sure he was in the house.

Heard her take the last step on the stairs. "Kenneth!"

He sat stock-still, didn't even breathe, ignored the pain in his legs and lower back. She opened the bathroom door. It must still be wet on the floor from his shower. Didn't necessarily mean anything, they had no floor heating, it could stay wet for hours. As long as the fog on the mirror had disappeared.

A second later he heard her enter the bedroom. Seemed content to stand quietly and listen for what seemed like an eternity, before turning around and walking back down the stairs again. Kenneth exhaled as gently as he could, trying to change his position but space wouldn't allow it. Heard her walk into the living room, then it went quiet. Complete silence.

She didn't move. He didn't move.

A quarter of an hour passed. Then another. His body ached so much he thought he might start crying. Was she even still here? He hadn't heard anything for a long time. Waited another ten minutes, but then couldn't take it anymore. He carefully lifted the lid and tried to straighten out. His muscles were screaming in pain at the slightest movement, but he came out of the basket in slow motion. Stood completely motionless for a while, not sure that his legs would obey him, didn't want to fall with a loud thump. Made an attempt. Had a plan now. Slowly he crept over to the bedroom window where the fire escape attached to the wall outside. Peeked out carefully. The Audi was still there, she wasn't in it, so he assumed she was still in the house. Silently waiting.

He unhooked the window catch, stopped and listened when he was done. Not a sound from downstairs. He put his hand on the window frame and pressed. The window didn't move an inch. He was just about to put more effort into it, when he saw Sandra skidding into the driveway. Heard the woman downstairs start to move. Wanted to scream at Sandra, but didn't dare. Could only see how quickly she left the car, opened the trunk, leaned in, and straightened up with a rifle in her hands.

It was loaded. She knew that, but still Sandra checked the rifle as she approached the house determinedly.

So many thoughts on the road home, which had never seemed longer. Mostly about Kenneth, about what she would do if he was hurt or dead. Sure, she'd played around with different future scenarios in which he didn't always play such a prominent role, might not even been present at all, but during the forty-five minutes it took her to get to Norra Storträsk, she couldn't think of anything other than that he needed to make it. Especially now, when it would be her fault if not.

She wouldn't even say anything about his stupid PlayStation if only he survived.

The Audi in the driveway must belong to the woman. She was still there. Good or bad?

She couldn't find Kenneth, or killed him without finding out what she needed? Sandra leaned toward the first. If the woman had gotten hold of him, it wouldn't be so difficult to make him tell her everything he knew, Sandra thought, taking a few quick steps up the stone stairs, turning the safety off her weapon and opening the door. Stepped in, stopped right inside. Totally focused and more comfortable standing in her hallway with a loaded shotgun than she ever would have guessed. The house was dead silent. Sandra had no idea what she should do. With her back still against one wall, she approached the kitchen. Peeked in quickly. Empty, what she could see anyway. She heard a familiar sound. The moment it took her to identify what must be the sticky basement door opening was long enough for the woman with the Audi to come forward and press her weapon into Sandra's back.

"Drop the rifle, please."

Sandra obeyed, didn't have the skills for close combat. Placed the weapon on the nearest countertop.

"Where's your boyfriend?"

"I don't know."

"Didn't you rush in here to save him?"

"If you had him, but you don't."

The woman tilted her head a little and looked at her with a slightly amused smile on her lips. Sandra surprised herself, wasn't sure where she had gotten her courage.

"Kenneth!" the woman shouted, pushing Sandra a few steps into the kitchen. "Come out, or I'm going to hurt Sandra."

Both waited. Sandra wondered if she should tell him to stay where he was, but apparently he understood that himself.

Not a movement, not the slightest sound.

Or had he managed to sneak out? Sandra turned to the woman with a hint of a contented smile. A small win. But before she could react, the woman grabbed her arm, twisted it up, put her hand against the wall, pressed the muzzle of her gun against it, and fired.

The shot was silenced, but Sandra screamed loudly.

Looked at her hand. A hole. Straight through. Strangely enough, the pain subsided somewhat when the blood began to flow.

"Kenneth!" the woman shouted into the house. Sandra moaned helplessly, pressing her wounded hand against her stomach, pressing down on it with the other. Her new sweater soaked up some of the blood, but not all, the rest dripped onto the floor. But no Kenneth.

The house was as quiet as before.

"Sit down," the woman said, pushing Sandra toward the kitchen table. Sandra did as she was told. Her hand still pressed hard against her stomach, breathing heavily, finding it difficult to think clearly, her earlier bravery long gone. The woman grabbed her chin and forced her head up.

"Do you know where the money is?" she asked calmly. Sandra nodded eagerly. "How much is there?" At first Sandra didn't understand the question. How much? Didn't she know? Or was it a trick question? So that she didn't waste time on someone who couldn't lead her there.

"Two bags. About three hundred thousand euros."

The woman nodded in satisfaction and pulled her to her feet. "We'll wrap that up, then you can show me."

Only after he'd heard the car back out and drive away did Kenneth dare to move. A ball of anxiety in his stomach made it difficult to breathe. *Whatever happens* Sandra had said. He obeyed her, it was always for the best. It had taken all his will-power not to rush down when he heard her scream, but somehow he managed it.

Closed his eyes, covered his ears, bit down hard.

Understood that this was their best chance for survival. The woman only needed one of them to show her the money. The other would be redundant. Now they'd managed to convince her that he wasn't home, so she didn't think anyone would do something.

But do what? What should he do? What could he do?

Drive after them? Then the same situation would arise again.

Besides, she'd get the money, and then there was no reason for her to keep either of them alive. But she'd taken Sandra with her. He had to do something. With trembling hands he searched for his phone. Scrolled to a number and called it. Wandered around while the phone rang, but froze the moment he heard a familiar voice.

"You have to help me, I'm fucked."

She turned the speed on the windshield wipers up, glanced over quickly at the material lying in the passenger seat. Didn't get much from the meeting with Elena other than what she brought with her from the station this morning.

Just one thing. One word.

The Academy.

That was all there was, the only thing Elena could give her that was little more than guesswork and speculation.

She had opened the door and shown Hannah into her hotel room in Torneå, when Hannah arrived at the appointed time. Only the two of them there.

"Where's Henric?" Hannah asked as she stepped in.

"The City Hotel, he's with the forensics team."

"I see," Hanna said and sat down. Elena offered her coffee, which she refused, then Elena also sat down and put a notepad in her lap.

"So, you said you have information that might help us," she said, straight to the point, no small talk.

"Yes, but I lied." Elena looked up in surprise. "I don't know any more than what you learned at the station last night."

Elena slowly closed the notepad. Tense, on guard, as if Hannah were suddenly a threat.

"Why are you here then?"

Definitely suspicion in her voice. Hannah knew the question was coming. Was ready for it. Thought she'd continue to be honest and hope that was the best way to get what she wanted. She needed it.

"I met her at the station when she was cleaning my office."

"OK."

"There was something, I couldn't put my finger on it then, but then when you came…"

"Yes…"

It was time. The hardest part. Hannah kept her gaze steady, important that she not be immediately dismissed as crazy, and continued on with the truth.

"My daughter disappeared in Stockholm in 1994. She was two years old. I think I see similarities."

Elena's reaction revealed that Hannah hadn't completely avoided seeming crazy. Elena flicked her eyes to the side briefly and a slightly uncertain, indulgent smile appeared on her face.

"That is indeed a strange coincidence."

"I know, and you can believe whatever you want. You can think I'm crazy, my husband does, but can you please tell me what you know?"

"That depends." More relaxed now, but definitely still on her guard. "What do you plan to do with that information?"

"Nothing," Hannah lied freely. "What can I do? You work full-time with every European resource, and you still can't find her."

"So why…?"

"I want to know as much as possible. Everything I can. I may realize that it couldn't possibly be her. That would be good, too… Better, actually," she corrected herself, not sure if the last bit was true.

Elena took a deep breath, let out a sigh. Considering it. She studied Hannah as if to determine if there were any ulterior motives, if she'd missed something. In the end, she made up her mind.

"Like we said yesterday, we don't know much, but there is a little..."

The Academy.

That was what they had, what there was, Elena told her.

The place where they took the children to train. For ten years. If they survived. A word people whispered, mentioned in only a single document, mostly rumors and hearsay, but it popped up often enough to be worth taking seriously. They didn't know where it was, whether it was in one place or several.

The Academy.

This was where Hannah was going to start when she got to the cabin.

Sandra sat in the passenger seat, the pain in her bandaged hand pounding in time with her heartbeat. The normal painkillers they had at home didn't help at all.

At first she had tried to explain. How they ended up with the money, given the drugs to UV. That it was an accident, that they never meant to do anything bad. They just didn't think. Got overwhelmed and rushed ahead.

"It was dumb," was the woman's only comment.

"What happened to UV?" Sandra asked after a few more kilometers.

"Do you really want to know?" was the response, and Sandra took that as answer enough.

They continued in silence. For a moment, Sandra considered throwing herself out of the car, trying to escape on foot, but a glance at the speedometer made her abandon that. Giving the wrong address, trying to deceive the woman, hadn't seemed like good options either, so now they'd soon be there. If Kenneth hadn't come up with a way to help her, the only thing she could hope for was that the woman would let her go when she got what she came for. She had a feeling that was too much to ask for.

"You can pull over here," Sandra said, pointing to the road ahead. "It's up there."

They parked at the edge of the road, and both left the car. The woman nodded to Sandra to go first while taking out her gun. The sky was an even gray, the trees, the moss, the grass, everything in the forest was wet. Her hair stuck to her head and face, the bandage around her hand turned a light red in the rain. A thought flashed through Sandra's mind: she hadn't waterproofed her new shoes. Dumb, but better than thinking about what was going to happen once they arrived at the shack.

"It's there," she said, pointing to the four dilapidated walls as they came into view. The woman nodded, and they continued. Stepped through where the front door once stood, and Sandra showed her to the closed hatch in the floor. The woman stopped a few meters from the side, nodded to the ground.

"Open it."

Sandra fell to one knee and with some difficulty pulled the hatch up. At first she thought she must be seeing wrong, that the dark sky and rain were playing tricks on her eyes. She didn't see the bags. It took her a few horrible seconds to realize they weren't there.

"What the fuck?!" She straightened up, completely uncomprehending. The woman took a step closer, looked down into the hole, immediately raised her gun. Sandra threw her arms over her head and came clumsily to her feet.

"No, no, no, they were here! I promise. This is where we hid them. I promise."

"Your boyfriend…"

"No, no, or maybe, I don't know, but in that case we'll get them. If it's him, we'll get them. Then, then, then we just need to call him."

"It's not Kenneth."

The woman quickly turned toward the voice with her gun raised, while she slid in behind Sandra in a single smooth movement, holding her like a shield in front of her. Sandra tried to take in what she was seeing and hearing. Couldn't make sense of it.

Thomas in the rain. With a rifle aimed at them.

"I have the money. I intend to give it to my children."

"Give it to me, or she dies," the woman replied calmly and turned the pistol for a moment to Sandra's temple instead of at him.

"Let her go, and you'll get it. You can go back to Russia. Mission completed. No one needs to die."

Sandra didn't understand what was happening. None of it. Why was Thomas here? When did he take the money? Did he know who the woman was? She didn't seem to be the only one who was surprised.

"You know who I am," the woman behind her said in a questioning tone.

"No, but I know why you're here. My wife is a police officer."

"Hannah."

"I'm the only one who knows where the money is. Let her go, and I'll show you."

"If I let her go, you'll shoot me."

"I've had plenty of chances to shoot you, if that's what I wanted."

Then silence. The raindrops falling on leaves and the collapsed roof were the only sound. Sandra hardly dared to breathe, certainly couldn't turn her head to see if she could figure out what the woman behind her was thinking. She kept staring at Thomas. The rain glued his hair to his head, ran down his face and neck, but he didn't seem to care. Just blinked it away every now and then. Stood firm, legs wide, ready to shoot the rifle.

"Are you going to let me go back?" The woman behind her broke the silence. "Your wife must have told you what I did."

"They'll keep chasing you. All I want is to save Sandra and my nephew. Enough people have died."

Silence again. Then Sandra felt the firm grip on her upper arm start to loosen. She was pushed to the side with a powerful movement and almost stumbled. The woman aimed her weapon at Thomas instead.

"Very well, let's go."

Katja didn't trust him, of course, didn't relax for a second as she walked a few steps behind him. He had sounded honest when he said he didn't want more people to die, and thinking back he did have the opportunity to shoot her when she was on her way to the tumbledown shack with Sandra, but he let her be.

So if he led her to the money now, what should she do?

The mission was clear.

Find the goods, kill the people who took them.

Could she mislead Uncle about who really had them, say it was UV all along? UV who was unquestionably dead. Not that she cared what Hannah's husband wanted, but it would be nice to grab what she needed and head back to St. Petersburg. Not have to hunt down Sandra and Kenneth and kill them. She didn't have to decide now.

The money wasn't hers yet. A lot could happen.

"How did you know we were here?" she asked as she caught a glimpse of a red cabin through the trees.

"Kenneth called me and said you were on your way to get the money."

So he'd been home all along. Katja had to admit she was impressed that he didn't expose himself when she shot his girl-friend. The right decision certainly, but not many would have understood that.

"When did you move it?"

"Last night?"

They came out of the woods, walked around the corner to a parked car that she assumed belonged to Thomas.

"What's your name?"

"Thomas. What's your name?"

"Louise."

"What's your real name?"

"I don't have a real name."

"Not even Tatjana."

She stopped abruptly. Gripped her wet gun even tighter, aiming at his head. Who was he? Hannah's husband, he'd told her, but he could be anyone at all. The police had found her, but they couldn't have gotten so far that they knew the name her "parents" had given her.

Unlikely.

"You know who I am?"

"No, but my wife thinks she knows."

"Stop!" she said coldly.

"We can talk about it in the car," he replied, and kept walking.

"No. Stop. Drop the rifle."

He stopped, turned toward her, the rifle still lowered. Looked like he was about to say something when she heard the crackling of tires swerving into the driveway. Katja kept her weapon aimed at Thomas, who seemed at least as surprised as she was when the car door opened before the car had come to full stop, and Hannah jumped out. Her hand already on its way to her holster. Katja turned the gun on her instead, heard Thomas shout "*No!*" and saw out of the corner of her eye as he raised his rifle. Close range, a weapon with a greater spread that did more damage. She quickly shifted back, aiming at him.

"Elin!" she heard Hannah screaming through the rain. No idea why or what that meant. "Elin!"

She squeezed the shot before he had time to get his rifle in position, the bullet entered above his right eye, and he stopped mid-movement and collapsed quietly to the ground. Hannah screamed. Katja heard a shot go off and turned to the car again. Saw Hannah take cover behind her open car door, a gun in her hand. Fired another shot. Missed again. Katja was completely unprotected. Hannah's legs beneath the door made a small, hard-to-hit target. A third shot from Hannah's weapon, and Katja felt how close the bullet passed by. Made a decision. Fired three quick shots at the car without really aiming, then turned and ran into the woods.

Hannah saw her disappear into the trees. Straightened up, stared emptily around her, as if trying to orient herself before she started walking. Was having a hard time pulling air into her lungs, something was in the way. Exhaled in short, desperate moans.

She shot him.

Hannah tried to understand what had happened, how this could have happened, if it had even happened. The two of them, both armed, as she pulled up in front of the cabin.

My God, she shot him.

She still had her weapon in her hand, it struck her now. Dropped it in the gravel, continued forward. Sank to her knees beside Thomas's lifeless body, didn't know what to do with her hands, hesitated before gently placing one on his wet chest. The rain fell straight into his staring eyes, diluting the small stream of blood that flowed from the hole on his forehead.

Everything stuck in her chest came suddenly loose. The force that held her upright left her, and she collapsed onto him. Wept, just wept, inconsolably.

"Hannah?"

She jerked, turned toward the voice. Sandra had come around the side of the house. This was completely incomprehensible, too. Just like her husband lying on the ground with a bullet hole in his head.

"What are you doing here?"

"Is he dead?" Sandra asked, slapping a hand over her mouth as she slowly approached. Hannah merely followed her with her eyes. When she got there, she sank to her knees in the gravel. "Oh my God…"

Hannah looked at her, still no idea why she was there.

"What are you doing here?" she asked again.

"Where is she?" Sandra said, avoiding the question for a second time and glancing around anxiously.

"She ran."

"Aren't you going to follow her?"

"I don't know…" Hannah answered honestly, mostly because she didn't really understand how she could. It felt difficult to do anything at all, difficult to stand up, difficult to think.

"My car is a few hundred meters away," Sandra said, pointing. "You can catch up with her."

Hannah hesitated, looked down at Thomas, her chest began to tighten again, her breathing getting heavier, her eyes flooded.

"I'll stay with him," Sandra said softly. "You have to catch her."

Hannah met her gaze. Surprisingly calm and collected. Nice to have someone here to tell her what to do. Avoid making any decisions on her own. The ones she had taken so far were bad, wrong, and fatal.

She got to her feet again and walked back to the car. Managed to start it, shifted into reverse and drove out. The headlights lit up Sandra, who was on her knees beside Thomas. She thought that might make her lose what little grip she managed to have on reality, but to her surprise it made her more determined, more rational. As she shifted into first and pulled away, she could even feel an incipient rage forcing her thoughts in another direction, away from an abyss of sorrow, even though she knew it would only be temporary—grief would be her constant companion for a long to come.

Barely out of breath, Katja came out of the forest and jumped into the car. She'd had time to think through her situation while she ran. It didn't look good. If Thomas had been telling the truth, and she believed he had, there was no way for her to get the money now. No reason for her to stay. Going back with only half of what she'd promised to deliver wasn't really an option, but what else could she do?

She had failed. It was as simple as that.

This Swedish shithole had made her fail.

For the first time. That was her saving grace. She was an asset, one of the absolutely best from the Academy, if not *the* best. She'd be punished, but allowed to continue. They'd invested too much in her for them to get rid of her.

She started the car, turned off the road, continued forward at high, but not too high speed. Out toward the bigger roads. Would her fake IDs still work? Could she risk buying a ticket of any kind? They would have sent out the name Louise Andersson to every conceivable place of departure. Would she have to drive the whole way? In that case, she needed to change cars, they'd soon issue a description of this one.

She was sunk so deep in thought about possible escape routes and transportation home that it took her until she was out on highway 99, on her way back to Haparanda, to notice she was being followed.

Hannah caught up after only a few kilometers. Assumed she'd been seen and recognized, so she kept a distance that meant never losing sight of Sandra's car while also allowing space to react if the vehicle in front of her made any kind of maneuver. Prepared for the worst. In everything.

She pushed her phone on the radio, called Gordon.

"I know where she is," Hannah said as soon as he answered.

"Who?"

"Louise or Tatjana or whatever the hell her name is. Her!" she almost screamed. Heard Gordon catch his breath and get up from his office chair. "She's on Highway 99 on her way back to town."

"How come—"

"She shot Thomas," Hannah cut in. Didn't know why. Stupid. Saying it out loud made it more real, and sometimes she wasn't very good at dealing with reality. But she had to say it, to tell him. "He's dead," she continued, hearing her voice thicken, the words stick.

Silence at the other end for a few seconds. Felt like she could see him in front of her as he struggled with how to continue this conversation. *Who* should continue it. Gordon, the caring colleague who would like to ask questions, comfort her, listen, or Gordon, the police chief who was hunting a mass murderer.

"You're following her on 99, have eyes on her?"

The police chief apparently won. Temporarily, at least.

"Yes."

"I'll round up the others, we'll call you back in two minutes."

"Hurry up, we'll be in Haparanda in ten."

"Be careful, don't do anything stupid." It was clear that he wanted to say more, not leave her and this conversation, so she helped him by hanging up and giving her undivided attention to the car in front of her.

Gordon looked at the phone in his hand, trying to make sense of what he'd heard. He snapped out of it quickly though and ran out into the corridor, down toward Morgan, who was standing behind his desk, forewarned by the sound of someone running toward him.

"Gather everybody, right now, quick," Gordon said as soon as he got to the doorway.

"What is it? What happened?"

"Hannah called."

"What did she say?" There was worry in Morgan's usually calm voice as he took a step closer to Gordon.

"Thomas is dead." That was not what he'd asked. Information he didn't need, but Gordon had to get it out. "The woman who blew up the hotel shot him."

"What? When? Where?"

Morgan could absorb information faster and better than anyone Gordon knew, but Gordon could see in his colleague's uncomprehending gaze that even he was completely at a loss.

"Don't know, I never asked. They're on their way here."

"What? Together?"

Clearly he still didn't understand anything. Gordon felt his impatience bubble up.

"No! Hannah is following her car. They'll reach town in ten minutes."

"OK, then we'd better hurry."

"Where's X?"

"The hotel. Should I call him in?"

"Fuck it, we don't have time. Gather everyone in the meeting room."

He was just about to rush on when Morgan stopped him.

"Gordon…"

"Yeah, what is it?" Gordon snapped, unable to keep the stress and thus irritation out of his voice.

"She'll be fine." Morgan took a few steps toward him. "I know how you feel about her. She'll be fine. We're going to help her."

He put a firm hand on Gordon's shoulder, squeezed briefly, and looked steadily into his eyes. He knew. Of course he knew. Morgan Berg knew everything. Gordon should have realized that by now.

"Gather everybody," he said more softly, hoping his gratitude was in his voice. Morgan nodded, and Gordon hurried down the corridor, took the stairs to the meeting room two steps at a time.

Katja glanced in the rearview mirror. Hannah was a hundred meters behind, making no attempt to get closer, turn around, or to stop her. At the moment, Katja was fine with maintaining a distance. She had just murdered Hannah's husband. Killing or hurting those who had hurt you was satisfying, Katja knew that from personal experience, and some people were willing to take great risks for revenge. So keeping Hannah at a distance was not altogether a bad thing. But it also indicated that Hannah had called for reinforcements, probably was in constant contact and could direct them according to whatever Katja decided to do. She needed to shake her off, but that wouldn't be easy with Hannah keeping her distance. Impossible to get closer, clearly didn't want to risk anything.

Katja made up her mind. If she turned around sharply, drove back, she'd drive right past Hannah, get close. Close enough to make her car unusable at least. Disappear down the small roads. Take the bridge over to Finland to Övertorneå instead. Was there even a police station there? Not one with much of a staff or many resources in any case, of that she was sure. She was about to carry out this maneuver on an empty county road, but she saw in her one last look in the rearview mirror that Hannah had been joined by a police car from the north.

The blue lights were flashing, but no sirens. She wouldn't be able to get past both. For a moment she'd toyed with the idea of stopping, leaving the car and trying to escape on foot, but that was no longer an option. Swearing, she kept going, hoping a new chance would pop up along the way.

Five men leaned over a large map that lay unfolded on the conference table, all serious and focused.

"As far as we know, they're headed this way," Gordon said, putting his finger on the map where 99 came in from the north.

"And we have two cars following now?" Lurch asked.

"Yes, that will make it harder for her to turn around, but we don't want her out on the E4."

"So we stop her there," Morgan said, pointing to the round-about near Ikea. "But we don't want her in Finland either," he continued.

"No," Gordon confirmed.

"Then we'd be forcing her toward downtown," P-O stated, staring at the map. Gordon looked up when he perceived the criticism in his voice. "There are people there, what if she takes the hostages?"

Gordon thought briefly. P-O's objection was absolutely justi-fied. What little they knew about the woman approaching their city proved she had no respect for human life.

"It's raining. There aren't usually many people there anyway. We'll have to keep our fingers crossed. I want her there," Gor-don said, putting his finger on the map again. Hoped the tone of his voice indicated he wasn't expecting any more objections. Clearly there were none. The others looked to where he was pointing. Nodded, glanced at the clock on the wall.

They didn't have much time.

★ ★ ★

Hannah maintained her speed and distance. Reinforcements were behind her, no sound on, but blue lights flashed comfortingly into her car. Gordon was back on the speaker. Had made contact with all available cars, got the Finns out on the bridge too, so that was no longer an escape route.

"We have a plan."

Hannah listened intently.

She hated this little town, the feeling washed over her as soon as she saw the old water tower rising against the darkened sky. She hoped she'd never have to see it again. She was still convinced she'd be able to get out of this situation, but it would require a lot more now that she was so close to Haparanda. More police, a bigger effort. Had they received any reinforcements from the south? From Stockholm? Probably. Someone must have told Hannah about her. About Tatjana.

Everything had gone spectacularly to shit, and she was facing real problems now. Uncle, Zagornij, the fact that her face was known, that someone knew facts about her childhood. Major problems.

Getting away from a small-town police force, even with reinforcements, shouldn't be one of them. She just needed to pay attention, spot an opportunity when it presented itself, and react quickly.

The first police car she saw came roaring onto the E4 at high speed. Skidded to a halt and effectively blocked both lanes west of the roundabout. Armed cops jumped out and took up position.

The cars behind her peeled off at the roundabout, forcing her to turn left, toward the Finnish border. No longer an accessible route, she realized at the next roundabout, when she saw the blue lights flashing on the bridge. Forced to turn right, down onto Storgatan.

Hannah and the other car were still behind her. Closer now. They were herding her somewhere, had a plan.

She continued through the center of town. The few people who had defied the weather stopped on the sidewalk as she whizzed past at far too high a speed with the other cars trailing behind her. Past the shops, the banks, HM Hermansson's, and then on until the street was lined by houses and apartment buildings. She was getting close to the railway tracks. At the end of the street she could see the small stone railroad. Got an idea. Only one lane under the bridge. If she crashed into the wall on the right in a controlled manner, parked her car across it, made ready to jump out quickly, she could disappear into the houses on the other side. It didn't look like they'd sent any cars to that side, and she'd neither seen nor heard a helicopter.

This was going to work. She was fast.

By the time her pursuers left their cars, made it past hers, and got out on the other side, she'd be well hidden, she'd wait them out.

She was good at waiting.

She quickly went through the plan again. Not the safest, but she was forced to improvise, it was time to end this. Still had two cars behind her. One behind the other, so the car closest to the bridge was Hannah. She surely wasn't that fast. The odds were better and better. She unbuckled her belt, turned her attention forward again, and slammed on the brakes. A police car had arrived from the other side and effectively blocked the single-lane passage beneath the bridge.

Fuck, fuck, fuck!

This was where they wanted her.

There were no other exits—she'd just driven past the last one. She cast an eye in the rearview mirror. The cars behind knew what was about to happen; now they were side by side, effectively blocking any possibility for her to double-back. On the right side, she saw an old abandoned, boarded-up factory building, so it would have to be left. Down toward the river. She quickly shifted into first, and turned onto the gravel plane that ended in a hill, which led up to the tracks and the centuryold railway bridge to Finland. Katja drove as far up the slope as she could. Defenses from some war stood to the left, a fence with an opening onto the rails to the right.

She threw herself out of the car, got up on her knees, and shot at the cars coming toward her. They stopped when bullets hit their windshields. The police crouched behind their dashboards. Katja stood up while reloading, then started running, through the opening in the fence, out onto the bridge.

Hannah remained in her car, looked in near shock at the two bullet holes to her right in the windshield. Gordon and Morgan rushed by.

Gordon stopped, looked at her and made a questioning thumbs-up. She nodded in response, and he continued running, soon catching up with Morgan on his way up the hill. Hannah unbuckled herself and climbed out. Should probably run after them, but she'd never catch up and her weapon was still at the cabin, so what good could she do?

But at the same time...

She had to see how this ended. Didn't even know what she was hoping for anymore. Did she want to know? Did she want to be right? The woman had shot Thomas without blinking. Wouldn't it be best if she just disappeared?

On her way up the hill, she heard Gordon shouting to the fleeing woman to stop, and Hannah increased her pace. One shot was fired. Gordon shouted again, more shots. As she reached the top, she saw both Morgan and Gordon standing with weapons drawn. Aimed straight ahead. Hannah went through the fence and walked over cautiously to her colleagues. Saw what they saw.

A few hundred meters out on the huge metal structure, she was on her knees in the middle of the track. Hannah could see how hard she was breathing. Her whole back moved with each breath. Slowly, with great difficulty, she got to her feet.

"Drop your weapon and lie down!" Gordon shouted while walking toward her, gun raised. Hannah stood rooted to the spot, noting that the woman was still holding onto her weapon as she straightened up. She took a swaying step to the side, toward the massive metal beams. She'd been hit by at least two bullets. One in the leg, one on the side of her abdomen. Gordon shouted at her again, ordered her to drop her weapon and lie down.

She did neither.

Suddenly she steadied herself and raised her gun. Morgan and Gordon fired at the same time. Both hit her. The woman staggered, looked for a moment like she might regain her balance, then fell to the left. Where previously there had been a beam to lean against, now there was nothing. She seemed surprised as her hand fumbled against only air, then she plunged into the swirling water. Gordon and Morgan rushed forward.

Hannah turned and left.

Down the hill, slowly back to the car. The rage that had driven her, the adrenaline rush of the pursuit, her total focus.

All of it was gone.

Only an enormous emptiness remained.

More police cars from both Sweden and Finland arrived. People rushed toward her, past her, out onto the bridge, down toward the river. Orders were given, rescue efforts were coordinated. Hannah watched it all as if through a filter. It didn't concern her, it seemed to be happening to someone else, somewhere else. The sounds were muffled, the movements slow.

She sat down in the car again. They would ask. What Hannah was doing at the cabin. What Sandra was doing there, with Thomas. Why the woman had been there, the woman who was now in the river.

Why had Hannah driven there? At a critical point in the investigation? Immediately after the meeting she'd had with the security police? Was there some connection?

There was no doubt they would ask, but she wouldn't say what she really thought. What led her there. Who killed Thomas. That it was Elin. That her lost daughter had caused everyone so much grief and pain. Hannah most of all. Again.

It didn't matter what she thought. Everyone was gone. It was over.

Everything was over.

A beautiful summer day in mid-July, the kind most people spend on the beach, by the water, eating an ice cream, lying in the shade. Too hot to shop, but people into the stores seeking a place to cool off.

A day most people wouldn't associate with grief, with loss, with a funeral.

She's seen so many.

Five thousand years since the first, and since then a rapid, never-ending stream. If there's one thing she knows for sure, it's that if you choose to live in her, you will also die in her one day.

That's life.

Of course, that doesn't make it any easier for the ones standing by the open grave. The woman and her two nearly grown children. Grieving for her husband and their father. She's stoic, struggling, fighting to keep it together. The son weeps, remembering and missing his father. The daughter weeps too, but in her grief there is also suspicion, a silent accusation, that her mother might have had something to do with her father's death.

There are other funeral guests. The man who loves her. Who

can't decide if he should take that job in Umeå. Or stay here. For her sake.

More colleagues of hers. Some neighbors. No friends really. No one who is really close.

After the burial is complete, they disperse. Each in their own direction, no gathering afterwards. The mother and her children go home. To the house they've never lived in without him. The man they've left in the cemetery.

She sees them, feels for them, but what can she do? She's a city.

She just exists and keeps existing.

Like she always does. Always has.

She welcomes the new and grieves for those who leave, while quietly, patiently lying beside the river's eternal flow.

"**T**hink!"

"I've been thinking, I don't know."

"You knew him best."

Kenneth didn't answer, just shrugged tiredly. Sandra held her tongue. She believed him. Believed he really was making an effort to be helpful. Had asked him the same thing every day for almost a month. He simply didn't know.

Where the hell could Thomas have hidden the money?

Her money.

The money that was going to give her a new, easy life. So she would never have to worry about things like the bills lying on their kitchen table. She was on sick leave because of her hand; Kenneth, as usual, wasn't bringing in any money. Life was anything but easy.

The police had been here, asking a bunch of questions. Why was Sandra at the cabin when Thomas was shot? Why did she go there with the woman who shot him?

Fortunately, they'd managed to talk to each other before the first interrogation, and both stuck to the story they'd practiced: the crazy woman just showed up at their house, convinced that they had something to do with the run-over Russian in the woods. Why she thought that, they didn't know. They'd had to get her out of the house, play along, say they'd lead her to what she was looking for. Kenneth had called Thomas, who went there and...well, the rest they knew.

Why hadn't they called the police instead of Thomas?

Kenneth hadn't been able to hold back the tears when he told them he wished he had, but he didn't think of it. Thomas had always helped them before, with everything...

At first they seemed skeptical, but when they found the drugs in the woman's car, and UV dead in the trunk of his, they seemed to lose interest in her and Kenneth. Probably came to the conclusion that if UV had the drugs, he also had the money, they just couldn't find it.

As soon as the police stopped being interested in them, Sandra and Kenneth went back to the shack, made sure the money wasn't still in their hiding place, then they started looking. Spent days walking around the property and through the woods. In wider and wider circles. Searching for any signs that someone had dug, dragged, or hid anything. Nothing. They even broke into the cabin, combed every inch of it, and the outhouse. Nothing.

"Could he have hidden it at home, do you think?" she asked him now, well aware that she'd dropped the subject only moments ago. But it occupied all her waking hours.

"Then Hannah would have found it."

"Not necessarily. He said he was going to give it to his kids. Do you think he had time to tell them where he hid it?"

"No."

"Call Hannah, say we want to go over and visit, check how she is, and then we can look around a little."

"Sandra..."

She turned toward him. He didn't like it, she knew that, especially since he felt guilty about Thomas's death, but his feelings were of secondary importance right now.

"What is it?"

It was clear in those three small words that she was in no mood to be contradicted or questioned right now. He understood immediately.

"Nothing," he said, taking out his phone with a sigh.

Good. Hannah, Gabriel, and Alicia first, then she'd talk to Thomas's colleagues, maybe some of the neighbors. She knew at about what time he must have picked up the bags, could work on mapping out where he'd been after that up until the moment he was shot. Could a private person retrieve data from his phone? Where had he been? It was worth a try.

She would get that money back.

Her money.

If it was the last thing she did.

The other bed was empty. Of course it was. That was always the case nowadays, no matter what time of day. Hannah got up, put on jeans and a sweater, went out into the kitchen. Most days that's as far as she got.

What should she do? Why should she do it? Why do something instead of nothing?

For the sake of the children? They were both still at home. Seemed to be finding it easier to cope than her. More in touch with their feelings, found it easier to talk. To each other. To their friends. They fell apart sometimes, but on the whole they were taking it well.

With her it was different. She felt halved. A cliché, but she couldn't come up with any other way to describe it. Their lives had been intertwined for so long. Now he was gone, and it was up to her to carry all of it, all those memories. Just her.

That's what grief was.

Bearing the unreasonable weight of keeping their time together alive, so afraid those memories might fade until one day she wouldn't even know if they were real.

That was what it meant to be left behind.

She had been left behind. She was alone.

The questions had been asked sure enough.

Hannah explained that she went out to the cabin to go through the investigation in peace and quiet. No other reason. Not a word about Elin. They were content with that.

Kenneth and Sandra's answers also seemed to have satisfied her colleagues. Now they were working on the assumption that UV had driven into Tarasov. The drugs had been found, but not the money. They questioned Stina, his girlfriend, but she didn't know anything, she said.

Hannah didn't know either. There were definitely still question marks.

They had to get that woman out of the house, Sandra had said, so that Kenneth, who the woman didn't know was there, could call for help. Why did the woman think Kenneth and Sandra were involved? How did Kenneth know where they'd be going? Why take her to the cabin? What was the plan? To play along. But for how long? What really happened right before Thomas showed up?

Questions.

Kenneth knew UV from his time in prison. His Volvo, which they'd had for several years, was missing. Sometimes Hannah suspected Kenneth and Sandra had driven into Vadim Tarasov in the woods. That they took the money and the drugs. That the Russian woman was right.

Anything was possible.

She didn't inquire into it any further. Did very little. Nothing.

Gordon had visited a few times. Been the caring colleague. Offered to help in any way, inquired if she needed anything, showed he cared. Let her know she could call at any time.

She had called. Hadn't helped.

She was alone. Left behind.

But more idle days with too much time to think weren't going to change that, nor make anything better. It was enough now.

Nothing gets better from dwelling.

Whatever she felt, no matter how she felt: she had to move forward. Knew how and with what. Put on the coffee maker, and while she waited, she took out the material she'd brought with her from the station before heading to the cabin. Before she watched Thomas get shot. By the woman whose body they never found, but who Hannah still believed might once have been her daughter.

Someone had taken Elin from her, destroyed her, trained her to become the murderer of her husband. Someone somewhere was responsible. She was going to find them.

The Academy.

That was all she had.

That's where she would start.

★ ★ ★ ★ ★